BEFORE SHE C[...]
SHE MUST SOLVE A DARK SECRET . . . .

All these years later, lying in bed, I remembered that day in Africa. Why did my father protect my mother so ardently? Why did he never visit his parents who loved him? What had my mother done that there were no pictures of her at all in my grandfather's massive collection of photographs?

Then I received a mysterious letter, perhaps the first piece in the puzzle that was my mother . . . .

Dear Mary,

My name is Mary Higgins, but you can call me Aunt Mary. I knew your mother many years ago. I also knew your father's parents. I'm sure you've grown up lovely, but I want to see you for myself. You can visit when your school's ended. Your mother probably likes to keep her past in the past, so I wouldn't tell her about this. Or anyone else. Let's keep it between us. All right?

Love,
Aunt Mary

Who was Aunt Mary? Maybe she would be the person to tell me of my mother's past. I might as well take a chance and meet this woman, whoever she was. I felt that the beginning of an adventure was waiting for me . . . .

HarperPaperbacks
by Erin Pizzey

The Snow Leopard of Shanghai

Erin Pizzey

The Consul General's Daughter

 HarperPaperbacks
A Division of HarperCollins*Publishers*

This is a work of fiction. The characters, incidents, and
dialogues are products of the author's imagination and are
not to be construed as real. Any resemblance to actual
events or persons, living or dead, is entirely coincidental.

HarperPaperbacks   *A Division of* HarperCollins*Publishers*
10 East 53rd Street, New York, N.Y. 10022

A hardcover edition of this book was published in 1988
in Great Britain by William Collins Sons & Co. Ltd.

Cover photograph by Herman Estevez
Cover illustration by Michael Herring

First HarperPaperbacks printing: March 1991

Printed in the United States of America

HarperPaperbacks and colophon are trademarks of
HarperCollins*Publishers*

10 9 8 7 6 5 4 3 2 1

DEDICATION

This book is dedicated to my dear friend and editor, Marjory Chapman, and all at Collins; to Mr. and Mrs. Nolan Foster, who first invited us to visit the Brac; to District Commissioner James Ryan, who welcomed us; to Mr. Burnard Tibbetts, who facsimiled our contract with our thanks; to David Feinberg, whose hotel—the Tiara Beach—has the best bar in the world; to Audley Scott and to Joy Tatum who have helped us settle in; to Moses Kirkconnell and Billy Bodden, who feed us; to Lona Grizzel, our angel at Cayman Airways; to everyone on the Brac, particularly the children. This book is for them.

As always, our thanks go to our British solicitors David Morris and John Elford, our American lawyer John Faure, our accountant Alan Cohen, our friend Jeff Flook at the Lloyds Bank, Eddie Sanderson—one of the world's finest photographers and purveyors of sushi, and to our agent Christopher Little and his tireless secretary Pamela Overnell. And of course my thanks to my beloved husband Jeff Shapiro.

May God bless you all.

Prologue

The peperoncini were hot. I was making a salad for my mother, cutting everything into small pieces so she would be able to swallow easily. The tomato I held in my hand was red and, twenty minutes after I picked it, it held the heat from the sun and I smelled it, like the smell of my body after love has been made. But I remembered with a shock that there was no longer a man in my life to make love to me, neither husband nor lover.

I was standing in a flat in Chelsea overlooking the River Thames. It was a gloomy old-fashioned kitchen. Down the corridor my mother was dying slowly. She fought each day with all her strength. I could tell by the determination in her eyes that she was fighting.

She had had a severe stroke, strong enough to put her in hospital, paralyze her body, and pull me back to England. (*Someone* had to look after her full time.) And her stroke had left her silent. The doctors said she had no hope of recovery. So now she lay up the hall, unable even to readjust her position in the bed, making no sound.

How strange to hear the silence! Never, in all my memory, could I recall silence and my mother ever to have remained in the same room. Any room my mother was in was full of her commotion, her bustle, sometimes her anger, always her energy. I remembered that when her sounds were angry, any silent room I sought out to hide from the dangerous sharpness of her words never felt entirely safe, for at any moment my mother could intrude through the door, bringing her noisiness with her, to desecrate the peaceful sanctity of my own private and secret imaginings.

I could remember also the other times when the effervescent strength of her presence gave life to any party or social occasion. She always was a great entertainer. People always seemed to gather around her, just to be near the glinting silvery light that she radiated whenever in the company of others.

Now my mother was suddenly and simply silent, deathly silent. Her silence did not lie quietly in bed with her; it pushed up the hall and filled the flat. At times I felt as if her silence, like her eyes, watched me, still allowing me no place to hide in the world of quiet thoughts.

There were moments, even now, when I found myself feeling that her silence, as her mouth once had done, accused me. Of what? Perhaps it was the crime of not being born a son, a son whom she could spoil and make into a mate more perfect than she ever believed my father to be. Perhaps it was the crime of being born the wrong kind of daughter. I could never share her delight and fascination in the minutiae of socializing, of serving the right drinks in the right glasses, of finding the perfect handbag to match the perfect hat. Or perhaps it was the crime of ever having been born at all.

But there were other moments when her eyes seemed strangely to need me, to be asking something of me. What did she want from me? Forgiveness, understanding, love? And what did I want from her? Perhaps the same emotions, an understanding that would make us feel less alone in each other's company. Why, I wondered, had my mother always had the power to create such confused ambivalence in me?

I felt I was beginning to know what we wanted from each other: the crumbling of the wall between us. I could not say for certain how the wall had ever got there. I remembered that early in my life the wall often seemed impermeable.

Lately I'd had instants of panic as I realized that there was not much time left. Would my mother die while the last stones of the wall still stood, before we were able to reach each other? The last brick remained between us and it was the most difficult to move. It was the mysterious cornerstone that had separated us, one from the other, since my earliest memory: Who was my mother? I did not know for certain. So much of her own life she had kept secret from me, and I only now began to understand the cause for her secrecy. And a suspicion had been growing in me that I was more like my mother, in hidden and surprising ways, than I ever would have believed. But until I understood her, how could I know myself?

Every day I fed and bathed her and tried to make her comfortable. When my father sat beside her bed and held her limp hand in his own, I watched him watching her. My father became thinner and thinner. I knew he found it unthinkable that a creature of such energy—to him, such *dazzling* energy—now lay so still. He held her hand as if he gladly would have pushed all of his own energy, his own life-force, from his body into hers, even at the cost of his own life. But all he could do was to sit, tired, worried, and frustrated.

My father was a small man and it seemed as if his hair was falling from his head like the needles off the pine trees in the park where, when I could get away, I walked with my dog, a Pekingese puppy called Taiwan II. Thank God for Taiwan. Taiwan was a very busy male dog. He threw himself about, huffing and puffing in the park near our Chelsea flat. As I prepared the evening meal, he sat at my feet, reassuringly, trying to absolve me, or help me, or merely to love me.

Would there ever be a man to really love me? I wondered. I remembered a time nearly four years ago when I felt young and was married to a phantom. My husband, in many ways, was a phantom which I created. Of course he was a person in his own right, but I created in him everything that I had hoped would fill me and complete me, to make me feel wanted and loved. That was not the same thing, I learned all too painfully, as truly being loved by another person.

When I thought of the past I found it hard to conjure a clear image of my mother. For so many years my mother had felt to me like a stranger, beautiful, proud, and obstinate. We had huge expensive photographs of me as a baby, Mary Jane Freeland. My mother had black hair and violet eyes. My father was hardly ever at home. He was a Consul in the Foreign Office then. He loved me in his own quiet way, but he adored my mother. A calm shadow of despair hung about my father until my mother came into the room and then his face would light up and his eyes shine. How I wished I had that effect on my father, but I never did.

I was a quiet child. What my parents did not know, however, was that I had a vast repertoire, a long bridge that I built, an escape world in which I lived nearly all the time. Perhaps it was because of this escape world that I also felt so isolated from the real world around me. But I believed there was a love in me, a love that I never felt safe enough to express.

And now, as I prepared to spoon-feed my mother after another day, I felt myself retreat to the familiar refuge of memory, of a life far away from the moribund atmosphere of this Chelsea flat. I began to walk up the corridor towards my mother's room; my thoughts, independent of my footsteps, ran from the future and flew to the past.

Book One

Chapter 1

The memory of Africa filled my mind with joyous brightness and the strong steady warmth of the African sun. My father then was the British Consul to South Africa, not the most senior Foreign Office rank, for there were a Consul General and an Ambassador above him. Nevertheless, the Foreign Office provided him with a generous colonial house seven miles outside Johannesburg, and with lots of servants.

I remembered the servants best and also loved them best. My earliest memories took me back to a time when I could not have been more than three or four years old, in the early nineteen-forties. A terrible war was going on in other parts of the world. But life for me, in the sunlit haze of distant childhood memory, felt happy and at peace. Not the life inside our wide white house; my mother's unpredictable moods made the house feel unsafe. But I spent as few hours as possible inside the house. Instead I lived my life and found my peace and my love outside our house in the blissful company of the servants.

There were many servants; a few were to me the most special. Sam was our huge black bodyguard who doubled as our gardener. He loved his gardens, and often I would follow him around as he raked a path, watered a bed, shoveled a hole to be filled by a young flowering bush, picked some vegetables, or protectively plucked the odd offending weed that threatened to steal water and earth from Sam's beloved selected plants. (I especially loved the bed of snapdragons that stood tall and high, big and strong and meaty like the big toads that sat in the lily pond putting out their long long tongues and trapping the flies as they sailed past.) Sam's manner was invariably unhurried, yet the work he managed to do in his steady relaxed pace was enormous. He could be sweating while hoeing a vegetable bed, or straining to heave away a boulder from a spot where he wanted to plant a new fruit tree, but he never showed me any temper. Always he had time to talk to me as I trailed after him, and when we ran out of things to say we were both happy for me to play with handfuls of dirt beside him while he carried on with his work.

When the sun set, a nightly excitement seemed to fill Sam, a quickness which he kept hidden from the hot noon sun. Ever guarding us, he would take out his gun and smile at me and shoot big fat rats off the barbed wire that fenced us in and kept us safe from whatever it was out in the black South African night. I was frightened of the rats, with their fleshy claws and the reflected lights from the house's windows shining red in their eyes, but I felt sorry for the poor creatures as they scrabbled and squeaked and died. Sam told me the rats were bad, and with his smile and his gun he would see to it that nothing bad came to bother me.

Sam lived in a group of bungalows, the servants' quarters, near our house. In the bungalow next to Sam's lived Saul, our houseboy. While Sam took care of everything outside our house, Saul tended to everything inside. He was there to see that things remained in the proper place ordained to them by my mother's divine rules of order. When my mother was in a bad mood, she would find something to complain to Saul about. "Those plates aren't where they're supposed to be," she would suddenly snap at him. Or "The rug in the hall is a mess. Take it outside and beat it," or

"I've decided I want that table moved over there." Always with the greatest humility, Saul would bow his head politely and do what my mother instructed. But when she wasn't looking, he would turn his eyes to me and wink.

Saul and Sam both loved me and I loved them. They took turns giving me rides on their shoulders when they had a break from their work. They laughed with each other, and teased each other, and gave me little presents—a pretty flower from the garden, a small lion carved from a piece of wood, a string of beads to wear around my neck under my dress—and they each pretended to be jealous if the other had given me a nicer gift.

Max, our cook, was a different matter. He seemed to have no time for playing; always busy cooking one dish and preparing another. He guarded his kitchen as if it contained jewels that the world was trying to steal. If any other servant dared to enter the kitchen without first being invited by Max, Max would growl and act fierce. Even my mother seemed hesitant to walk into the kitchen of her own house. When she spoke to Max to order her menus, she spoke cautiously, as if to an animal not fully tamed. But for all his menacing fury, Max liked me. I could wander into the kitchen any time I pleased. I would climb up onto a stool and watch Max as he boned a chicken or cut up vegetables with his long sharp knife. He would peer at me silently from the corner of his dark yellow eyes, and then—as if doing something he ought not to—he would glance around and, seeing no one was looking on, slip me a choice slice of vegetable or sweet piece of fruit. Clutching my treat and sucking on its juicy sweetness, I would hop down from my stool and go running off to find Bertha.

Of all the servants, I loved Bertha, my nanny, most. Bertha's body was soft and it smelled edible, a fragrant mixture of coconuts and molasses. She had marvelous soft warm breasts. Upon seeing me, she always would pick me up in a hug, my arms as far around her as they could reach and my cheek turned gladly against her breasts, and swing me in a circle, lifting my feet high off the ground. Bertha was beautiful, black, and wide and tall as a carob tree. She carried me on her hips for as long as I can remember and she sang songs to me. I loved Bertha with all my heart. And she loved me.

Bertha lived in her own bungalow near the house (my mother insisted always that I should be grown up enough to sleep by myself in my own room), but I spent most of my days with Bertha in her bungalow. I don't think there was ever a time I ran through Bertha's door when some boiling pot or other could not be smelled cooking. Freshly plucked chickens bubbled slowly in a creamy white sauce of coconut milk, or a spicy chickpea curry grew darker and spicier with the popping of every puffed out bubble. Bertha fed me my lunches from her own food. Wondrous lunches! Bowls of strong smells seeping up my nose and filling my head, and peppery tastes heating my tongue and warming my stomach. Why didn't my parents eat food like this all the time?

After lunch Bertha would sit with me outside in front of her bungalow while I played on the ground with the children who had the other servants as parents. These children were beautiful in their blackness, and it never seemed fair to me that I was not born black like them. Their skin had such a deep blackness, like liquid onyx, and glistened where their necks met their shoulders in the afternoon sun. Because I was always in the sun myself, my skin grew light brown all over and red on my shoulders, on my cheeks, on my upper arms, and on the tops of my feet, for I wore no shoes whenever my mother wasn't looking. (My mother's skin was the whitest white. Never did she allow the sun to touch a bare inch of her skin. "It causes wrin-

kles," she explained, and she was forever scolding me
for my darkening complexion. ("No proper English little girl," she told me, "wears a suntan.") But try as I
might, I simply could not get my skin to go the same
solid black as the African children. I felt pale and less
beautiful, seeing my own white knees beside theirs.

I did become very good at squatting. The African
children, when playing, squatted in a circle, squatted
with their heels firmly on the ground. I learned to keep
my balance without picking up my heels. And into the
center of our squatted circle we tossed pebbles. I don't
remember the rules of our game, something like trying to hit the big pebble with all the smaller pebbles
that we squeezed tightly in our hands until the
rougher edges of some pebbles left little dents in our
palms. Pebbles were to be treasured. The better one
became at tossing them, the more of everyone else's
one got to collect. I showed a natural talent for
pebble-tossing, even at such a young age, so my pockets always bulged heavily with my prized pebble booty.

However much I tried to darken my skin and improve my squatting and pebble-tossing techniques, I
still did not have a proper doll like the African little
girls. I was forced to play with perfectly awful dolls,
all delicate and useless. My mother had them sent to
me from shops on the other side of the world, and any
of my parents' friends coming to visit kept giving me
more of the same wretched dolls. The dolls did everything I hated doing. They wore frilly white dresses; I
wished I could wear few and light clothes like the African children. The dolls kept their feet in shiny black
party-shoes; I thought feet were meant to be bare. The
dolls hid their silky hair beneath lace bonnets to keep
their vacuously staring porcelain faces forever pale
and Britishly white; I disdained hats and was cross with
the sun for not making me black enough to become
African.

But the African children's dolls were beautiful. The

African dolls were themselves African. They were carved from dried corn-cobs, relieved of their kernels. No floppy arms with delicate porcelain hands had these dolls; they were straight erect figures, hard and strong, with necks as tall and as beautifully shaped as those of the African children. The children's fathers carved the dolls for them. Although I knew my father loved me, he was never home long enough to carve a doll for me. When he was home, he was always busy reading, writing letters, or having meetings with other English men.

One day, a day I remembered clearly because it proved to be one of the worst in my life, I sat with the other children in front of Bertha's bungalow. We had eaten our lunches and had tossed many rounds of pebbles. Growing tired from our games, we sat down from our squats to play dolls. My prissy dolls sat unloved and ignored on a shelf in my bedroom in our house. I was interested only in the African dolls. All the girls had their proper corn-cob dolls, but I had none. I borrowed another girl's doll and pretended it was mine. The whole afternoon I kept the doll in my arms pressed hard against my chest.

When the afternoon began to grow cool, and the white sunlight of the day turned to its softer evening colors, Bertha came to take me back into my house, my English house, my white house, away from the happy and lively African bungalows that smelled of good food. I did not want to go. I did not want to leave the other children or to release the beautiful corn-cob doll. I think I started to cry. "Come, child," Bertha said, picking me up in her arms and handing the doll back to its rightful African owner. She hugged me close. I smelled her body's smell, spicy like the smell of the food she cooked. I stared into her face. She did not have her usual smile. Bertha looked sad. I knew why: my mother had been very cross with her. I had heard my mother screaming at her, "You're ruining her! You're trying to turn her into an African girl, and I won't have it! I will not raise my daughter to have her stuck in Africa her whole life. I want better for her than that!"

Bertha looked at me now with a sadness that made her eyes wet. Her smooth black cheeks curved down into deep lines around her soft mouth. "You have to go back to your house," Bertha cooed at me. Then, reading my mind, she smiled and shook her head. "You can't live here with us," she said. "Your mother wants you to be a fine English girl."

"I want a doll," was all I could say, feeling her tears drying on my cheeks. Bertha sighed and leaned her head to the side, as if in agreement.

Bertha took me inside the house. Max gave me dinner alone, for my parents were dining out at some Foreign Office affair. Max was especially kind to me. He did not say much, but while I ate he sat across the kitchen table quietly drinking a glass of the wine he used for cooking.

When I put myself to bed my leg kicked something hard beneath my sheets. Reaching down, I lifted the object and, in the moonlight through the window, beheld a corn-cob doll of my own. Bertha must have put it there during my dinner. I don't know where she got it from or who carved it—Sam or Saul or another of the servants—but I knew it was mine. It was beautiful and I loved it at once. My own real African doll. It put my horrid porcelain dolls to shame. I wanted to let them know that I no longer needed them at all.

I lay my new doll on my pillow and jumped out of bed. With one arm I swept all the other dolls off the shelf. They fell in a pile on the floor. One doll's china head hit the leg of a chair and the sound of the porcelain shattering was loud. "Serves you right," I said to the doll with the broken head. Then I remembered my mother. She had given me the fragile doll. She would be upset if she found out I had broken it. I slid the broken bits into a little pile and then covered them with the doll's headless body, and then a mound of the other dolls. I would ask Saul to clean up the mess tomorrow.

I climbed back into bed and hugged my wonderful corn-cob doll. But I could not sleep. I sat up in my teak bed under a thick musty-smelling mosquito net and surrounded by more dark teak furniture. I waited for the sound of our chauffeur bringing my parents back home.

When at last I heard the car crunch up the drive, I lay down and closed my eyes. When my mother was in a good mood, my father always slipped in and kissed me goodnight. He knew I was awake every time, but that was our secret. This night was a bad mood night, and he did not come in.

I could hear my mother clicking furiously in her high heels, pacing the front hall. "How could you?" she was yelling. I knew it by heart. My mother was jealous.

My father did not answer back.

At last I heard a door shut. It was my father's door, for he and my mother had separate bedrooms. My mother, I hoped, had calmed down. But no, for I heard her heels clicking up the hall towards my room. She was still cross. My door flew open and the light went on with a loud snap and I could *feel* my mother standing behind me. "You're still awake! It's no good pretending. I know you're still awake."

I rolled slowly towards her. "Hmmm?" I said, trying to make my voice sound sleepy.

"Don't even try to fool me. I know you're still awake and it's way past your bed time and you're still awake. You're spoiled. That's the problem. Everyone spoils you. Your father spoils you, that Bertha spoils you, Sam spoils . . . What's that?" she said suddenly, seeing my corn-cob doll held tight in my arms. "Oh, Mary

Jane! What on earth are you doing with that horrid statue? Where did you get it?''

"Bertha gave it . . ."

"Bertha? I should have known. She'd make a little nigger out of you, if I gave her half a chance. Here, give it to me." And she grabbed the doll from me. "This is not the sort of thing a proper English girl should play with. It's horrible and ugly. And you have such pretty dolls." She looked across my room at the empty shelf. "Mary Jane! What have you done? What on earth have you done?" She went across my bedroom and started collecting the dolls in her arms. I shut my eyes. Inevitably she came to the broken doll.

There was silence. I opened my eyes. She stood with the dolls in her arms and the headless one hanging in her hand. My mother's pale cheeks were spotted with red. "I ordered this doll especially for you. You've broken it and thrown it away. Why, if I'd had a doll like this at your age, I'd have treasured it forever." She looked sad for a brief moment, and then she hissed, "That does it. That finally does it." She dropped all the dolls from her arms and walked quickly out of my room.

I got out of bed to put out the lights, then, trembling with fright, I climbed back in. I could hear my mother's voice, shrill in the night. I lay motionless until at last I fell asleep.

In the morning, before breakfast, I ran to Bertha's familiar bungalow in the servants' quarters. I stood in Bertha's doorway, blinking into the darkness from the bright South African morning light. The bed was empty. The rickety wooden cupboard was empty. A tremendous sorrow struck my heart. Where was she? Then, remembering my mother's harsh voice in the night, I knew Bertha had gone far away, farther than the gate, farther than the giant rhododendrons that lined the drive, farther than the barbed wire that kept us all safe. I knew I must find her and I set off down the drive. Sam the gardener saw me. He caught me struggling and kicking and carried me back with such a sad look on his face. He handed me to my mother. "Bertha! Bertha!" I cried.

"Bertha's gone," my mother said. "She's a bad influence," she said to Sam. Sam's face remained unchanged. Then, as if to strengthen her explanation to Sam, she added, "And she stole my jewelry."

I knew then that my mother could lie. I looked at Sam. Sam had the most beautiful eyes in the world, wide shining black eyes that sloped in his head. They reminded me of the dates that glowed in the garden. I saw his mouth droop but his brown eyes snapped like the snapdragons that I squeezed between my fingers. "I hate you!" I screamed at my mother, for at that moment I felt only intense hatred. She had taken from me what I had loved, Bertha and my doll. "I hate you!"

And Lavinia Freeland, my mother, laughed her sharp, silvery, tinkling laugh. I saw her nostrils flare and the pupils of her eyes tighten. She was going to hit me. I knew because I was her daughter and I was behaving badly. I roared and screamed. "Go now, Sam," my mother said. "Chop chop." Sam reluctantly left me, and my mother took me into the hall of the long cool house, still quiet in the morning. "You stupid girl," my mother hissed. "You stupid little girl." It was too late to run. Her blood-red fingernails dug into my arm. Her hand slapped my face. "I'll make a proper little girl of you, if it kills us both," she said. In the explosion of that blow, her ring caught the edge beside my eye and blood trickled down my face.

Seeing the blood, my mother suddenly changed. She knelt down and hugged me passionately and started to cry. "I'm sorry," she said. "I'm very sorry."

I started to cry as well. My face hurt and I knew that I had hurt my mother with my words of hatred. "I'm sorry, too," I said. Holding each other, we both cried.

When my father came to the breakfast table, where my mother and I were already quietly seated, he saw the cut beside my eye. He did not comment. Instead, he led us in saying grace, the three of us sitting at the table, Saul the houseboy standing behind my mother's chair. I was grateful Saul was still there; Bertha, my beloved motherly Bertha, the one woman on earth who, I knew, loved me, was gone. And I knew that I would never see her again.

My father looked at me after grace. I realized that he knew she had hit me. My father said nothing. He did nothing. He was my father and he was supposed to be my protector, no matter how badly I behaved. From that day on, I decided to make Max the cook my protector, huge fierce Max who always seemed to have a chopping knife in his hand.

When Bertha left, I felt I was cut dangerously loose from the main anchor that had steadied me on the high-waved seas of my mother's moods. Without Bertha to keep me safely grounded in all that was real and nurturing and indigenously African, I had little choice but to drift into Foreign Office life as prescribed by my mother. This must have made my mother quite happy, although I think she always sensed that the responsibilities of being a British Consul's daughter did not come naturally to me. I was a fairly perpetual disappointment and cause of irritation to her. Still, during the middle years of my childhood I behaved more like the other Foreign Office little girls in South Africa, and from this fact she derived some satisfaction.

As if in compensation for my loss of Bertha, I was given a pet by my mother shortly afterwards, a present that surprised me. I was not allowed a dog, but it seems my mother believed a cat to be an appropriate companion for a Foreign Office daughter. My cat I named Marmalade after the delicious jars of orange jam that arrived every six months in that mysterious thing called the diplomatic pouch. This pouch disgorged my mother's silk stockings, treasures from Harrods, and cashmere sweaters to wear on a cold crisp night when it was necessary for Saul to light the big fire in the drawing room and I would sit at my father's feet on my small chair and gaze into the magic mysterious flames. Far away in the flames I saw castles and princes, queens and kings.

❧ *Chapter 2* ❧

When I went to school I realized I found it difficult to make friends with other girls. I was shy and awkward. They all seemed absolutely thrilled to be dressed in dollish pretty frilly dresses, while I minded having my feet stuffed into shoes and my body bedecked in what seemed to be perfectly useless outfits. (A dress was hardly right for playing in the garden or tossing pebbles.) And the girls giggled. They laughed at me because I was always far more interested in finding out something new from a book than in joining their gossip.

Entering school at six, I had read many of the books in our house. I had worked my way through a marvellous set of the *Encyclopaedia Britannica,* spent hours staring at Gray's *Anatomy,* looked with wonder upon a morbid yet fascinating dictionary of abnormal diseases, and was beginning to open our volumes of Hardy and Dickens. Reading was the first love that I shared with my father, Peter Freeland, an Oxford scholar. His great joy in life was to read. First at breakfast he read *The Times* from London and I listened as he discussed English politics with my mother. She, I could tell, seemed distracted. I was interested. The

War halfway across the world was exciting. The Germans all wore helmets and I eagerly read accounts of the War. It all sounded glamorous. The English soldiers always seemed to be smoking and their blond hair was forever sticking up at right angles to their scalps. They all grinned in the newspaper pictures.

My father was decorated at the beginning of the War. For what, I was never sure. He never talked about that. I was proud of him though, and I came to look forward to spending an evening hour or two with him each day after I returned home from another boring day of reading about two irrelevant fictitious children named Peter and Jane (how boring they seemed compared to the criminal yet loveable characters in *Oliver Twist!*) and their terminally obedient dog Spot. Were I ever allowed a dog, I promised myself, I would find better things to do with it than make it wear a napkin around its neck while I pretended to serve it tea. But I did have my cat Marmalade, and he was good company in the afternoons spent waiting for my father to come home from the Consulate.

My father was my favorite companion. We shared our love of Africa, of books, of new bits of information, of the garden, of many things. Sometimes I seemed to share with him many more things than my mother. Perhaps that was another crime for which I felt accused by my mother. I was not girl enough to be her daughter, but I was boy enough for my father to enjoy me as a daughter/son.

On some evenings when my parents were not entertaining or being entertained, we sat as a family in our drawing room. While I watched the fire and handed over my imagination to its flames, my mother sat on the other side of the hearth and embroidered chairseats, her sharp needles flashing in and out, glinting cold in the firelight. By her side was a box of Harrods chocolates. Every few minutes she popped a chocolate into her mouth. She had slightly protruding front teeth and she wore bright red lipstick.

My father usually lay back in his chair with a massive political tome in his hand, or he wrote letters to his Oxford friends. He collected all the anecdotes about his beloved England from the afternoon post, and sometimes in the evenings he would read the amusing parts of his letters aloud to me. I saw pictures of the lovely house he was born in, a very stately home called Milton Park in Somerset. I knew some time, when I reached eleven or twelve, I would be sent home to school in England, a country I had never seen. It was both an exciting thought and a terrifying one. All the English children were going, my mother told me.

I think because I had not been born a boy, my father dealt with this sad blow by treating me like one. We fished together on some weekends. Big bright catfish. We played cricket together and while, unlike many of the other men, my father refused to shoot the deer and the elephants, we went (when my father had the time) together with Saul and Sam to photograph the animals. I loved those trips. My mother stayed behind. I know she found it hard enough living in Africa at all, never mind being imprisoned seven miles away from the city. To venture voluntarily even farther from civilization seemed to her, I'm sure, the greatest of incomprehensible folly.

But my father and I loved South Africa. At night we often walked around the garden together. We watched as the vegetables ripened through the year. Harvest was a joyous time for us both. Sam did all the heavy work: my father said he had green thumbs, which he certainly had. When I read of Eden in my Bible, I thought of our garden. To both my father and me, our garden was our Eden. As it moved from the house, it grew in height and lushness and fragrance. Near to the house were the beds for the flowers and the vegetables, all very vibrant but also very civilized. Beyond the neat beds, beyond the waist-high row of night-scented stalk, were the fruit trees growing not in proper regimented rows but in a chaotic African order of their own. As each evening the sun sank and the sky darkened, the stalk was the first to release its evening vanillic smell, throaty and rich, more dangerous and alive than the sun-blanched smells of daylight. The blossoms on the fruit trees—mangoes, pomegranates, and plums—mixed their spicy sweetness in the wind. And past the fruit trees, in blackening crepuscularity, spread the looming shadows of the forest.

After dinner my father usually did some translating from Latin, and then he rolled a Havana cigar between his fingers and I knew it was time for the walk. The walk was a peaceful time of refuge for me. I did not do well at school. I was never naughty; I was far too quiet, the teachers said. I knew what the problem was. Being an only child, I was used to discussing everything with my father: books, the Bible, what was happening in Africa. My father was famous for his ability to prophesy accurately the events of the future. He wrote books on war, on the history of war, and on the evolving history of Africa.

"This lovely country," he once said passionately to me, "is like a sleeping animal. Millions of people across the land are starving and dying because of the color of their skin. Isn't it ironic? Slavery abroad is banned and considered a horrible crime, but here, in his own homeland, a black man and his family are enslaved by a handful of white people. One day, the animal will stir and shake himself, and the door of South Africa will be shut to the white men for a very long time." I saw pairs of animal eyes gleam from the darkness of the forest. We stood as the big stars lit the ground and the moon, full, scudded past wrapped in clouds of darkness. I trembled at what he said.

All this I shared and loved with my father. It was always a mystery why my mother could not share with us our love, why we could not be a family in which love spread evenly among us all, as the ocean spreads its waters to every shore. But my mother seemed excluded from the love between my father and me, an exclusion which, I am sure, must have hurt her. No doubt she could not understand why I had been created more in my father's image than in her own. I suppose it must have been lonely for her to have a daughter who could not join in her passions.

My mother was a mahjong fanatic. She and her friends seemed to hate South Africa. They complained all the time about the heat, the flies, the provincialness, even of the city. But they loved their mahjong games together. On several occasions when I was in the drawing room quietly reading or pretending to read, I looked at the women, my mother's various rouged and pomaded friends, and I listened to the endless tap tap tapping of the mahjong pieces. Sometimes the fearsome dragon carved on the black ivory pieces seemed a lot less dangerous than the women who grasped their tiles in their weekly manicured nails. "He is a little *timid,* darlings." This was my mother's opening maneuver. "Do you know Melitta?" (She was the Australian Ambassador's wife.) "Well, she tried to make a pass at him. I thought he'd die."

Crow Number Two (I, on those occasions when my mother had been cross with me, thought of my mother as Crow Number One) was Mrs Biddle, a loud harsh American woman. She replied, "Jerry's too boring for anyone to want to sleep with him." She sniffed. Mrs Biddle was a face-pincher. She was at that age when she would plug her face to your cheek and pinch the other cheek with her hand. She was flashy and hard like the black widow that hung outside my window. She had lots of raspberry lipstick which ran into the crevasses over her mouth, and by the end of the afternoon, after several White Ladies, the red tide slipped over onto her quite protruding teeth and she made me think that she had perhaps just bitten her poor quiet husband Jerry.

Crow Number Three, Madame Derlanger, was French. She had a daughter of my age, Geneviève. Geneviève was perfect at everything. She and her mother were elegant mice. They had glossy hair and glossy bodies and they went everywhere and did everything together. Madame Derlanger was my mother's mentor, because Madame Derlanger was the French Ambassador's wife. My mother was merely a Consul's wife. Usually an Ambassador's wife would never deign to play mahjong with a Consul's wife, so my mother was in awe of this weekly event. Her mahjong day reflected the hours of cleaning and polishing required, the making of seemingly hundreds of little cucumber sandwiches, white bread, white as Madame Derlanger's fingers. Also confections of chocolates, each woman vying with the other.

Crow Number Four, Connie Wiseman, was the least senior of all the wives. Her husband was in the Air Force, and the Air Force to a man was considered "common." Actually I rather liked Connie. She seemed to be a fantastic mahjong player, as she always won money off my mother. When they played together in tournaments they were largely undefeated.

While the four women, the four Crows, played I sat and listened. I heard them, through subtle dismissals, exclude their husbands from their hearts. This was the world of women. This was my mother's true world. Indeed she would pretend to take an interest in the evenings in my father's day, or in whatever history book he currently was working on, or in his political opinions towards a quickly changing world, but in my father's company she was the pale twin of the vital woman she became in the presence of other women. And this whispering, gossiping, hinting, innuendoing world of women, I grew aware, was the world to which she wanted me to belong.

But how could I belong? What could these women offer me compared to the truly alive, truly vivid, truly breath-taking colors to be found among the flowers of our garden or among the birds of the bordering forest? What bits of gossip from their lips could possibly be as fascinating as information I could learn from my books or from my father? I began to wish I *had* been born a boy, for then there would have been no question of my inclusion in the women's circle . . .

The tiles clicked and the women talked. I kept my eyes on the book in my lap. Then, with a sharp clarity, I heard Madame Derlanger's French-accented voice ring like a newly polished bell. "The reports from Geneviève's school are brilliant. How wonderful that she should be a leader among the girls of her class. And Mary?"

An awful silence fell among the women. I kept staring at my book but I waited carefully for my mother's words. Her voice spoke quietly. "Mary? Oh, she does well. She just hasn't found her place yet."

"Not surprising," Madame Derlanger, the Ambassador's wife, continued with momentum, clearly on the attack. "One must be born to one's place. Geneviève knows our place and it has always suited her like a fish in the ocean."

I could tell from my mother's silence that the words "our place" had stung her. I knew that she knew that the Derlangers' place was higher than the Freelands'. It meant so much to my mother to move among the right people in the diplomatic world, to play mahjong with an Ambassador's wife as if she were an equal, but here she was, reminded of her lower position. My mother, for once, had nothing to say. She continued with the game and made her move, silent as if she had not heard Madame Derlanger's intentional snub. A subtle snub to be sure, but still a snub. And I knew my mother was embarrassed, because how could I compare to Geneviève Derlanger?

Suddenly I felt sorry for my mother. How dare Madame Derlanger speak to her with that awful French tone of superiority in her voice. I wanted to defend my mother, but who was I to defend her? Just a small girl who hardly knew how to put two words together when other people were around. I found myself wishing I was a grown woman. Then I could have pulled up a chair and joined in the mahjong game and said something terribly clever and cutting to hurt Madame Derlanger as she had hurt my mother. Or if I had been a boy, I could have done something properly naughty, like take my slingshot and aim a pebble at the back of Madame Derlanger's head, then run out of the room, laughing at what a good shot I was. Instead I was just a girl, a useless girl, and I could think of nothing to do to help my injured mother.

There was another reason that I wanted to be a boy or, more precisely, *not to be a girl*. Only with difficulty can I remember this reason at all, as if the memories themselves, mercifully trying to protect me from their own painful truth, prefer to remain hidden and beyond my mind's reach. This reason was other men.

As my mother came to new life in the company of other women, so she radiated with a special brilliance, a glow brighter than she showed around my father, when entertaining other men. It was in the nature of our Foreign Office life that my mother frequently was called upon to play hostess to many men: visiting foreign dignitaries, more senior diplomats from our own corps, and, of course, the King's Messengers. The ubiquitous King's Messengers, "Uncle Richard" and

"Uncle Thomas." (The avuncular tone of their nick-names had been assigned to them by my mother.)

Whenever these bearers of the diplomatic pouch, and of all other official mediums of contact between us and the rest of the world, were due to visit us yet again, my mother seemed to dither around the house with a special agitated excitement: the "Uncles" would carry with them treasures from other worlds, worlds where I knew my mother would rather be. Moreover, Uncle Richard and Uncle Thomas brought with them their own maleness, a maleness that loved to be doted on and fussed over by a woman as beautiful as my mother. When they arrived and had delivered their pouches, their envelopes, their messages, they would be entreated by my mother to sit down, to relax, while she ran to tell Max in the kitchen of their special re-quests for the dinner menu (a subservient service I never remember her performing for my father). "Be nice to Uncle Richard," my mother would say to me over her shoulder as she left the room. Or "Why don't you and Uncle Thomas sit and have a chat?" And once they had had their many cups of tea and shared our dinner, they remained with us longer than their offi-cial business necessitated. Or so it seemed to me.

In my mind, the faces and bodies of the two Queen's Messengers blurred and merged into one. I can re-member neither their individual voices nor their dis-tinctive faces. All I see when I try to recall my "Uncles" are thick lips and even thicker fingers, trying to touch me. I remember the lips that used to try to kiss my childhood mouth in a dark hallway. Or, if Uncle Thomas or Uncle Richard sat next to me at dinner, I remember finding a thick hot hand on my knee.

I was afraid to tell my mother. Tell her what? And would she believe me if I were to complain about any of the men who, so obviously, brought her excitement and joy? As for my father, however much I loved him and our hours together, he had proved long ago his uselessness as my protector, either from my mother or from the men who came to be near my mother. It was my other fathers, my black, strong, African protectors—Saul and Sam and Max—who made me feel safer whenever my "Uncles" were around. When, at dinner, a hand found my knee, I was at least reassured to feel Saul's guarding presence behind me.

Wanting to be a boy became an obsession to me, and this longing reached its culmination one day. I had already, and after much practice, got quite good at peeing standing up, but it was the "Dreadful Penknife Day" that shook me to the core. DPD, I called it.

The boyscouts and the girlscouts in our region of South Africa were all called together, along with the cubs and the brownies. I was two days off my eighth birthday. There were about forty of us all lined up in front of the British Consulate. The grass was so green it was blue. Fortunately a wind blew, depriving the fainters of a chance to draw attention to themselves by hitting the deck, thus further preempting the Red Cross Ambulance's opportunity to rush about with stretchers and race with bells a-clanging to the nearest hospital.

My father, in full regalia (that is, white suit, medals on, and a sort of Napoleon hat with funny feathers sticking out of it), walked up and down inspecting the ranks of children. My mother accompanied him and gave a very good imitation of the Queen accompanying George VI, except that my mother always looked distant and distracted on these occasions. So at the end, we all saluted and then Gray Owl came down the lines and handed out wrapped presents. Across from me I could see the cubs tearing off the paper and holding up shiny pen-knives, not just a one-blade but a two-er. I was shaking with hope.

To my dismay, I got one of those dreadful kits to make long ropes of knitting by poking a roll down a hole surrounded by little pegs at the top. Some of the cubs looked at my present and laughed. That was too much. I threw the thing in the bushes and ran home.

Saul saw me run into my bedroom and he followed me. "What's matter, missy?" he said.

I thought I would die. "I want to be a boy," I said. Saul grinned. "I want . . ." I waited.

Saul patted me on the back. "Go see Max. He has made a big cake."

I usually invaded the big kitchen after Max had made a cake because he always left me the bowl to lick, but this time even chocolate wouldn't ease my pain. All those prayers every night for a pen-knife unanswered. How could God do this to me? Jesus must have had a pen-knife.

Then a miracle occurred and I could resume my relationship with God. After supper and an emphatic reminder from my mother that I was not to be "a bad sport" for sulking over my knitting kit, which was a mortal sin in her eyes—as we were not practising Catholics, it constituted bad form, which was a dreadful crime at least as onerous as sin—I went to bed disconsolate.

I liked to sleep on my face with a pillow over the back of my head, dead flat under the sheets so if a burglar or a pirate (I had read *Treasure Island*) were to slip through my window he wouldn't know I was there. I put my hand under the pillow to lift it up, and I felt a fairly large object. I lifted the pillow and to my joy saw a big African hunting knife with blue beading on the shaft, lying encased in a perfectly beautiful sheath made of real-smelling leather. So much better than those cheap little pen-knives. I got down on my knees and thanked God for the miracle. Another miraculous present hidden in my bed, just like the beloved doll that Bertha had secreted for me. Another saving African treasure. The secrecy of *this* treasure, I promised myself, would be preserved at all costs. I thought my mother might confiscate the knife if she saw it, so I hid it under my mattress. Only Marmalade, my cat, knew where it was and he promised me he wouldn't tell.

Safely assured of my boyhood rather than girlhood, and with a real knife of my very own, I now could pretend fully to be a boy, my father's son.

 # Chapter 3

The year when I was ten proved to be a year of crisis, if *crisis* is understood (as it should be) to mean *change*. Everything changed for me in that year: my security in feeling I would always be allowed to live in Africa, my unquestioning relationship with my father.

Late one afternoon, I sat by the window in the drawing room, reading as usual, waiting for my father to come home. It had been a day like any other. I had sat quietly through the school day feeling awkward and alienated among the other girls, and also slightly cowed and intimidated by their easy social graces. Then, leaving school and feeling that daily sense of liberation when running away from the open school gates, I had arrived home to the sanctity of my own safe world. I talked with Sam, I joked with Saul, I was kindly shooed out of the kitchen by Max—he was busy cooking for a big dinner that night—and I watched Marmalade stalk a lizard amid the dangerous miniature-jungle-like stems of sun-faced African daisies. Finally, as the moment of my father's expected return approached, I sat with my copy of *Swallows and Amazons* by the window. I could hear my mother bustling in the dining room, overseeing Saul and other servants in their preparations of the long table for the evening's guests. That night they were having a huge dinner party for the Spanish Ambassador from Johannesburg.

When the front door opened and my father stepped in, I greeted him with my usual gladness. But my father's face held a strange look, a look that seemed to ignore my hug of greeting. His face was at once preoccupied, nervous, and excited. "Where's your mother?" he asked.

"In the dining room," I said.

I walked beside my father as he strode quickly to find my mother. "We'll be moving to Paris," he, standing in the open doorway of the dining room, announced to her back.

Immediately my mother turned and was frantic with joy. Immediately my heart sank. Never had I felt such a sudden panic, as if all that I loved as home would be taken from me in an instant. "Can I take Marmalade?" I asked.

"Of course not, Mary Jane," my mother said. "He'll have to be put down."

My father looked at my mother and said very firmly, "We can find Marmalade a good home, can't we, Lavinia?"

My mother's head went up, as it always did when she was annoyed. "Yes, dear," she said evenly. "Of course."

That night, though grieving inside, I had to play my role in entertaining the Spanish Ambassador. By now I, too, was part of the entertainment, a dutiful actress in an endlessly repetitious play. I was to be polite and poised at all times, and already I had learned from my mother the practiced art of *noblesse oblige:* Keep your thoughts and your tears to yourself; propriety is the priority.

Dressed in frilly dress and long white socks, my outfit was complete with my shiny black party shoes. I had long fair hair and I had inherited my father's deep blue eyes. I wished I'd inherited my father's eyelashes and his long slender hands. Instead I had short fat hands and wide peasant feet. Mercifully that night I only had to stay around for the introductions and the picture-taking. The press always came and took a picture of Peter and Lavinia Freeland out on the patio shaking hands with this Ambassador or that famous actor or racing driver. In the back there was always a blob, like a round dumpling. That was me. I hated having my picture taken. "They take your soul away with the picture," Sam the gardener told me and it did indeed feel like that to me.

After the last flashbulb had popped, and after I'd kissed hundreds of cheeks—some were soft but most were withered—I ran off to find Marmalade and tell him we were leaving. I lay on my bed with Marmalade sitting on my chest. Marmalade blinked his marmalade eyes and gently licked the tip of my nose. I clung to him and I cried myself to sleep.

It turned out to be a year before we moved to Paris, but the months leading up to the move seemed to be spent interminably packing. Enormous crates occupied the house. My mother considered she had an eye for African art, so she had a huge collection of statues and belts and beads. The new house in France, my father told her, was very grand and he was going to be promoted to Consul General. My father showed me his promotion paper from the Foreign Office and I did feel proud of him. The order was signed by George VI.

For years I had come to think of the King of England as a protective guardian, watching over us all even from distant London. I had my father in my family.

Then there was Our Father who was in Heaven, and then there was Our Father who was in London, George VI. I felt I knew the whole Royal Family well, for my family represented that Family abroad. "If in doubt, do what you think the Queen would do," my mother always said. I spent a fair amount of time thinking about this. I loved Elizabeth, the Queen Consort, as a grandmother. The beautiful young Princess Elizabeth, whom I knew from newspapers and photographs, seemed to me a lovely maternal aunt. My scrapbook on the Royal Family and their children grew, but the subject of Edward and Mrs Simpson was never discussed in our house.

Neither was sex. I got what little information I had from overhearing the girls at school. But by the time we were packing to move to Paris, I knew more than I wanted to know, thanks to the night, shortly after I learned the news of our eventual move, when something happened that changed my life.

I had a nightmare one night. I was fleeing from a horde of grotesque-looking gnomes in my dream. Waking, I ran down the corridor to the far side of the house and into my father's bedroom. I switched on the light and I stood there. My mother was in my father's bedroom, in my father's bed. The night was hot. My father lay on his stomach beneath the bedclothes, but above the sheets I could see his bare shoulders and back. Despite the lights, he remained asleep. The eyes of his head, turned towards my mother's pale smooth underarm, were shut and his mouth, pressed to the softness of the pillow, was open in deep and undisturbed sleep.

My mother, awake beside him, looked straight at me. My mother was naked. In an instant I knew they had been doing "it," that thing I had overheard the girls giggling about at school. Until that moment I had assumed that my parents did "it." How else would they have had me? But never had I had a picture in my mind of my parents engaging in physical love, of my mother sharing herself with my father.

Frozen forever in my memory is the sight of my mother's eyes. She looked at me, her languid eyes full of amusement. Her lips without her usual blood red lipstick were still red, her body a pale scarf broken only by her patch of peculiarly bushy hair between her legs. Very slowly with her hand she reached for the sheets and covered her exposed body. All the while my mother's eyes remained on me. In her eyes was now the strangest look I had ever seen, a look of ownership. In a very special way, a very grown-up way, my mother had a part of my father all to herself. Yet her body, first bare then covered, looked to me, as ever, porcelain: like the heads of my imported dolls years before. Beside her my father looked small and vulnerable.

I stood transfixed. A huge bolt of pain pierced my heart. No, no. My lungs felt as if they had atrophied. Breath squeezed past my lips. Outside the calls of rasping cicadas exploded. I ran, no word exchanged between my mother and me, and I threw myself on my bed. Many hours of troubled thoughts passed before I fell into an even more troubled sleep.

When I awoke, dawn was coming through my window. I realized I had been crying in my sleep. I knew I would never be the same again. Part of me was locked away. My father's relationship with me, his exclusive daughter/son, would never be the same. As the indigo nightsky receded and the early birds called, I lay half asleep, clogged with sweat under the mosquito net. I felt a new confusion towards my mother.

So many times had I assumed that it was I, not she, who appreciated my father fully. I even had wondered whether or not she loved him. Oh, I knew she loved the lifestyle he gave her, the endless rounds of balls and parties, the dinners, the big stylish house, and she loved her diamonds inherited from the Freeland family. Yes, she loved the Freeland diamonds. The Freelands were originally Dutch, she said. "And these are Dutch diamonds, Mary Jane. When you marry, go to Holland for your engagement ring. You choose three one-carat diamonds set in white gold. The white gold shows them off best. A yellow setting discolours diamonds." There was no end to my mother's knowledge about the proper way to live a proper life, the life she had because my father gave it to her. She had a mind like a magpie's nest, bits of information sticking out like straw here and there. And of course she had a little machine on her dressing table that cleaned her diamonds so they shone and glittered. And I had seen my mother at times pat my father's cheek when she walked behind his armchair. But I had also seen her at her mahjong games, dropping her little implications to her friends that somehow she just managed to tolerate her life with her husband. Until now, I had felt a special confidence that only I truly revered my father's great mind and loved him as he deserved to be loved.

Last night I had seen the possibility of another kind of love between my parents. Maybe my mother did love my father after all. Did she love me? I felt too confused to say for certain.

I did not know what to feel about my father. He had looked so young and contented in his sleep last night. What did he feel for my mother? Sometimes when he sat in his special armchair at night reading Catullus or listening to Beethoven on his gramophone, there was a lost look on his face, as if my mother, infinitely attractive, as I knew her to be, to my "Uncles" and the rest of her male admirers, was a beautiful parcel all tied up with many colored strings, and all he had to do was to find the right string, tug it, and he could have her totally and completely to himself.

I suppose I felt a sort of jealousy. More than anything, I simply felt confused.

I lay in my sweat-sticky bed that morning when I was ten. I watched the rising sun lighten my windows and then my room. How, I wondered in light of my discovery of my parents' special relationship with each other, would my own relationship with them change? To my child's mind, my new confused knowledge threatened to change everything, for the knowledge brought with it a guilt. I felt guilty for having trespassed in my parents' secret world.

I feared there might be no walk with my father in the garden tonight. Perhaps never again. And I dreaded the thought of facing my parents at breakfast. My mother, I was sure, would tell my father in her amused and sometimes amazingly husky voice that she had seen me seeing them. And my father and I would both be too embarrassed to look at each other. I sat up in my bed. My life lay in splinters of bamboo around my room.

Everything felt like it was leaving me, and I soon— too soon—would be leaving everything, leaving Africa. I felt sad to leave Sam and Saul, but glad that Max would accompany us to France. My mother, with her usual flair for the original, fancied a gigantic black cook. Max was the best cook in Africa, and he looked magnificent with his white coat straining across his chest and a tall white chef's hat clamped on his head. At least I would have one friend in the world.

Uncle Thomas and Uncle Richard, I knew because my mother had told me, we could not lose. As King's Messengers, they traveled across the world carrying the diplomatic pouches. No doubt my mother would also find other men in Paris to occupy her with luncheons and to arrive in time for tea.

My father was so besotted by my mother he never questioned the numerous men that littered our lives. My father, I decided, was oblivious to what really went on in our house when he was away, to the often cruel way my mother could behave when she was not around him. Only I knew the truth. In my father's trusting blindness, he left the house every morning at eight, after reading *The Times* carefully, kissed my mother goodbye, shouted "Be good, Pumpkin," to me, and then went to the office where Miss Linden, his secretary, awaited him. Miss Linden loved my father with all her intense spinsterly heart. I had been to his office enough times myself and had watched the fondness with which she brought him his tea, straightened his desk, took his dictation, and smiled any time he talked to her without lifting his eyes from his blotter. But my father never noticed. At one o'clock punctually, if he were lunching at home, he would arrive. School finished at lunchtime many days, and Saul would serve the lunch to the three of us, in which case my father discussed with my mother unclassified events that occurred. "The chaps at Carlton Terrace really liked the last report. Very pleased with it."

"That's nice, dear." My mother had a way of saying "That's nice, dear" to everything my father said. Once the postman left a small box in the hall. My father opened it at lunch-time. There were three shiny medals with lovely ribbons in recognition of the work he had done for his country. Exactly what work I did not know. My father could be so very secretive about the work he actually did. "That's nice, dear," my mother said. I wanted to throw my arms around him and hug him and celebrate, even if I didn't know why he had received the medals, but my father would have died of embarrassment at such an unEnglish display of affection.

My father's family, I had heard, were very proper

and his schooling had taught him to hide his emotions. It was in his writing that he really came to life. Beautiful lucid prose. Wonderful delicate sentences. Words that reflected like double-rainbows, dew drops scintillating in the sun. I loved to read his books on history. I felt I'd always known the speeches of his hero, Winston Churchill. "I have nothing to offer but blood, toil, tears and sweat . . ." My skin crawled with excitement at these words. And I knew my father's skin, too, prickled with the same excitement at the same words. We had shared so much. I had loved my father completely. For these first ten years of my life, he was my life.

And now, facing the first move in my life to another country, I feared that my special relationship with my father, like my security in Africa, had changed forever.

I didn't get up to have my breakfast with him. I stayed in bed and said I had a headache. Saul brought me my breakfast on a tray. The end of the beginning of my life, I thought, had come.

After I finally did emerge from my bedroom, the incident, which to me had been so important and shattering, was not discussed or mentioned. My father treated me no differently—maybe my mother had told him nothing—and that night we did go for our usual walk, only now he felt a bit unfamiliar to me. My mother carried on as always: planning her dinners, playing her mahjong, ignoring me mostly and correcting me endlessly. And then, about a week after my fateful night of awakening, she with her characteristic whim, for her moods could change as suddenly as the African weather, did something to confuse me even more.

After another day of school, feeling more isolated than usual, I sat in my window place reading. My father was still at work and my mother, Saul told me, was in Johannesburg shopping. Suddenly the car pulled up in the drive and my mother stepped out looking particularly gleeful. She entered the drawing room and, to my surprise, greeted me with a kiss on my forehead. "I bought a surprise for you, Mary Jane," she said. "Sam?" she called, turning over her shoulder. And Sam came through the door smiling hugely. In his hands I could see a tiny blonde ball of fur with two gleaming black eyes. "It's a Pekingese puppy," my mother said, hardly able to contain her own excitement. "I thought he could keep you company in Paris after you leave your cat—Marmalade?—here."

Warily, for I had not been aware that my mother's ban on dogs had been lifted, I silently walked to Sam and took from him the creature, so very small in his large hands. The puppy was by far the funniest animal I had ever seen. As soon as it was within my arms, it started its Chinese head-rocking. He, for the dog was a baby boy, bulged his eyes and stuck out his tongue and panted with delight. "He's mine?" I asked my mother incredulously. Why, I thought nervously, was she giving him to me? Whatever her reason, I felt my heart beat faster with joy. He was such a beautiful amusing puppy. And he obviously loved me from the very first moment.

"Yes," my mother said. "He's yours. But if you want to keep him, you'll have to see that he's house-broken and properly trained. And you must never feed him from the table or let him get in the way when we have guests."

The Pekingese puppy was mine. "Thank you, mother," I said.

I took the tiny dog to my bedroom and played with it until it was time for dinner. After dinner I ran back to my room and spent the rest of the evening lying on the floor while the puppy pranced about and chewed on my hair. His name, I decided after giving the matter considerable thought, would be "Taiwan."

When I put myself to bed that night, I reconsidered the changes in my life. Leaving Africa, I began to feel, need not be the end of my life. It would be sad to leave my beloved Africa, sad to leave the garden which was my special joy, sad to leave Marmalade. But I reminded myself how much Marmalade would hate Paris. He would never settle in a city. He belonged with the snakes and the spiders that he stalked so stealthily in the garden.

My life, I decided, surely would change, but it would go on. And now I had Taiwan to go through it all with me. As I slept that night, Taiwan curled up on my pillow and nestled beside my ear, breathing little puffs of puppy-breath across my cheek.

Chapter 4

We were ready to leave for Paris. As each room of our house was stripped of its wall-hangings, its paintings, its antiques, its statues, its *objets*—and the walls themselves could do nothing but stand immobile and watch defencelessly while they were denuded—I thought of a quotation from the Bible that my father had recited to me once during an evening walk: "How doth the city sit solitary, that was full of people! How is she become as a widow!" Leaving our house and its surrounding bungalows, the only home I ever had known, felt like leaving a kind of mother.

For all that I reassured myself that my life would go on however much it might change, for all that I was comforted to be taking Taiwan with me, I was both saddened and frightened. My father, too, seemed nervous. Part of his soul, I knew, would remain forever in South Africa. My mother, however, anticipated our move with nothing but exhilaration, as if she could not wait to say goodbye to all that was African. She, I felt sure, could leave and never look back. To her Africa was a hell, and I felt she would suffer no Persephone-like longing (I had developed a great interest in Greek mythology at the time) to peer over her shoulder for a final loving glimpse, regardless of the beauty of the African pomegranate trees.

For her the hills held no magic, nor the forests any mystery. Never had she seemed to feel at home with the Africans themselves.

I remember a night only about a week before we left. We had been invited to a farewell dinner at the Chinese legation in South Africa. My mother had a memorable conversation with Madame Yeng. Madame Yeng and her husband were ardent Communists and I liked them. They lived very simply in the grand legation, surrounded by beautiful Chinese furniture and precious silk rugs. There was a particularly beautiful blue bowl. It had several washes of blue, so one moment you saw the deep South African blue sky in it and the next the palest of blues, a hint of robin's egg blue, and then a quivering passionate blue.

I sat at their table with my mother on one side of me and Madame Yeng on the other. Despite my great efforts to be mindful of my manners, I caught myself clamping my teeth and tightening my jaws to suppress a late-in-the-evening yawn. Madame Yeng smiled at me. "I wish," she whispered to me, "I had a daughter to keep you company."

"Do you have children?" I asked, trying not to overstep the boundaries of polite conversation.

"Diplomatic life is no life for children," Madame Yeng said with her eyes looking down. "We decided not to have any."

I hadn't realized there could be a decision. I thought you had babies if you liked it or not. So, forgetting for a moment my manners, I asked Madame Yeng, "You mean you can decide?" My mother scowled. Madame Yeng laughed her silver laugh, silver like the wine goblets left over from the Imperial days. "When you marry, if you don't want children, you take precautions."

"Oh," I said, realizing we were on perilous ground. Chinese Communists, I had been told, followed a different code of etiquette. But my mother's rules, I knew, remained forever the same.

That was when my mother, somewhat shaken and eager to change the subject, leaned across me. "We're all looking forward to our move to Paris," my mother intruded. "How lovely it will be to live in a country where everyone smells of perfume."

Madame Yeng, despite her different Chinese manners, was a very sophisticated woman. I knew all about sophistication because I'd read all the P. G. Wodehouse books and I thought Jeeves was marvelously sophisticated. Madame Yeng, catching the hint of a dart shot by my mother, leaned forward and said very sweetly, "If I had to leave Africa, I know how I would miss the lovely smell of Africans."

"I'm sure," my mother smiled, "it is an acquired taste."

Madame Yeng seemed to sit up straighter in her chair. I felt she did not like my mother.

"Of course black people smell different to white people." Madame Yeng laughed again. "But then, we Chinese consider the white smell to be an acquired taste, rather difficult to acquire. Perhaps it's all the meat you eat." Madame Yeng turned to her next-seat neighbor on her other side and discussed the weather.

This was one of the rare times I saw my mother discountenanced, and I found myself feeling sorry for her. She did try so very hard to get everything right. That night I kissed her goodnight on her cheek and she was so astonished, she kissed me back, a shy dry peck, but it was a kiss. I went to bed feeling that maybe she, too, wondered how she would fit in to a new country with new people.

On the day of our move I awoke with a tight feeling of panic in my stomach. The last time I would ever wake up in my own African bedroom. I felt like a chameleon about to change to an unknown color. I remembered the collection of chameleons I had kept a few months before. Sometimes, when I was lonely, I'd take them all out to the veranda and sit them down on different cushions so that some would go yellow, some green.

A girl at school had told me that if I put a chameleon on a multi-colored rug, it would explode. I'd chosen my worst-tempered chameleon, to experiment. I hadn't really wanted to do it, but I was very interested in science at that time. The chameleon didn't explode, which was just as well. But as I got up that last morning in Africa, I wondered if my impending change would be so great that I might explode.

I dressed and then took Marmalade, with Taiwan skipping on short Pekingese legs behind us, for a goodbye walk in the garden. Marmalade did not show his usual interest in catching insects and lizards. I was sure he knew I was about to leave him forever. To distract myself from the pain of leaving him, I watched beside a tall clump of pampas-grass as a pale, green, elegant praying mantis ate, with intense concentration, her partner. She had long arms and she crammed the head of her mate into her mouth. I lay on the ground, pressing myself to the earth, feeling sick. But she looked at me crossly and I thought of my mother and my father again. Exactly, I said to myself as I went back into the house, now empty of furniture, the last tea-chests all packed. Exactly. Now it will all happen again in Paris.

When the moment of our leaving inexorably arrived, I kissed Marmalade goodbye and thought I was going to die, but Saul promised he would keep Marmalade himself in his bungalow behind the house. Our house, I was told, soon would be filled by the next family the Foreign Office sent as my father's replacement. I hoped that a daughter of the new British Consul to South Africa would love Marmalade well. I knew it was the right thing to do because Marmalade thought he was a tiger and the garden was his own personal jungle. Paris, I reminded myself, had nothing to offer Marmalade. Paris didn't have lily ponds stuffed with fat African toads. And I was sure it would not have, swaying majestically through the bushes, chameleons.

 ## Chapter 5

We left Africa. The boat was extremely crowded. The War was several years over and if you were me you would have found it hard to believe that there had been a war. Had it really happened? All those pale faces, those dead bodies in the mud, gone. All forgotten in the luxury of the great European liner.

My mother was disgruntled. She expected to be on the Captain's table, but she was outranked by several Ambassadors and their wives. So we ended up on the Doctor's table. My mother fussed and called him "common," but my father liked the Doctor: he, too, was an historian of vast learning. The Doctor liked me and he said on our second day out of port that I was bright and I would go far. My father laughed but my mother sniffed. The Doctor smiled a big warm smile.

Later that night I saw him sitting by himself with a glass in his hand. I went up to him and said, "It's windy tonight. Look at the gulls. They are pushed about by the winds."

"Ah, child," he said in a very sad voice. "We are all pushed about by the winds." I could see he was crying. I wondered if the green liquid in his glass was making him cry. But he saw me looking and he said, "My wife died. I loved her so much. So I gave up my private practice—just couldn't bear to stay in the house we had loved together—and I took to the sea." His face was red and his lower lip quivered. She must have been a good wife. I put my hand on his shoulder. "Do you have anyone to love you?" I said. "I think it is really important to have someone to love you." Like Marmalade my cat, I thought.

"No," he said. "We didn't have any children." He stopped crying and looked out to sea.

"I'll love you," I offered. "After all, we're on this ship for six weeks."

Dr Paulson was his name. Just then my mother called in the fading light. She saw me and made an impatient gesture with her hand. When I walked to her side she said, "Don't talk to the Doctor on your own. How do you know you can trust him?"

I thought of the King's Messengers and their hot hands. "I can trust him," I said. "Anyway, he needs someone to love him. His wife died and he has no one left . . ."

My mother interrupted, "Run along to bed. It's late."

I fell asleep with the sea churning in my ears and the Doctor's face looked very like Marmalade. Poor Taiwan was locked in the quarantine end of the ship and even poorer Max was down in the hold.

I had a wonderful time with Dr Paulson, and I resolved to be a doctor. Dr Paulson was from Scotland. After a few of his special glasses of absinthe, he said he'd sing. He taught me the "Blue Bells of Scotland," "Speed Bonnie Boat," and "Loch Lomond," and he showed me how to do the Scottish Reel. He showed me all his instruments. The bandages were clean white with a wonderful smell of disinfectant.

My mother found a set of mahjong friends, nearly as crow-like as the ladies we left behind, so I had a lot of my time free. The bad news was that Madame Derlanger and her husband would be returning to France a few weeks after we arrived, and the dreadful Geneviève would haunt my life. Geneviève Derlanger: the perfect Ambassador's daughter, a girl with whom I had nothing in common. And once we were both living in Paris, I knew I would be expected to be friends with her. But for now I was happy. Taiwan needed a lot of visiting and when my mother was deeply engrossed in her mahjong party, which took place every day at three o'clock, I'd slip down down down the long shiny ladders into the exciting black oil-smelling world of the hold. Max looked at me with worry in his usually opaque eyes. "What if some bad white man take you away?" he said.

I thought the whole idea was a huge joke. Soon the men and the few women in the hold got used to my visits. Some of the young students from Africa were going to Paris, also to study. I helped them with their English. They kept small bowls of rice and spices with plantain for me, or chicken and peas in milk scented with coconut, and I realized how much I was missing Africa, how silent and cool were the white people on the top deck. Here in the hold were real people like Max and his friends, all excited about going to France.

"I make your mother best food in Africa, now France," Max said happily.

And on the boat I met my first serious boyfriend. Before I met Quentin Franshaw, I really felt there had been a dreadful mistake and I was really a boy. Getting to know Quentin, I began to feel happy that I was a girl. But we still shared a mutual love of beautiful knives. On the ship I kept my treasured knife, the glorious African hunting knife that Saul had given to me after the DPD (Dreadful Penknife Day), hidden in my school satchel. The knife was the first thing I showed Quentin Franshaw. He was wildly jealous because he only had an unextraordinary three-er: two blades and a bottle opener.

Quentin had blue eyes and blond curly hair. He was thin. He ate a lot but he rushed about. We committed ourselves to being engaged, to be followed by marriage, and fortunately my mother seemed to approve of his parents. Quentin's father was going to Rome as a First Attaché. Obviously my mother thought Quentin's mother worth talking to. I overheard Quentin's mother having endless conversations with my mother about buying leather in Florence, crocodile handbags in Singapore, and how to find the best milliner in France.

About this time I began to understand that when my mother stopped her idle chatter she could be very astute. But when she asked a pointed question, my father laughed and said, "Don't worry your pretty little head about that, darling. That's men's work." My mother would let out a small tinkle of a sound and my father would feel proud of his beautiful wife. But now I knew my mother better. I knew that she would have her way in the end, however much my father thought of her as just beautiful. I was sure she already was planning the first expensive French creation that would sit on her pretty little head.

I sighed and looked at Quentin. Being a boy, he was unwise in the ways of women and he had not studied them the way I had. My mother, I opined—a good word underlined in my dictionary (I learned ten new words every night so that I could have a vocabulary like my hero Winston Churchill)—my mother, I opined, was a clever woman, and she was being quite nice to me, glad that I at last had a friend who wasn't common or dropped his *h*'s. Quite what she would have said if she'd seen us sneaking off to kiss each other in the lifeboats was another matter.

I had to admit to myself that I was beginning to feel happy. I was eleven and at sea and in love. Life, though changed, was good.

ᔑᓫᓬ *Chapter 6* ᔑᓫᓬ

I don't think I had ever experienced such pain in my life. The pain got all tangled up with the thing that changed my life, and with my cat Marmalade and with losing Saul and Sam. The pain curled in my heart like the small shoelace snakes that inhabited our garden in Africa. The shoelace was a deadly snake and once from my bedroom window I watched a wild mongoose in the flower bed under my window rise on his back-legs and puff to twice his size. His quick paws milked the air, a wild high-pitched chattering sound left his mouth, wide open. His sharp teeth gleaming, his tiny pink tongue swollen and protruding, he pounced on the little snake. There was no contest. The snake dangled from his mouth and, with a muffled stutter of self-congratulation, the mongoose galloped a hump-backed gallop into the tall grass behind the garden.

But I had no mongoose next to my heart to protect me. Just as I got control of the pain, the little snake inside me uncurled and struck again.

Quentin and I had planned to run away. We were to slip off the boat together and run into the streets of Paris to live among the dustbins and to sleep behind the restaurants, eating the leftovers from the great meals the Parisians enjoyed. We had been perfecting our plan for a very long time, really from the moment we knew we were in love and knew we eventually were to be parted. Quentin was not as sure as I about living on the streets, but then he had been very sheltered in his life. His nanny Heida sounded from his stories about her to be a rather supercilious Swede, and he talked about her all the time because the family sent her back to Sweden when Lady Franshaw, his mother, said he had reached the age at which he needed a French governess. So Quentin was miserable when I met him, but soon he cheered up as we explored the boat and I introduced him to Taiwan and we slid down the hold and talked to Max.

Quentin rather envied my free life. His mother was always fussing over him and sending him off to wash his hands. Or suddenly she would whip a silver-backed brush from her bag and, in front of *everyone*, brush his hair. His hair would then settle in a neat gold halo around his head, and he'd make a face and run off. I'd have to find him and cheer him up.

The night before we docked there was a big good-bye party for the grown-ups in the ship's lounge. Quentin and I watched our parents waltzing. Dressed in white tie and tails, the men wore white gloves so as not to put finger marks on the ladies' silk dresses. My mother wore a long white dress. Her shoulders, white as the sand on the African seashore, rose out of the dress. Tonight she wore her hair down to her waist, black and shiny. She had beaded some of the strands with pearls. My father, who was a rotten dancer, fumbled his way through the waltz. Soon a handsome young man stepped between them and, bowing to my father, he swept my mother into his arm, gazing darkly down at her. They swirled away and soon were no more to be seen. I felt sorry for my father. I had seen that look so many times on his face. He looked as if an unseen hand had reached into his face, pulled a string, and switched off his light.

The boat was to dock at six in the morning. Quentin and I were to slip out of our cabins at 6:30 and meet at the main gangway.

We kissed each other goodnight. Quentin was rather quiet and subdued. I supposed that never seeing our parents again was a rather subduing thought. We went to our cabins and I began to pack.

First I unearthed my knife and took it from its sheath. I went to my dressing table and put the knife, shining in the light of the cabin, to my heart and I vowed that when I grew up, like Peter Pan I'd look after other children who weren't loved by their mothers. I had always loved the story of Peter Pan, though I never saw myself as Wendy. Rather, I was Peter Pan, but when *I* left my mother's house and flew to Kensington Gardens, I never went back to the house. I was perfectly happy in the Round Pond in my boat nest.

After the vow I kissed my knife that was sure to protect us. I packed three pairs of clean knickers, one nice dress for Sundays, and two ordinary dresses for everyday use. I laid out the jodhpurs and a cardigan—the one with the pockets—that I would wear the next morning. I had a few African coins for my pocket money, and that would keep us for a while, though I would have to find a way to get them changed to French money. I slipped into bed and said my prayers.

"God bless mummy and daddy. God bless Sam and Saul. God bless Taiwan and Marmalade and make me a good girl." Taiwan, Quentin and I had decided, had to stay with my father. Taiwan loved my father and he was used to being fed at the table, despite my mother's ban. My father always cut a little of what he was eating and put it on a plate at his feet for Taiwan. At tea-time, Taiwan always had his own bowl of tea with a little sugar. I knew our new life was not going to be able to give Taiwan the standard of luxury he enjoyed. So I said a heartfelt goodbye to him before supper.

I finally did fall asleep and my bedside traveling clock woke me. I felt a huge surge of excitement. Escape! Freedom! All Paris would be at my feet. I stopped the alarm from ringing and pushed it into my knapsack. I slipped on my jodhpurs and my yellow turtleneck riding sweater, and over that the pocketed cardigan. Then quietly I walked through the sitting room of my family's suite. I smelled the slightly corrupt smell of roses past their peak. I opened the door and suddenly I was a new me. I was this other grown-up person who had taken her life in her own hands.

The deck was ablaze with people and lights. The sun was attempting to rise from a sluggish gray ocean. The cavernous hold was now thrown open. The smell of wet tarmac hit my nose and the brine mixed with the tarmac, and my new found freedom sent me into a state of exaltation. Huge steel hooks hung in a state of suspended animation. Thick steel chains clanked. People bustled, instructions were shouted. As I turned the corner of the deck I saw porters with trolleys filled with luggage dashing about excitedly on the dock. All was gray, with the exception of the yellow of the lamps on the docks, cutting the gray light with their phosphorescence. I soon reached my destination and I waited for Quentin.

I waited and he didn't come. I waited from half-past

six, each minute agony. Then it was seven. I could wait no longer because my mother had her tea sent up at a quarter past seven. So I walked slowly, to give Quentin time, from the gangway to his suite. I stood outside the silent door feeling sick. I looked in the window. The sitting room of the Franshaws' suite was empty. I pushed the handle of the door down. The door was locked. The snake, uncurled, bit deep. I went to the side of the ship and threw up. Then I walked to our suite, all noise silent in my head.

My mother was sitting in the armchair next to the marble fireplace. The roses had not moved since I left, except for a fat brown-at-the-edges petal that lay on the walnut writing desk. My mother was smiling. "Where have you been?" she said, arching her eyebrows.

"For a walk," I said.

Her eyes were cool. She knew. I knew Lady Franshaw must have found out and told my mother of our plan. How they must have laughed, and what an idiot I'd been to think that Quentin would need to leave his warm loving family. "Go and take those ridiculous clothes off," my mother said, sipping her tea. "You're not going riding, are you?"

"No," I said. "I'm not."

"Put on your gray dress with the matching hat, and your knee-length white socks and a pair of gray gloves. Remember, you're the Consul *General*'s daughter, for better or for worse."

"I will," I said.

Later, my blue suitcase neatly packed, I looked at myself in the full-length mirror in my cabin. Gray face, gray eyes, my light hair looking mousy and short-cropped—a style my mother insisted upon. I looked awful. No wonder Quentin didn't want to run away with me. I sighed and left the room. I never saw Quentin Franshaw again.

Chapter 7

Paris seemed like a series of plunges through vast tunnels. I came up for air only to catch a momentary view of Notre Dame. To my eleven-year-old heart, it looked just like any other cathedral, for that heart had recently been broken.

As the car dashed in and out of the frenzied French traffic, Max and I sat in the two guest seats facing my mother and my father, who sat together in the huge cushiony seats that swallowed them up in gray leather and plush. I, preoccupied with my sorrow, and Max, big and black, contrasted sharply with the luxury of the car. Max looked very lost and very lonely. He knew my mother well enough to know she would sack him at a moment's notice, and then he would be out on the streets of Paris. He also knew my father was a compassionate man and would give him a reference and his passage home, but Max, I knew, had a dream. He also loved my father and very much wanted to attach himself to my father's rising star. As cook to a Consul General, and maybe someday even Ambassador, Max would benefit from my father's status.

I put my hand on Max's arm. We knew each other so well there was no need for words. He knew I was hurting and I knew he was feeling isolated. I saw my mother frown. "Fraternizing" I knew she called it, and I really do believe she thought that the black might rub off.

We arrived in front of an elegant pair of gates, newly painted shiny and black.

Chapter 8

I fell in love with the gates first and then with the rest of the house. A generous gravelled courtyard, bordered by glorious beds of roses, lay inside the gates. The gray-stone front of the house was strong and square and simple, topped by a row of ornate stone-carvings beneath the roof. Tall rectangular windows reflected sunlight on the lower story, and the windows at the top of the house were smaller and had rounded tops. Sun-bleached oak shutters, faded to nearly the same color as the gray stone, hung open on either side of every window. In the very center of the flat stately façade opened brightly polished wooden double-doors, with brass knobs that seemed wealthily inviting to the touch.

Inside the door lay an immense marbled hall with a wide stone stairway across the polished floor leading to too many upstairs rooms to count. The downstairs rooms, like paintings of antique luxury come to life, were huge extravagances of polished floors, stone in some, wood in others, tall mirrors between carved columns on the walls, and brilliant chandeliers hung from painted and moulded ceilings. The house seemed held always in a remarkable silence, as if it had nothing to do but, in quiet, contemplate its own lavish beauty.

The house—*our* house, I had to remind myself many times during the first few weeks to make our living in it feel real—stood on the outskirts of Paris. Quite where it was remained a mystery, because I was not allowed out of the gates by myself. I left the house in one of the chauffeur driven cars, usually the Daimler, and I returned from school in a car. All the streets looked the same as I, imprisoned, gazed passionately at the children playing on the pavements and sitting with their parents. Even if I was a prisoner, I loved the house for its stony strength and beauty and for the security the shutting of the solid front door offered me every day when I came home from school.

Most of the diplomats' children went to the International School, but my mother, on the advice of Madame Derlanger who would soon arrive with the loathsome Geneviève, insisted I be sent to the local school where I would mix with the French children and very quickly learn to speak French. She had a point. I was the only English child in the school.

On my first day there, dressed in a pleated blue tunic with thick white cuffs, I felt alone and abandoned. Most of the children ignored me. It was, I remember, a Wednesday, and Wednesday was the school's half-day. Everyone went home at lunchtime, and I put my head on my desk and cried. My teacher, Mademoiselle Pétain, put a sympathetic arm around me and said in perfect English, "Don't cry, little one. I will take you out and we will have lunch together."

She took me in her little Renault and we putputted across the busy streets to a real corner café, the kind of café that I had seen in my mother's big books of paintings by famous artists. As soon as I could read, I devoured those books. My fingers trembled with the joy of the colors. I don't know why colors always have affected me so deeply that a good painting tears my soul apart. Almost like my father's records. Beethoven at night singing out into the garden, my father with his conducting baton, the great crescendos and then the anti-climactic diminuendos. My favorite piece of all, however, had to be William Byrd's *Sacred Service*, the voices throbbing in the night. Such ecstasy frightened me.

But here we were, this kind lady and myself, sitting on two stippled chairs with rush matting seats bristly with old age. I felt I was at last in France. Africa lay like a beautiful dream behind me.

"You must have our onion soup." Mademoiselle was smiling. "When I was at Oxford, I always went to the Black Swan for lunch, and I ate your marvelous cheddar cheese and thick white bread. Do you know Oxford?"

I shook my head. Suddenly I had lost my voice completely.

Mademoiselle took my hand. "Don't be shy, child," she said. "This is your first day at our school. It's always hard. You ask if I can come to your house and give you extra lessons in French. Soon you'll be chattering like a starling. And you will enjoy our school."

I wasn't shy really. I was just bursting with happiness. Mademoiselle was little and pretty. She had the face of a kitten with a small arched nose and button black eyes. She had full round breasts, a tiny waist, and red hair piled on her head. She wore a black pencil-skirt that reached halfway down her calf and a white sleeveless shirt. Outside the buttoned neck of her shirt hung a simple gold cross. Over the back of her chair she had draped her black woollen sweater with glinting black buttons. She had the smallest feet I'd ever seen, fitted prettily into black high heels, and she was as French as French could be. And she smoked Gauloises. I looked at the blue packet, familiar to me from the French magazines I had stared at when, in Africa, I had been called upon to spend an afternoon with Geneviève. My mother had the *Tatler* delivered from England, but Madame Derlanger used to have *Vogue* delivered from France. I died every month when Geneviève visited to pass on *Vogue* to my mother. I loved the feel of the heavy thick magazine, the smell of the pages. I loved the cut on the bias that made the clothes hang, and I could imagine the catwalks, the tall stately models swinging impudently down in the brightly lit show rooms . . .

My thoughts were interrupted by a waiter who put

two steaming cups of soup in front of us. Mademoiselle laughed. "Come along," she said. "We haven't got all day. When we get back, I'll explain to your mother that at our school we finish at lunchtime on Wednesdays. This way, you go home and do your homework and then you have time to play."

Everything seemed wonderful. The soup was thick with golden onions. A little raft of fried bread carried a cargo of yellow cheese, beginning in the heat of the soup to cast long slender anchors to the bottom of the white china mug sitting serenely on its saucer. Before me sat a fat complacent jug of wine. Mademoiselle, catching my glance, took the jug in her hand and poured me half a glass of wine and then filled the rest of the glass with water. She lifted her glass and she said, "*Santé.*" *A votre santé,* she explained meant to my good health. "*Santé,*" I said, returning her toast. Suddenly I felt very grown up, very sophisticated, sitting in a Paris café, drinking red wine, a generous piece of French bread on my sideplate.

"Look." Mademoiselle showed me. "Dip the bread in the soup and eat it. The English are always dreadfully prudish about sex and food." She stretched and I realized that, unlike my mother's bare hollow armpits which reminded me of the yellow plucked chickens in Max's kitchen, Mademoiselle's armpits had black hair that I could see peering from the openings of her sleeveless blouse. Mademoiselle smiled. "Yes," she said, guessing my thoughts. "European women don't shave." She stretched again like a cat. "Hair under the arms is very sexy, don't you think? My boyfriend Jacques has not only the Renault but also a *vélo* and we go to the Bois to make love. He loves my armpits."

I sat there changing color like a traffic light. No one had ever asked my opinion about anything, certainly not about whether armpits were sexy or not. Sex was a forbidden subject in my family, and Quentin and I had only embraced and kissed each other on the cheek.

At last my mug lay empty. The hot sun shone down on us. Other families sat around us, blowsy with food and drink. Little children scampered past us and I felt in love with the world. "Come along, Mary." Mademoiselle got up, pushed her chair back, and wiped her mouth and chin with an enormous white napkin. "Let's go. *Allons y.* I'll telephone your mother and I'll drive you home."

I asked God to create a miracle and allow Mademoiselle into the house to tutor me. We drove back along the tree-lined streets, leafy in their spring underwear awaiting their summer dresses, and my nose filled with the smell of Paris. The city smelled of honey tainted with a faint taste of garlic and sweat. It was a wonderful smell, rich and warm. We putputted again up to the house. The butler, a Frenchman named Barzon, opened the big door and Mademoiselle's self-assured shoes rat-tat-tatted across the marble floor, up the circular staircase, to my mother's sitting room.

There my mother, in one of her afternoon dresses, awaited us. In front of my mother, Mademoiselle, her black sweater now buttoned all the way up, turned into a mousy little woman with a schoolmistressy manner. She explained my academic needs and my heart somersaulted with joy when my mother nodded her head. "Do you know," my mother enquired, "of a good music teacher? We have inherited a baby-grand in the drawing room. It would be a good idea and certainly high time for Mary to learn to play an instrument. After all, she does not have much to offer in the way of beauty. But if we give her enough social graces, we may be able to find a suitable man to marry her."

"I don't want to get married ever," I said.

Mademoiselle nodded. *"Mais oui,"* she said. "I have

a colleague, Monsieur Jacques LeFarge. He plays the piano and the guitar and he gives piano lessons, Madame.'' She turned her head and I saw her left eye wink. Jacques, I thought. That's her boyfriend.

I realized Mademoiselle and Jacques were to be my saviours. No longer was I cast at sea, adrift on some vast lonely vessel that sailed in the diplomatic waves of Paris. I had allies on my side. Mademoiselle did not appear to accept my mother's version of who I was. Two people were going to invade my mother's fortress and rescue me. I had friends.

When Mademoiselle left I saw her to the door. As she kissed me goodbye, she whispered, ''We will have fun.''

I went to bed that night in a daze of happiness. To my prayers I added, ''God bless Mademoiselle and Jacques,'' and then I slept.

❧ Chapter 9 ☙

Jacques made an immediately good impression on my mother. He told her he was an existentialist, a word too long for my mother to understand, but she was impressed. To show my mother how good a musician he was on his first visit, he asked us to sit quietly while he unpacked his guitar. The guitar was in a case, and when he had lovingly opened the case, he paused and smiled. Jacques was tall. His long dark hair fell to his shoulders. I'd never seen a man with long dark hair, but it suited him. He had broad shoulders, a full mouth, and the kind of gray eyes that are very arresting because the gray is the gray of a seashore just before the sunset, or the same gray as Paris. The eyes look at eternity.

There was something ethereal about Jacques. He had a low soft rippling voice and his fingers were long and intimate. He held his guitar as if it were human. With such love and tenderness, I thought, Mademoiselle was a lucky woman. My father looked at my mother like that. My mother, however, was mesmerized by Jacques. I knew she would be. Jacques was exactly what my mother dreamed a Frenchman should be, only Jacques didn't wear a beret; he wore a big soft brown floppy hat and a big brown cloak. Altogether, the day was a huge success. Jacques was definitely more than acceptable, as far as my mother was concerned, and I left her grilling him about his views on literature.

Mademoiselle and I went up to my bedroom for a lesson in French. *"Qu'est-ce que c'est que l'amour?"* she began.

I had no idea what she meant. I shrugged. I thought we did *"plume de ma tanté."* I answered that I had a book all about aunt's pens and where the windows were.

"Non," Mademoiselle replied. "You'll learn much faster this way. I asked you what is love? Now here is your French dictionary, so you can look up the words that describe love, and next time we will put them into sentences."

"What kind of love?" I asked. "Love for animals? For my family?"

"No, goose," she laughed. "Love for a man."

"Oh." I was disconcerted, but I told her all about Quentin.

"Good," she said. "You know love, you know abandonment, you begin to feel feelings."

She didn't know about my father, and she didn't know that I had made a vow never to allow my true feelings to show.

She looked at me and sighed. "Poor little rich girl," she said. "You live in prison. But," she stood up,

"Jacques and I will get you out. Next lesson we go to the park."

"Thank you, Mademoiselle. I'd love to go."

Downstairs again, Jacques was waiting in the hall. My mother was beaming. Not only did she have Jacques, she supposed, as her left-wing intellectual, but also octopus-handed Uncle Richard was passing through. So she had yet another man to hang about the house.

Madame Derlanger was installed in her own private house, for her husband was on leave. I had an appointment with Geneviève. I say appointment, because as a child of the Foreign Office, I had learned to write my engagements in my own diary. Meetings between a British Consul General's daughter and the daughter of a French Ambassador, like all other aspects of diplomatic life, were arranged well ahead of time. I watched Geneviève's arrival from the little window seat at the top of our house. The limousine drew to a halt in front of the door. I always felt you could tell how rich people were by the amount of pebbles they had lying on their drive. Our drive—the whole courtyard, in fact—positively reeked of wealth, but of course it was not "our" wealth. We only owned a few African figures and our clothes. I knew that the rest of the furniture and the house belonged to a rather dreary department of the Foreign Office called the Ministry of Works. When my father had been a Vice Consul before I was born, he was only worth a flat. Then, as a Consul, we got a house. In Africa, because we were a Consular residence, we got our first carpet. Such a relief from the uniformly disgusting wall-to-wall carpet, usually bright orange. Now, I thought watching Geneviève alight and her chauffeur making a great performance of opening the door for her, we actually lived in luxury.

I knew I must get up and go downstairs and have tea with Geneviève. I so much wanted to race outside and run across the road with some sandwiches and a thermos, but a Consul General's daughter may not treat a French Ambassador's daughter with such frivolous behavior. So I reluctantly lolled down the long white-carpeted stairs, dragging my hand along the polished banister as I walked. What would I talk to Geneviève about? We were so different from each other.

Because we were children of diplomatic parents, we were different to other children. Because we moved lock, stock, and barrel when our fathers were told to move, we had no real friends. We hadn't read nursery stories because our mothers were never around at bedtime. But as soon as we were old enough to attend dinners, we both had to learn politics. I was my mother's conversation piece at six. I had learned to sit straight, to speak when spoken to, and never to leave the table for any reason until my mother rose to lead the ladies away while the men passed the port. I so much wanted to stay with the men. My father, after a few glasses of port, grew expansive. And just as he was about to go into the intense political happenings of the day, my mother invariably rose and like obedient dolphins the other ladies trolled behind my mother and I followed, cursing under my breath that I'd been born a girl. Taiwan usually trotted out behind me.

Sometimes the women's gatherings so far in Paris had been quite fun. My mother sat in her sitting room and poured coffee from a large silver coffeepot. The smell of the freshly ground coffee mingled with the smell of expensive perfumes, all vying for attention. The perfumes faded into a flurry of powders being applied to faces that, by that time of the evening, began to glow. Next a batter of lipsticks were touched to mouths and last of all came the indefinable smell of women in a group together. I sat in the corner next to the curtains where I could be quickly forgotten. Soon the prim chit-chat degenerated into full-scale gossip: who was seen at the opera with whom; my mother complaining about the servants; which parties were coming up; and then a final flashing of little diaries as dates for bridge, mahjong, hairdressers, or shopping expeditions were made. Then there was rather a lot of cheek-kissing and the ladies were ready to go home.

Geneviève's life, I knew, was even more formal than mine. The difference was—and this really was a big difference—she loved every moment of it and I didn't. I saw girls of my age play hopscotch in the parks. I saw them running home with baguettes under their arms. Some of the girls were poor. They ran barefoot or with their soles flapping, hair loose, whipping over their faces. My mother was as fierce about my playing with the street children as she was about my fraternizing with servants. "Remember," she said until the words were seared into my soul with an ice pick. "Remember, we represent the King of England. England will be judged by your behavior." The prospect terrified me.

At public occasions my body was gripped with fear. Always my mother mentioned the little princesses. She had a picture of the young Princess Elizabeth hung in my bedroom. "Why," she said in an exasperated voice, "can't you be more like her?" My mother had a way of staring at me as if she could inject sufficient shame into my body to rid me eventually of the various unconforming devils that beset me.

But Geneviève loved every detail of diplomatic life, and she was completely at home and included in the world of the powdered, perfumed, fashionable gossiping women. Geneviève belonged. Madame Derlanger had no need to frown at Geneviève.

Geneviève stood waiting for me at the bottom of the stairs. Her blonde hair was in an immaculate chignon, her dress simple, but so well cut that I knew it must have come from a very expensive shop. Geneviève did not have to wear socks. She wore nylons. I knew, because when I first met her in Africa, she lifted her skirt to show me her stockings. They were attached to a black lace garter belt. Her long lean thighs had flashed, as she did a couple of high kicks and she said, "When I'm ten I get to wear a brassière."

"Well," I had said defensively, dressed in my horrid party dress, a dreary blue as usual, "I don't want to wear that sort of thing anyway." That was four years before.

Now we stood in marked contrast still, but at least the carpets weren't bright yellow or funereal green. We moved to the drawing room where my mother sat waiting. She loved having Geneviève for tea. "Well, Geneviève," she said, "how does it feel to be back in Paris?"

"Very well, thank you, Madame."

The thing that annoyed me about Geneviève was that she could be any age, though she was only a year older than I. She never blushed, never stammered, and was always surrounded by all the boys, some of them even fifteen or sixteen years old.

"Your mother tells me," my mother said, "that Madame Mauriac is making her hats this season. I think Mary Jane and I had better pay a visit."

I tried to look pleased. I saw no point in hats unless you had to go out in the sun.

Geneviève gave her pretty little all-captivating smile. "Yes," she said. "I have two on order. Will you be going to the collections for the autumn?"

"Of course," my mother replied. "I can't wait. Now, girls," she said in the bright frosty way she had. "I'll leave you two together. I must change for dinner. Mary, we have the German Consul and his wife for dinner. Uncle Richard will be with us, and Father Joseph from the local Catholic church. I do hope he doesn't drink as much whiskey as the last RC we had." She left the room making loud mental notes to herself.

Left alone by my mother, we sat ourselves on a feathery plump sofa, and a lace-aproned parlor-maid placed a Wedgwood tea service before us.

Geneviève looked at me and smiled while I poured her cup of tea. "You haven't changed," she said.

"Nah," I replied.

"What have you been doing?" Geneviève said.

"Nothing much," I said. "I go to the local lycée. I have French lessons from Mademoiselle Pétain and music lessons from Jacques . . ."

"Jacques LeFarge?" Geneviève looked at me for once in my life with respect.

"I think so," I said casually. "He's an existentialist."

"Yes, that's right." Geneviève nodded. "He's very well known in Paris." She grimaced. "My father hates him. Says he's a revolutionary."

"Really?" That sounded more interesting than regular politics.

"Do you have a boyfriend yet?" came Geneviève's next question. I was busy contemplating an assault on the cherry cake which the parlor-maid carried in to accompany our tea. I loved maraschino cherries, and Max had a way of mingling the sweet-bitter taste of the cherry with amaretto liqueur. "Yes." Secretly I was thrilled I had something to boast about.

"Indeed?" Geneviève leaned forward. She was the sort of girl that always leaned forward, pregnant with secrets. Or she would put her hand to her mouth and whisper into an ear. Life for Geneviève was a series of events, most of which her thirteen-year-old self seemed to observe wide-eyed and innocent, but I knew there was nothing innocent about Geneviève Derlanger. She, more than I, had been brought up in the fashion world, endless whirling partying at the French Embassy. She was truly an Ambassador's child. Like sugar almonds, always in a heap in a rose-leafed silver bowl on the desk where my mother used to write her daily instructions for the staff, Geneviève was brittle on the outside, but underneath she built a wall of stone. I tried to build my wall, but there were crevices.

Now both of us were in Paris, maybe we could be friends. Certainly for children like us, there were no casual telephone calls to meet in a park, no going to see a film. If I wanted to see a film, I was driven to the cinema and a suitable chaperone sat with me and I was returned to the house after the film. I was not allowed to chew gum. Gum was vulgar, and so was popcorn. So I sat surrounded by gum-chewing popcorn-mouthed cinema-goers all furiously chomping and chewing. I alone, and my attendant, sat in the best seats, usually visited by an obsequious cinema manager.

Geneviève said she was in love with Rollo. "Do you wish to meet him?" she asked. Since my love was unrequited and somewhere in Italy, I said I'd very much like to meet him. "Lovely. We can meet at my house for a swim." Geneviève's house, I was told, had the most magnificent swimming pool in Paris. "He has a friend, you know."

By this time, both of us had finished sipping our cups of tea from my mother's treasured Victorian Wedgwood tea set. Geneviève placed her saucer and cup on the tray, sat back, and crossed her legs. Geneviève could cross her legs in such an elegant fashion. My fattish legs refused to drape one over the other, so I settled for crossed ankles. Already I began to envision how embarrassed I would feel to meet someone while swimming: I wished that I did not have to wear my ugly and sensible black wool British bathing suit. Geneviève, I *knew* without doubt, would have the most fashionable swimming costume that money could buy, and she would look fabulous in it.

"The friend is called Patrick Johnson," continued Geneviève, smoothing her skirt over her knees. "His father is a banker. They have a big house on Rue Monmarché, and his father drives a Rolls Royce."

"What sort of diamonds does the mother wear?" I asked, knowing that she would know the answer.

"One baguette. Three carats."

"Whew," I said. "You do your homework."

Geneviève laughed. "I'm a French girl and soon I'll be a woman and have to find myself a husband."

"What about Rollo?"

Geneviève smiled. "No. Rollo is for practice."

I laughed. Geneviève and I for many years had known each other, attended tedious formal children's parties, stood in lines shaking hands or, in our cases, curtseying. All along I, rebellious and flushed with boredom, envied her calm pragmatic cool personality. Geneviève, with her thick natural corn-colored hair and her midnight blue eyes, slender-bodied and usually tanned, was everything I'd always wanted to be.

Now I was approaching my teens. This was the last innocent summer for me. After the summer, real life began. "Okay," I said. "I'd love to swim."

"And meet Patrick?" Geneviève looked at me.

"And meet Patrick," I agreed. Two girls interested in boys but still, underneath it all, we were two girls. A summer of secrets and a pact.

Geneviève called on the phone for her car to be at the door. I followed her down the stairs. She stood before me on the doorstep of the house and she smiled. "Next week," she said, her eyes shining with the promise of laughter. "How about Monday for lunch and a swim?"

"Lovely," I said. "I'll put it in my diary."

❧ *Chapter 10* ❧

I served drinks that evening. There were so few of us, the house staff were given the evening off. My mother said that Father Joseph might attack the whiskey, and whiskey was expensive. She didn't much like the German guests, and Uncle Richard liked champagne, so all I had to do was to mix the champagne cocktails and carry the glasses prettily on the tray.

Father Joseph turned out to be a large gentle bear of a man. He had a big moustache and he loved his food. "Madame," he said, bowing low at the waist. *"Enchanté."* I watched fascinated as my mother's little hand disappeared into his moustache. My mother smiled graciously. She did not like large hearty men with thick red sensual lips. She preferred rather pale slight men, most of whom wore pointed shoes.

The German Consul and his wife were new in Paris. It was our turn to invite them to dinner. They were exhausted and looked pale and drained. Frau Hilda Liebman was a sweet dumpling of a woman. She had a nice shy face and red cheeks. Her husband was far more formal and had a very thick accent. I felt sorry for Frau Liebman, who immediately asked me to call her Hilda. I could feel my mother wince. I wasn't allowed to address anyone over eighteen by their first name, and I was supposed to know all ranks and titles by heart. Behind me, as I sat at the dining table, stood row upon row of books on etiquette from countries all over the world. I knew that the major rule of protocol was not to embarrass your guest, so I smiled and said, "Thank you."

Soon my father and Father Joseph were deep in conversation with Herr Liebman and I was left to talk to Hilda. My mother certainly wasn't going to take it upon herself to entertain an insignificant Consul's wife who looked like a country peasant. "Where do you come from?" I asked politely.

"Buchenwald," she said.

"Oh." I had heard all about the concentration camps and had watched in bone-shaking horror as the camps were opened by the American Army. "I didn't know anyone lived there, except for the camp."

"Oh, yes. Before they built the camp, we were just another small town."

"Did you know what was happening?"

"Not really." Frau Liebman smiled at me. "They took away the Jew who ran the pawn shop at the end of our road . . ."

"Did you mind?"

"No, not really," Hilda said. "You see, he took all our money. The whole town owed him money."

I gazed at her in amazement. "Did he die?" I asked.

Hilda shrugged. "I don't know," she said. "It was war-time. Nobody asked questions. I like to forget all that now . . . Tell me, do you go to school?"

I nodded. I knew that I was forbidden to ask political questions, but every so often such a question burst out unbidden from my mouth. My father usually forgave me and laughed. "She'll be an Ambassador yet," he'd say. But my mother said, "We are here to entertain, not inform." She'd always remind me of my role.

This time I had been informed. And suddenly the whole world of diplomatic intrigue looked no different, in its preoccupation with delicate social niceties, than the shrug of Hilda's shoulders which said, "A man's death is none of my business." At our table we would entertain men and women who had committed various crimes. Those French that fought for freedom mixed with those who had collaborated with the Germans. A large gray cloud of depression settled on my shoulders. I looked across at my father listening intently to Father Joseph. Even if he were bored, no one would ever know. We were all actors in this huge game carried on all over the world. I hoped passionately that I could escape.

When I withdrew at precisely nine o'clock, I curtseyed to the assembled company and wished them all goodnight. I found it hard to look at Hilda. Her face was no longer pastoral or innocent. As I walked up the stairs, I remembered that Mademoiselle was due to visit the following afternoon. Thank goodness she had my mother trained to allow her to take me out in her little car. We were supposed to go to her apartment and study French, but this time she had promised me we would abandon the apartment and spend all afternoon in Paris. I suddenly felt an awful lot better.

✌ Chapter 11 ✍

That summer I became two people. There was the good obedient me who played the piano with Jacques and seemingly did my lessons with Mademoiselle and no longer argued with my mother or was rude to my father. I no longer agonized if I didn't see my father before I went to bed. Now I felt a strange indifference, an almost inevitable distance that grew wider as I grew older. Sometimes he came home from work looking white and tired with dark rings around his eyes, and I'd feel guilty for not loving him as passionately as I had when I was in Africa. But I consoled myself, as I listened to my father endlessly agreeing with my mother, with my secret world.

The only shadow on my happiness was that Max was going back to Africa. Max had tried to make a success of his position of cook to a Consul General, but even Max—dear lovable dependable Max—was defeated by France. He spent afternoons, while I watched him cooking for the numerous dinner parties, talking about his frustrations with communication with the French cooks who shopped beside him in the big regional markets in the city. "Not like African cooks," he explained. "No drinking, no smoking, *no women.*" This he said with great emphasis. *"No women."*

He certainly was a success. He quickly learned to make his own prosciutto which even my father insisted was as good a ham as any from Parma. My mother, who spoke of sex only rarely, and even then obliquely as a curse laid upon women, also had no interest in food. She had a shelf of cookbooks and numerous recipes which she eagerly swapped among her friends, but on Max's night off we went out to eat or she boiled a few eggs. The family joke was that the eggs could be used as ammunition, should revolution ever threaten the Consulate. My father found the joke funny, but I didn't.

Later, as always, my mother slipped into my room and I awoke with a jump. There she was sitting on the end of the bed in her beige silk nightgown with her handmade beige nightdress. What instinctively woke me up was her smell. My mother had a musty smell about her. My father had a wonderful woodsmoke mixed with African daisy smell.

When my mother used to sit on the end of my bed in Africa, I was often confused. "You see, Mary," she would say plaintively, "I'm strict with you for your own good."

I had come to feel that it was unfair that I had been born my mother's daughter, unfair to both of us. If only my mother's daughter had been a girl like Geneviève Derlanger! Then my mother would have had a companion to share all her tastes, a proper daughter who would equally relish shopping for clothes, a social creature who would delight in small talk and prefer to read book reviews rather than the books themselves, a child who would wish for nothing more than to grow up as beautiful and as charming as her mother. Instead I felt myself my mother's embarrassing shadow. So why should she love me? She was gregarious; I was shy. She was graceful; I was awkward. She was shapely; I had no shape. She revelled in the *beau monde* of Paris, I rather in the architectural beauty and rich cultural history of the city. It was unfair that my mother should have such a gap in her life—the position of daughter—filled only by me. Perhaps there was an empty place in my life, too: the place that should have been filled by a mother to love me for my awkward, self-doubting, ugly-feeling self. Perhaps this had something to do with why I split myself in two.

Now, in France with my mother sitting on the end of my bed, my new secret self, whom I called Françoise, giggled. Françoise openly resented my mother. "Old bitch," Françoise thought. "Silly old English bitch. *Tant pis . . .*"

Mary—good old plain Mary—sat up in bed and said, "I'm really sorry, Mummy. I'll try to do better." As I went off to sleep, Françoise lay beside me worrying about what bathing suit she could wear for next week's swimming date with Geneviève, and she fervently hoped Patrick was handsome.

Being two people was not at all easy. Françoise followed me about everywhere. The only other memory of this kind was when I had a "friend." She had been a little fairy who sat on the top of my wardrobe when I was three. Because I had no friends, I invented my fairy. I called her Thumbelina from the Hans Christian Andersen story my father read me. In those days, however tired he was, if my mother was in a good mood he would come to my bedroom and read me a goodnight story. My favorite was Peter Pan, but his was *Wind in the Willows*. My father had a wonderful funny laugh. It was like the snickering of a horse. Soon both of us would be convulsed with laughter. My fairy watched from the top of the wardrobe and then, when my father kissed me goodnight and shut off the light and I lay in the dark, I talked to my friend and she listened. Sometimes, if my mother had hit me or simply spoken unkindly to me, my little friend glowed with sympathy and I felt better. Someone cared. I could certainly never tell my father.

Now it was Françoise who sat beside me at the table, only she, unlike Thumbelina, made naughty remarks about my mother. "What are you smiling at?" my mother said sharply the day before our swimming date.

"Nothing, mother," I said. "I'm thinking about the swim with Geneviève tomorrow."

"You will practice your breaststroke, won't you?"

"I hope so," Françoise said. I tried not to giggle. "I will," I promised.

"I'm off to the office." My father always finished breakfast the same way. Pushing back his teacup, he meticulously folded *The Times* to coincide with the arrival of the car at the front door.

"Monsieur, la voiture est prête." Barzon the butler, who was not only immaculate but also completely unapproachable, opened the dining room door.

My father kissed me on the forehead and my mother on the cheek. "I'll see you tonight, darling. Where are we going?" On the rare day, when my father was told they had no social engagements, his face lit up. His idea of heaven was an evening devoted to reading books and listening to classical music.

"We're at the Johnsons' tonight," my mother said. I looked up. The Johnsons were Patrick's parents. "Not you," my mother said to me. "You can stay home."

"Never mind," Françoise reassured me. "We can spend the evening getting ready for tomorrow."

That evening I stood in front of the cheval mirror in my mother's bedroom and looked at myself in a smart very French swimsuit. Françoise suggested quite sensibly that I ask Mademoiselle's help over the swimsuit problem. Mademoiselle took herself off to the store called *"Printemps"* and bought me a really wonderful red swimsuit. All of a sudden my twelve-year-old body didn't look like a skeleton in a boiler suit. My legs and arms, I noticed for the first time, were beginning to fill out. When I was out with Jacques and Mademoiselle they fed me and I ate. When I was alone with my parents, my mother measured every mouthful I took in case (horror of horrors) I got fat. With Jacques and Mademoiselle I ate like a horse. Free of my mother's reproachful eye and oblivious to her comments about my increased weight, I indeed was filling out. "Men like women with a little meat on their bones," Jacques had said, pinching Mademoiselle's bottom.

Mademoiselle, away from the classroom, her hair swinging around her head, shook with laughter. "Leave her alone, Jacques," she had said sitting in the middle of the picnic blanket strewn with Camembert, bread, and a bottle of red wine. "Go and play, child." But I didn't go far to play. I hid behind the biggest tree I could find, and I watched. I watched Jacques and Mademoiselle roll themselves into the blanket. Whatever he was doing to Mademoiselle, she enjoyed herself very much indeed. So did he.

As I stood in front of the mirror, I wished I had long hair. I wished I didn't have boring blue eyes, and I wished I had a bust. No good wishing.

For the first time in my life, directed by Françoise, I rifled through my mother's creams and thoroughly creamed my face. "Now your body," Françoise instructed. Thoroughly embarrassed, I started to argue. "Don't be silly," Françoise said. "You don't want your legs to be like sandpaper, do you?"

"No," I said meekly.

"Well, then. Take off your swimsuit and start rubbing." I took my swimsuit off and looked at my flat chest, really two pink studs sitting on two beans, and I looked at my hairless pubic area. I felt bleak. Geneviève had pubic hair. Every girl in the world had pubic hair. And I was just bald. "Don't worry." Françoise was reassuring. "You'll grow up. Just get on with it. Your mother'll be here soon."

To be caught naked in my mother's room put me in such a panic I hurriedly applied cream all over myself and began to rub it in. I heard the car in the drive. I grabbed my swimsuit, put the jar back on the night table, and fled naked down the hall.

I blessed my mother's policy of not having female live-in staff. There were no maidservants policing the hall, so I ran down the dark corridors to my room, threw the swimsuit under the bed, jumped into my nightdress, leaped into bed, switched off my tablelamp, and pretended to be asleep in case my father decided to say goodnight. I lay in the fragrant silence feeling my silken skin. "Well," Françoise said. "Aren't you going to do it?"

"No," I said.

"Why not?"

"Because," I said.

"Because what?" Françoise giggled. "Everyone else your age does it."

"Well I don't," I insisted crossly. "It's a sin."

I went to sleep with Françoise chuckling in my ear.

Chapter 12

Max was leaving for Mombasa the same summer morning I was leaving for Geneviève's house. I found it hard to be sad. Max was crying, big tears welling up in his big gentle brown eyes, slipping slowly down his cheeks. My father hurrumphed when Max shook his hand before my father left for work.

"I envy you, Max," I said. "Just think. Mombasa, those lovely white beaches, mangoes, papaya . . ."

But Max still looked mournful. "I don't want to leave you, Missie," he said. He handed me a picture of himself with Taiwan in his arms.

"Taiwan will miss you," I said. The new cook was French and didn't look as if he'd allow us in the kitchen. As I flung myself into Max's great warm arms, I felt as if my childhood was gone. My former innocent joyful life was to return with Max to Africa.

I read somewhere that an Arab will bury his son's afterbirth in the sand outside the tent. My grandfather was in the Army, my father said, and he traveled with the bedouins across the desert. I felt as if my afterbirth was buried in our garden in Africa. Tears came to my eyes now. In Africa everything was simple. Max and Saul lived and worked. We lived simply. Here in the sophisticated world of the French Embassies, we lived a complicated multi-faceted life. If I wore shoes in Africa, it was to avoid snakes or scorpions. Now I wore shoes so as not to scandalize women who could be far more dangerous than the snakes or scorpions. I had a huge wardrobe of unwanted clothes. No longer could I lounge about in shorts and a T-shirt. Nice girls didn't wear shorts. Nor did they wear trousers. We wore horrid prissy dresses. Today, a ghastly pink dress.

I knew Geneviève would be wearing a very white pair of tennis shorts and a stunning designer T-shirt. When I protested and described Geneviève's outfit to my mother, she arched her eyebrows. "The Derlangers are French. We are *English,*" she said with fierce pride.

"Take another outfit and stick it in your swimming bag," Françoise whispered. I did.

Now Max was in the front hall. The car ground to a halt on the pebbles outside. Max gave me one last hug and picked up his battered suitcase and was gone forever.

"Well," my mother said, standing on the stairs. "It's just as well. Mary, you're much too old for all that hugging and kissing." She approached me nervously. "Dear," she said, "now that you are nearly thirteen, you may have need of this." She pressed a paper parcel into my hands. "Take this upstairs and put it in your drawer. If you need to ask any questions," she said, "do consult me. But there is a little booklet enclosed in the box. All you need to know," she said hurriedly, "is that it happens to all girls. Now I must go. I'm due to play mahjong with Mrs. Biddle."

"Mrs Biddle?" I said, still thinking of the woman as Crow Number Two.

"Yes." My mother nodded. "Her husband's been posted to Paris."

"Oh," I said. "I'll take this upstairs . . . Thank you." On the way up the stairs I thought of Mrs Biddle. "Wait 'til she pinches *your* cheeks, Françoise," I said silently.

Françoise was laughing. "Open the box," she said. I didn't really want to open the box. It was all a bit Pandora-ish. I hated the Pandora story. Poor girl opens her toy-box and dreadfully ugly things fly out. I'd always been nervous of opening boxes ever since I learned of poor Pandora's plight.

I rushed to my bathroom and slowly opened the parcel. I laughed. Mademoiselle had explained all about the facts of life ages ago. Jacques, she said, was going to marry her and then they'd make babies, but as they were both Catholics they used the Roman Catholic method of only making love on safe days of the month. Mademoiselle was very advanced in her views. Most French women did not make love before they were married. Why, she said, should a man drink milk from one cow if there is a herd available? "Mark you, little one," she said darkly, "if women ever make themselves available without a promise of marriage, overnight there'll be a revolution and marriage will go out of the window. Women will have everything to gain by marriage and men everything to lose." I listened carefully because Mademoiselle was very clever and Jacques loved her very much. I wanted to be loved like that by a man as handsome as Jacques.

All the way in the car to Geneviève's I thought about love, and when I saw Patrick I fell in love for the second time in my life. Patrick was tall for fifteen. He had a wide smile and freckles across his nose. "Hi," he said and squeezed my hand.

I was so glad I had my red swimsuit with me. Before I had left, I had changed out of my dreadful dress. I wore a dirndl skirt and a black turtleneck sweater. I sneaked a pair of my mother's sunglasses out of her drawer and tried to look as if I was at least fourteen. It was awfully hard to see through the glasses. They were for skiing, but they looked fabulously sophisticated.

Geneviève's boyfriend Rollo was smoking a cigarette, and every so often Geneviève leaned forward and took a puff. We four were the only people at the pool. Time stood still with slightly jagged edges. It felt as if the moment was captured in a bubble. There I was at one end of the pool. Patrick was beside me and across the pool, lounging in two long white chairs, were Geneviève and Rollo. "Come on," Françoise said. "Look sexy." I'd never tried to look sexy before, so I said hello to Patrick in a low voice and then walked beside him rolling my hips in the way I saw Marlene Dietrich roll hers at the cinema, only Marlene Dietrich had hips to roll.

I lay down on the long chair next to Geneviève feeling silly. Geneviève lay sprawled, her long perfect brown legs emerging from very short tight shorts. Her yellow T-shirt matched her corn-colored hair, and her eyes gleamed with amusement. Rollo, dark with sleek black hair, had a possessive hand on Geneviève's arm. "You're late," Geneviève said. "We'll have to swim after lunch."

"I'm sorry. I had to wait for the car. Max left for Africa." I was awfully conscious of my two matchstick-like legs sticking out in front of me.

"Ah, yes," Geneviève explained. "Max is, or was, your African cook. My mother says you have Armand now to cook for you." She grinned. "I hear he's a beast, but a good cook. Anyway, let's see what we have for lunch."

I always enjoyed lunch at the Derlangers. Geneviève led the way through huge rooms to the family dining room, a pretty room filled with French country wicker furniture. I always envied Geneviève her poise. We, of course, did not live in the sort of grandeur that Geneviève lived in. And Geneviève made friends very easily. She must have broken at least a hundred hearts since we'd been in France. Rollo, I thought looking at the back of his head, didn't look as if he'd have his heart broken. In fact he looked a little too predatory for my taste. But Patrick looked wonderful. "Come and sit by Patrick," Geneviève said.

She pushed a buzzer by her plate. "The chef says the lobster is excellent today, and we have smoked salmon from the north of Scotland. We use the same source as the Savoy in London."

"Ah," Patrick sighed. "I do so love living in Paris." His blue eyes clouded. "English food is the pits."

I looked at him. "Really?" I said. "I have to go to boarding school next year. Is it really that awful?"

"Yes," Patrick said firmly. "I tell you what. When I go back, I'll write you vivid descriptions of the most frightful dishes, and you can write me long letters about French food and cakes, and I can lie in my bed and die of desire for a pot of French chocolate or a huge squishy fresh croissant."

Just then two maids dressed in black with white starched aprons and little frilly caps carried in the first course. Lovely, moist, pale apricot, smoked salmon. A mound of green mayonnaise, and a pile of toast so thin the pieces lay on top of each other as though racked with pain. My little pepper mill spat specks of spicy black pepper onto the smoked salmon. And then I sneezed. Not the delicate sneeze of a well-bred girl, but an awful huge explosion that sent my glass of water splashing across the table and my face buried into my thick white napkin. I never had been able to sneeze quietly.

I sat motionless while Geneviève laughed, and I could hear her moving the plates around. "I say," Patrick said. "That was quite a sneeze. Do you often do that?"

I nodded.

"Don't worry," Geneviève said kindly. "I've mopped everything up. Don't be a goose. It was an accident."

I had to put my napkin down. I would have preferred to have kept my bright red face covered and to have quietly left the house. Rollo was looking at me in quiet amusement. *"Les anglais,"* he said.

"Hey," Patrick laughed. "That's enough. We may not be as sophisticated as you lot, but we try."

Lunch passed and I did not make any other embarrassing *faux pas.* I remembered the right forks and knives for each occasion, and I drank out of the right glasses. We had three different wines: white with the smoked salmon, a Portuguese rosé with the lobster, and a sweet pudding wine with the meringue base stuffed with puréed greengages. I was full when we finished and happy. The wine gave me a warm glow and restored my lost confidence.

After coffee we walked to the pool. I went off to change into my new suit. Geneviève simply slipped her shorts off and her T-shirt. She was wearing a very slinky black swimsuit which clung to her ripe breasts. Both boys stared at her in a way they would never stare at me. But then, as I looked at my bare pale self in the dressing room, I wasn't sure that I wanted any man to look at me in that way. Especially Rollo. There was a fire in the way he looked at Geneviève, a fire he looked as if he intended to extinguish. I hoped Geneviève knew what she was doing.

When I returned to the pool I felt self-conscious, especially because, when I felt nervous, I always got the most dreadful goose bumps all over my legs and arms. So here I was in my bright red swimsuit, white skinny legs, and an army of goose bumps in attendance. I was mortified. So I recited "The Rime of the Ancient Mariner" to myself as I walked the length of the huge pool to the chairs at the end. I slipped into my chair as gracefully as possible, and I put my hand into my swimming bag and put on my mother's dark glasses. Anonymous at last.

I listened to Geneviève, Rollo, and Patrick discussing a party they had been to the night before. Unlike my mother, Mme Derlanger loved her daughter to go to parties, as she explained to all and sundry. Indeed, Geneviève and her mother could be taken for sisters and they often dressed alike. My mother and I would never even remotely resemble sisters. She, with her beautiful face and perfect figure, and I, looking more like nine than nearly thirteen . . . "How about coming to my birthday party?" Patrick's voice invaded my thoughts.

"I can't," I said. "My mother won't let me."

"Well," Patrick said, taking off my glasses and looking at me quizzically, "we'll get round that one. We'll ask both your parents as well. Then we have two parties. My parents entertain everyone else's parents, and we all go off in my father's boat. That way the parents stay up all night and we get to have a party without parents."

I laughed. "Really, Patrick," I said. "That's very clever."

Patrick grinned. "Come on," he said. "Let's swim."

The water was warm and my goose bumps melted away. Rollo and Geneviève were having an intense conversation that involved a lot of *nons* on Geneviève's part. I swam slowly down the middle of the pool. I loved to swim, and the crawl is a beautiful stroke. I felt the water part under my arms, and I felt like a knife slicing my way through the water. The edges of my hands were dangerous weapons. Finally I stopped and stood up.

Patrick was trailing behind me. "Hey," he said, standing up. "You're a good swimmer."

I smiled. "I swam an awful lot in Africa."

"You must miss it," he said. "We had to leave our tea plantation in Ceylon." He made a face. "My father knew there'd be trouble, so we got out before anyone else. Now he's a banker, but our hearts are still in the tea plantation." We both got out and sat side by side with our legs dangling in the water. Patrick's feet were long and thin. I felt the warmth of his body next to mine. "You know," he said, "it's the nights I miss. We had a huge wide veranda, and most evenings we spent sitting out there, my father with his stengah in his hand, my mother sewing, and my two sisters and I playing or listening to music on the old radio." He sighed, and I sighed, too.

"Yes," I said. "The nights were so alive. The bushes had eyes. Everything is so quiet at night here, except for the traffic." We spent the afternoon talking about Ceylon and Africa.

When my car came to pick me up I was quite upset. "I'll get your invitation out tomorrow," Patrick promised. "I'll speak to my father's secretary. She handles all that sort of thing." Suddenly we both felt shy. "I enjoyed talking to you," Patrick said.

"So did I." Shyness gripped my throat, and I fled. "Good-bye, Geneviève," I called behind me. "I'll telephone you this evening." I got into the car and I sat back in the seat and thought "This is love, the second time round."

Chapter 13

I was not as shy on the telephone as I was in person, because no one could see me. I waited for my mother to go out before I made my calls. I loved the ring of the Paris telephones. In Africa, when I telephoned my grandmother and grandfather in England, they sounded a million miles away. I imagined my voice miles up in space. I suppose it was the closest I got to feeling how vast the universe was and how tiny and unimportant I was—just a speck, a bit of dust. My mother didn't like the telephone at all. She used it only to give orders to shops and if she had to change an appointment. She sat every morning in her sitting room, and at ten sharp the new chef Armand came nervously to the sitting room and took his orders for the day. Barzon came in after Armand and my mother told him who was coming to visit or what uniform my father was to wear, how many medals, which stars on his collar. My father looked very romantic in his uniforms, particularly if we were entertaining or being entertained by the French government. Somehow the old French government buildings breathed a dramatic life of their own. To be going-on thirteen and to attend a ball with Geneviève, who was so poised, seemed like a very special magic.

One evening, as I waited for my mother to go out to *le cocktail* with my father, I decided to spend the evening thinking about myself. Life seemed to have accelerated itself so fast since I met Mademoiselle that I, Mary, and I, Françoise, seemed to be not two people like my fairy friend in Africa, but two people in one person. Sometimes I felt out of control, with Françoise dictating events or making suggestions that I, Mary, would never have thought of. However, I did intend to borrow some of my mother's bath milk and spend the evening floating about in my own bath, just thinking.

I liked to think. I found it difficult to think about school. School was a place I went during the day, and I sat in a neat row with other boys and girls my age. I had been there long enough to have become accepted by the other students. One of the boys fancied himself in love with me, but I didn't have time for all that then. The girls, on the whole, tolerated and teased me about being English, but thanks to Jacques and Mademoiselle my French was getting good. Mademoiselle made me make sounds at the back of my throat, so that I didn't speak French with an English accent. "Such an abomination," she said crossly. " 'orrible." I hung my head because my father spoke grammatically perfect French, as he did German and Russian, but always with an impeccable English accent. Now I could hear the difference when he spoke French on the telephone or to a guest at the table. It hurt me to realize that my father was not perfect.

During dinner I sat in the library. The dining room was too big for a lone person, so Barzon served me chicken and salad followed by a peach sorbet. The sorbet was astringent and cleaning. Then I went to my mother's bedroom and opened the door. Her smell was always there. Her room breathed in and out. I felt eyes watching me, but Françoise said, "Don't be silly. Get the bath milk. No one is here." In fact, I realized as I stood on the threshold of her room, this was the second time I had violated my mother. I took the large bottle with the lilac design and I carried it to my room in triumph.

I filled the bath full of hot hot water, and then I dropped a few drops of the pearly white milky liquid into the bath. Instantly rings formed. The liquid joined with the water in a sensual embrace. The fragrance of white thick-leafed roses assailed my nostrils. I put the bottle down and I slipped slowly into the water, my feet—pink—first, then my ankles, down through my legs, to my waist, and then past my breasts, their nipples puckered at the hot embrace, and then up to my neck, and my head back, afloat in a big French bath somewhere in the universe. "Ahhhh," I sighed. Little things are made in heaven.

When I raised my head, I saw that my fingers were quite water-logged. I now sat up and began to reason with myself. You are nearly thirteen. You are good at your lessons. You love Mademoiselle and Jacques. You have a best friend Geneviève and you are in love with Patrick Johnson. How wonderful to have all that in your life at once!

It was getting late as I lay in the bath. The window of the bathroom was black with the sky. Tonight Paris was besieged by a storm. I loved Paris when the forks of lightning leaped about the city. Wonderful ballerinas of light. Amazing tightrope walkers, they flashed and clashed in the heavens, around the cupolas, and in and out of the streets, stamping their feet on the dry pavements, filling the air with the excited smell of ions, and then came the rain. Huge balls of unexploded moisture, and then the sound of the drops spat on the hard pavement. Splat, splat, splutter on the pebbles outside the house. In the downpour I dried myself and hurried downstairs to phone Patrick. "Isn't it exciting?" I said.

"Yes," Patrick said. He understood exactly what I meant without my saying anything more. "Wow!" he said. "The lightning just struck the ground by the river."

"Wow."

"Listen, I must go now, but I waited for your call. I'll see you Friday. Okay?" And he said, "I'm really looking forward to seeing you."

The "you" lingered in the air long after I'd put the telephone down. The "you" lay in my arms as I slept deeply and peacefully until the light was on and my bedroom door was open. My mother stood there in her dressing gown. "Where is my bath milk?"

Then I remembered in the middle of the storm and my haste to ring Patrick, I'd forgotten to replace the bottle. Before I was fully awake, my mother—more out of control than I'd ever seen her—pounced on me and began to strike me with her fists. I had my sheets and blankets tucked firmly around me, so I lay as still as I could . . . Then I felt a searing jolt of anger. The anger felt as electric as the storm that crashed outside my bedroom window, the lightning lighting up the window. "Hit her back, you fool!" Françoise's words summed up the feeling in my body.

I leapt out of bed and I swung my hand back as far as it would go, and I hit her with all my weight, all my breath. I hit her in the chest. She gasped and put her hands to her chest protectively. "How dare you?" she said.

"I *do* dare! You will never *never* hit me again." I put my face close to hers and spoke in a grating voice that was not my own.

My mother, for the first time in her life, backed off from a fight. She stared at me. I stared back. This was the woman whose body I had inhabited unwillingly. Just as unwillingly she had given birth to me. For a land-locked moment we were one, but then the plates deep under us both separated. A shudder tore us apart and my island, myself, broke free.

She looked at me and then walked out of the room without closing the door. I went into the bathroom and I picked up her bottle of bath milk, and I stood over the lavatory. I let every single last drop leave the bottle, and then I flushed the lavatory and threw the bottle in my waste basket. Old Madame Charpentier who cleaned the rooms every day would appreciate such a pretty bottle. As for my mother . . . I lay in bed triumphant. As for my mother, I vowed I would never be hurt by her again.

And then, before relief and freedom had even a moment to settle on my soul, guilt raged within me. I had

hit my own mother, surely the worst sin in God's eyes.
I started to cry and I prayed to God for forgiveness.
Hours of tears, prayers, and guilt passed before I fell
into a black and dreamless sleep.

❧ *Chapter 14* ❧

I awoke instantly the next morning. I felt as if I lay in
the middle of the flower bed outside my window in
South Africa, as if the black window that hung under
the eaves in her untidy shroud-like web swung over
my face, her large elegant body made obvious by the
bright splash of red on her abdomen. And I felt as if
the wedge-shaped head of the deadly cotton-mouthed
viper also lay beside me, a yawn exposing two curled
fangs dripping with venom. I couldn't breathe. Death
and convulsions were all around me.

Slowly I opened my eyes and breath once again
filled my lungs. There was the door so recently shut
by my mother. Still shut, there was the other door to
my bathroom, the scene of my most recent crime. But
wonderfully the room surrounded me in a warm loving secure embrace, just as Mademoiselle would when
I told her. I could see Jacques's dark head nod in sympathy. I wouldn't tell Geneviève.

If my mother told my father of my behavior there
would be a silence over breakfast, my father buried in
The Times before he left for work. He would look at me
reproachfully. "I don't know, Pumpkin. I really don't
know why you do these things. I think we'll have to
find a good boarding school." The idea of a good
boarding school terrified me. I was shy anyway, and
had no friends apart from Geneviève. Even she was
not my confidante. I kept my own counsel now Max

was gone, and if I cried, I told Taiwan my troubles. Sitting up in bed sobbing into his coat, he licked my tears away with his little energetic Peke tongue. He snuffled and whuffled with understanding, but today the second big event in my life was about to stare me in the face. Last night I hit my own mother, a crime so abhorred that not one of my books which I read so avidly ever hinted at such a felony.

Before HM (Hitting Mother) I had been reading Dornford Yates's *Jonah and Co,* a book that reduced me to tears of laughter. Brothers, sisters, and cousins shared a summer in France, never a mention of family sadness. The book comforted me as much as it made me laugh. Here was a world before war had decimated Europe for the second time. The people in his book loved each other and teased each other in a way that was not possible in my family.

As I walked down the stairs to the dining room, I looked first at my mother. She gazed back at me. My father was talking to my mother. His face was alight. "Do you think," he was saying, "we should keep some of our own bees, darling?" So she hadn't told him.

I smiled at my mother. "Good morning, Mother," I said as cheerfully as I could manage. "Do let's keep bees, Daddy," I said. "I'd love to be an apiarian."

My father laughed delightedly. "Good girl," he said. "Splendid word. I have a marvellous word for you." My father threw back his small neat head and shut his eyes with the thrill of passing on a new word. "The word is *thigmotropic.* Take a shot at it."

"Thig . . ." I said slowly. "Well . . ." I was watching my mother through Françoise's eyes. My mother hated this sort of exchange between us. Her right hand fluttered over her breasts where I had hit her the night before. A sudden guilt threatened to overwhelm me. I struggled to keep my mind on my word-game with my father. "Let's see," I began. "Thigmo would come from the Greek *thigma*, meaning touch. And tropic would be from the Greek *tropos*, 'turn.' So thigmotropic must mean 'turn towards touch,' '' I said triumphantly.

My father let out a snort of approval. "Quite right, old sport," he said. "Top of the class."

"Yes," said my mother. "She's really doing quite well for a slow beginner." She stared at me with a dare in her eye. Would I, her mother-hitting child of last night, take her on again, now in the arena of verbal blows? No, I would not. I said nothing and my mother smiled as if in victory over this small battle. "Darling," she turned to my father, "today I feel I must write to England. Mary is really old enough to go to a good boarding school." In her eyes lay a promise of a time shared together without me.

My father blushed and looked hurriedly at me. "Of course. If you say so, dear," he said. 'Don't worry, pumpkin,' he said. "You'll have to like the place. I loved Winchester. Best time of my life."

I smelled defeat; I knew better than to fight. Perhaps I vanquished my mother last night, or perhaps she had won last night through her secret weapon of guilt. Surely she must have known how awful I felt. Now, however, she was seizing again the position of victor. She, in the nicest possible way, was shipping me off: the last laugh, if ever there was one. "That'll be lovely, Daddy," I said, feeling a genuine awe at my mother's cunning strength. Then, in an effort to regain some of my footing: "Can I have a horse?"

Glad to be free of a possible fight, glad for the promise of the return of his wife, my father got up and kissed my cheek before leaving. "Don't worry about a thing."

"I'm not," I said to his retreating back, trying to sound nonchalant. "Maybe they'll have bees."

We sat, my mother and I, in silence. She sat at the

head of the big table, elegant in her morning gown, my father's family crest enjewelled on the gray-green *eau-de-Nil* robe. I, in my Peter Pan collar gray school uniform, sipped Earl Gray tea from the Wedgwood morning tea set. In our home, the hours ticked by obsessed with the time of day. I gazed intently at my big morning cup of Earl Gray tea. The thin wedge of lemon floated on the top of the pale tea. Where was the tea picked? Whose brown hands took the tea off the bushes? Was it in Ceylon with its huge rubber trees, or Persia? Isfahan? If I kept my mind intensely occupied, I could maybe block out my mother as a person sitting at the end of the table, make her vanish like the old fakir that visited us once a year in Africa.

He claimed he was invisible. "How can you be invisible?" I said when I was five. He had just put a lighted stick down his throat and charmed a huge cobra from his round wicker basket. "How can you be invisible? I can see you."

"Ah," he said in his soft brown Indian voice as ancient and as cracked as the shoes he wore. "If you couldn't see me, you wouldn't know I wasn't there. Would you?"

From then on I practised disappearing people who frightened me. Even if my mother could see me this morning, I couldn't see her. Too many busy thoughts got in the way. First the lovely blue of the peacock on my cup reminded me of the peacocks in the garden outside. They preened and strutted, and the peahens rushed about drab and silent. Unlike my mother. The sound of the car returning to take me to school broke the silence.

I got up and left the room, my mother watching me all the while. She won in the end. She had the power to send me away. I sighed as I reached the school. My world was going to fall apart again, just when I'd met Patrick, I had Mademoiselle and Jacques as friends, and Geneviève. I found Mademoiselle in the empty classroom and, seeing her, the pretence of stoicism I had practiced to protect myself from my mother and my guilt toppled and an urgent sob arose from my throat and tears from my eyes. "Was it bad, *ma petite?*" Mademoiselle asked, her hand on my shaking shoulder.

I shrugged. "I have to go to England to a boarding school," I answered. The class was filling up.

"Why so suddenly?"

I sniffed and wiped my eyes with the palms of my hands. "I hit my mother last night," I said.

Mademoiselle, to my surprise, smiled. "We all have to hit back sometimes," she said, showing her white little teeth. "Otherwise we never grow up. Hunh," she grunted. "We'll celebrate. I'll tell Jacques."

I went to my desk relieved. Someone in the world understood me.

❧ *Chapter 15* ❧

Patrick's party was marvelous. He was quite right: the parents very quickly lost themselves in his father's vast apartment. All of us who lived abroad tended to collect the same furniture. Patrick's father had a superb collection of carpets stretching across the tiled floor in permanent prayer to the God they served. The walls were lined with huge heads, the biggest of which was a lion's head glaring at the visitors. I could see my mother was impressed. My father made straight for the bookshelves. He took out a green marbled first edition Jane Austen. Reverently he ran his finger down the spine of the book, and then he put his nose to the book to smell the words that lay between the covers.

I, too, had the habit of smelling books. Each book had a different smell to it. Jane Austen's books smelled spicy, almost like nutmeg, whereas my Dornford Yates smelled of the south of France. Summer. New wine.

"Ah, there you are!" Patrick looked fabulous in black-tie. He put out his strong hand and fairly pulled me through the crowd. "Come on," he said. "Let them get on with it. I've got the boat tied to the landing dock on the river." And so he had.

We fled like two conspirators down in the ornate lift, past the porters, and across the busy road. It was the butt end of a lazy Saturday in Paris. People were talking and walking. Saturday evening was yet to come, that unique celebration of a day squashed between busy Friday and holy Sunday, a rather louche day, Saturday. A day devoted to eating and hopefully, when I was married, to sex. I always thought of Saturday as the look of barely concealed delighted satiation on the face of a Rubens nude, the food congealed on the plate, the wine imbibed, the woman reclining, all lust sated, the painter satisfied to take up his long sable brush again to paint the rosy fingers of his desire on canvas for those of us who would gaze so many centuries later at a moment shared between them and would hope for the day to come when we ourselves would lie on white sheets or a shore lost in the bliss. "You'll get run over!" Patrick screamed in my ear.

I shook my head and avoided a tram. We ran down the steps and onto a gangway. The teak rail was rimy with salt. I put my fingers in my mouth. The crystals crunched and let loose the pungent taste of the sea. People were coming towards us. I saw Geneviève and then I came back to reality. "*She* looks wonderful," Françoise said in my ear.

"I know," I protested. "But Patrick made a special effort to find *me*."

"And what special effort are you going to make for him?" Françoise snorted.

"I'm not," I said . . .

Geneviève sauntered over to me. She wore a little white dress, Roman-style, all the rage this summer. The whole year's sun kissed her round shoulders and her delicate forearms. The pleats folded beautifully across her breasts and then hugged her thighs possessively. Rollo stood behind her glowering. "He says I'm flirting," Geneviève pouted.

"Well, are you?" I asked.

"Of course," Geneviève said. "Every woman should know how to flirt."

"You'll have to give me lessons," I said.

"At least," Geneviève laughed, "you have decent shoes."

I nodded.

"Phew. You *have* changed since I last saw you."

"Yes." I nodded. "I have. I'm going to England to boarding school."

Geneviève gave me a funny look. "I'll telephone you tomorrow," she said. "But now I must *embêter* Rollo," she giggled.

Patrick returned with a glass of cold champagne. "Here," he said. "Bottoms up."

"I have to go to boarding school," I said.

"In England?"

"Yes. My mother doesn't approve of European schools. She says they let the girls grow up too fast."

Patrick smiled. "Well," he said. "I'm going back to Rugby in September, so instead of writing to you in Paris, we can write to each other at home." I took a sip of champagne. I suppose England was technically my home, but really Africa was in my heart and my soul. "Come to the dining cabin. My mother's chef has done a super job with the langoustine."

The evening flowed as gracefully as the Seine. My

head and nose were full of champagne bubbles. I saw little of the river except when I danced the last waltz with Patrick. We were on the bow of the boat as she nudged her way back up the great river to the landing dock. Under us the Captain of the ship brought all of us home safely to our parents. Pulling me gently into his arms, Patrick said, "I will never forget tonight. Just stay as you are, Mary." Safe in his arms and conscious of his face close to mine, I promised. Then he kissed me, a light fairy-moth of a kiss. I breathed deeply. I was in love in Paris, and somehow boarding school didn't seem such a bad idea after all.

Chapter 16

I missed my father dreadfully. No one to say "Did you know?" in his punctilious English fashion. Or he said, if he wished to contradict me without hurting my feelings, "Oh! Do you really think so?" Then I knew I must think again. For a going-away-to-school present he gave me a big box full of silks, a packet of the sharpest needles, and my first chair-seat.

I wasn't as lonely as I had expected because Rollo bashed poor Geneviève and split her lip. For once Madame Derlanger was not amused, and she said, "That's enough." Geneviève was out of hand, and a good English boarding school could do Geneviève the world of good. I was ordered to attend the Derlanger house when the news was to be broken to Geneviève. *Well.* I've seen my mother make scenes, but Geneviève outdid even my mother. She screamed, she yelled, she threw herself on the floor and rolled about with her legs in the air so everyone could see her knickers. She obviously didn't have to wear the horrid black bloomers I had to wear. Françoise was laughing like a train, but I was horrified. Finally Madame Derlanger marched out with a final *"c'est fini"* and slammed the door behind her.

Geneviève sat up and grinned at me. *"Pas mal?"* she said. "What do you think?"

"Goodness," I said. "Gosh. You're an awfully good actress. Why did Rollo hit you?"

Geneviève smiled. She covered her thumb with her forefinger and giggled. I looked at her little thumb sticking up with its bright red nail. I frowned. "It's Rollo's penis, you idiot," Françoise said crossly. "Oh," I said.

"Too small," Geneviève laughed.

"You mean you saw it?"

"Yes. Yes, of course." Geneviève was bored with the subject. "I've seen lots."

"Well, I haven't." I was indignant. "I seem to be the only penis-famished girl in Paris," I said.

"Listen," Geneviève laughed, her eyes alight, her split lips bruised. "If there's girls' schools, there must be boys' boarding schools."

"Oh, yes," I said. "Patrick goes to Rugby."

"How far is Rugby from Sherwood Park?"

I shrugged. "I don't know."

"Okay." Geneviève got off the floor. "I'm going to marry an English lord. I have decided."

Huh, I thought. She probably will. I watched Geneviève mope her way up the stairs and then I left. In the car I reflected on my awful lack of talent. I already had my Dornford Yates book, my book of Edna St Vincent Millay who was an imagist, and my first edition of Jane Austen's *Mansfield Park*, and last of all my Bible from Jerusalem, a gift from my father, with everything Jesus said in red.

Saying goodbye to Mademoiselle was awful. My last

piano lesson with Jacques was horrible. I had to like Jacques. There was the respectable Jacques that came to the house and sat beside me on the piano bench. He didn't exist. He sat three times a week solid and reassuring while my mother prowled about. She was attracted to Jacques. I could tell because she came up behind him and rested her fingertips on his black alpaca jacket. My mother always touched the men she was interested in: patted a pocket or straightened a tie. But Jacques never never responded, which was a relief. After all, he had beautiful warm loving Mademoiselle.

"Why don't you get married?" I asked on my last visit. We were sitting at the little kitchen table covered with a green checked cloth. Huge napkins hung from our necks. I had an unbearable pain in my heart. Mademoiselle cooked my favorite, *coq au vin.* The chicken lay positively drowned in the lees of many bottles of wine. The flesh was blackish-purple. The mushrooms looked as if they'd soaked sufficient gravy to explode in my mouth. And the fresh leafy salad, praying mantis green, glistened with the brown-yellow fat drops of olive oil. On my plate sat a huge mound of perfectly boiled little nutty potatoes. "When you come to see me, you won't be able to share a room in the hotel," I explained.

Jacques laughed. *"Mon chou,* by the time we get the money to come and see you, we'll probably be married. Anyway we have a secret to share with you." He put his big hand on Mademoiselle's stomach. "Monique is to have a baby."

"Really?" Suddenly the whole world brightened.

"Yes." Mademoiselle blushed. "So we will get married."

"How wonderful!" I said, and I looked at Mademoiselle. She looked so happy. I knew she was glad to be getting married.

So arriving at Sherwood Park wasn't too much of a shock, because I started my *hibiscus rosa sineusis* design on the boat. The embroidery kept me calm. I knew most nights my mother sat by my father doing embroidery and eating her chocolates. Now I, too, would be able to embroider and keep a bit of my father to myself. Geneviève had no time for sewing at all. "I won't have to sew," she said. "I'm going to be so rich, I'll order everything from Harrods." She had the use of her parents' account already. She had a purse full of fat white five-pound notes. I had three dingy brown ten-shilling notes. I was only going first class because the Foreign Office paid, otherwise I would be sitting with everybody in the third class, and Geneviève would be lording it away in the first class all by herself. The difference between Geneviève and me was that she was the Ambassador's daughter, and I was only a Consul General's daughter, so I suppose I always felt a third class person.

However, I did have my grandparents to stay with in the holidays, and Geneviève was to spend the Easter and summer holidays with us at Milton Park. My father told me shortly before I left that he had applied for a post in London. He said he couldn't tell me much about the post because it was "hush hush." I knew all about "hush hush" from our African days, so I just nodded. "Does that mean we have to live in London?" I asked.

"During the week I will, if I get the post, but I can't wait to get down to Milton Park." My father's face shone. I loved it when his face lit up, his eyes particularly. I knew it was the trout-fishing. He badly missed his fishing rods. He'd had them since he was a child. He and his father fished in Scotland every year. That was where my school was, in Scotland in a place called Loch Hey built on the site of a terrible battle. "When the salmon run," he said, "it's like a miracle before your eyes. Great solid walls of fish leaping and jumping out of the water, the sun catching the jewels of water . . ."

But my father's reappointment never came. He let slip that he had hoped to do some work in London and then be promoted to Ambassador. To where? Wherever they sent him. "It would appear," he said upon hearing the news, "that they're quite satisfied to keep me as Consul General." I could see the disappointment on his face. I felt terribly sorry for him.

I missed him. Oh, how I missed him! Now I was in England and about to be in school.

I would like to say that Geneviève's first impression of England was a happy one. What actually happened, however, was that we were escorted to the train by a man from Thomas Cook. Now any English person knows that the world begins and ends with Thomas Cook, also that one's father has an account with Thomas Cook who then, anywhere in the world, looks after you. I always imagined Thomas Cook to be a man who resembled Mr Pickwick, one of my favorite English characters. I also imagined Mr Thomas Cook, stopwatch in hand, rushing about all over the world rescuing people and steamer-trunks from overzealous ships that gobbled up luggage. He must have had a terrible time with our luggage when my family moved from Africa.

My mother made it her business to get the huge vast packing cases made out of teak and mahogany. Then, when we were in Paris, she made a handsome profit selling her wood to a furniture shop. My mother could make a profit out of bottletops. She also arranged flowers beautifully, but I hated to cut the flowers in our garden. I loved gardens, and when the gardener took my mother's silver secateurs in his hand, I went to my room. Poor flowers, cut just as they had achieved their moment of destiny. Especially roses.

Now she had arranged to separate me from the family, and the man from Thomas Cook turned out to be young and handsome, so handsome I had to yell at Geneviève who tried to suggest we stay the night in London. "English penises look just like French ones," I said crossly. "Besides, I'd be in the room."

Geneviève sighed. "I didn't know we'd cross the Channel and you'd become a bore."

Still, all across London in a Thomas Cook car, she persisted in fascinating him, which she did very well. Beads of sweat were beginning to form on his head. We pulled into the station and clambered aboard the train. A convenient gust of wind caught Geneviève's skirt. The poor man went very red. "Showing your knickers again?" I said.

Geneviève was madly cheerful. "Well, you can't show those dreadful passion-killers you wear," she said. *"Mon dieu.* You'll die an old maid before anyone puts their hand down there."

"Don't," I said uncomfortably. "Anyway, I'm not getting married unless I meet a man like my father. He knows everything." I lay in my bunk looking at the dark night clattering by. The view was not of animals, their eyes catching the refractive light. The steam and the hiss and the clickity-clack sounded the same, but the whine of the wheels said, "I want to go back. I want to go back." Back to what? I thought. My father loved me, but couldn't protect me. My mother had insisted that a "lady" had to travel with her own silverware and plate. So tucked into one of my massive suitcases were a set of Puiforcat silver—even fish knives. The box lined with velvet said "Puiforcat. 1820. Silversmiths. Paris" and my dining set was a particularly ornate collection of Victorian Chinese design. The pattern was bright red, and a vulgar gold strip descended upon everything and dripped all over the plates.

I now owned several thousand drab dresses. The school uniform was even drabber. Geneviève's answer to the uniform was to give the stuff to her mother's seamstress to take in every dart and seam until the dress looked as if it had been painted on her. "Look," she said before we left. I did look and realized she was not wearing any underwear. I was so depressed with the sight of myself looking like a discarded sack of potatoes, I didn't bother to argue with her. After all, we were about to be incarcerated for thirteen weeks in an all-girls' school.

I lay looking out of the train's window, wishing I were back in Africa in those golden years when I was loved by my father and our servants. That was a long time ago. I fell asleep in tears.

Chapter 17

The school was a surprise for me. All my reading life, I'd imagined an English boarding school to be a huge gray institution. Here, in the bright pleasing Scottish Highlands, I was pleasantly surprised to see a lovely manor house appear at the bottom of a long carriageway lined with immense oaks, some so old they were propped up with sticks and hung bulbous and warted with age. Geneviève said very little. She sat sulking. She announced over breakfast that she was now forced to live life like a nun, and already the prospect did not suit her.

Geneviève sat with me in the back of a very old car driven by a wizened little man with one tooth, a dripping nose, and a coat stiff with age and ill-use. He smelled as if he never bathed, and his breath was redolent with whiskey. "Those trees," he said proudly, "have been there since the Doomsday Book." I was curious at how beautifully his voice rose and fell with a gentle lilt. My father always said that the art of speaking now belonged only to the Scots. My father often imitated his own Somerset dialect with its burring and buzzing of the words. "Ay, the trees are written in the Book," the man continued, "and they've outlived the terrible violence of the English to the Highlands."

He spat out of the window. This also did not surprise me. My father warned me before I left not to discuss any wars with the Scots. Or the Irish, he added. To this day, no Scot, Welsh, nor Irish have ever forgiven the English. Neither had my father. I was curious to see how "the English" behaved. Certainly we had English visitors, but they were on business. They all dressed alike and sounded as if they were all processed like the English sausages they brought with them.

By now we were approaching the house. Our house in Paris was beautiful, but this house was magnificent. Wide soft-colored steps rose to embrace a huge double mahogany door. The house sat comfortably protected by a balustrade. The roof, severe and elegant, behatted the four stories of windows that gazed with joy. The stately trees casting shadows on the green lawns, looked as if they were women at a ball with their skirts spread about them. The poplars, lean and slim, stood about like courtiers bowing in the wind, an invitation to the dance that must occur when all of us who attended this establishment were asleep. Across to the right side of the house crouched little broken-down cottages. "That's where they seized my people."

"Oh really?" I said.

He, the driver, turned his face. "Ay," he said. "My great-grandfather was dragged out of there and set alight by the redcoats." He turned his face to me and pointed to an eyeless socket. "I lost that in the trenches in the mud of France." The other brown eye looked at me. "I wasn't fighting for the bloody British. I was fighting for my own people."

I nodded. Suddenly I felt less alone. "What is your name please?" I said breathlessly.

"My name is John MacAllister," he said. "I'm a groundsman here. I drive you back and forth to the town."

I smiled. "Well, John, I'm pleased to meet you. My name is Mary Jane Freeland."

"And I you," he said. "You'll be seeing a lot of me. If you want to learn about the flora and fauna of this area, I'll be telling you."

"Do you have any snakes?" I asked. We were drawing to a halt. The massive doors opened by magic, and a couple of girls ran down to meet us.

"Yes, we do," he said. "Stay away from the adders, and I'll find you some slow-worms."

I was grateful because I missed Taiwan more than I ever imagined. My mother said that the English always locked up foreign animals for six months to deter foreigners from entering England. So I left Taiwan with my mother and father, but now with a snake as a possible pet, and the broken-down cottages full perhaps of mice and birds, I might not be as lonely as I expected.

"Hello there. Let us help you with the luggage." The first speaker was tall and blonde. "I'm Georgina. This is Liz. We're your house prefects." Both girls smiled and we smiled back, except I knew Geneviève was dying inside. Both girls wore shorts down to their knees, white socks, tennis shoes, and blue air-tex shirts. Even Geneviève couldn't unbutton those unyielding shirts low enough to show off her bust or do much on the leg exposure front. I tried not to laugh.

John took the cases out of the boot of the car and

smiled. "Off you go, gerls," he said with a delightful roll of his rrrs. "You'll have a good time here." And he left us standing on the steps ready for our next adventure.

Miss Standish was the name of our headmistress. We were to be taken to her study after lunch. Lunch was held in the Great Dining Room, a beautiful room which must have once been a ballroom. The walls were lined with full-length mirrors. The floors were highly polished, and the long refectory tables, marbled in oak, looked as old as the trees outside. As we were ushered through the door of the dining room, four hundred curious eyes looked at us and a sudden hush descended upon the crowd. Geneviève smiled faintly and I tried not to bolt for the great front door. But the lure of food was more urgent than their curiosity, and immediately a hum and a babble swelled again.

Georgina moved through the room and sat us down at the last table right next to the tall window that looked out over a large rose bed. Further back I saw a lake with willows leaning sorrowfully over the water. I was overjoyed. Lakes meant frogs and newts and fish. More companions. Also I could see a few black faces among the pale white blonde heads. Liz appeared with two plates in her hands. "Cook says he's sorry. He didn't expect you 'til tea-time. But here are some Cornish pasties and salad."

Geneviève disdained the pasties. She was on yet another diet. "Besides," she said rather loudly, "it looks as if it rolled over and died."

"You're quite wrong," I said, sinking my teeth into the pasty's delicately swollen belly. The gravy and the meat were in communion with the onions and rushed down my throat to comfort my starving stomach. My father talked earnestly and with great delight on the food served in English public houses. Fisherman's pie, pasties, pork-pies . . . The mere mention of these words brought a light to his face that even the most finely executed Beef Wellington did not. "I'm a meat and potatoes man," he said firmly and on many occasions. "I need good English food." I was glad to be able to tell him that he was certainly right about Cornish pasties.

I ate mine and then I ate Geneviève's. Then we were summoned to meet Miss Standish in her study.

Miss Standish was short and squatted behind her desk in her wood-paneled study. She gazed at me through her thick horn-rimmed spectacles. Then she looked at Geneviève. "I see," she said, "you two girls are from Paris."

Geneviève smiled her pretty smile and curtseyed. I wished I could curtsey like Geneviève, but I had spent years fighting with my mother over curtseying. I always fell over my feet and blushed with shame, so I usually spared myself the humiliation and just shook hands. "My name is Mary Jane Freeland," I said. I took Miss Standish's seated hand in my own. Her hand was small and plump and pleasingly warm. I was surprised because I expected a cold wet hand, but it was not so at all.

"Mademoiselle Derlanger—"(Miss Standish's French accent was perfect)"—your parents tell me they have been worried by your conduct in Paris." Geneviève looked at her lovely high-heeled shoes. "While you are here, Mademoiselle, I expect perfect behavior. For a start, you will spend this afternoon in the sewing room. See that your uniform conforms to the school dress-code. Here, run to the end of my study." The distance was about twenty-five feet. Poor Geneviève tottered off, her bottom wiggling and her feet tapping. I tried not to laugh. Geneviève shot me

a filthy look on the way back. "You see, dear—" Miss
Standish almost allowed a smile to touch her rather
sad brown eyes"—here you will be doing gymnastics
and taking part in the educational activities of my establishment. I run a tight ship, you know. Everything
ship-shape and Bristol fashion. None of this modern
nonsense. *Gels* like you refuse to use your noodles
when boys are around. Can't have that, can we?"

"Huh, no," Geneviève replied, a slight tremor in
her voice. "Not at all."

"As for you," Miss Standish smiled at me. "I gather
from your father you love to read." She frowned. "But
your mother says your behavior requires correction.
We will have to work on that. What books have you
both brought with you?"

Geneviève spread her hands, for she never read
books except for *Gone With The Wind.* She was in love
with Rhett Butler, which was why she got into such a
mess with Rollo. I was bursting to write to Patrick and
tell him all about my school. "Dornford Yates," I said.
"And a book of poems by Edna St Vincent Millay. Also
my Bible."

"Ah," said Miss Standish. "I love Dornford Yates.
And in your Bible do you read Isaiah?"

"Yes. When my mother is angry with me, I read the
end of the Book of Job."

Miss Standish took off her glasses and rubbed her
eyes. "Run along, Mademoiselle, and sew your uniform. I'll have to see that you have a more suitable pair
of shoes. Miss Freeland, I'm about to have a cup of
tea. Would you join me?" Her eyes without the glasses
looked like the eyes of a baby gazelle. Miss Standish
looked oddly vulnerable. I wondered what had happened to her to make her so sad.

"I'd love to," I said.

Miss Standish pressed a button on her desk. She
nodded to Geneviève. "Off you go," she said. I heard

the sound of stiletto heels tapping up the corridor. Then, as Geneviève left the room, a slim pretty woman slipped into the study and smiled at me. "This is Margaret," Miss Standish said. "Margaret dear, we need a nice pot of tea and a few digestive biscuits, I think, for my guest Miss Freeland. Would you see that Mademoiselle Derlanger sees herself safely to the sewing room? And then join us, if you will, for a cup of tea."

Margaret looked at Miss Standish with such a look of adoration that I was forcefully reminded of Jacques and Mademoiselle Pétain. But then, so far, I felt that Miss Standish could easily arouse a feeling of adoration. She was kind and correct. She was surrounded by beautiful objects and had a fabulous library. I could see a whole row of bound editions of Kipling. I loved Kipling, especially *Stalky and Co.* I very much hoped I could read her books. "You can, dear." Miss Standish was smiling mischievously. I was startled. Added to all her other virtues, she could mind-read.

Margaret laughed. "Miss Standish is very good at soul-searching. I'll run along and sort something out with Bridget. She's the sewing mistress. Then I'll bring up tea. Cook is off this afternoon, and so is Matron."

"All right, dear. Come along, Miss Freeland. We'll go over to my drawing room and get to know each other."

Getting to know each other, I discovered that afternoon, meant Miss Standish got to know all about me and I left knowing nothing about her, except that she had once lived in India and always had a school. Tea was served in a pink Limoge teapot. The cups were the daintiest things imaginable, and the biscuits made me homesick. My father always had his chocolate digestive biscuits ordered from the Army & Navy in Victoria Street. Even if the French patisseries were stuffed with every kind of biscuit you could imagine, my father very firmly explained to my mother that family tradition was family tradition. The Freeland family ordered their digestive biscuits from the Army & Navy, their Christmas crackers from Harrods, and the big round Stilton and port from Fortnum and Mason's. That was the way life was. Miss Standish understood my father's attitude at once. "Quite right," she said, smiling at Margaret. "It's our British heritage that keeps us going." She sighed. "I'm afraid we are far too quick to pick up bad habits from those Americans. I won't have American *gels,* you know. All that chewing, and those clothes . . . You know, Margaret, American *gels,* I'm told, are dreadfully fast."

I rolled my eyes. If Miss Standish thought American girls were fast, wait 'til she sees Geneviève in action. I sat back and felt the beauty of the drawing room surround me: two plump sofas by a small marble fireplace, a blue Chinese washed rug. Pretty curtains hanging snugly by the windows let us know that outside there was a perfect autumn day. Upstairs somewhere my suitcase lay waiting for the moment when I would put my belongings into my locker.

Miss Standish put me in a room with five other girls. My dormitory was called the Lily Dormitory. Both Margaret and Miss Standish were talking over school details. Suddenly I felt sleepy. The day seemed endless, and I was tired from the train journey. Miss Standish smoothed her hair with her hand. Her hair was a soft mahogany color streaked with gray. "I think Miss Freeland is a little tired," she said in her sensible English voice. "Margaret, why don't you take her to her dormitory and she can unpack in time for supper?" Miss Standish stood up and took my hand. I very much wanted Miss Standish to call me Mary. She took my hand and she said, "By the way, dear, I think I know you well enough to call you Mary."

At that moment I fell in love again. All those aching years of loneliness seemed to roll away like a fog leaving the seashore. Ahead of me lay a completely clean beach, a new life, and Miss Standish. "Come along, dear," Margaret said.

I heard her voice through a lovely crimson cloud tipped with gold. "Good night, Miss Standish."

"Good night, dear," she said. "God bless you. And sleep well."

I floated after Margaret down a corridor, up the stairs, and into a room I'd never seen before, but it didn't matter. I was home. Far more at home than I'd ever felt in my mother's house. I knew Miss Standish might be strict, but also, I could tell, always fair. Miss Standish's anger, if ever shown, would arise only correctly and predictably in righteous response to some legitimate offense, not suddenly and whimsically like my mother's labile moods. I knew Miss Standish would never shout at me or hit me. That was enough.

Nobody was in the dormitory, and Margaret left. "I'll send Phoebe up," she said. "She'll help you." I sat on the bed and waited. Before I knew it, I was asleep.

❧ *Chapter 18* ❧

"So, you're having a kip."

I woke up with a start. "What," I asked, "is a kip?"

"Army term. Slang, you know."

I obviously didn't know. "I don't know very much," I said. "But I can see I'll have to learn."

Phoebe (at least I assumed she was Phoebe) threw her six-foot self onto the bed next to mine. "I'm Phoebe Balfor. My people are from Mayo." She frowned. "I had a bloody aunt who did things in the Irish theater, so I'm supposed to be a playwright and write yet more plays about the Irish fighting each other. Oh dear," she moaned.

I'd read about English schoolgirls, and as I watched Phoebe pull a pillow over her face and wave her legs in the air, I reflected that Phoebe must be a prize English specimen. Not only was she tall, but she also had immense thighs. Her face was very white. She had a long nose and close-set blue eyes. Really, I thought, she looked like the ladies at the court of Henry VIII. Very Plantagenet. The life of Henry VIII was one of my favorite reading books. Poor Anne Boleyn, and even sorrier Catherine.

Phoebe sat up. "And who are you?" she asked sternly.

"Well, I'm Mary Freeland. I live in Paris." A memory of my father sitting at the table made my throat burn and my eyes fill with tears.

"Don't blub," Phoebe said plainly. "We all feel homesick at first, but you'll like it here. I'm the hockey captain. You look as if you'll be good at games." She smiled. Phoebe had a nice warm smile. Her teeth were pointed. "We play matches every Saturday." Phoebe put her capable hands on her knees. "We play away matches at the Air Force base." Her grin widened. "That way some of the girls meet boys who are at the base."

I smiled. "Then Geneviève will definitely want to play hockey." I laughed. "She's afraid she will have to live like a nun that has none."

Phoebe shrieked with laughter. "Here you don't have time to think about boys. Anyway, I'm not interested in boys."

"I'm in love," I said.

"Oh really? Who with?"

"Patrick Johnson. He goes to Rugby."

Phoebe stood up. "Well, you can write him jammy letters. At this school we can write to whomever we like."

I asked, "What is Miss Standish like?"

"Well," Phoebe stretched, "she is very strict. But we all love her. Actually, I prefer school to going home. I live in Wicklow in Ireland. My mother has to run our house on a pittance. My father was killed in the war."

"Oh, I'm sorry," I said. The idea of life without my father was unthinkable.

"I don't really remember him," Phoebe said. "I sort of remember him in uniform. When I go home, it's all mucking out the stables and cleaning up after the cows. I have three brothers, lazy brutes. Mother works far too hard. How about you?"

I shrugged. "We have servants, but it's pretty lonely because I'm an only child . . . Do you know where Geneviève is? She went off to do something about her uniform. Miss Standish didn't like that Geneviève made it cling to her."

Phoebe snorted. "I'll bet she didn't. Miss Standish doesn't have any nonsense at all. Listen, I'll go and scout for your friend. What's her name?"

"Geneviève Derlanger."

"Oh. French. That explains it. Whenever we get a new girl from the continent, we expect trouble. Miss Standish says they're all oversexed."

"Well," I said, trying to be loyal to Geneviève, "Geneviève is only a *little* oversexed." My goodness, I thought. If Phoebe thinks Geneviève is oversexed, what would she think of Mademoiselle and her informative talks on the virtues of unshaven armpits?

Phoebe exited with a loud clatter, and I sat on my bed and looked around the room that was to be my home for a very long time. The six beds lay pristine. We were in the Lily room, and all was white. The huge windows were hung with white brocade curtains.

Lovely swags of brocade flowers lay lost in the heavy silk embrace of those curtains that looked as if they had witnessed the lives of the rich family that at one time must have owned this gracious house. The floor was the same tongue-and-grooved pine that shone softly in the evening light. Some of the beds had teddy bears. Phoebe's bed certainly didn't. I put out my picture of my mother and my father in a silver frame by my bed, next to a smaller picture of Taiwan. Phoebe had a picture of her mother looking very tired. The three brothers were in a separate frame. They were good-looking boys with jolly smiles and Phoebe's nose.

My mother looked at me in her usual stern fashion. My father was always embarrassed to have his picture taken. He agreed with the African dictum: cameras steal your soul. So he stood beside my mother smiling awkwardly. But I had a secret picture of my father in my writing case, which was a secret place in itself where I kept my poems and my diary. This picture was taken when we were on holiday in Nîmes. There I took a picture of my father, sitting unaware on a Roman ruin of a palace. Because we were on holiday, he had not shaved that morning. I remember the bristles as they brushed my cheek and the quiet amusement in his eyes as he smiled, glad to be among his beloved Roman ruins. In his hand he had his book—always a book—of Catullus. Ever since I was little, he read me excerpts in Latin from that and other ancient Roman books. The fact that all Gaul was divided into three parts was a source of never-ending fascination. I preferred to read the stories of the Norse and the Greek gods. The fact that Prometheus was tied to a boulder and an eagle pricked at his liver for aeons fascinated me. However, I loved my father so much that I learned to decline in Latin: *amo, amas, amat, amamus, amatis, amant.* I still remember the warm hug and the smell of my father when, as a small child, I declined that verb.

I opened my suitcase to unpack my dreadfully sensible English clothes. At the bottom of the suitcase, I knew, my "plate and silver" lurked. My mother, determined not to be outdone by Madame Derlanger, also had ordered a vast amount of vests and knickers from Daniel Neill. To my embarrassment, just before I left, my mother gave me a package. Upon opening the package, I had gazed with surprise at three brassières, but these were not ordinary brassières. They were satin, and one of the brassières was black. "I don't need these," I had said, putting the brassières back in her hand.

"Yes, you will," she said. "And you'll need to talk to Matron about women's matters." I didn't tell her I already knew. "Besides," my mother said, "you'll be a woman some day, and then we can go shopping together."

Now the package lay in my suitcase. Françoise seemed to have vacated for good. Now, I realized, I'd have to rely upon myself. I unpacked the case, leaving the brassières and the plates with the silver at the bottom of the trunk. John MacAllister was going to collect the trunk and put it away in the store room this evening. I wrapped the plates up in a spare towel and hoped they wouldn't break. Then I heard the gong for supper.

Geneviève, with Phoebe behind her, sauntered into the dormitory. Her uniform hung about her. I laughed. "You can laugh," she said. "I feel like a pregnant cow. Thank God Rollo can't see me."

"We'll make a decent respectable girl out of you yet," Phoebe teased.

I walked down the main stairs of the old house marvelling at the frescos on the walls, enchanted by the beautiful hunting tapestries. There were dogs in the tapestries, and again I missed Taiwan.

The food was good but lacked the tang of garlic. There was salad marred by plain boiled eggs split in half on a few lettuce leaves. I missed our huge exuberant French salads tossed with yellow-green olive oil, black olives lurking in the depths of the bowl. I realized, as I sat among the chattering girls, I was going to miss a lot of things. Even, to my surprise when I climbed into bed to say my prayers, I missed my mother. I fell asleep without writing to Patrick. I was too tired. I was grateful to John that when he came to take my trunk, and I said there were a few things I didn't need, he nodded, understanding at once, and then he winked. Miss Standish came to the dormitory and stood in the doorway and smiled. "Good night, girls," she said. "God bless you, and sleep well." I felt blessed and I did.

৯৯৯ *Chapter 19* ৬৩৩

I grew to love my bed. My bed was the first safe place I'd ever had to myself. It was a little white railed bed, next to Phoebe who was fast becoming a good friend. Geneviève soon made friends with a crowd of Belgian girls, and they wandered about talking about the boys in their lives. Thank goodness Phoebe did no such thing. Instead we found a wall riddled with slow-worms. I learned to play hockey and loved the game. I also practiced at the cricket nets. Phoebe was a fiend of a bowler. She had learned to play with her brothers in Ireland, and the crack of the bat became a reality for me. The day I hit my first six was a day of joy. Geneviève thought I was mad. Her athletic efforts consisted of her staggering up and down the hockey field. She was fast, but she only played to get on the bus and play away teams, in case she could meet a young English lord. Her best friend was indeed the daughter of an English earl, and Geneviève was sucking up to her as hard as she could.

Miss Standish was kind to me. I always felt as if my heart were going to melt like a chocolate bar when I saw her, and I would do anything for her smile. I worked terribly hard at my lessons. I loved French and was well ahead of the class. In my time off I read Molière, Flaubert, and Racine. I absorbed poetry like blotting paper. *I Wandered Lonely as a Cloud,* a Wordsworth poem, filled me with warm yellow buttery love. "And is there honey still for tea?" from *The Old Vicarage, Grantchester* gave me a feeling of Rupert Brooke's sharp wistfulness for safe days when there was tea and the clock yet stood at ten to three. Life was now thrilling. I had excellent teachers. Latin became alive, algebra a code to be cracked. I knew my father would be pleased.

When I returned home for Christmas, he was. I brought home a handkerchief embroidered with a small dancing Chinese dragon that looked like Taiwan. Taiwan was so pleased to see me that he coughed and sneezed, stood on his head, and went round and round like a corkscrew.

I was nervous when I saw my mother. We had parted so badly, so coldly. I was still haunted by confused memories of the night I had hit her: relieved to feel I had stopped her from dominating me, yet remorseful to have hurt her. Had she forgiven me? Would she ever? Could we think of relegating pains to the past and begin to approach each other in a new way? I gave my mother a box of Christmas crackers from Harrods, and I very much hoped I'd get the cracker with the penknife this Christmas. I also gave her a runner I had embroidered. All through the long hours of careful embroidery, I had wondered if my mother would like this specially made gift. Might she accept it as a peace-offering? "Very nice, dear," she said the first evening I was at home, and she put the runner in the top drawer of the bureau in her sitting room where she put things she never used, usually presents from the "Uncles." Particularly Uncle Richard, who always brought her jewelry which she said was vulgar.

We spent the first evening I was home together. The meal was quite silent because I think my parents had been arguing. My father seemed to be smarting from whatever my mother must have said to him; he said very little. My mother as usual picked at her food and her movements were like those of a startled bird. I tried to make conversation. I told my father all about the wonderful teachers, about my Latin lessons, and about how I was placed second in the school. Only Georgina, the head girl, had higher overall marks. "Do stop chattering," my mother said. "Really, you're giving me a headache."

I had forgotten that as a family we did not speak. Hiding my heart, I concentrated on the food served and decided I might as well savor the tastes that had been missing in Britain. Food comforted my hunger for a nurturing mother. I was grateful for the salad and the tiny medallions of steak surrounded by *pommes frites*. The cheese was an excellent *chèvre* with fine herbs strewn across its white back. The herbs, fresh from our kitchen garden, were a balm to me. Taiwan's little black lips smacked loudly as I slipped bits of goat cheese to him. "I hope you're not feeding that dog," my mother said.

"Of course not," I answered. "He's just happy to see me home." Lying to my mother became second nature to me after that night.

"You smell nice, pudding," my father said as I bent over to kiss him goodnight.

"Thanks," I said. "Phoebe gave me a bottle of Appleblossom for Christmas."

My father looked up from his book. "Well, I say. You *are* growing up, aren't you?"

"Yes," I said, happy that I had not lost my father's tenderness. "I'm growing up. Maybe I'll even ask for a pair of stockings like Geneviève's for my next birthday," I said with a light laugh.

"Certainly not." My mother sat by the fire in her chair, a chocolate suspended in the air. "No daughter of mine wears lipstick or stockings until she is eighteen."

Very well, I thought, over to Mademoiselle's. "Of course, mother," I said demurely. "I was only joking about the nylons."

"Don't say 'nylons.' Dreadful American word. Say 'stockings.' Geneviève is French, and all French girls grow up too fast. You mark my words. She'll come to a bad end."

If coming to a bad end meant marrying a lord, I thought walking up the stairs, she'd better be very bad indeed. I could see myself ending up an old maid with my school knee-socks. I entered my bedroom feeling lonely, far more lonely than I had ever felt away at school, away from what was supposed to be my home.

I got into bed and took out my writing case which I kept hidden under my mattress. I didn't trust my mother not to find it and read my diary or my letters from Patrick. I had written to Patrick every week on a blue pad with matching blue envelopes. He wrote to me on Basildon Bond white creamy paper. I had a Platignum fountain pen with a broad nib, a present from my father, and Patrick had a Parker fountain pen. His last letter said how pleased he would be to see me at Christmas, and the letter ended "Lots of love. Patrick." There were three kisses and four hugs.

I kissed the letter tonight and then wrote a little in my diary. My code name for my mother was now "Starling." Since she had left Africa and had become even posher in Paris, she looked less like a crow and more like a starling.

It was a week before I got away to visit Mademoiselle and Jacques. I knew they were married while I was at school. Mademoiselle was more pregnant than they had at first thought, so they couldn't wait for me to come back. As Mademoiselle explained, she didn't want to be married with a huge stomach. I understood and was dying to see them both. As the car glided back home through the now familiar streets of Paris, I was glad to be back because it was Paris, but I was lonely again.

During the week I spoke to Geneviève on the telephone. She had her cousins staying for Christmas and was too busy to see me. So I sat or read in the house, or I looked outside the windows into the hibernally dry garden and felt alone and isolated. Revolutionary politics deemed that I should not walk the streets alone, and so I had to sit impersonal in the car. I did my Christmas shopping with the chauffeur at my shoulder. He kindly carried my packages for me and I returned home to the same silence I had left.

I was reading Einstein's theory of relativity, a subject of great interest to my father who patiently explained the whole concept of explosion to me. I asked him, if the equation of atomic explosion was expressed in the statement $E = mc^2$, then surely there must be an equation for implosion. If I discovered the equation for implosion, then we had an answer to nuclear power. My father loved this sort of discussion and we shared many evenings just talking together, though as it was Christmas-time we were very busy. The English Ambassador to France had a son called Myles who was kind to me. I helped my mother wrap the endless presents for the diplomatic community and wrapped countless Fortnum and Mason jars of Stilton in their uniform gray containers with the royal crest. My mother made (the only time she ever worked in our kitchen) little *petits fours*. I learned from a very early age how to pick the delicate violet leaves and put them in icing sugar. She also dipped big fat scarlet strawberries into a mixture of chocolate and Grand Mariner. These were to be eaten immediately. But as we worked on our Christmas projects side by side, we hardly exchanged any words.

I took the boxes of treats to various diplomats' houses. And, to my delight, Patrick's house.

I was dreadfully shy about handing the *bonbons* over, but Patrick devoured half the box before his mother returned from Christmas shopping. "Oh, Patrick you greedy pig," was all that Mrs Johnson said when she arrived. I was amazed.

Patrick grinned. "Well, I'll leave the rest to you and father. Come on, Mary. Let's go out."

The idea of just "going out" was new to me. I knew I was always supposed to have the chauffeur with me at all times, and he had been specially trained. My father once nearly got shot. He kept the Panama hat he was wearing at the time as a souvenir. There was a hole with sulphurous stains straight through the brim of the hat.

I hesitated and then I said, "Hang on a minute. I'll go and get rid of the car. Can you drop me off at the house?"

"Sure," Patrick said with the ease of a boy who had never been a prisoner.

I went downstairs and I told the chauffeur that I was

staying for lunch with the Johnsons. The chauffeur clicked his heels and smiled. *"Au revoir, mademoiselle,"* he said, and I watched him climb into the car and drive off. Lying was becoming remarkably easy, and I was good at it. I surprised myself. I found myself behaving as formerly only Françoise would have behaved. Now it was *Mary* who lied to get her way.

Mrs Johnson did invite me to lunch. I remember it was Cook's day off, so Mrs Johnson cooked a light fluffy omelette with a large green salad and a plate of fat ripe tomatoes. I always remember food, particularly when I'm happy. And that day I was marvelously happy. Mr Johnson returned for lunch and was delighted with the strawberries. "Wonderful woman, your mother," he said. "Famous in Paris for her food."

"Yes," I agreed, suddenly full of pride for my mother's achievements and glad to be thinking something nice and loyal of her. "She really is. Our parties are the best attended in town." Then I blushed and looked at Patrick. I hoped he didn't think I was bragging. He smiled his lovely smile.

Mr Johnson talked to me about my father's extensive knowledge of world politics, particularly his knowledge of China in the old days before China was torn apart by revolution. "A much needed revolution," Mr Johnson said. "The foreign concessions were raping China, the drug-rings destroying her heritage. Don't let anyone tell you that Mao is anything but a great visionary for his people. When he dies, there will be no one to replace him, and the Chinese—who are the most pragmatic people on this earth—will return to their old family ways."

"Don't lecture the girl, Derrick," Mrs Johnson scolded, but I was sure I detected warmth and almost laughter in her scolding. To be in the company of parents who spoke to each other with respect and affection seemed to me a rarity to be coveted.

"I'm not, Sally." Mr Johnson smiled at me. "I can see she's an intelligent girl, and goodness knows they're hard to find these days." He passed me the plate of tomatoes.

I popped a slice into my mouth and bit into the lovely sweet rind. Here I was, called "intelligent" by Mr Johnson, sitting opposite the boy I loved. A blue day dotted with high white clouds, the chill of winter in the air. And I was going to spend the afternoon all by myself with Patrick. Happiness, never a complete emotion in my soul, visited me that day with no wicked witches in her retinue. Rather, she put her wand upon my shoulder and a chink of light lit up inside me. I fell in love with Patrick's whole family.

Lunch ended with a big steaming bowl of coffee in a French cup. I dipped my face into the thick creamy steam and inhaled the smell of French coffee, so dark and velvety and deep, so unlike the smell of African coffee. African coffee smelled of the hot summer cricket-leg-rubbing nights. Paris coffee smelled of dark alleys, high fashion, and sex. Not that I knew much of sex, except for a forbidden feeling at the pit of my stomach. Geneviève said she felt it all the time, but I didn't. And if I did, I felt it too dangerous an area to explore. So I read an absorbing book on poisonous animals or consulted Gray's *Anatomy*. The precise clinical drawings, with their correct Latin origins, always brought a sane order into the world of messy human emotions.

But now, looking at Patrick's neat square hands, I imagined mine in a short time in his, as we walked together down the Rue de Fontaine. I remembered a song I heard our housekeeper Madame Charpentier sing: *"Sur la claire fontaine . . ."* I forgot the rest of it, but the final stanza haunted me. *"Jamais je ne t'oublirai."*

Never will I forget you. That *never* hung inside me like an unfinished note. I heard that song before Patrick. Before Patrick (or "BP") I was alone. I never imagined a boy could or would love me ever, with my awful shoes and dowdy dresses. Now I was loved and I desperately hoped our love was forever.

I couldn't really understand how Geneviève spent her life breaking boys' hearts or having hers broken. Already this Christmas she was in love with the American Consul General's son. How long it would last I had no idea. But for me, love for Patrick was an intensely deeply felt love. And now I was getting to know his mother and father and hopefully, eventually, his three sisters who were married and scattered abroad. Two of his sisters in picture frames were captured in happy poses with several children each. I was content.

Sally Johnson was a big blonde easy-going happy woman. When Mr Johnson left to go to the office, Mrs Johnson walked to the door with him. "They really do love each other, don't they?" I said.

"Yes. They dote on each other," Patrick agreed. He grinned. "Come on. Let's go. I have a really lovely little church for you to see."

We walked out of the block of apartments into the gray wintery afternoon. I pulled my Daniel Neill school-coat around my shoulders and wished I had a little mink jacket like Geneviève. The wind was bitter and cut through the cloth like a steel lathe.

"Let's run." Patrick took my hand. At the moment his hand touched mine our energy seemed to fuse. We didn't run; we flew. My feet hardly ever touched the ground and we arrived at the portals of a small gray-stoned church with the prettiest flying buttresses in all of Paris.

Inside, the Virgin Mary in a blue and gold star-spangled niche smiled down at us. Patrick made the sign of the cross and we dipped our fingers in the font of Holy Water. Jesus gazed down upon us as we walked up the narrow aisle to the altar. As it was siesta time, no one else was there. The pale sun pushed through the leaded windows. The light refracted on the altar. The tabernacle was flecked with reds and blues. Incense hung in the air, and the only sound was our hushed feet as we approached the altar rail. Both of us bent our knees in prayer. Patrick was still holding my hand. I prayed to the Blessed Virgin that I would marry Patrick and his family. I prayed to St Jude, the saint for hopeless cases, that I could marry Patrick, and I prayed to our Lord, the final arbitrator of my life.

Phoebe was the one who taught me how to pray. She was a very devout Catholic and I enjoyed attending mass with her several times during the term. My religious knowledge was confined to my Bible and saying my prayers at night. My father was a lapsed Catholic and my mother believed in no religion at all. We never discussed religion because it made my mother angry. She held God personally responsible for all the trouble in the world.

But today I promised God I'd try harder to get on with my mother, and then I looked at Patrick through my eyelashes, which were far too short, unlike Geneviève's. Patrick was also looking at me. We knelt for a moment of perfect harmony between us. And then Patrick lifted the hand he was holding and he kissed my hand, and something inevitable was cemented between the two of us for eternity.

We walked out of the church still hand in hand. Across the street was a small *tabac.* "Would you like a pot of chocolate?"

I nodded, still full from lunch but eager to spend as much time as I could with him. We sat, Patrick and I together, surrounded by several families and a few students alone in the middle of Paris, with two bowls of hot chocolate. Both of us, content, had little to say. He told me about the rugger games he had played, how the Irish rugger team had "licked the Scottish team off the face of the earth." And I told him a more humble tale of how we boarded the buses to take us to other schools and how the one time we were to play an all-male team twenty miles away, and in spite of Geneviève's pray-in—she had all two hundred girls on their knees. Even the cook got caught up in the drama, but then Cook was very dramatic anyway . . .

Patrick said he loved school but wanted to be a banker like his father. The British Oriental Bank in Hong Kong had always been his dream. I smiled. Hong Kong had always been my dream, too. "Maybe we can meet in Hong Kong," I said airily.

Patrick smiled and asked for the bill. "Maybe," he said, "we can go together." My heart raced out of control. And then the waiter came to the table. "Let's go," Patrick said. "I have to be back for cocktails at six."

We walked back arm in comfortable arm. "Your mother called," Mrs Johnson said.

"Oh." For a moment I panicked.

Mrs Johnson smiled. "I told her I'd sent you round the corner to buy a *baguette,* as it's Cook's day off." She nodded. "Did you have a good time?"

"Lovely," I said, relieved. "Lovely." Mrs Johnson had lied to protect me. I wanted to hug her, but I didn't know how to.

"I'll call the car," she said and left the room.

Patrick gave me a quick hug and a kiss on the cheek. "Goodbye," he said. "I'll see you after Christmas." And he put a little package into my hand.

"I haven't got you a Christmas present," I said. "I don't have any money . . ."

"Don't worry," Patrick said. "Write me a letter. I love your letters."

"And I love yours," I said, feeling my heart would burst.

The Johnsons' car was ready. It wasn't until I sat in the back seat, remembering Patrick's kiss and holding onto the little package in my coat pocket, that I also remembered with a feeling of shame that I hadn't put my mother's visiting card in the card-tray in Mrs Johnson's hall. That was a very serious omission, because at the end of every few days my mother collected all the cards of the people who called on us. A list was made of all the names and then the list was checked with the big diary so that people who called went onto the invitations for cocktails, dinner dances, and the balls. Also the names were checked with the cook's diaries to see that no menus were served twice to the same people, and that the same people did not dine too often together. I'd let my mother down.

I slipped into the house. As I crossed the floor my mother was standing on the balcony. "I telephoned," she said, "when you sent back the car."

"I know. Mrs Johnson sent us out to get some fresh bread."

"Oh yes?"

"We weren't long."

My mother had that look in her eyes that she always had when she had done something I didn't know about. "Interested in Patrick?" she said, and it was then that I knew my mother must have found my writing case.

"He seems very nice," I said, and then a huge rage threatened to overwhelm me. But I held onto it with both hands. Firmly, holding Patrick's present in my coat pocket, I walked up the stairs to my room.

"Wear your blue dress," my mother said. "We have the Russian Ambassador and several of his staff for dinner."

I liked the Russian Ambassador, and I liked his wife.

We always had a marvellous time at the Russian Embassy. When I got to my room I put the package under the carpet in the left-hand corner of the room. I lifted the mattress and took out my writing case. I had left a piece of hair between two of Patrick's letters. The hair was not there any more.

I felt invaded and sullied. But Patrick's love for me, I reminded myself, could not be sullied. I had found a safe clean family, a comforting world apart.

I took off my coat and ran the bath, and I lay there feeling clean. A strange feeling, half of love and half of lust, spread over me. As I immersed myself deeper into the bath, I imagined what it would feel like to be lying in the bath with Patrick. I knew it would be a very good feeling.

I lay thinking that there were times, particularly when we had visitors—I was not allowed to say "company," or, for that matter, "couch" or "toilet." Only common people used those words—when my mother was interesting. She knew all the diplomatic gossip. Nothing happened in London without my mother's knowledge because the uncles kept her informed. But even when she was being kind to me, I was always nervous around her. She could turn like a London taxi which, I believed, were famous for turning on a sixpence. Even if I was a dreadful disappointment to her, with my mouse-brown hair and shapeless body, she treated me like a possession.

I got out of the bath, took out my blue dress, and decided that I would make a rebellious point—small but significant—by not wearing it. Instead I chose a dress with yet another Peter Pan collar. I ran downstairs to stand beside my father and mother while Barzon the butler announced the Russian visitors.

Chapter 20

The Russian Ambassador gave a bellow of delight, after grandly bowing over my mother's hand. He picked me up and swung me into the air. In the ensuing noise and chaos, I was glad of his bear hug. He smelled wonderfully of cigars.

My father, who spoke Russian fluently, particularly liked the Russian legation. My father explained his position this way: "I may not like Igor's politics, but I like him and the people of Russia enormously. One has to think historically. And the Russians as a people, like the Chinese, are an individual people. They have and will spend years under the Communist rule. Then they will shrug off Communism and embrace their own new destiny with freedom. What began as a revolution of a huge peasant class with no future under the Czars, progressed as it always does through to a huge bureaucracy. And then, the young who are now educated will bring about the rebirth of a middle class and a culture. You watch," he said. "As the west struggles—particularly England—as the middle class deserts, and a totalitarian state asserts itself."

All this I dimly understood, but here and now I loved to see the Russian wives soberly dressed, as were the men, but such warm women as they laughed and chattered among themselves. Some of the women spoke a smattering of English. The Ambassador's wife, called Monica, pressed a large tin of caviar into my mother's delighted hands. Several bottles of best Russian vodka appeared. I was thrilled. We always had a tin in Paris in the fridge. My father loved caviar, and so did I. The pop and the instant taste of sea always pleased me.

I knew Cook would be very happy tonight. He made delicious *quenelles* of smoked salmon, and he liked to stud the *quenelles* with real caviar. He made our meal, and then he took a couple of shots of vodka home with extra *quenelles* for his family. I knew because he told me and we trusted each other.

Dinner was also a riotous affair. We had put up the Christmas tree the day before. I always wanted a real Night-Before-Christmas tree, with lots of cotton wool balls and yellow and red tinsel, but my mother thought that was vulgar. How I longed to be vulgar. I know she thought Igor was vulgar. He belched when he felt like it. Other members of the legation had exquisite manners. They were scholars and equal to my father in affairs of diplomacy.

I sat next to Monica at dinner. I talked about her two daughters, one of whom was going to go into the Foreign Office and follow her father's footsteps. The other was an artist. Apparently both girls were part of a woman's movement, Monica told me, to free women from slavery to men. Monica smiled when she told me that. "You see," she said, "I stayed home and looked after my family. My husband works hard and we have a good life. My girls live with their loves, go to work, queue for food, clean their apartments, and I laugh. Remember, men don't change. They just take a long time getting home from work." And Monica laughed uproariously. So did I. Personally, the idea of going to work never appealed to me, and the right to drive a tractor seemed foolish. As for sitting in interminably boring committee meetings, my mother had enough of those in our house to put me off for life.

I sat in my seat and I thought about Patrick. Around me people ate, talked, and argued. "Always keep lines of communication open" was my father's creed, and he was good at it. Everybody liked and respected my father. Unlike some of the British diplomats, who really only had inherited titles going for them, my father knew the customs of the people he served. At the end of dinner, we toasted the Queen and then Igor toasted the Premier of Russia. I liked toasts. We all felt happy and close together that night.

After they left I went to bed. "Happy, pudding?" my father said as I kissed him goodnight.

I looked at the severe tall Christmas tree with the matching silver lights frowning in the stairwell. Underneath the tree were big parcels. I knew in three days' time I'd be undoing the boxes all morning with a claw-hammer. All the silver teasets and all the silver ashtrays, as well as the silver cigarette cases, would be taken back to the shops they came from, and the money they cost would be left on future credit or would be handed over in cash. The diplomatic community was always diplomatic in the giving or receiving of favors. We always did far better than the Ambassadors my father served because my father was a great deal cleverer than they were. But because he was only the son of a father who served as a Brigadier in the army, he was NQOUD: "Not Quite One of Us, Dear." So he was often excluded from the dinners where they all talked about Eton, possibly Winchester, but never Harrow. Harrow was "trade," my mother said . . . "Happy to spend some time with you," I said to my father and kissed him goodnight.

Upstairs I took out my little parcel from Patrick and looked at it, but I decided to wait to open the box at midnight when the big clock struck in the marble hall and sent its vibrant news of a new day resounding where my sleeping parents lay. I slept well that night. I dreamed of Hong Kong, a place I'd never been to, a place I'd never seen.

When I awoke, it was two days before Christmas and I remembered my birthday. I had had an unremarkable birthday at school, unremarkable because my mother and father had forgotten. Phoebe, only Phoebe, left a little package under my pillow. It was a new bottle of pink nail polish. I sat up with my torch and painted my nails, all of them, with this enchanting shade of pink. Phoebe was snoring loudly. I looked at my hands and my feet and felt quite charmed with myself. And wicked. We were not allowed to paint ourselves or to use lipstick. Miss Standish's *gels* were not to show off, paint ourselves, or chase boys. All of which most of us did, except for myself and Phoebe. By the time I had painted my nails and read more of *Far from the Madding Crowd* under my blanket, taken a quick peak at *Mansfield Park* (Jane Austen always had the ability to make me laugh), and then said my prayers, I forgave my mother and father.

Today, however, I was going to spend all day with Jacques and Mademoiselle who soon would give birth. Jacques arrived to pick me up in his wonderfully battered Renault. I loved his car as much as I loved John MacAllister's old car, because unlike the Consulate's sleek Daimler that wafted me about the city, these cars had a character of their own. In the Daimler whenever I was locked away in the back, the sliding door shutting off the chauffeur, Paris glided by like a huge fashion show or like a magnificent fish tank, with me lying, drowning from lack of contact with the real world, or how I imagined a real world would be, full of people and different smells. Our house was as immaculate as the cars we sat in. No dust floated in the sunlight that shone through the windows. Nothing smelled except the excellent smell of polish on the furniture. Servants took care of everything. Even ashtrays were emptied every quarter of an hour. A huge beautiful tomb. A silence, as the servants were forbidden to talk to each other outside the servants' quarters, and I was usually to be found in the library with my head deep in a book.

But today was special. Once in the little car, Jacques smiled down at me. "Thank you for your letters," he said. "We really enjoy them."

"And I yours," I said in French, so he knew I'd not forgotten his lessons. "Oh, it's so good to be out," I said.

Jacques looked at me and nodded. "You are perhaps a little confined."

"Yes. But then, not for long. I'm going to marry Patrick and go to Hong Kong."

Jacques laughed. "Has he asked you yet?"

"No. Not yet. But he will." Jacques gave a great shout of amusement. I settled back and did what I liked doing best: looking, breathing, and smelling Paris. My beloved Paris, my best loved city.

Before we arrived at Jacques's apartment we stopped at a grocer's to pick up some food. "See?" Jacques said. "Look. Elephant garlic." His eyes shone. He took out a pocket knife and neatly sliced a piece for me to try. I expected it to taste bitter, but it didn't. The taste was similar to cloves of garlic but far sweeter. "If I want to make Monique happy, I just buy her elephant garlic and get her a bottle of virgin-pressed olive oil. See?" He picked up a bottle of oil, thick and green. "This is the most expensive because this is the first pressing. *Un demi-kilo, s'il vous plaît,*" he said, pointing to a huge sack of thick-skinned red ripe tomatoes. Then he bought some olives big and black.

Supper would be a fresh *baguette,* a plate of sliced tomatoes sprinkled with sea salt, fresh basil, those big black olives, and a carafe of rough red burgundy, and oh how I looked forward to these meals! My stomach was in rebellion against the food at home. I longed at times to tear a crab apart with my fingers, instead of looking at the creature gazing at me with startled eyes from my plate, the white meat neatly striped with the dark. Soon we were home, or the place I liked to think of as home.

Everything was blessedly the same. Mademoiselle hugged me. I had grown taller during the term, and

I felt awkward with my big hands and feet, but the smile in her eyes told me that she still cared about me very much. I asked her questions about school and the girls I knew. Lunch was a delicious affair of white beans, courgettes, onions, mushrooms, all cooked in white wine and cream. "A dish from Tuscany," she said, clipping fresh parsley from her pots. The smell of the fresh-cut parsley is so exquisite. The smell always took me back to Africa where we had a huge bed of it growing luxuriously green and broad-leafed. My mother didn't like English parsley. We planted French parsley, and she was quite right. When I got to England and tasted the English parsley from the kitchen garden, I saw at once what my mother meant. English parsley was a poor cousin. The taste could not compare with the broad leaves of the parsley in France. But chiefly I remembered the parsley in Africa because my cat rolled in the bed, if he could avoid Sam who chased him off, but the aroma remained in the air.

Mademoiselle was definitely roundly and prettily pregnant. She did not look like Melitta, the Australian Ambassador's wife. The Australian Ambassador's wife was considered extremely vulgar by my mother, but I rather liked her. She was extremely vulgar by any standard, but she brought a fresh life into the rather stuffy world of diplomacy. Melitta was pregnant at a late age, but she happily attended the parties billowously pregnant, varicose veins from her three previous children's births sticking out militarily on her legs. She talked about "dropping the little brat." My mother would not let me even visit her other children. It was as if vulgarity rubbed off like paint. Charlotte, the eldest daughter, once told me what she called a dirty joke in a corner. I laughed, but I didn't understand the joke. Still, I liked the three girls. They didn't take my world at all seriously and they were very proud of being Australian.

Now, in Mademoiselle's kitchen, I had a feeling that maybe my world was all wrong, that I knew spending hours in milliners, shoe fittings, dress fittings, did not make me or my mother happy. Not happy in the way I was now happy, buying the fresh vegetables, watching Jacques tenderly kiss his wife and put his hand on her belly. "Here," he said. "Feel."

And indeed I felt the baby kick my hand. I so hoped I'd have a baby, or maybe six, to make up for my lonely childhood. All of them to look like Patrick. "Do you want a girl or a boy?" I asked.

"Oh," Mademoiselle smiled. "I don't care. Whatever God sends me, I'll be thrilled. Maybe a girl first. They're easier to bring up at first, but then when they are teenagers . . . ay yie yie yie yie!"

"Then it's my turn with the shotgun!" Jacques laughed.

"But, Jacques," I said. "You said sex was all right without marriage."

Jacques looked at Mademoiselle. "Well, if it's a boy, it's all right. But if it's my daughter, it's a different matter altogether."

Mademoiselle giggled. *"Mon chou,"* she said to me, "you have just learned a lesson. Men never change."

"Nor do women," said Jacques. "Now she's married and about to have a baby, all we hear about is knitting, nappies, and we even have a pot. Look." He put a bright yellow baby potty on his head. "Who would ever have thought that Jacques LeFarge, revolutionary extraordinaire, the terror of the Paris streets, would one day come home with a potty? And," he paused dramatically, "I chose the pram myself. Come. You must see it."

Beside their bed was an amazing contraption, a veritable Rolls Royce of a pram. "How wonderful!" I said. On the table, beautifully laid out, was a bright cascade of knitted fresh vestments. I remembered the awful jerseys my mother knitted, the dreadfully scratchy vests, scratchy because the African washerwoman washed all our clothes in cold water and then boiled everything furiously. Here lay fine lawn, hand-stitched by relatives. As far as I could understand, we had no relatives. Other people had aunts and cousins and even second cousins. We lived alone, except for my grandmother and grandfather with whom I was to spend a week before I returned to school. Even that was better than nothing. At least they sent ten pounds, usually at Christmas.

This little baby was a lucky baby surrounded by people who wanted a baby very much, and a large family of aunts and uncles. I felt very envious, as I did of Phoebe who moaned about her family but couldn't wait to leave for Christmas. I put my little present for the baby on the table. I had bought a silver mug on my mother's credit at Niemann Marcus. I knew there would be a dreadful row when she found it on the bill, but I didn't care. For Jacques I got a silver cigarette box from under our tree, remembering to thank the German Vice Consul for a present my father wouldn't get, and a gold cigarette lighter, heavy and handsome for Mademoiselle. When they saw the presents, they both looked solemn. I smiled. "Jacques," I said, "you left the revolution, yes?" He nodded. "Well, mine has just begun. I'm not the Mary you once knew. I'm a different Mary. All the presents go back to the shops anyway." When Mademoiselle hugged me my eyes were full of tears, but they did not see them.

After a wonderful well-remembered supper, the taste of the virgin oil in my mouth, Jacques drove me home. It was a Sunday night and the people of Paris, I imagined, were in church, all kneeling and praying for a peaceful New Year. My mother and father were not in church. "Hello, pumpkin," my father greeted me from behind the *Sunday Times*.

"Hello, dear." My mother was already writing thank you letters and wrapping the last of the presents. "Here, lend me your finger. Your breath does smell, you know," she said. "Why must you eat garlic? Ladies shouldn't eat garlic ever."

"I really don't want to be a lady," I said. "I want to grow up, marry, and have children, and eat garlic whenever I want to."

"No one will marry you, Mary," my mother said.

My father said, "I'll be landed with you for life, pumpkin." He lowered the paper. "The pound is up again, darling."

"Really?" My mother raised her eyebrow. "How interesting."

Nothing ever changes in our house, I thought as I trailed upstairs in the dark of the unlighted corridors. My mother might spend money with impunity, but when it came to lights or doors, she was a fanatic. Lights were not to be left on, nor doors left open. I always felt I lived in the dark behind closed doors. Goodness knows why, or what an opened door might reveal, but in our huge empty house, I nightly groped my way to bed.

✎ *Chapter 21* ✎

It was twelve o'clock and Christmas Eve. Christmas was always an exclusively family occasion. Not even visitors darkened our doors. There were two cocktail parties after Christmas, and then I was being sent to my grandparents whom I had never met. My mother, from what I could tell, seemed to hate both of my father's parents. My grandmother was her main enemy, and my grandfather, she said, was an alcoholic. He sounded quite frightening and he looked even worse, a big man wearing a brigadier's uniform. My grandmother, in her photograph that stood along with the many famous people my mother knew, on the piano, stood next to my mother being presented to the King. That was my mother's proudest moment of her life. In a carved chest she kept the silks she bought in Bangkok and Saigon. She bought the silks before I was born. If I had been a boy, the silk would have been made into ball gowns for my mother. When I was born the silks over the years became ball gowns for my mother anyway, ever hanging reproaches at my failure to be brilliant and beautiful.

Dinner, like all Christmas Eve dinners, was a tense affair. The tree's lights shone readily enough. The traditional smoked salmon, the little rounds of toast heaped with caviar, followed by three small sweet henlobsters, the bottles of chilled hock chosen by my father.

My mother always had a lost look on her face at Christmas, half angry, half resentful. I knew nothing of her life as a child. It was a subject seemingly of no importance to her. She was born the day she married my father. I knew she had a vast amount of luggage, so I imagined she must have been very rich. My father always laughed when he described her forty suitcases, her matching hat boxes all loaded on the ship for their honeymoon that took them around the world.

Tonight these happy times were forgotten and I thought towards Christmas Day. My father and I had bought my mother a lovely blue bed jacket. The arms and the neck were lined with swan's down. On Christmas Day, it had been the family tradition for me to go to the kitchen and make breakfast in bed for the three of us. Now I was older, I sat at my mother's writing desk in the bay of their bedroom window, and I was glad I did not have to get into their bed. I was always made uncomfortable by the musk-smell of my mother, and I didn't feel comfortable that close to her. Christmas Eve dragged on.

We all were allowed to open one present and my father opened a bottle of Piper-Heidsieck '45. My mother's fingers picked disconsolately at the pretty knot of bows tied on her present. I ripped mine open and I had a matching pencil to my Platignum pen. I was thrilled. I loved pens almost as I loved stacks of paper. I particularly loved fresh *cahiers*. Even the word pleased me. I spent a lot of time in French bookshops just looking and feeling the books. And if I had a little money, I bought one of the spiral notebooks with the enchanting blue squares, and I wrote my short stories and my poems which I showed to no one, not even Phoebe.

Finally my mother unwrapped a very little box of blue velvet and then she opened it. There lay a brooch, a wondrous object to my eyes, a little gold pin with two diamonds suspended. My father was red with excitement. "Shall I pin it for you?" he said to my mother.

"No, thank you," my mother said. Then she said something else softly, so softly that my father couldn't hear. "Those are my tears," she said, but I caught the words and held them in my heart.

I went over to my mother's chair and I kissed her on the cheek. "Good night, mother," I said. "We'll have a very happy Christmas."

"We will?" she said.

"Good night, pumpkin." My father gave me a big hug. "Sleep well." My father was holding a pigskin wallet that I had bought him. He was a dreadful squirrel, his pockets always bulging and his wallets torn in the corners, filled with little notes he made for himself as he read omnivorously from his collection.

Now with the midnight bells pealing across Paris,

I could hear Notre Dame from my bedroom. At least I was not going to end up in the embrace of the hunchback of Notre Dame. Patrick had saved me from that fate. I opened my little box and my soul flew out of the window and up over the city. There, on a bed of velvet, lay a gold ring with a small sapphire. "Our secret," said a note in Patrick's handwriting. I kissed the ring and put it on my engagement finger. The ring looked so pretty and fitted perfectly. But I knew I must find a way to hide the ring from my mother, and I had just the place. In my *armoire*—so old it was undated— I had come across a tiny secret drawer, and that is where my ring would lie safe until I escaped to England.

⤜ *Chapter 22* ⤛

I was happy when I awoke on Christmas Day. I ran downstairs and made the breakfast: hot boiling Earl Grey tea in my mother's favorite teaset, brown toast with lilac-scented honey, and a plate of bacon and eggs for my father. I plonked the silver salver over the bacon and eggs and carried the butler's tray upstairs to my mother's room. My mother slept in the big bedroom and my father had his bed in the dressing room, because my mother said my father snored so loudly he kept her awake. Today they were both in the same bed, my father looking remarkably pleased with life, and my mother less desolate than the night before.

I put the tray across my mother's knees and wished them both a happy Christmas. Snow had fallen for the first time that year. The garden was swathed in a shawl of pure white angora wool. The trees hung low with the weight of the snow, and as I ate my toast I watched the snow slide from the branches, the sun releasing the trees from the snow's icy grip. Then I heard the soft muffled explosion as the snow hit the covered grass. The colors were dazzling.

Time to change for dinner. Cook always served Christmas dinner at 12:00 noon, and then he went home to his own family, and my father and I, after the Queen's speech, washed up together, a task we both enjoyed. I went upstairs, looked at my ring, gave it another kiss, and wished I was spending the day with Patrick and his family. Suppressing the wish as disloyal, I hurried downstairs. My father was reading and my mother embroidering, waiting for me to open the presents; ten pounds for me from my grandparents, a pair of plain pajamas from my mother, and a bracelet from my father, which pleased me. My mother opened my present and said that the swan's down would shed and make her sneeze. Then the doorbell went.

My father opened the door himself. Barzon had the day off. My mother's face lit up. Behind a lovely bunch of mixed spring flowers was the smiling face of a boy from a florist shop. "That'll be from Tom," my mother said.

My father walked back with the flowers in his hand. "You and your boyfriends," he teased her.

My mother took the bouquet from him and opened the little envelope. Her face changed. "They're for you. There's no signature on the note."

I shrugged and spread my hands the way Geneviève did when she lied. "I have no idea," I said, "who sent the flowers."

"Let's face it, darling. Pumpkin is growing into a young lady. She's entitled to an admirer or two."

I walked up to my mother and I took the flowers out of her hand. We both stood looking at each other, she just beginning to get lines around her mouth and the freckles on her hands looking a shade darker. I walked slowly up the stairs, my back aching and pricking in case she lost her temper and came running up after me.

I put the flowers in the water by my bed. I smelled the sweet smell of a winter-forgotten spring, and I knew Patrick had sent the flowers. I felt very alive and in love. I went downstairs and we ate Christmas lunch almost in silence. We watched the Queen, radiant as ever, make her speech. We stood with our glasses of champagne raised to toast her, and my father who adored her always got a lump in his throat. Then it was to the kitchen with my father. Behind the huge door that separated the servants from the house, we laughed and we joked.

Soon I would be back in England. Soon I could write to Patrick and even talk to him on the phone. Miss Standish let the girls call their boyfriends, if they had an understanding with the boy.

I left Paris with Geneviève on the train that stood in the Gare du Nord and hooted under the great glass dome. Jacques and Mademoiselle were at the station with a present. *"Oh, là!"* said Geneviève as I opened the package. Inside was the prettiest garter belt I'd ever seen, and six pairs of silk stockings all with a black line down the back. I laughed and laughed, and then I read my favorite novel again, *Journey into the Mind's Eye*, by Leslie Blanche, a wonderful tale of a young girl bewitched by a much older man. I read into the small hours of the morning under my small brass lamp safe in the bottom bunk of the train. Dawn was just breaking when I fell asleep.

Chapter 23

As soon as I arrived at my grandmother's house, I asked if I could telephone Patrick. He had left for Rugby a few days before. He wanted to go before the term started because he was going to be his house captain, and going to row for his house, so he had much organizing to do.

My grandmother's name was Caroline Freeland. We looked alike. She was smaller and bent with age, but she had very bright blue eyes and silver hair. I knew I would like her very much indeed. A car was waiting for me at Taunton Station, and I felt the excitement growing as I approached the gates of a very fine Georgian house called Milton Park. I have always loved trees, and the trees at Milton Park were no exception. Tall graceful pines escorted us up to the front door. I thanked the chauffeur whose name was Ned. He had a good-natured face and fair hair cut short. He told me on the drive to the house that he had served in the War and his brother lost his life at Flanders in the First World War. He had been too young to serve during that war, but the women in Taunton handed him white feathers. Even after all those years I could feel the hurt in his voice. He had gentle eyes and obviously adored my grandparents.

I was nervous, but the beauty of the house and the lovely lush green lawns and the roses in the beds in front of the house reassured me. I always felt that gardens reflected their owners' souls. Our garden in Paris was stiff and formal. Patrick's mother had bowls of hydrangeas. I didn't like to tell her that my mother thought that both hydrangeas and dahlias were common. I liked both plants, but dahlias did house rather large earwigs. Geneviève said earwigs crawled down your ears when you were asleep and ate your brain.

Today there were no earwigs in sight and I was greeted at the door by my grandmother and grandfather.

My grandfather, Lawrence Freeland, was very tall, unlike my father, but then my father looked much more like my grandmother. We all shook hands formally and Ned took my two suitcases up to my room. I smiled as I saw my blue cases climb the stairs. In one of them lay my illicit parcel containing the sinful suspender belt and the silk stockings. "If you get a run in a stocking," Mademoiselle said before she waved me off to England, "use a little clear nail varnish to halt the run." I still felt her warm hug and wished I could hug my grandmother, but I knew the English did not show their emotions. Nonetheless I felt my grandmother's affection. "Hang up your coat," she said, "and we'll have a cup of tea in the kitchen."

All along the walls of the hall portraits of my family gazed down at me. People who were part of my history. There was an Admiral Freeland, lots of Army Freelands, and one looking like T. E. Lawrence of Arabia wrapped in a djellaba and sucking on a hubblebubble. From feeling like a rather lonely only child, I suddenly felt I had a huge family. Grandfather Lawrence went off to his library to read until dinner.

"We live very quietly," my grandmother said. "Ned doubles as a chauffeur, and he does the heavy work. And Mrs Smyth-Jones, a widow, lives in and acts as our housekeeper." She smiled kindly at me. "Do you want to help me dip marzipan strawberries?"

"I'd love to," I said. "Since Max went back to Africa, the new chef doesn't want me in the kitchen, but I love to cook."

By now we had walked through the house, down a long corridor again hung with pictures. "That," said my grandmother, "is a Russell Flint."

I looked at the etching of a camel in a marketplace.

How wonderfully clever of him to draw such a camelly camel. The haughty imperious nose of the camel was exactly right. I laughed. "Only camel-owners love their camels," I said.

"I know," my grandmother agreed. "When we lived in Baghdad, one of the brutes spat at me. Your grandfather had his own fleet of racing camels when he was fighting in the First World War. He and his regiment raced the bedouin Arabs for bottles of whiskey if they lost, and if they won they got the pick of the carpets." I looked down at my feet. "That," my grandmother said, "was your grandfather's saddlebag. Aren't they beautiful?"

"They really are."

"I'm so glad you're here at last." My grandmother pushed open the kitchen door and I found myself in the most marvelous room I'd ever seen. My grandmother, seeing my face, laughed. "My kitchen," she said, "hasn't changed since we first came here. There." She pointed to a stool. "That's the stool your father sat on. I accompanied my husband in all his posts. I had Peter when I was in Teheran, and I swore that I'd have no more children. The climate and the diseases meant that many English children died. I always took Peter away into Shimran for the summers, and Lawrence came up to the summer house at the weekends. Peter was a dear little boy and no trouble at all. The Embassy and the Army entertained a lot in those days. Every few years all this was packed up and off we'd go to another part of the world."

It was then I told her about Patrick.

She said, "He sounds splendid. And Hong Kong is a glorious place. My people were old China hands." She shook her head. "All gone," she said. "The bad and the good, all gone. The telephone is in the pantry. We don't approve of the telephone. We use it to order things from the shops and we write letters. Dreadfully old-fashioned of us, I know. But then, there are several families I'll introduce you to who are from abroad. Go and phone, and we'll talk while we make the marzipan strawberries for the spring bazaar to collect money for black babies. Oh, "black babies" is a term used to collect money for African baby clinics. We all participate."

Life, I thought as I found the phone, was obviously busy. I looked at the bottles of plums and bottles of red cherries, peaches, tomatoes, cucumbers . . . The phone brrrrred in my hand. I imagined Patrick running to answer it. Finally a voice said, "Who, may I ask, is calling?" The voice was funny and flat North Country, I knew. So different from Ned's soft round words which signified Somerset.

"May I speak to Patrick Johnson? My name is Miss Mary Freeland."

"All right, Miss Freeland. Just a minute."

The minutes felt like ages, but I contented myself by looking at the patterns of the blue cheese and the thick creamy rind of the Stilton. They sat very English and secure, imprisoned by their helmets of wire net. Above them hung hams of all colors. Particularly a prosciutto ham still covered in its necessary coat of mold. Eventually the mold would be brushed carefully twice, much airing and drying, and then painted with a special seal. Then, at the end of the summer, a final inspection, and the day arrives of great excitement when the first delicate pink slice of ham is tested and pronounced a success. I knew about that because Max was unable to keep the hams at the right temperature in Africa, but when we got to France, he did his own curing and I got quite expert at it. But I could see my grandmother was a master cook.

Then I heard Patrick's voice and my heart shone. Good, secure, safe Patrick. Patrick knew who he was, what he was doing, and where he was going. I was going to marry Patrick and the British Oriental Bank, all safe and very secure. "Hello." Patrick was breathless. "I've run all the way from the tennis courts. Give me a second to catch my breath. How are you?"

"I'm fine," I said. "Grandma and Grandpa are lovely people, and the house is beautiful. I'm going to learn how to dip marzipan strawberries. I'll make a box for you."

"Thank you." Patrick was not very good on the telephone. There was a silence. "Well," Patrick said, "I'd better go."

"Patrick?" I said.

"Yes?"

"I love you," I said.

"I love you, too," Patrick said. His voice was choked.

I put the telephone down. (My mother wouldn't let me say 'phone.) I walked into the kitchen.

My grandmother was just dipping a bright scarlet marzipan strawberry into dark brown almost black chocolate. "Here," she said. "Try one. I made that batch yesterday."

I picked up the strawberry and I bit into the chocolate and then tasted the sweetness with the bitter aftertaste of almonds. It tasted like love felt.

My grandmother smiled at me. "Are we in love?" she said. I nodded. "Ah, how wonderful! I remember meeting your grandfather for the very first time." She paused and stared into space. "He was so tall and so handsome. I thought he'd never notice me. I lived at Ripham Lodge, and the first time he came to ask my father if I could go to the Ripham Hunt Ball, he brought me a dozen white roses and a box of chocolates from Winona's Chocolate Shop. Oh, how envious my older sister was of those chocolates! They were *very* expensive. She only got Black Magic chocolates. I always stole the one with the hazelnut. Here, dear.

Let me show you how to put the African violets, both blue and white, into confectioner's sugar."

"I know how to do that," I said. "Max taught me."

"How wonderful! Then let's make the chocolate truffles together."

I loved chocolate truffles. I loved to roll the truffles in the powdery chocolate and then stud them with little black beads of shiny chocolate. We worked in silence, I sitting at the pantry table, my knees hard against the table knob on a high stool, my grandmother at the other end of the table carefully moulding and dipping the marzipan. I felt safe with this woman who had known of me and my existence but who never had met me. I already felt far more part of her, than of my mother's, world. My mother's world was all sharp edges and black. In my grandmother's pine kitchen, with all the shelves alive with Wedgwood and Spode, the aga old and redolent with meals cooked by my grandmother for my grandfather, I felt included.

Here, doors were left open and I had caught glimpses, on the way into the kitchen, of other enticing rooms. My father traveled with a few pieces of priceless Chippendale, but my grandmother's house was a joy to behold. Soft shiny satiny writing desks, the drawing room full of huge Victorian wickerwork overstuffed furniture. Pretty swags of flowers invited the sun to shine on the rose red carpet. I recognized the furniture that they must have brought back from China.

"Mrs Eldridge and her husband John are coming to lunch today. Let's go and pick a salad." We washed our hands in a big Victorian sink in the pantry and then, picking up a basket, my grandmother chose a pair of secateurs. "For my roses," she said. "This basket is really for roses as well, but my salad basket is so old I have retired her, but I keep her in happy memories of gardens all over the world." She laughed and I followed her out of the kitchen into a conservatory that ran across the back of the house. The flower beds were full of scented flowers, except for the beds at the far end of the house. "I like my vegetables to be fresh all year round, so I grow lettuce and cabbage, Brussel sprouts and tomatoes. Above all, tomatoes. Anyone who doesn't enjoy vegetables as much as I do is no friend of mine. Remember, Mary, you can tell a woman by her kitchen, and a wife from her vegetable garden."

"Oh, I will remember," I said. "I adore gardening and growing things. When I was little in Africa, I had my own patch. I remember my corn. It grew so much taller than I did. You know, Grandma, I miss the blue sky of Africa. You don't know how much I miss it."

My grandmother paused. "Yes, I do," she said softly. "Africa is a state of mind, just like China. You'll see, when the Eldridges come to lunch, we'll talk about our days in China, our years in Africa. Thank goodness," she said, "the Africans finally got a grip on Africa and now are beginning to run things for themselves. All our friends were African and Chinese. Your grandfather always had African and Chinese visitors and we all ate together. Caused an awful stir in those days. Whites tried to keep everything segregated. We didn't ever believe that nonsense. Your father was the only white child at his local school. He didn't know what racism was 'til he went to his prep school. There they bathed the boys from abroad in water that was already used by the white children. Really," she said, "he was so upset. He had nightmares for a week."

The basket was full of filmy green lettuce, a few tomatoes, little bullet-like dark green Brussel sprouts. "Darling!" my grandmother called out. "Lunch will be ready in half an hour!" We were passing the library windows. The double door was open.

My grandfather looked up and smiled. "What's for lunch?"

"Your favorite ham," she said. "I'm making fresh mustard with white wine."

"Lovely," my grandfather said. He looked at me from behind his horn-rimmed spectacles. "Peter tells me he calls you 'pumpkin.' So I shall call you 'pumpkin.' We have waited a long time to get to know you."

A shadow crossed my grandmother's face. I felt the years of sadness sweep across me, years my grandparents lost of my life, their only grandchild. "Never mind," I said. "I'm here now, and no one will ever take me away." I was fiercely determined.

Lunch was served on white plates with pretty fish floating about the plates. Mine was a big blue fish with a wide open mouth. We started with tiny delicate shrimps in a bed of bright yellow butter, a little curly green leaf under the small brown ramequin dishes. Mr and Mrs Eldridge were a plump roly-poly couple. They arrived laughing and joking with two adorable white Sealyham terriers at their feet. "There, Caroline. I brought two dozen brandy snaps. One box is for the bazaar, and the other is for pudding."

"Lovely," said my grandmother. "I'm busy dipping chocolate, and I didn't have a pudding. Are you making lemon marmalade this year?"

"Yes. And I've got a pantry full of cherry-choke apples, so I'll swap you apples and marmalade jam for two large Christmas puddings."

The men had gone into the library and we went into the kitchen to deposit the booty. "I say, Caroline." Bridget looked at the rows of strawberries, the pile of marzipan bananas and apricots. "These look all rather splendid."

My grandmother laughed. "I'm determined to beat Mrs Rogers this year. Last year I took a second ribbon and Mrs Rogers's silly hat fairly nodded with joy. Let's go and join the men. And I want you to try this particular bottle of sherry. Of course, Lawrence is the expert when it comes to wine, but I do love a glass of sherry before lunch. So good for the digestion."

I remember the spicy taste of the sherry as I sat listening to them talk. I helped to clear the plates. Ned carried out the soup tureen as the turtle soup also became a fond memory, and the ham, pink, moist and trimmed of fat. I hated fat of all kinds, especially the white lard-like substance that adhered to ham in our house. My father always trimmed his off, but my mother ate ham fat, every scrap of it, and because I refused the fat began the litany of the millions dying of starvation. My father never interfered.

There were key words and phrases in my mother's tirades. One of them was "You don't know how lucky you are . . ." Today I felt lucky, happy to be alive. I had my ring, Patrick's letters, and two grandparents who obviously loved me. There were pictures of me all around the dining room. When we went to the drawing room for coffee, there were more pictures of me and my father. There were none of my mother.

Mrs Eldridge discussed the state of the world. That all sounded terminal and dreadful, until my grandfather got on to the subject of the etiquette of eating sheep's eyeballs to amuse me. "You have to eat, you know," he said. "It's considered dreadfully rude if you don't. The Sultan of Morocco once leaned over and took the eye out of the socket of the sheep's head and handed it to me. I ate it," he laughed. "I don't remember what it tasted like, but I ate it. In those days we really settled our business in the tents. Today, these young wallas wouldn't know how to sit cross-legged for hours bargaining a point here, a point there. You argue differently. You argue with an African wearing an African hat. An Arab, a hat and a long stick. They're clever. The Arab and the English go back a long way, but a Jew and an Englishman can never do business the way a Jew and a Jew do business." I listened fascinated. I could see where my father got his ability to negotiate.

Mr Eldridge had been the head of the harbor in Hong Kong. He was wizened, as if he were a prune dried in the sun. But he had gentle eyes.

As a fire cracked in the grate, I sat back in my armchair and closed my eyes. Paris, our house, our afternoons, were never spent this way. My grandmother I could hear discussing the cake contest at the church, and the two men talked. For me, who fervently read Hardy, this was the England I imagined. Small, pretty, happy. And I fell asleep.

I awoke with a start, not sure where I was. Grandma smiled. "You were tired, dear, so we let you sleep. I'll put on another log, and then I'll make a nice cup of tea. I know everyone has a favourite brand of tea, but I prefer Lipton's every time. You just sit and look at this magazine."

She passed me a glossy thick magazine called *Field and Stream.* In it, elegant women in immaculate hunting clothes looked busy with their horses, or at balls and dances. I didn't ride because my mother wouldn't let me. She didn't ride, or ski. I was not allowed to ski, in case I broke my neck. I always envied the girls and boys who shot down the slopes, my father not far behind. He was excellent on skis, and we went to the Austrian Alps. My mother said the *hoi polloi* went to Gstaad. I dearly wished I could be the *hoi polloi.* We stayed in very authentic apple-strudel houses with very heavy food and even heavier maids.

Now, as my grandmother returned with a silver tray and a silver fluted teapot, I could see how my father must have loved his childhood. Everything was certain and secure. Grandfather came into the drawing room, scenting the air with his long beak-like nose. "Muffins," he said. "I can smell muffins."

"You can smell muffins a mile away," my grandmother beamed.

"Only *your* muffins, my dear."

Grandma lifted the top of the muffin dish. There the muffins, like little fat hens, lay above the base that was filled with hot water. The butter was yellow and the Devonshire cream sat in a dish beside fresh homemade raspberry jam. The kind of homemade jam with pips that stick between the teeth. "You leave the pips in," said my grandmother. "The pectin in the pips sets the jam." Lesson number one, and one of the many my grandmother taught me.

I slept well in my room in the attic. The room wasn't at all as luxurious as the one I left behind in Paris. The little room nestled high under the eaves of the house. Originally the house was Georgian, but an over-enthusiastic Victorian landlord built servants' quarters, and so the lower part of the house contradicted the upper story. But somehow one didn't mind too much. Grandfather kept his souvenirs up in the room next to mine. A huge elephant foot, like one in the hall, which was filled with walking sticks, umbrellas, and shooting sticks. My room was small. The walls were a bit shabby, but the wallpaper was alive with blooming clematis, blue and pink. The curtains matched, and from the window I could look out across the Somerset hills, now changing to purple shadows to greet the night. I unpacked my traveling suitcase, my present from Jacques and Mademoiselle hidden securely in my trunk. When I got into bed I began to think about myself and Patrick.

After musing and planning my wedding (white, of

course) I read my Bible, the end of the Book of Job where God gets cross with him and talks to him out of the whirlwind and asks him why he is whining. "Where were you," He says, "when I hung the stars?" Quite right, I thought. Poor Job. I lay back and felt my Job-years were over. I had grandparents who loved me, and Patrick, and of course Taiwan, and my father. The list was getting longer. And soon we were going to the cake competition. I'd never been to one before.

ᘒᕯᗂ *Chapter 24* ᘒᕯᗂ

Grandma was already up the next day in the kitchen stirring dough in a yellow cracked-glaze baking bowl. Her hands were mired with dough. "Pass me those raisins," she said, and I carefully poured them into the mixture. "I'll clean off my hands and you take over while I get breakfast."

Soon I was stirring the dough while my grandmother fried bacon and freshly picked horse mushrooms. The mushrooms were enormous. They filled the frying pan with their lacy black edges, and the black fragrant smell of soil tilled by horses seeped around the house. "Breakfast, darling!" Grandma shouted.

"Coming!" And my grandfather arrived with a double-barrelled shotgun under his arm. From his hand swung two dead rabbits. I felt sorry for them; but at least we'd eat them. "Ned can dress these while we're out," my grandfather said.

"Oh good!" Grandma exclaimed. "I'll make rabbit in a mustard sauce for tonight."

"How's the cake going? I can see you have Pumpkin occupied."

"She's got natural pastry hands." My grandmother smiled at me.

I was thrilled with this compliment. Even if I had a bad seat, at least I had good pastry hands. I washed them clean of the dough and sat down at the breakfast table at the end of the kitchen in a chair that had a scratchy rough seat. The mushrooms and bacon were delicious, the pieces of bacon so much thicker than anything I'd seen in Paris. When bacon was served at our house, two pieces each lay politely across a piece of toast. Here the bacon coiled among the mushrooms and deposited itself in an impolite pile on the thick piece of white toast. I had never been allowed to eat white toast. It didn't exist in our house because my mother said that white toast, along with chocolate, was the cause of allergies.

So I bit into the white toast and was surprised to find it delicious. We had more toast in a toast-rack, and homemade marmalade, rough and chunky. Grandma said, "I hope Mrs Rogers's hat won't be too dreadful this year." Mrs Rogers evidently was Enemy Number One for Grandma.

The day was clear when we got into the old green Volvo and drove to the church bazaar. The main event, the cake-judging, was to take place in the tent on the main lawn in front of the church. The vicar was a young man. He had his wife at his side, and two little boys darting about the crowd. There were many elderly retired people like my grandparents. My hand was shaken, it felt, by everyone there. They all seemed genuinely glad to see me. "Peter's girl," my grandmother said with pride in her voice.

My grandmother's cake was magnificent. It sat on a big platter of faded blue roses. The raisins, submerged in the perfect brown of the cake, gleamed black. No icing despoiled this cake. I saw Mrs Rogers before I realized who she was. She was tall with black hair, and she wore an abominable dark blue velour mess on her head, with a veil that covered her eyes but stopped just short of her over-large nose. Her mouth, a lipsticked gash, never stopped moving for a minute as she bore down upon us. "Hello, hello," she smiled, and I watched the lipstick smear itself across her teeth. "How are you, Caroline?"

"Very well," my grandmother replied. "Very well indeed. Do let me introduce you to my granddaughter. Say hello, Mary."

"Oh, how wonderful! You're the grandchild we've all heard so much about! You've turned up at last like the proverbial bad penny! Fortunately we don't have that sort of trouble in our family. By the way, Caroline, I'm giving a party for Angela on Wednesday. Do bring your little Mary. It's Angela's birthday. She'll be fourteen. You will come, won't you?"

I looked and felt trapped. Grandma, to my horror, nodded. "Why?" I whispered when Mrs Rogers left. "I don't want to go. I hate parties."

"*Noblesse oblige,*" my grandmother said. "We are a small village, and we all do what we can to make life harmonious. We will make a nice bookmark tomorrow for a birthday present, and you shall go and be a good girl and do us proud." I mulled over the need to be dutiful at all times.

The judging started and three very senior looking matrons walked up and down the rows, taking little samples off each cake. The owners of the cakes stood behind their offspring and waited. The air was thick with excitement. I stood beside my grandmother and I felt her tension. The judges did stay a very long time before our cake, certainly longer than before Mrs Rogers's cake, a mishmash of cake, cream, and concentric orbits of dyed curlicues. Another long wait before a lovely looking ginger cake . . . And then the judges left and grandfather arrived. "Let's have a cup of tea," he said. "We have an hour before the results."

In another smaller tent there stood trestle tables covered with white cloths. Two shiny urns disgorged hot tea, the other hot milk. A basin with a spoon tethered to it was full of sugar. We each carried our cups carefully to a card-table set neatly with four card-chairs. "Can't stand these damned chairs," my grandfather grumbled. "Feel as if they're made of matchwood."

Grandma just smiled. I could tell she was anxious. We drank the tea from the thick white mugs. The cups reminded me of the café at the end of Mademoiselle's road. They, too, were thick and white, quite unlike anything we owned, but I loved the thick white churchy cups.

Soon people crammed back to the tent. My grandmother and I stood side by side behind our cake. The elder of the three women judges took out a list and put up a pair of lorgnettes. "Mrs Rogers," she said, "third prize." She approached Mrs Rogers and put a red ribbon over her head.

"Thank goodness. She's out," my grandmother whispered.

"Mrs Jessup—" ("She's American," my grandmother hissed.) "—second prize." And then we held our breath. "First prize this year goes to Mrs Freeland."

Then the clapping started. My grandmother had two patches of red in her cheeks. The grand lady came over and shook her hand before she put the blue sash over Grandma's head, and a gold medal glinted in the sun. "Well done, Caroline," she said. "Really excellent cake."

"Vera, do meet my granddaughter Mary Jane. She helped me."

"Ah," Vera said to my grandmother. "So you're

Mary. I see." She nodded to my grandmother. "At long last," she said.

Grandma put her arm around me. "Now she's here, I'll never lose her again."

"So like her father, isn't she?" Vera said. There was a long pause.

It looked as if there was a secret that was shared by everybody but me. I resolved to find the answer, however long it took. I sensed that Grandma was not going to tell me. Perhaps, I reasoned, if I began by looking through the old photo albums . . .

Grandpa was so pleased that Grandma won first prize he took us to have lunch at the Duck and Hounds. I was allowed to drink a half pint of beer, not out of a mug but out of a glass; ladies didn't drink beer out of mugs. There were a few women in the room off the bar, but my grandmother and I were not allowed in the bar itself because, she explained, men had to have a life of their own without women, which seemed perfectly sensible to me. Grandpa came back with a tray of drinks, a pint for himself, a glass of white wine for Grandma, and my glass of beer. We ate crusty porkpies that had a boiled egg in the middle of the pie. I asked my grandmother how they did it. She said, "They pour aspic into the middle and then, when it begins to set, they cut a boiled egg in half and slip it in . . ."

✣ Chapter 25 ✣

I heard words in my grandparents' house like "Suez" and a man named "Anthony Eden." My grandfather said he was "a wet," whereas Churchill was a true hero, almost in the ancient Greek notion of the word:

an individual so stellar as to surpass the standards of mere mortality, approaching instead the stratum of the gods. It sounded as if Churchill had won the War all by himself. Grandpa often walked the library with Churchill's speeches. The "blood, toil, tears and sweat" speech, also one of my father's favourites, was engraved on my heart. Mr Churchill, I realized, practically lived with us. My grandfather after dinner wound up his gramophone, which had a huge tin ear, and sent Mr. Churchill's voice booming across the lawn, a habit that made our neighbors, the Lovel family, very cross.

Apparently they weren't speaking because the Lovels sent a letter from their lawyer asking my grandfather to desist, but my grandfather said, "They are Communists and Churchill is good medicine for Communists." Evidently in the last election the Lovels walked about with red ribbons on their coats while everyone else in the village wore blue. Nice people were all conservatives and the nasties were labor. Even Mrs Harding, who arrived three times a week to clean, was a conservative. Grandpa predicted that within twenty years nobody would be working. All the people who were coming to England looking for streets paved with gold, and searching for a good education for their children, would end up living off Grandpa's and Grandma's taxes, and their children would take to the streets and loot and riot. It was difficult to take him seriously.

When we went home from the church bazaar, triumphantly carrying our cake, we—my grandmother and I—after a lovely dinner and before a cup of hot chocolate, made a little bookmark for that awful girl Angela. The party was in two days' time, and Grandma promised to stay with me.

My first week passed quietly. The peace and the hum of insects in the conservatory were a delight to me.

My grandmother introduced me to *Dick Barton, Special Agent.* First, at six o'clock, the three of us sat in the library, where there was a big radio, and we listened to the BBC news. After the news Grandpa turned off the radio and we discussed what was happening all over the world. "Good fellow, Jomo Kenyatta," my grandfather said. "Knew him myself. Stupid colonials don't understand Africa. Jomo does, though." My grandfather passionately and indiscriminately hated South African white people. "All ought to be shot," he said. But I loved my Africa, and he and I talked about Max and Sam and walked the winter garden while Grandma got the chocolate for me.

Then every evening at 6:45 I ran to the other big radio in the sitting room. I turned the chunky knob on the huge brown dial, and sat close to the big secure rounded shape and listened to the story of *Dick Barton, Special Agent.* "Dum de dum dum . . ." Marvelous. The end of a perfectly lovely day.

Tomorrow the perfectly awful party was going to take place.

I put on one of my dowdy dresses at lunchtime and went downstairs. "What a perfectly awful dress," my grandmother said. "You are much too old to wear dresses like that. Who bought you that dress?"

"My mother."

My grandmother's head gave a slight twitch as if she'd expected that answer. "We'll go into town and buy you two party dresses and an everyday dress." I was so relieved my eyes filled with tears. And we did go into town.

The shop was full of modern dresses. I chose my three dresses myself. One, my first evening dress, was white with flowers on it. It had a large elastic belt that cut my waist off, and it came with a great big petticoat. The sleeves were baggy and came halfway down my

arms. It was quite the most beautiful thing I had ever
seen, and I twirled about the shop admiring myself in
several mirrors. Then I chose an off-the-shoulder
party dress. The dress was pale blue, my favorite col-
our. The final dress I chose was a deep, dark red day-
dress. At last, at last, I had clothes I was proud of. And
to make my day heaven, Grandma took me to a shoe
shop and bought me my very first pair of shoes with
a heel.

We hurried back in time for me to change. I had the
great joy of snipping off the labels and taking my new
shoes out of their box. The shoebox was green and
smelled of leather. My grandmother gave me one of
her shoe-bags and a shoe-horn. She also gave me a set
of shoe-trees and some white polish.

When I was dressed I went downstairs and looked
at myself in the pier-glass in the hall. I looked all right,
I thought. "You look wonderful," my grandfather
said. "Really, Pumpkin. You're nearly a young
woman."

I smiled. Just then my grandmother came up. She
wore an afternoon dress of crêpe de Chine. The lace
collar was ivory with age. "Come along," she said.
"Let's get this over with."

The party took a lot of getting over with. As we walked
up the drive, Mr Rogers arrived in his Bentley. My
grandmother hurrumphed. "A Rolls, maybe," she
said. "But never a Bentley." Apparently Rolls Royces
were for country and Bentleys for trade. I quite like
Bentleys, but obviously Patrick eventually would have
to settle for a Rolls. I made a note of the difference.

Mrs Rogers's house was a shock. I had never lived
in or visited a house so ugly, and I sincerely hoped I
never would again. Mr Rogers looked rather nice. He
was "trade," my grandmother said. My grandmother

didn't really approve of "trade" and "country" mixing their social life, but we were a communal village.

Angela Rogers looked like Mrs Rogers' cake. Her white dress was layered and she wore a white sash, earrings and a string of pearls. "How perfectly dreadful," Grandma whispered. Grandma's whispers were really rather loud.

The party soon split up with Grandma taking refuge in the depth of the shiny, new, mock Chesterfield sofa. The whole house was blanketed in wall-to-wall carpet of a curly design. The house was "modern." Mrs Rogers, my grandmother warned me, had more money than taste.

We had tea in what Mrs Rogers called the *lounge.* I thought my grandmother might faint right into the huge bowl of sherry trifle. The word *lounge* could be used only if referring to a ship's drawing room. There was an awful lot of *lounge*ing and *couch*ing and *toilet*ing, and Mrs Rogers insisted on taking us for a tour of the house. The boys and girls mostly stood about talking in monosyllabic sentences. The parents stood about clutching teacups and eating the failed cake from the competition. Angela wore make-up. Angela's boyfriend had slick black hair and he had long pointed toes to his shoes. He had a string tie and was my first introduction to a Teddy Boy.

We were to leave at six sharp, as Grandpa—who didn't approve of women driving—would be at the gate to pick us up and he hated waiting.

Grandma did not look happy when Bill, Angela's boyfriend, shook her hand. "Where is the bathroom?" I asked, and Mrs Rogers escorted us to the "guest toilet". Grandma shot across the room and plunged her hands into the basin and washed them vigorously. "What a disgusting smell," she said. The soap was pale pink and highly scented. I thought the bathroom was rather fun. The bath was modern and had a shower. The lavatory was swathed in shaggy orange rug, like the carpet under my feet.

I sat on the furry lavatory with the lid down and looked at the loo-roll. Not a roll but a slit in the wall, and little bits of paper with piano notes on it came off in my fingers. No rasp of the loo-roll as it tore itself loose from the wall and cascaded onto the floor, which meant much of my time in my bathroom was spent rolling it up again. My bathroom at my grandparents' house was on the third floor. A little tiny room with a hot geyser that had a mind of its own. There was no self-willed geyser in this room. All was new and exotic. "All this modern rubbish," my grandmother said.

She streaked into the sitting room to say goodbye and then screeched to a halt as Billy threw Angela into the air and we got a full shot of Angela's lace knickers. My grandmother's nostrils quivered. So we went over to Mrs Rogers, who was surrounded by a gaggle of other women. "Rock and roll," Mrs Rogers cheerfully explained the sounds striking our ears. "Isn't it wonderful?"

My grandmother gave a very faint moan and we left the house.

"My goodness," said Grandma over supper in her own kitchen that evening. "Whatever next?"

My grandfather nodded. "I hear from Eldridge, who's on the bench this year, that they had an Elvis Presley film. Some damn fellow from America. The children tore up the seats."

I would have loved to see an Elvis Presley film, but I knew I had to wait until I went back to school and maybe sneak into the local cinema. I loved the cinema. There in the quiet darkness I could dream my romantic dreams. My grandparents hated the cinema. All of it. They really lived as if the modern world did not exist, except for the white Citroën Safari, which grandfather loved. It stood in the garage and he lovingly polished that car every Sunday.

And after lunch on my first Sunday we all climbed into it to go for a drive. It had a big chair in the back which could turn in a circle. My grandfather had used the car for his shoots on safaris in Kenya. I sat in the back seat listening to African safari stories and the names of famous hunters. For me, those stories were as romantic as any told by Ernest Hemingway. I read *For Whom the Bell Tolls* and all of Hemingway's books. My grandfather refused to read American literature. He lived among his English books and really had nothing in his library after Dickens. Dickens, Thackeray, and Boswell were his constant companions. I was so intent on listening, I do not remember where we went on our drive.

My grandmother read Victorian gardening books or cookery books. She was a wonderful mine of information. When one day Mrs Harding was considerably worse for wear, my grandmother took a jar of asparagus from her pantry and cooked it for her lunch. Mrs Harding looked at the pile of seemingly foreign vegetation with the deepest suspicion. "Eat it," Grandma said firmly. "If one is under the weather, asparagus is just the cure." My grandmother poured butter over the pile.

Mrs Harding ate the first one as if she might die at any moment, but by the time the pile was gone she was smiling. "Ever so good," she said. "My Jimmy's got nits."

"Oh really?" Grandma stood firm. "I'll get you some tincture of larkspur. That'll get rid of them."

That night we all washed our hair with tincture of larkspur. I scratched all night. But apparently my grandmother cured whole villages of nits and scabies. "Awful things," she said.

The two weeks passed both slowly and in a flash. On my second Sunday my father telephoned my grandmother. Her face became flushed and happy. I talked to him and I realized that he was in his office. Why didn't he telephone from our home? I looked at my grandmother, but now there was a hurt look on her face that made me hesitate to ask. I could see she loved my father very much. My grandfather didn't talk to my father, but then he never went near the telephone.

What was the mystery about my mother? I went to bed thinking about it all. Then I wrote to Patrick and fell asleep dreaming of school. This term I was on kitchen duty with Maximillian.

❧ *Chapter 26* ❧

I awoke with a jump and I saw Phoebe's large form snoring gently in the next bed. I lay in my bed looking at the other beds filled with girls. The Lily dormitory was composed of Sandy and Jenny (both girls were from Kenya, so we had a lot in common), Phoebe who was crazy Irish, and beastly boring Marian Pool. I didn't like her or her smiling friend Ruth. Ruth was boring and smelled bad. We tried being nice and gave her soap. We suggested baths. I even shared some of my Apple-blossom, but it didn't help. She was so virtuous with it all, a goody-two-shoes with both laces tied. Even if I said, "Pooh, do go and have a bath," she just smiled back sweetly and said, "You're quite right, Mary." It reminded me of the passage in the Bible where Jesus is told that Lazarus "stinketh." At least Jesus knew he could do something about it.

As for Marian Pool, she usually said, "Do we have to talk about Africa or Paris?"

"Well, no one wants to talk about bloody boring Eastbourne. Do they?" Phoebe got very cross with Marian when Marian said anything nasty about Ireland. "If you don't shut up, Marian," Phoebe warned, "I'll do an Irish keen for your death and we'll all have an Irish wake. You'd look good in a coffin. Then I'll do an Irish reel on your grave." Usually Marian shut up when Phoebe got cross, particularly as Phoebe played defense in netball and flattened Marian to the ground.

Ruth didn't play anything. She had a weak chest, her mother said. She also had a nose with a permanent drizzle. At least, I thought, it's the Easter term.

Patrick had written a letter which I put under my pillow. Miss Standish was pleased to see me. I had my tuckbox stuffed full of goodies by my grandmother, and my grandfather had put a brand new pound note in my hand just before I left. Mrs Harding had popped by. "Ta," she said and gave me a whole bag of wonderfully nobbly jelly-babies. I still had my garter belt and stockings. John did the usual vanishing trick with my dishes and my silver, and I felt very much at home. All was well with my world.

I got up quickly the first morning because I was on kitchen duty with Maximillian. Max, another Max in my life, was a very quiet man. He was tall and thin. He wore horn-rimmed glasses and was a magnificent cook. The food at Sherwood Park was much better than at any other school we visited. Max took very great pride in his cooking. After a particularly excellent meal we all demanded he appear and we clapped for him. I was really looking forward to my turn in the kitchen. Unlike the other girls, I even loved washing up. We had no machines like we had in Paris. We— Max and I and one other girl (Phoebe, thank goodness)—washed up when it was our turn: Max, his arms deep in the big white sink, me standing next to him, and Phoebe usually dried.

Maximillian talked a lot about the war. He was in a destroyer when a bomb came hurtling down the smokestack and he was blown up. "Poor Jimmy. Blown to bits," he said. "I always felt loved. My boys . . ." He said, "I was older, so I listened to them. I knitted socks for them. I comforted them when they cried."

Sometimes Max's eyes filled with tears. He never married or had any children, but he had shared his house in the village of Loch Hey with a man he called his "partner." He, too, died a few years ago, and I could tell Max missed him very very much. He told us terribly funny stories about how his partner dressed up as a woman and sang funny songs in the local pubs, and how in the early days, when Max and his partner had no money, Max had to help push the piano from village hall to village hall . . . "And we looked ever so funny," he said. "Me in my suit, and me partner in his dress and high heels, bending over showing his knickers for all the world to see!" We all laughed hysterically.

Max was very fond of Miss Standish, though he always treated her like the Queen Mum. Max loved Miss Standish, but he adored the Queen Mother. We had pictures of her all over the kitchen. I had my scrap book of the Royal Family, particularly the new Queen. I always remember when she had her first child, Prince Charles.

Max and I talked a lot about the Royal Family. Not so Phoebe. She hated the English, she said. I was forgiven, but all of Ireland's troubles, she said, were because the "bloody English" wouldn't mind their own business. "They destroyed Wales and Scotland, and they are still messing about in Ireland." We tried to keep off the subject of Ireland.

Max was making porridge, thick cream, and toast

and marmalade. I helped make the tea. There were two hundred girls, and this term I was delighted to see that I was on Miss Standish's table. Miss Morgan, the French teacher, had Phoebe at the next table, and smelly Ruth shared another table with Marian at the other end of the refectory, thank goodness. It was a bright sunny day. The kitchen shone. The big aga gleamed and the broad pantry table reminded me of how much I was going to enjoy the term ahead. Phoebe brought an extra horse over from Ireland for me because my mother had made my father change his mind: I was not to have a horse. I had been bitterly disappointed, but Phoebe surprised me. "Anyway," she said as I stood beside my horse, "I had a double horse-box and I missed George dreadfully when I left him behind the last time. He and Spice are such good friends. The Mater said it was all right. Now you'll have to clean tack."

I was only too willing to clean tack. I had longed for a horse of my own. My father was still embarrassed by his betrayal. He included a white five-pound note in his letter to me. He always put "Your mother sends her love." I planned to spend some of my five pounds on two tickets to see Elvis Presley. On the way through the village in John's car, I had seen the film advertised. John had snorted. "They're tearing up the seats, I hear," he said. A film that made people tear up seats must be good.

Also the local boys were wearing extravagant suits and blue suede shoes, "brothel-creepers," as Phoebe explained, "to creep round brothels," she added. I knew there were brothels in Paris, but not in this part of the world. "Oh, yes," Phoebe said. Still she was impressed with my five pounds and even more impressed with my garter and stockings. "Good heavens!" she said. "We can open our own brothel."

After breakfast we all had an hour to go outside and

groom our horses. Those girls like Ruth and Marian, who didn't have horses, had to run or play games. Jenny and Sandy couldn't bring their horses from Kenya, but they helped us with ours and in return they exercised Spice and George. Usually I lingered over breakfast, but today I nodded to Phoebe and asked to leave the table. "To groom your horse?" Miss Standish said.

"Yes," I said, blushing with happiness.

Miss Morgan, the French teacher, scowled. She didn't like me because my French was much better than hers, and she went on and on about boring old Stendhal when I preferred Proust or Flaubert. Phoebe didn't care about either writer. She liked books about horses. Phoebe's French was excruciating, but my father promised I could spend half-term with Phoebe in Ireland. This time he swore he would not break his promise. I felt this time he wouldn't. I was pleased to be going to Phoebe's house for half-term.

Both horses were pleased to see us. Spice put his big warm nose in my hand and blew sweet hay-breath at me. George nuzzled Phoebe. We stood with the sun on our backs, grooming the horses. I knew how to ride because Sam taught me in Africa. Sam had a huge old roan, but to have access permanently to a horse was like an answer to prayer, and I had prayed for years for a horse. I always loved the greasy horsey smell that comes on your fingers when you run the curry-comb through a horse's back. I did great long sweeps. Spice was a strong cob with a red coat. It took all of an hour to do him properly and then to polish each hoof. Our stalls were in the main barn. There were twelve stalls all filled with horses.

Phoebe's groom Jake left the horse box at the school and took the night boat back to Ireland. John MacAllister looked after the horses at half-term. As it was only a week, Phoebe explained, it wouldn't be worthwhile for George and Spice to make the trip to Ireland with us. Besides, she had several other horses on their farm.

So much happened these first few days, so many friends to swap stories with. I wrote a short story about my grandmother winning the cake at the cake show. Miss Standish sent it to the local paper and, to my amazement, the editor gave her two guineas which she handed on to me and in the middle of the term he published it. I sent a copy to Patrick, a copy to grandmother and grandfather, and a copy to my mother and father. Everybody wrote back except my mother. My father was particularly pleased because he wanted me to be a writer like he was. Patrick was ecstatic and said that I could write my stories while he was working in the bank all day. Then I could read him the stories at night. That sounded marvelous.

I was really happy at school. I loved the routine. I loved having friends. I was very well behaved because I never never wanted to upset Miss Standish. She was the kindest person I'd ever met, apart from Mademoiselle who had had her baby, a baby girl. She sent a picture of Jacques holding the baby, a little crumpled pink blob. They called her Marie, after me, which made me feel proud.

Phoebe was dreadfully naughty. It was like having Françoise back again, only Phoebe was real-life. We always sat together and Phoebe copied all my work. I didn't mind because I loved to study and Phoebe never read a book, if she could help it. But she was a demon giggler. I always had a frightful time not giggling. I never understood the other girls' need to giggle and whisper in each other's ears. I'd always been told that whispering was bad manners. Well, Phoebe's manners were non-existent. Not only did she whisper in a loud voice, but she also snored and giggled loudly. "You'll never get married if . . . ." Miss Standish said.

The "if" covered an endless list of don'ts. Like picking your nose, another of Phoebe's habits. She said snot was medicinal. And anyway she had no intention of getting married because of "it."

The snot, she said, was like a vaccine. I didn't believe her, and I didn't habitually sneak out at night to ride in the moonlight as Phoebe did. She was fearless. As far as marriage went, I was determined to get married. So I took Miss Standish's sermons seriously, very seriously. I crossed my legs at the ankles. I drank my tea without making a sipping noise. And I walked slowly and elegantly, unlike Phoebe who gallumphed along beside me, talking nineteen to the dozen about everything under the sun.

I also took my music lessons very seriously and learned to play songs that Patrick and I could sing. I had to hide away in the practice room. If Phoebe found me practising she interrupted and banged *Chopsticks* out on the piano. I sang in the school choir. We were doing Gilbert and Sullivan, and I had a very high voice. My mother and I sang flat. So it was quite a surprise when Miss Donovan asked me to audition and I got the part of Angelina in *Trial by Jury.* "O'er the seasons vernal time may cast a shade . . ." I loved the choir rehearsals nearly as much as I loved the play rehearsals.

Phoebe hated it all. She just wanted to live forever in Ireland and hunt all day. Half the school felt the same way: they were all addicted to their horses and never talked about boys. The other half never stopped talking about boys. Geneviève was definitely among the latter crowd, comprised largely of other European girls. I really didn't have much to say. I spent a lot of my time in the library, unless Phoebe dragged me out to play tennis, or I rode. To be happy, that happy, was so fragile I always feared I would wake up with my mother bending over my bed hitting me.

But that term I did go out for a ride one night. It was unusually hot. Jenny, Sandy, Phoebe and I decided to sneak out and ride in the immense moonlit night. Marian was asleep, and we thought Ruth was too. We dressed quietly and slipped out. Night encircled us and the shadows lay deep and silent. We had to tiptoe. I wore my gum-shoes. The others had riding boots. I could hear owls hooting and bats chirping. The house looked large and the windows glared sightlessly at my folly. I was enraptured.

I saddled Spice who was as excited as I was, and we took off before the others. We agreed to head for Dedem Wood and to meet there. I felt like the *Highwayman* in one of my favorite Alfred Noyes poems. Spice flew, his hoofs barely touching the ground. The barn was well away from the main house, and the moss lawns absorbed the hoofbeats. We were alone in the universe, my horse and myself and the black velvet night. I rode into the path of the moon, closer and closer to the big "ghostly galleon," and for a moment we were in the moon, Spice and I, and then we were out the other side. I could hear the other horses behind me.

Finally we all drew rein and the horses puffed and huffed. Slowly we turned and ambled back to the stables. We didn't talk much, but when we slipped back into the pantry door, Miss Standish was waiting for us. I nearly died of fright. Miss Standish said, "Sit down, child. I'm not going to hurt you." I think I must have flinched.

The others hung their heads. "You are very silly *gels*," Miss Standish said. "I'll see you in my study tomorrow."

We realized that Ruth must have sneaked. "Telltale-tit," Phoebe said and turned over Ruth's bed. Ruth fell on the floor and began to snivel. "Shut up, sneak!" Phoebe said. We all got into bed but I couldn't sleep. I was so ashamed. I'd upset Miss Standish.

After breakfast, which I made with Max and Phoebe, I told Max all about the night before. He smiled. "She won't be cross, duck," he said. "You are hardly ever naughty. Not like *you*, madam," he said to Phoebe who grinned. "You know," he said, looking at me, "you don't have to be perfect."

When he said that, I felt a pang inside. So often in my life I had tried to be perfect. A perfect daughter, a perfect little girl, and now a perfect teenager. I tried so hard to be all those things. I was so used to worrying about being disapproved of for my inevitable failure that now, with no one to condemn me, I'd find something else to worry about, like Latin, or an algebra equation. If I wasn't worrying I felt afraid that the sky might fall on me, like Chicken Licken.

"Anyway," Phoebe said, "last night was great fun." That was true.

Phoebe wasn't nearly so perky when we were in Miss Standish's study. I was told off, but not much. Phoebe was in real trouble though. Sandy and Jenny both cried. So did I. But Phoebe refused to cry. Miss Standish gave me a week's work with John in the kitchen garden during break. I was pleased. Jenny and Sandy had to clean the house, and Phoebe was confined to the library and no riding for a week. That really upset her. "Bloody bitch," Phoebe said. "Ugh. I'll go through the Bible and look up all the dirty bits. That'll teach her a lesson."

As it was spring, I got to watch John transplant the lettuce from the cold frame into the ground, and to learn how to pot geraniums. "You break off the side shoots at an angle and then repot the cuttings." I was terribly proud of my little shoots, and I gave the best shoot I had to Miss Standish. "Suck-up," Phoebe declared. I didn't care. Miss Standish was awfully good to me. And I was reading *Stalky and Co.* again and rolling about with laughter. If Phoebe couldn't love books as I did, it was her fault. I was beginning to learn that I was not always wrong. John, Grandpa, Ned, and Maximillian somehow seemed stronger men than my father. I was beginning to learn that my father was not perfect, and that hurt.

Chapter 27

John took us to the night boat to Ireland. I loved the busy docks and the smell of the salt. I remembered a line from one of my favorite poems: "Dirty British coaster with a salt-caked / smokestack / Butting through the Channel . . ." Actually the word "bustling" seemed more appropriate to me than "butting." The little tugs really bustled and the lean northern sailors looked so very different from their southern brothers who had larger bucolic faces and seemed to have more food at their disposal.

Jeremy, Phoebe's oldest brother, was also at the boat. He was a student at Oxford and a rugger blue. His ambition was to play rugger for Ireland at Twickenham. He was even taller than Phoebe and they looked very alike. He had a fringe hanging over his blue eyes, and his smile was lovely. As it was the night boat, Phoebe and Jeremy shared a cabin. Dinner was excellent. I ordered Dublin Bay prawns and Jeremy let me have a sip of his bitter dark beer. Guinness, he called it. We pulled out of the port and lurched on a slightly choppy sea.

Ireland. I'd always been interested in Ireland. My mother said I was related to George Bernard Shaw. She embarrassed me by saying that I had inherited the

"Shaw head." I couldn't see any resemblance myself, but I did like to write. I'd been writing plays since I was six and in Africa, and I still wrote whenever I had peace and quiet, which was not often at school. Hopefully at half-term I might find a room in Phoebe's house, write to Patrick, and then attempt another short story. I wrote best when I was sad, and I realized that now I was no longer sad much of the time, and my stories were not so gloomy. Phoebe at first had laughed at the idea of my writing stories, but now she enjoyed them. I was in a phase of writing horse stories. I was so in love with Spice. He, in turn, loved me. We always talked about everything, his big nose against my cheek and his wonderful long eyelashes blinking sympathetically when I told him of my childhood, how nervous I always felt at the prospect of going home, back to my mother's elegant prison and her often prickly presence. There was something of the porcupine in my mother. If stroked the right way, she was enjoyable to be with, but I could never feel completely safe, for a word or touch out of place could, in an instant, bring about the raising of sharp and painful quills. Even if I missed my father, I was happy to be going to Phoebe's house. I fell asleep under a full moon and slept dreamlessly, my letters from Patrick in my writing case under my pillow.

Phoebe's house was a major shock. It was actually an enormous gray stone castle. "You didn't say you lived in a castle, Phoebe."

Jeremy laughed. "We don't live in a castle," he said. "We live in the servants' quarters at the back."

"Oh." I was disconcerted, but even more disconcerted when I met Phoebe's mother.

Bridie Balfor was huge and fat but had a nice, if tired, face. She wore thick lisle stockings like Miss Standish, and an immense pinafore wrapped itself around her ample form. "Come along," she said, shooing us in front of her. "Breakfast is ready."

"Good," Jeremy beamed. "I'm starving. Are the others here?"

"Yes. Joe and Charlie are in the kitchen, all waiting."

We deposited our suitcases in the great front hall and Phoebe walked swiftly through the castle while I ran to keep up, wishing that God had obliged me by granting me lithe long legs like Jeremy's or Phoebe's. As it turned out, Joe and Charlie Balfor were also tall, blonde, and blue-eyed. Bridie and her family looked like a race of giants. We all sat down for breakfast and Bridie said a prayer. Of course I knew Bridie was a Catholic, but Phoebe wasn't keen on church-going and hardly ever went when we were at school. She did go to confession after we went to see the Elvis Presley film. I loved the film. He had a big deep gravy voice that poured over the four of us and he did sexy things with his hips that caused Sandy and Jenny to scream. I didn't scream, and Phoebe said it was all a lot of bloody nonsense, which was hurtful since I was paying. However, she did go to confession and we both went to Mass on Sunday. In a way I wished I was a Catholic and could go to confession and tell the priest what a sin I felt it to be that I was uncomfortable in the presence of my own mother, and, in the confession and the absolution, my deep awful pain might go away. But today the pain was less.

The kitchen was large with an old-fashioned range, and the range was hot and threw a wet warmth around us as we ate porridge oats with cream. Through the kitchen window I could see cows and horses grazing. Charlie and Jeremy were joking and Joe sat quietly getting on with his breakfast. Both Joe and Charlie wore jodhpurs and jackets. I knew from Phoebe that they both ran the farm and that Joe was engaged to be married to a local girl called Sandra. Phoebe liked her. They were to be married in the summer. I wished I were older and could get married.

Here was another group of happy people, laughing and joking together, Jeremy teasing Phoebe, Bridie smiling affectionately at her handsome brood. I didn't feel any dangerous undertows. No need to flinch at the sharp edge of a question. Here was peace and calm, an oasis, and I loved the gray-blue color of Ireland. The shadows of the lawn, the blue-gray sky, all reflected in Bridie's tired gray eyes.

I helped Bridie and Phoebe wash up, feeling guilty for the wealth of our house in Paris and for the fact that I only washed up once a week with my father on Cook's day off. The big thick white plates piled high and the mugs, blue and white banded. We soon finished while Phoebe and her mother chatted. Phoebe grunted answers in a shorthand which Bridie seemed to understand. I listened to a country litany of how many cows calved this spring (ten, I gathered) and how many chickens were laying.

After breakfast and a climb up a winding long staircase, I was given a small round room in a turret. I had a stone guest bathroom next door, and to my surprise the water was steaming hot. Phoebe slept in the room underneath me. She had a small four-poster bed and a really lovely writing desk which I asked if I could borrow. "Okay," Phoebe said. "I'll get the boys to move it up and you can scribble your stories."

"You have a smashing family," I said.

"I know." Phoebe grinned. "I'm sad Dad died, but we all love each other and do the best we can. I feel a bit guilty about being away so much at school. I'd much rather be here on the farm helping the boys. Anyway, mum is making butter and cheese this morning. We sell all our stuff at the market on Saturdays, so let's change and we'll give her a hand."

"Grandma would love this dairy," I told Bridie when I got up enough courage to speak.

"Would she now?" Bridie smiled. "Come with me."

And I followed Bridie and Phoebe to the end of the long white shiny dairy. I helped Bridie by holding the milk-churn while she scooped out curds for the cheese. The curds for cottage cheese were swathed in porous cheese-cloth and hung over buckets for the whey to drip into pails which then fed the pigs. I marvelled at the huge pots of fresh butter, both salted and unsalted. We worked in silence, but I liked the silence. It was as smooth as the butter, not a tense cut-of-the-knife silence but a comfortable concentrated silence of people working well together. I could see why Phoebe sometimes minded the school. Here she was at home and useful, her long arms and legs not crammed under a desk. Unlike my useless hands, Phoebe had quick nimble fingers and she patted and prodded everything into shape.

I dropped a fat pat of butter and Bridie laughed. I was relieved and I blushed. "No need to flinch," Bridie said, and I realized she knew my secret, and I blushed even harder. "No one will touch you here," she said. "I'll see to that. If anyone hurts you again, you telephone me and I'll deal with it. I'm a local justice of the peace in this town. I don't allow anyone to hurt children for any reason at all."

"Not even at school?" I asked in amazement.

"Not even at school," she said. "I know boys were beaten at Rugby. When my boys were in school, I told the head-master that if anyone so much as touched my boys, I'd be after them with my shillelagh." And I believed her. Bridie on the rampage would be a terrible sight. I imagined her storming the house. I suddenly felt very comforted. Bridie was much more forceful than even Miss Standish, and that day I knew I had an ally.

We worked happily all morning. Then I helped cut soft pink ham onto big chunks of white crusty bread served in the kitchen. The boys came back and Phoebe made a large bowl of yellow mustard. I watched quietly as they talked of farming.

The afternoon was ours and Phoebe saddled two ponies, Paint and Smokey, and we ambled about the grounds now sadly run down. "Black and Tans did their job well here," Phoebe said bitterly. "Our family once owned all these lands and we employed the whole village, all craftsmen. Look." She pointed to a desolate formal garden. "That was a real Italian belvedere. See the broken marble? Well the English did that . . . We don't have the time or the money to restore the garden. We all just do what we can to keep the farm going." I could sense the deep sadness in Phoebe. "The boys and I made a promise that our mother would end her years in the castle. To her, the place is a shrine to our father. She still sleeps in the bed she shared with him, and all his clothes are in the cupboard, just as he left them. To think, he survived the horrors of the First World War and nearly all of the second, and some bloody sniper got him in Aden . . . Come on, let's gallop."

And we fled down the fields and jumped a ditch. I followed, trying hard to stay on. Phoebe had ridden all her life. I had not, but I realized that she, too, had her sadness in life. I couldn't imagine what it would be like not to have a father.

I fell asleep immediately that first night and slept deeply. How Patrick would have loved this castle. And tomorrow I could explore.

Explore I did. Phoebe helped her mother gather eggs and pick the early vegetables for the market. I lost myself in the main part of the castle and walked the seemingly endless miles from one end to the other. How much history the walls contained! The pain and the sorrow of the centuries lay behind me, but at least, I reminded myself, now the castle can experience the joy and happiness. I pushed open big heavy doors and gazed into great rooms still full of furniture. Phoebe's school fees had been paid from the sale of a seventeenth century dining table, Oxford for Jeremy by the sale of a blue Ming vase. Currently a set of sixteen Baccarat crystals awaited sale at Sotheby's. All this family discussion reminded me how different our life was from theirs. (Our silver was safe in bank vaults. If my mother needed it, the chauffeur collected all of it and it was polished, used, then put away. My mother had jewels also in the bank vault. I hardly ever saw her South African diamond necklace with its sunburst of diamonds. "A wedding present" was all she would say.)

Here, in the huge gloom of the castle, priceless objects lay about to be sold if necessary. I felt that Bridie wouldn't mind if these objects were sold, as long as her children and her animals were safe. They came first. Several suits of armor stood in dark corners and it all began to feel spooky, especially in the portrait gallery where rows and rows of Balfors, all looking like Phoebe with her long nose, stared down at me as if I were intruding in their dialogue. Long dead, they still were very much alive and their eyes followed me as I walked past.

I found steep stone steps at the end of the castle and I realized they led directly to my turret and my room. I climbed and climbed, catching fleeting glimpses of blue sky and cloud as I climbed. And then I was back in my dear little room. I sat down and wrote a letter to Patrick telling him all of what I'd seen, and I began a ghost story set in the picture gallery. I quite frightened myself, so I went downstairs for lunch.

The days slipped away. I helped in the market on Saturday. What a difference from the markets in Africa and France. Here the men sat about and conversed amiably, the women sold their produce, but it lacked the great heaps of food, the implicit feeling that huge meals were to be cooked. No smell of garlic wafted around. Instead the market was more a palate of greens and browns. The pub was open and I enjoyed my pint in a round beer mug. I knew Grandma wouldn't approve, but then this was market day. We also ate farm pie, lovely and juicy. Lots of laughing Irish people came up to talk to Bridie and I was happy.

The next day we caught the boat back to England, back to the soft gorse and back to the rest of the term. Next would come the Easter holidays and home. But at least Patrick would also be in Paris. There was that to look forward to.

❧ *Chapter 28* ❧

"You know," Jeremy said as we sat on the boat taking us back to school and Jeremy to Oxford, "you're not like other girls Phoebe's dragged home."

"I know," I said. "I'm rather boring."

"You're not boring." Jeremy's kind eyes were smiling. "You just seem to live in another world."

I felt elated that Jeremy even realized there was another world outside the one everyone else shared. "Sometimes I feel as if I live behind a thick piece of glass," I explained. "Only a few people can hear me.

Phoebe is wonderful because she just leaves me alone. But Ruth and Marian—they're two girls in our dormitory—they call me names. They say I'm ugly and stupid."

Jeremy smiled. "Girls are notoriously cruel," he said. "I think you'll grow up to a really lovely woman . . . Come on. I'll get you a cup of tea and we'll find Phoebe pigging out in the cafeteria." He took my hand and we walked across the deck to the first class dining room. I was thrilled. Here I was holding hands with a man from Oxford.

Later that night I made sure not to wash my right hand, and I looked at my hand so recently encased in Jeremy's handsome hand, and felt quite pretty really, quite attractive. I knew this was a secret and I mustn't tell Patrick in case he felt jealous. My familiar feeling of being a no-thing and a nobody was altering. I supposed in Paris the people that came to our house really saw me as an invisible creature. But this last week had been most amazing. Bridie listened to what I said and she took my opinions seriously.

I was happy tonight on the boat to England. Happiness was no longer an infrequent visitor. In fact, happiness was becoming present most of the time.

❦ *Chapter 29* ❦

"Shut your fat face!" I heard myself say.

Phoebe gave a great hoot of laughter. "Well done!" she encouraged.

Ruth looked shocked. "I see," she said. "We now have Irish bog manners, do we?"

Phoebe punched Ruth in the stomach and I took a swing at Marian. Within a minute all four of us were rolling on the floor punching each other. I had Marian's lank locks firmly in my fists, and I suddenly realized I was banging her head on the floor and enjoying every minute of it. *"Gels!"* Silence froze into hard drops of ice. "What are you doing?"

I was sitting on top of Marian. I jumped to my feet. Phoebe stood up. Marian and Ruth lay on the floor crying. "Ruth called Mary bog-Irish," Phoebe offered.

A look of distaste crossed Miss Standish's patrician features. "Patrician" was my new word and I loved the sound of it. "Well, Ruth?" Miss Standish's voice was sharp. In the tone lay a razor edge.

Ruth grizzled. "She told me to shut up," she whined.

" 'She' is the cat's mother." Miss Standish hated bad manners.

" 'Mary,' I mean," Ruth quickly corrected herself.

"How could you, as a Jew, call anyone bog-Irish? If you learned anything from history, it must be that discrimination of any sort is an abomination. You apologize to Mary immediately. And to Phoebe. Bog-Irish indeed! I'll be back in an hour for lights out."

I grinned. I had checked out Miss Standish in *Who's Who.* Her mother was an O'Connor from Sligo. Bog-Irish indeed.

Phoebe pulled me into the bathroom. "Quick," she said. "Slap this stuff on."

"What is it?"

"Horse liniment. Chuck it all over you, and you won't feel so sore tomorrow."

"I don't care if I am sore," I said. "I enjoyed that fight enormously." I went to sleep very pleased with myself. I was in love with Patrick, I'd held hands with a man from Oxford, and I'd had my first fight. All in all, life was wonderful.

I worked hard for the rest of the term. Maximillian taught me how to cook plum duff, Lancashire hotpots, and rare roast beef. For Phoebe's birthday I made a baked Alaska.

I first tasted baked Alaska in Africa at a birthday party. Cook brought in the ice cream covered with meringue alight with brandy. I was five then and the party was more for the adults than for the handful of children. The rains had arrived and the monotonous drumming of the fat raindrops on the roof made the adults unusually morose and bad-tempered. My mother and father lay in the long wicker armchairs out on the veranda. The rain pouring off the roof caused a strange effect of a waterfall between ourselves and the tropical green parrot-haunted vegetation. My father sat sadly with a whisky stengah beside him on a bamboo table. The air around us, I remember, was so hot and the drink so cool that wisps of condensation— the opposite of breath made visible in winter air— floated from the top of the glass. My mother sipped from a small glass a "white lady," her usual drink. I stood at the door watching, always watching. Bored men and women moved about the house, and on the table lay a heap of new toys for the birthday girl. She, tired, was asleep on the sofa and two little boys played a desultory game of soldiers on the floor. Then in the middle of the boredom that lay around the monsoon months, like a huge avocado too full even to offer the attraction of danger, came the cook carrying the cake. I thought it was one of the most beautiful moments of my life, that cake. The moment I tasted the chill of the ice cream on the edge of my teeth, the sweet crunch of the meringue, and then the heat of the brandy, I was filled with exaltation. Suddenly my mother's lethargic mood changed. She darted into the room and, with a shrill cry, took a plate and heaped it with the cake. That was probably the first time I thought of my mother as a puzzle.

All these years later, lying in bed the night after Phoebe's birthday and my very successful effort at making her baked Alaska, I remembered that day in Africa. Why did my father protect my mother so ardently? Why did he never visit his parents who obviously loved him so much? What had my mother done that there were no pictures of her at all in my grandmother's massive collection of photographs?

The term was near its end when I received a mysterious letter, perhaps the first found piece in the puzzle that was my mother. I sat alone on my bed while I read the letter. The handwriting was feminine and neat.

> *Dear Mary,*
> *My name is Mary Higgins, but you can call me Aunt Mary. I knew your mother many years ago. I also knew your father's parents. So I like to keep my finger in and see how you are. It wasn't easy finding you but I still have friends.*
>
> *I'm sure you've grown up lovely, but I want to see you for myself. You can visit when your school's ended. Your mother probably likes to keep her past in the past, so I wouldn't tell her about this. Or anyone else. Let's keep it between us. All right?*
>
> *Love,*
> *Aunt Mary.*

Who was Aunt Mary? It was impossible to tell from the letter what sort of woman she was. Curiosity compelled me to want to meet her and learn what I could learn. Maybe she would be the person to tell me of my mother's past. But who was Aunt Mary?

My first thought was to ask my mother, but the letter had instructed me not to. Would it be right to meet this total stranger? And the letter did not even have a return address. The postmark on the envelope said only "Ealing." I asked Phoebe to help me. Phoebe loved a good mystery. Together we found a Mary Higgins living in Ealing listed in a London telephone book in Miss Standish's library.

The telephone line to London was bad that day. The crackling on the line was so loud I could hardly hear the voice or the accent of the woman on the other end. I asked if I could see her. I heard a crackle back agreeing, and an invitation to stay the night. I didn't know whether to accept or not. Would it be safe? I hesitated and the voice through the crackle said, "I'll meet—" More crackling. "—Lyons Corner House." The voice named a date and a time. "For a cup of . . ." Suddenly we were disconnected and the line went silent. I hadn't had a chance to consent.

Phoebe said I should go anyway. Whoever this person was, I would be safe at least meeting her in a public place like Lyons Corner House. And if I didn't like the looks of her, I could slip away and not spend the night.

I decided I had to go through London on my way back to Paris for the summer. I might as well take a chance and meet this woman, whoever she was. As the term ended, I found myself increasingly eager and curious. I felt that the beginning of an adventure was waiting for me.

Chapter 30

I met Aunt Mary. Any dreams I had of being a secret princess were rudely shattered. Princesses didn't have Aunt Marys, or I supposed they didn't. We met at Lyons Corner House. I arrived early as always, and I queued, an English habit. I much preferred the push and the shove of Paris, the smell of sweat and hot coffee. Lyons Corner House was decorous indeed. The tables were neat and clean and stood all so obediently with metal responsible legs. No tea wobbled in its saucer.

The tea was awful, brown and bitter. Lyons Corner House looked like a refuge for the unfortunates of London. Sad men sat with their flat hats shadowing their eyes. Rimmed-red fingers traced the fate of their horses. A couple sat also across from me, so absorbed in each other they didn't talk. They just held hands, oblivious to the pile of chips and the mound of meat that slowly congealed on their plates. Two women in white uniforms were having an animated gossip too far away for me to hear what they were saying. Then I heard a cough, a dreadful terminal cough that filled the room, and a short old woman wearing a black bombazine hat erupted into the room. "Where is she?" she screamed. "Where's my Mary from Paris and Africa?" she said, sticking her face into the frozen lovers who jumped three feet.

I buried my face in my cup of tea and then scalded myself. Tears streamed down my face. "Choke up, chicken!" The apparition that was Aunt Mary banged me on the back. Festoons of ash rested on my head. I was to spend the night with Aunt Mary before going on to Paris. I had heard about cockneys. I had also read Dickens. There were two sorts of cockneys: those that were noble, loving, and full of service, and then there were the others like Fagin and Bill Sykes. Well, Aunt Mary was definitely one of the others.

"Wer's me fucking cup of tea?" Aunt Mary demanded of a young waitress who was passing by.

I felt the blood rise between my toes and move in waves of mortification up my body. "Oh, Aunt Mary," I said faintly. "You sweared." I couldn't worry about grammar at a moment like this. Phoebe said *bloody* and *damn.* That was bad enough. We all knew *bloody* was really *by our lady* and that was blasphemous and against the Bible. I once said *blimy* which means *God blind me.* Then I waited all day in a state ôf terror in case He did. And I decided that swearing was too dangerous and I didn't like the other thing that Phoebe hinted she did . . .

When my eyes stopped watering and I stopped blushing, I saw Aunt Mary was gazing at me. "Right little madam," she said. "Aren't we?"

"Am I?" I said.

"Yeah." Aunt Mary looked very much like my African marmoset. She had the same hairy face and mischievous eyes. "About bloody time, too," she said when the waitress put the teacup down.

I almost regretted having tracked Aunt Mary down with Phoebe's help. I now realized the crackling on the telephone wasn't all the line's fault. Aunt Mary crackled in person just like a bad telephone. We finished our tea. Aunt Mary paid for her cup after ages of fishing about in her bag, the same sort of bag in which Ernest was found in *The Importance of Being Earnest.* Poor Ernest, at least, was discovered in a reasonably clean handbag. Or maybe he wasn't, and that was why Lady Bracknell made such a fuss.

Eventually, with the cigarette sticking out of the side of her face, Aunt Mary dredged a tattered brown ten-shilling note out of the depths of the bag and handed it to the same young waitress. "All the change please, miss." Aunt Mary hissed her instructions. "All thieves these days!" she announced to the assembled. "If they're not thieves, they're all prostitutes! I'm glad to see you are still wearing knee-length socks and your knees aren't showing."

"Oh shut up, grandma!" The waitress, to my amazement, was laughing.

"Shut up? I'll give you shut up!" Aunt Mary replied archly. She checked the change and then she bit the sixpence. "Can't tell, these days," she said. "Forgers everywhere." She put the sixpence under her teacup, got up, and trotted out of the Corner House as if a posse of robbers were after her bag.

I decided to follow her and to spend the night after all. She was not the sort of person I was used to, but for some reason I liked her and trusted her at once.

We boarded a bus after half an hour's wait. Aunt Mary was one Englishwoman who did not believe in queuing. She pushed and shoved and cursed her way up to the top of the queue, with me apologizing furiously all the way. When we got on the bus she threw herself on the benchseat between two very fat people. "Bloody disgusting!" she screamed. "Four people are supposed to sit 'here, but you two are so fat you take up the whole bloody bus, don't you? There's a war on, you know."

"No, Aunt Mary," I said. "The war's over."

"I'll bet," she said, "those two 'elped Hitler." Both people glared at us and got up. I sat down, my face the same color as the purple-red seats. "I've always 'ad to fight," Aunt Mary announced loudly. "Oh look!" she said with horror in her voice. "A wog!" I thought I might try fainting. A night in the hospital was preferable to living like this. Aunt Mary was not only vulgar and common, she was also definitely OTT and she smelled like a very ancient ashtray.

Had I hopes that she was merely one of those eccentric millionairesses who really lived in a palace, these hopes were soon dashed. After swinging on the stopping bell quite illegally, and shouting "I get orf 'ere!" the bus stopped and we were the only two to get out.

Our second bus conductor on our second bus was also a "wog." "Actually," I said, "he is a Sikh."

"Sikh peek," Aunt Mary said rudely. "They're all wogs and should be sent 'ome." She carefully wiped her change on her filthy skirt. "Don't know where 'is 'ands 'ave been. Probably around some poor white woman's throat." I sighed. At least Aunt Mary had a vivid imagination.

Aunt Mary's door was painted bright glow-in-the-dark orange. She had a bed of dahlias that would have made my mother go white. I resolved to sit up all night with cotton wool in my ears in case we were invaded by earwigs. I took my suitcase up into the room that was to be mine for the night. The plump motherly bed was covered by a bright purple, shiny silk cover, but the sheets were clean. I was relieved. And I had a white bowl with a pitcher standing in it on a small black dressing table which had a runner that announced "Jesus is Lord." On the wall above my bed a picture of Jesus carrying a lamb in his arms walked towards me. On the floor a shaggy square of carpet said "Amen" to my feet. Obviously Aunt Mary was religious.

"Of course," she said, "I'm bloody religious. RC, thank you very much. Hate the Protestants."

"Why?" I asked.

" 'Cos they kill all the Irish, the buggers." We were standing in the kitchen. It was late evening and the lights across the street were dancing a lively minuet as people arrived home from work. Children's voices floated over garden walls. "Hummph," Aunt Mary sniffed. She took down two tall brass lamps and lit both of them. "I 'ave all I need," she said. "None of this modern nonsense."

Speaking of needs, I asked for the bathroom. Aunt Mary accompanied me to the end of the garden where a quaint shed laughed at me through a green mouth which resolutely refused to open. Aunt Mary gave it a flying kick and it responded immediately. It flew open. Inside I saw, by the light of my lamp, a commode—a very ancient commode—squatting comfortably on a white linoleum floor. "Don't fall in!" Aunt Mary cackled, and she left me with my lamp and the malodorous atmosphere. I decided to remain constipated until I reached the train. On the way down the little path we passed rose bushes that were blooming extravagantly. "Shit," said Aunt Mary. "My shit." I then and there resolved that no product of mine would enhance Aunt Mary's rose garden. I sat with the lamp at my feet and took stock. The lamp hissed and I realized that Aunt Mary made me laugh.

"Will you tell me about my mother?" I asked at supper. We had a salad for supper. The boiled eggs stared at me, shocked by the question. The boiled beetroot glared at me and the lettuce leaves shivered with apprehension.

"No," Aunt Mary grumbled. "I won't." But her voice was not convincing at all.

"How did you get to know her?" I asked.

Aunt Mary sniffed. "Nosy, aren't we?" she said. Then she got a faraway look in her eye. "I knew her in the Far East. But that's all I'll say. You stay 'ere and I'll wash up. Then we can 'ave a glass of port. You're old enough." She coughed and wheezed her way into the kitchen.

My lamp stood on a table by a bookshelf. I removed myself from the table and sat in a small Victorian nursing chair. At the bottom of the shelves lay several photograph albums. I picked one up and began to look at photographs. Lots of photographs of Aunt Mary with different children. Sometimes Aunt Mary with Chinese people. I finished the book and picked up another. The light of the lamp wavered. I felt comfortable in the little room with the fire—red coals with a headdress of fresh black coals waiting to sink into the bright red bed. So eternal was the fire. Each day the ashes gave leave to the new coals which reddened and then gave way again to the black briquets. I hadn't seen a coal fire before. I liked the nose-tickling smell of the coal.

I looked through three books until I came across a picture of a group of middle-aged women with children. One of the women made me pause. I felt an inexplicable affinity with this unknown strange middle-aged woman. She alone wore a cheongsam that fitted her full figure tightly. To say she was beautiful was too trite. She was more handsome, a tall woman with high cheekbones. Black hair fell in a waterfall down her back and her full painted lips smiled at me. "Aunt Mary?" I called. "Who's this woman?"

Aunt Mary shot into the room. She pulled the photograph album out of my hands. "Don't go looking through other people's things," she said.

"I'm sorry," I apologized, "but she reminds me of someone."

Aunt Mary crackled and popped with displeasure. "Just a friend," she said. "A White Russian . . . A long time ago, dear. An awful long time ago."

"What happened to her?" I asked. "She was very beautiful."

"Well," Aunt Mary sighed. "Those women were all kicked out by the Ruskies. They all 'ad an 'ard time of it. They 'ad to make their money any'ow they could. It's all right for me. I was a nanny. Minded my p's and q's. Said 'Yessir, no sir.' But 'er, she did it the 'ard way. She 'ad to. 'Er family croaked in Russia."

"Poor woman," I said.

"Yes," she said softly. "Yeah. She was a goer though." Aunt Mary's eyes shone. "A right goer." Her mouth stopped speaking. I watched her face as it seemed to carry on its own conversation with itself. For a moment her lips smiled. Then her eyes stared into the table and her head shook slightly. She wrinkled her brow . . . Aunt Mary straightened her tilted head, looked back at me and smiled. "Anyway, love, 'ere's the port." She slipped a fat bottle onto the table and she poured two shots of a sticky liquid into two small glasses. "Bottoms up," she said.

"Bottoms up," I said, happily aware my mother would have had a fit if she knew I was drinking port. Only men and prostitutes drank port. She would have had a fit if she knew I was here at all. "Aunt Mary," I said, "why did you ask that we keep my visit a secret, just between us?"

Aunt Mary looked at me sharply. "You'd *better* keep it a secret," she said, "or she'll kill you. Your mother is gone all lah-dee-dah these days. She won't want to know the likes of me."

"Will you ever tell me the truth about my mother?" I asked. The fire was burning down and it cast strange shadows on Aunt Mary's face.

Her face looked old, as the shadows deepened. She almost looked Chinese herself. I felt as if Aunt Mary was hundreds of years old and had been waiting for this day throughout all eternity to sit with me in this room, holding the secret of my mother's origins in her little wrinkled hands. "I 'ope I never 'ave to," Aunt Mary said at last. "There are things that are best forgotten. Not spoken about again. 'orrible things . . . You run along now, and I'll wake you in the morning. Give an old lady a kiss and run along."

I kissed her dry cheek and I took my lamp up the

stairs and climbed into the plump warm bed and fell asleep secure and cozy. I dreamed of the face I had seen. The smile and the warm eyes. Somehow, somewhere, I knew that face and the face knew me.

☙ *Chapter 31* ❧

"*Argaricus disporus.* White button mushrooms," I announced at breakfast.

Aunt Mary sniffed. "Too much education makes your brain rot, young lady."

I was happy. Aunt Mary's house was warm and safe. I knew it was dirty in the corners, and the teapot had a perfectly awful cozy with a bobble on the top, but the tea was hot and steaming, the bacon on my plate curled around a fried egg, and the little juicy mushrooms were excellent.

Aunt Mary was in a philosophical mood. " 'ow's your dad doing? 'e's ever such a nice man. I remember when 'e and your mum met in South Africa."

"But last night you said you used to know my mother in the Far East?"

"Did I say that? Well, I did."

"But you were just talking about Africa . . ."

"Was I?"

"Aunt Mary . . ."

Her face was red as if she'd been caught whispering a secret. "All right, child. Don't scold. Yes, I knew your mum in Africa as well. When your dad, 'e fell in love with your mum when 'e was a young man, and 'e went off to university in England and came 'ome and 'e looked 'er up and that was that. 'e went into the Foreign Office and they got married. I'll tell you, tongues wagged till they nearly fell off. There's no mystery to that."

"Really?" I was interested. "Then you *do* know about my mother's past."

Aunt Mary nodded. "But I promised not to tell. A person's past belongs to them. If they want to make changes, they can. But I've no business interfering."

I sighed. "Maybe if I knew more about her I'd understand her better."

Aunt Mary shrugged. "I don't know about that," she said. "Life's a matter of choices. You can do good or evil, or maybe nothing at all."

"I suppose so," I said.

"Anyway, how time flies! And we have to get you to the train. Hurry up."

I collected my suitcase and we left the little house with its narrow stairs. I washed that morning in the bowl in my bedroom. Aunt Mary filled the jug with boiling water. I felt very secure and permanent. Aunt Mary was self-sufficient. I could see into the back garden and behind the roses stood a small plot of tomatoes and cabbages, carrots, beetroot, and other vegetables. Even the mushrooms, she told me, were collected on Acton Green. "I've been collecting mushrooms since I was a child. You 'ave to know where to look. All this welfare makes people lazy. Worst day's work ever done when old Nye Bevan promised to look after the bastards from the cradle to the grave."

This homily was delivered at the top of her voice in the bus. "In the old days," she bellowed, "neighbors took you in, not snotty social workers." I prayed there were no social workers on the bus.

We alighted, Aunt Mary and I, on the station. Victoria was always my favorite station. The huge trains puffed and complained. Aunt Mary insisted on coming through the barrier and escorting me right to the train. In fact, she climbed in to inspect my cabin. I felt embarrassed. Here I was, a young girl in a first class cabin, and Aunt Mary had to struggle to live decently. Suddenly I felt very awkward. "The Foreign Office pay," I said defensively.

Aunt Mary put her hand on my shoulder as the train gave a warning hoot. "Who would 'ave thought," she said, "that all these years later . . . Lavinia's daughter!"

"That sounds better than being the Consul General's daughter," I said. "Though not much." I was apprehensive about seeing my mother again.

Aunt Mary smiled. "You have a place with me," she said. She put her finger on the side of her nose. "Keep it to yourself," she said, and she kissed me a dry rustling kiss.

I put my arms around her surprisingly small frame and felt immensely comforted. "I would really like to stay with you again," I said.

"You will," she promised. "I'll see to that."

The train gave a jerk and my aunt flew out of the door clutching her bag. As the train chuffed slowly out of the station, my aunt ran alongside shouting goodbyes. She ran so fast she stayed beside me until the edge of the platform.

I thought about Geneviève and how our lives had changed. I saw little of Geneviève now. At school she had her own set of girls. They were very aloof and very sophisticated. They thought of Phoebe and me as country bumpkins. But I was happy to be seen that way. Geneviève was spending the holidays in Spain with a member of the Spanish Royal Family. I was going home to the people I loved: my father, Patrick, and Mademoiselle and Jacques . . . I so wanted to include my mother in the list, but dare I? Now I felt I had other people to love also: Phoebe's whole family, and Aunt Mary. I thought of her as I went to sleep. Clackity clackity. My own Aunt Mary.

Chapter 32

I arrived at the Gare du Nord. The car, with yet a different chauffeur, awaited me. I used the word *awaited* because I was reading a book about Queen Elizabeth I. I admired her immeasurably. She also looked very like Phoebe, or Phoebe looked like her, as her people were Plantagenets. Ruth said that some of her people were on the Mayflower. Phoebe said that most of the people on the Mayflower were criminals or insane, which miffed Ruth dreadfully. Ruth always tried to pretend she wasn't Jewish, which I thought was very silly. Along with my Bible from Jerusalem (a present from my father, with a real olive wood cover) I also had a box made from cedar that smelled gorgeously when I opened it. That box was my new hiding place for my letters from Patrick.

I sat in the car and watched familiar streets flow by my goldfish bowl. I felt very much like a criminal must feel on his way to prison. I did have Patrick.

The streets were busy in the summer sunshine. Already the end of July, August was a hiatus between the world of summer and the long cold days of winter. August was an odd month for me. It was the month my mother had her birthday. I had packed in my suitcase a runner I had sewn for her. I did tell Miss Standish that, in spite of all our hard work, my mother could not admire anything I made.

I felt, as we reached the house, that life was harder now I had known freedom. Other people lived differently, and my mother scorned their lives, but now I knew that Bridie Balfor, in her careless but fond love of her children, was more the sort of mother I wanted. And Aunt Mary, in her little house, was a place that offered me respite. The doors opened and Barzon the butler smiled at me. "Lunch," he said, "is served."

My suitcases passed me on their way to my bedroom. I started to think of a way to get my cedar box, stockings, garter belt, and the nail polish out of the suitcase before my mother got into my room. "I'm going upstairs," I said, "to change my dress." And I raced up to my room with my keys in my hand.

I tore off the first layer of my open suitcase and hid the offensive objects under my mattress, which was not very nice, but immediate.

"So you're home."

"Yes," I said. "I'm just changing. It was a hot crossing."

"Oh. It's been very cool here."

"Well, it wasn't on the boat."

"Aren't you going to kiss your mother?"

I looked at her and hesitantly pecked her cheek, half waiting—hoping—for her to turn towards me and hug me. Instead her form remained stiff. (How silly, I thought, to dream of it being otherwise!) Evidently her feelings to me had not warmed in absence. And hugging never had been her style. I retreated from her cheek.

She stood, her eyes raking my body. "We are waiting to start lunch," she said.

"All right," I said, remembering that *okay* was American and everything American was considered rude and vulgar. "I'll be down in a minute." I felt the tension ease as I watched her back glide down the hall. If she took the first two steps down the stairs, she would not come back. She took the first two steps. I sighed with relief.

Quickly I removed my bundle of belongings and the box to my cupboard. My ring I put in its familiar place, and the rest I pushed between the two boards at the bottom of the *armoire.* A false bottom, thank goodness, had been put in hundreds of years ago, and for whatever reason the carpenter found the need to create a safe place, all those years later I blessed him.

"Well, Pumpkin," my father said when he saw me. "You look marvelous."

I hugged him tightly, remembering how much I had missed him.

"Where did you get that dress?" My mother's eyebrows were creased.

"I made it," I said. "Miss Standish says I'm one of the best dressmakers in the school."

"Really? How odd. Loosen the belt. You're far too young to wear a belt that tight."

"Darling," my father intervened, "she's only just arrived. Shall we worry about that sort of thing after lunch? My soup's getting cold."

The lunch was perfect, but I was now used to good food cooked simply. The fish that followed the soup was smothered in a white wine sauce. How I missed the fresh trout caught by Jeremy or Charlie, brought fresh to the meal and fried in butter, only a sprig of fresh parsley and a wedge of lemon embellishing its natural flavor. Suddenly the excellent French cuisine seemed *de trop*. I politely declined the pudding.

"On a diet, dear?" My mother laughed and then she leaned forward and smiled her confusingly warm smile. "This summer," she said, "you and I are going shopping. You are old enough to have a wardrobe, a proper wardrobe, because now you are old enough to attend functions with us. We have a busy summer this year. Not many people have left Paris for the summer, and of course there is my birthday. We must both look lovely for that."

"Yes, Pumpkin," my father agreed. "You and I must choose a present. Your mother is going to have a very big garden-party."

"Lovely," I said, unsure what to make of my mother's instantaneous and apparent change of mood.

The fitting for the dresses proceeded quickly because the dressmaker had our dummies already, but I had put on two inches around my hips and bust. I didn't like the dressmaker much. Madame Gio ran her hands slowly over my breasts and then over my hips. She always did that. She looked at me in a funny way. I stared back. She did the same to my mother, but my mother chatted away happily. She seemed to enjoy being touched by the dressmaker.

Madame Mauriac, the milliner, was quite different, as was the shoemaker Madame leChèvre. But Madame Gio the dressmaker had always made me feel uncomfortable. And Madame Gio made not only my mother's dresses but also her underwear.

My mother shocked me on this occasion by stripping off her dress, her slip, her brassière and her pants. She stood quite naked in front of me, getting measured. On previous visits I had been told to leave, but now she stood there smiling at my face which was rapidly turning crimson. "You have to grow up some time," she said. She lifted her arms and put them behind her head.

Madame Gio measured her, and when she measured her between her legs, I thought I'd faint. "My daughter has learned English bashfulness," my mother said. The dressmaker laughed and they shared a look that excluded me completely. It was the same look that Geneviève shared with her friends.

My mother had a chameleon's ability to change herself into so many different people. With the dressmaker she was light and flirtatious. With Madame Mauriac, she was very businesslike. I got a little hat that sat on the back of my head. "To show off your pretty little face," said the milliner.

Madame leChèvre welcomed me back. I was allowed to have a pair of shoes with a small heel. Closed in, of course. No such luck that I could have a pair of shoes with my toes peeping out. My mother ordered for herself a red pair of snakeskin shoes. The skin she chose from a rack of skins. The red snake must have been beautiful, and the black skin beside it contrasted with the shiny red and looked really evil but exciting. We were out sooner than I had expected and finally home.

A week for delivery and then the car brought home the dresses swathed in billowing clouds of white tissue, the shoes pristine in yellow boxes banded in green stripes, and the hats each in its own bright pink hatbox. My mother's underwear also arrived and I demurred looking at it. "But," my mother said, "it's a work of art."

"Underwear is private," I said, thinking of Miss Standish's standards of modesty.

All week long the telephones went. I was relegated to answering telephones and checking the boxes that piled through the door. My mother's new secretary was away on holiday, so I was the substitute. Thank heavens the invitations had been sent out ages before. Sending out hundreds of invitations by hand (of course) was an onerous job. All the lists they required . . . Checking all the decorations of all the different nationalities was a nightmare. Every time I got a whole batch ready, several of the guests got extra decorations or knighthoods. My mother was all of a twitter because the Marquise de Verdier Boudilliou had accepted, and if *she* accepted, everyone accepted. I had to learn how to curtsey.

Fortunately I had learned to curtsey at school. We all had to practice in case we met the Queen. Left knee behind right knee, and then down gracefully with a straight back. It took an awful lot of practice and Phoebe was dreadful at it. She had met the Queen anyway and said she was so excited she completely forgot to curtsey. Bridie only laughed. My mother wouldn't laugh, so I practised furiously. The thought of going down to the ground and then falling over in a heap at the Marquise's feet worried me dreadfully.

The acceptances flooded in. My mother ordered Maine lobsters. "Why Maine?" my father asked.

"Because Maine lobsters are the best," my mother said.

Sides of salmon from Scotland, Arbroath herrings, oysters, pheasants, Guinea fowl . . . The amount of food seemed enormous. The cook hired a *sous chef* and told me to go away. I lived in a maelstrom of place-settings. Drinks and hors d'oeuvres were to be served. The weather was too unsettled to risk a full dinner. Two hundred guests were invited and one hundred and seventy five accepted. My mother was ecstatic. I was glad that she invited the Johnsons because I'd see Patrick. And of course Geneviève would be there. My mother refused to invite Mademoiselle and Jacques. "One couldn't do that to them," she said. "They would be fearfully embarrassed. It would be too cruel."

I hadn't even had time to telephone them, I'd been so busy. But I vowed I'd collect a plate of delicious food and hide it in my room before the servants took all the left-overs home, and then visit them both with the food, and I'd see my namesake Marie. Personally I didn't for one minute think either of them would be at all embarrassed.

My mother selected the music for the evening. We had a very famous quartet coming to play. I was fond of Mozart, and I loved Tchaikovsky. But my mother had put Tchaikovsky on her vulgar list.

I overheard my mother talking to Mrs Biddle, the American cheek-pincher. Apparently Melitta, the Australian Ambassador's wife, was having "an affair." I pretended I wasn't listening. I was on my hands and knees on the floor, checking out the place-settings. My mother giggled. "Richard's awfully naughty. He says he did it for a dare. Melitta's been meeting him at the George Cinq."

How awful, I thought. I like the Australian Ambassador. He was a very kind man, and I remembered his children. I found myself wondering if my mother had affairs. I couldn't imagine any man other than my father in bed with my mother. And she seemed to disdain all things visceral. She even thought dogs' bottoms were rude. Taiwan was all right. Anyway he was Chinese Royal Family with a vast pedigree covered in winners.

I had a new collar for Taiwan. I made it at school in the book-marker class. I was going to give it to him on the night of the party because my mother said he had to be locked in the study. She said someone might stand on him. Poor Taiwan loved parties, and I knew he'd whine miserably all night. But I could climb in the window and see that he had so much to eat that he'd be busy all night. He rather fancied lobster and there were plenty of those.

On Friday morning, August 5, the house filled with people. My mother hired a special flower arranger who arrived with six florists and screamed instructions at the top of his voice. The girls scurried here and there carrying boxes and baskets of flowers, ferns, and green moss. The caterers arrived with all the plates, knives and forks, to say nothing of a jungle of glasses. Only the top two tables received our own personal plate and silver. Everybody else was considered below the salt. Of course my mother was so popular that, even though she was only the Consul General's wife, people fought to attend. Her table was famous, her food the talk of Paris, and what she would wear a matter for the newspapers to discuss the next day. Fortunately our Ambassador was her personal friend. His wife was a frump, and the Ambassador's parties even frumpier. My mother made fun of her, but my father was not amused. "She may be a frump to you," he said, "but Vanessa has one of the finest minds in England."

"Well, you might want to talk to the finest mind in England," was my mother's reply, "but would you want to sleep next to it all night?" I was amazed to hear my mother say something so forthright in front of me.

My father said, "You know, the thought never even crossed my mind."

My mother gazed back at him. And then she turned and left the room. "Come on, Mary," she said. "We have to see how the marquees look."

They looked lovely. Big white ships. And they billowed and they groaned as they were hauled by the men who strained and tugged and swore as they pulled. Now they were obediently awaiting the next day's events.

My father and I went to Asprey's and chose a ring, an eternity ring made with sapphires, although my mother's birthstone was sardonyx and her flower gladiolus.

In a final burst of effort, we finished the place-settings, slipped them into their little silver stands, and they stood in silent ranks on the dining room table next to the decanters for port, the sherry decanters, and the wine decanters.

My father instructed the wine waiters to strain and decant the red wine in sufficient time to breathe. He got quite cross with the head wine waiter who was rather superior. "We don't strain wine," the head wine waiter said. "You pour like this." He put a bottle of

Château Lafite up to the light and he gently tilted the bottle. The red wine slipped out of the bottle into the decanter until my father, with a grunt, saw the sediment in the bottom of the bottle. The head wine waiter, on loan to us from Madame Derlanger's household, looked down his nose. *"Quels imbéciles,"* he muttered under his breath, *"les anglais."*

We were all tired. I went to bed exhausted. Taiwan, knowing his fate, spent the night with me in protest. "Never mind," I said. "I'll see you get plenty of lobster, and I'll see Patrick tomorrow." With that thought in mind, I fell asleep.

❧ *Chapter 33* ❧

As if by magic, all the caterers, all the black and white flower arrangers, all the packing cases, and all the straw evaporated. Now the wine waiters stood to attention. Madame Derlanger's waiter still looked as cross as a rusty pair of old scissors. He was an Ambassador's wine waiter, and our house was not a patch on the Ambassador's house. The Derlanger wine cellar was a huge oasis of cool sensibility. I loved their wine cellar. Geneviève and I often sneaked down there among the cradled bottles of wine, Geneviève picking the best for rendezvous with various boyfriends. We, alas, owned a wine store-room with a temperature control mechanism, but what we had to offer was next to nothing compared not only to a true warren of a wine cellar but also to the Derlanger family château that produced the Derlanger family wine, bottled on the estate and crested with the family name. No wonder the wine waiter looked put out.

Poor Taiwan, elderly and miserable, was incarcerated in the library. I kissed him and put a full plate of chicken and a nugget of lobster before him. He gave me a very Chinese look of "I'll dine now and whine later." I knew he would. Hopefully the quartet already warming up would drown Taiwan's complaints.

Flowers arrived. The English Ambassador's wife sent roses. Sir Robert, the Ambassador, had always been a favourite of hers, and my mother usually reduced Lady Carpenter to a pool of green jealous fury. They had a son Myles, my age, and I knew that my mother's greatest wish was to see me married off to Myles. Poor Myles. He was goonish and pimpled and he gargled at the back of his throat. Certainly we discussed literature and poetry with great enthusiasm. He was a very bright scholar and wanted to be a writer, as did I. But he did not have the simple happiness in life that Patrick had, nor did he have Patrick's huge happy family. I longed and thirsted for family life. Myles seemed to be a tragically doomed poetic figure writing poetry up at Cambridge, now at the Sorbonne, quoting Sartre and smoking Gitanes furiously. Patrick thought the nihilist movement a lot of bosh.

I was torn, but I had no time to consider or philosophize. The afternoon stretched eagerly out for the night's events, and I had to change into my new and, for the first time, acknowledged position of the *grown-up* daughter of the Consul General. I was no longer a girl; I was *une jeune femme*. Tonight, though the party belonged to my mother, the night was mine.

After the bath and the powder and the perfume, I looked at myself in the mirror. I wore my red garter-belt and my first pair of nylon stockings. Thanks to Maximillian's cooking and my happy days at school, I had lost my nervous thinness and my bones were covered. I turned before the mirror to see a fluid line of fair flesh run down my body, and my thighs and bottom now looked more like that of a woman's body rather than the original bedraggled Bergen-Belsen body that greeted me in the old days before I met Mademoiselle and Jacques. They would not be there to see their own Pygmalion-creation, but when I saw them, the re-telling would be all the sweeter.

My dress slipped over my petticoat in a swish of lace and silk. For once the low cut of the dress emphasized the fact I did have the beginning of a budding bosom. The dress was white with a narrow waist and a voluminous skirt that swung and swayed with a myriad of net skirts pricking at my stockinged legs. Then came the pleasure of sliding my feet into my first high heels. I turned slowly and then faster and faster, until like a dervish divining the future through trance I whirled and twirled around the room faster and faster until breathless I had to stop. I collapsed on the carpet in front of the mirror, my cheeks flushed with unaccustomed color and my eyes sparkling.

I must go downstairs, I thought. I must join the evening. I must be who I am, this person who so politely stands and sits and dances with the assembled guests: the men in black tie, since this was a private party, and the women in fierce competition with each other, the cut of a dress or the glint of a diamond or the knot of pearls indicating at a practised glance the wealth and seniority of the wearer. I much preferred to remain in my room and imagine the night. If the night existed in my telling of it, how much more imagination, how much more vivid the night could be! A drowsy romantic haze in my head encapsulated the evening, the music, the food, the soft flowing clothes . . . I swaying in time to the waltz with Patrick, his hands brown from the summer sun. The clean smell of him. Others pass by our oblivion and the night goes on into the soft dawn and we gravely kiss each other goodbye, softly, secure in our permanence together . . .

But the reality was my mother's nervous knock on the door. "Hurry," she hissed. "The Derlangers are here." I sighed. Life would be so much more satisfactory if most of it were lived like St Theresa in a nunnery.

I hurried and joined my mother and my father by the door that opened to allow the guests to gust in, bringing with them shreds of mist and the smell of the city in August.

Quickly Madame Charpentier—our large hidden housekeeper, a creature of the other side of the green baize door—took the coats, the little box jackets, several silver foxes in terminal agony biting their tails and gazing beaded-eyed at the crowds of guests who arrived all at once. My face was frozen into a welcoming smile and my hand shook other hands with a separate will of its own.

My mother whispered instructions. "That is Madame Mercier, wife of the French First Secretary. Remember Monseigneur Salvator? Representative of the Papal Court . . ." I was pleased to see the Russian Ambassador. His was a friendly warm face. And in came the Yengs, the Communist representatives now to Paris. Both smiled warmly and Dr Yeng always took time to ask after my doings in England. "You must visit China," he said this time.

"I'd love to, Dr Yeng," I said. "I'd really love to. My grandfather lived there many years ago."

"It has changed," he said.

"My grandfather said China needed to change."

My mother hissed, "Mary, we have other guests to greet." My mother hated Communists, unlike my father who told me stories of the poverty and the starvation of millions of people. My mother didn't like Dr Yeng for reasons that were not clear to me, and the Yengs wandered off into the crowd.

They were replaced at the receiving line by Scot and

Melitta, the Australian Ambassador and his wife. Melitta was slim, no longer pregnant. Charlotte, her eldest daughter, was referred to as "Charlotte the Harlot" by Geneviève's set, but for all that gossip I liked her, and Melitta grinned as she took my hand. "Bloody boring, all this fancy dress, isn't it?" she said.

I nodded, casting a nervous look at my mother. Ever since Madame Derlanger told my mother Charlotte was not a virgin, my mother forbade me spending time with Charlotte, and she had invited Charlotte this evening only out of duty. My mother behaved as if loss of virginity was catching, like measles. I promised myself I'd find Charlotte later.

Then Patrick arrived. Derrick and Sally Johnson looked different from the other guests. Not any less expensive, but different. Watching them remove their coats and walk up to the bottom of the staircase where we stood, I realized that most of the guests were not only here tonight as themselves but as representatives of their countries, or churches, or the Army or the Navy or the Air Force . . . What was comforting about Derrick Johnson was that he was just Derrick Johnson, a businessman, and Sally was just Sally, his wife. My father was sometimes my father, sometimes a Consul General, a representative of the Queen of England. The Soviet Ambassador was a father, but also supposedly representing a Communist country in at least ideological conflict with our country. But here he was, partying with the enemy, laughing, joking, and teasing my father who laughed with him. But I saw a watchfulness in my father's eyes and heard a restraint in his voice as they joked.

I also knew that at parties such as this there were some people who were here to whisper a message or slip a piece of paper into a sympathetic hand. Perhaps a passport into a pocket. The difference was that Derrick and Sally Johnson could enjoy this complicated multi-layered diplomatic life one step removed. Derrick was able to sip his martini, the black olive innocent of espionage, while Dr Yeng watched the crowd around quietly. He sipped orange juice uncorrupted by alcohol, and he watched while his country sprawled, painfully evolving a new direction. He watched the glitter and the careless wealthy, immune to poverty, unacquainted with starvation.

I saw Patrick and now, most of the guests accounted for, my father called for silence and a toast. A hush settled on the crowd and they all turned towards my mother who stood beside me. I was taller now than she, and my white dress contrasted with her black-beaded evening gown. The long bugle-beads gleamed blue, purple, and black. My mother's hair also gleamed, piled high on her head. The neck of her gown swooped down and plunged between her breasts. She smelled of musk, a smell that made my nostrils quiver. "A toast," my father said, "to my wife." Glasses lifted and the toast repeated across the great white marble hall. The well wishes bounced off the walls and people mingled and talked, many moving out to the marquees in the garden.

I, grateful that the welcoming ordeal had gone smoothly, slipped off to find Patrick. I knew it was my daughterly duty to lurk on the sidelines and rescue obscure wall-flowers, but tonight I was unwilling to discuss Camus, such a pale shadow beside Hermann Hesse. I was unwilling to chatter with other daughters. I wanted to be me, not a puppet obedient to strings pulled tightly. So I slid off quietly. Patrick and I slipped into the dining room and took a chair each at a table.

The lights were still dim in the dining room, the tables laden with hors d'oeuvres. Outside in the hall guests chattered, waiters passed trays of cheese-puffs, small edible sharp-tasting food to make the gastronomic juices flow quickly. Here in the silence Patrick whispered, "I missed you," and his words were echoed in the baccarole now played by the quartet who, for the moment, were housed in a corner of the hall.

"I missed you, too," I said, and we held hands in the silence. Prawns hung pink and succulent, their whiskey heads buried in a tangle of green lettuce drowned in pink sauce in front of me. We gazed at each other intently. I looked into Patrick's eyes, blue like my own. His face so open and loving. "My mother is sending me away after O-levels," I reminded him.

"You said so in your last letter." Patrick smiled. "Anyway, a good finishing school will make a lady out of you," he laughed. "You can make me meringues and darn my socks." He didn't seem to be taking the prospect of my year's absence from his life very seriously.

"I'll be gone a whole year," I said.

"I know, but I'll have to do my time in London, and then we can be married and go to Hong Kong. You'd hate London on my salary." He squeezed my hand. "You'll be doing O-levels next year, and then a year away, and then we will be together for the rest of our lives."

"Well, that's wonderful." I looked at him, dear dependable Patrick. An ocean of peace and tranquility stretched out in front of me.

I heard Barzon declaim through the door, "Dinner is served," and we crept out of the dining room through the servants' door. I slipped past a closed door and whispered my apologies to Taiwan who was making miserable abandoned sounds in the library.

My father led the procession with the British Ambassador's wife on his arm, followed by my mother. I was escorted by the next ranking guest and we fluidly, with years of practice, led the guests in a precise and orderly flowing stream of people into the dining room where each chair claimed a bottom chosen by protocol, that demon of our lives. I thought of the hours and days that I spent in my mother's study working on those little white place-cards, and I breathed a relieved sigh when I saw the guests all sitting in their required order. My one fear was allayed: that of one single mistake, a protest, and then the whole plan suddenly exploding—a Vice Consul seated above his superior, or even worse, a foreign superior, a disaster. By now I was less apt to make mistakes. My mother smiled at me and nodded graciously, and I smiled back. She so far had made no mention of my stockings.

I spent the meal making conversation. My French was more fluent than my mother's, while my father talked of the problems in Algeria. My father had no small talk. He always discussed matters of diplomacy, and he was just as likely to monopolize a guest as he was to interview the dustman, often remarking he learned most of his information from the people in the streets of Paris. My mother was having a good time. She had two bright pink spots on her cheeks. I was glad she was enjoying herself on her birthday.

The night rolled on. Thanks to my mother, and to my own more recently acquired expertise, the night rolled on as if drawn by silken Arab steeds. Dinner finished. Liqueurs in hand, the guests moved around the house. Ladies floated upstairs to powder, while men pushed their chairs back and did whatever men do in the absence of their women, when excellent port is available. With a last look at Patrick, I left and climbed the stairs. Charlotte was in front of me. I took her hand and we ran giggling to my bedroom. I threw myself on my bed. "Isn't it splendid?" I said. "I'll be married to Patrick, and I'll never have to help organize another big dinner like this again."

Charlotte checked her lipstick in my mirror.

"Hmmm." She ran her tongue around her full mouth. "Have you slept with him yet?"

"Of course not. Charlotte, we're not all like you, you know."

Charlotte laughed. She sat down beside me. "Well," she said, "you get them any way you can. I'm in love with Richard Lucas. He's in the Navy, you know." She lay back and sighed, her large breasts trembling, her long arms behind her head.

"What does it feel like?" I asked. "I've read about sex, especially in Hemingway. But does it really feel like that?" I could see our two bodies lying close to each other on my bed, our dresses overlapping with each other, our arms pale moths, and our faces drowned. My hair short and hers so long and brown. Charlotte smiled a lazy smile. I envied her her wealth of knowledge in that smile. Mademoiselle smiled like that when I first met her: the luxurious smile of a woman from whom life has kept no secrets, and to whom men are no mystery. Charlotte was only seventeen, but she was old in her wisdom and knowledge. "What does it feel like?" I asked urgently.

"Sort of nice," she said. "It all depends on the man. If he's a good lover, it's nice. But if he isn't," she wrinkled her nose, "it's horrid."

Nice didn't seem much of a descriptive word for this awesome human pastime. "Nice?" I said. "Is that all?"

Charlotte laughed. "You see, there's so much more to sex than just sex. There is . . . There is . . . Let me see . . ." This interlude was becoming more profitable by the minute.

"What about getting pregnant?"

"Oh that. If you get pregnant, you have to get him to marry you. That's the most usual way to get married. But if he doesn't want to, well, you have an abortion. Geneviève had one."

"Did she really?" I suddenly regretted my estrangement from Geneviève. "Did it hurt?"

"A little," Charlotte said. "But," she shrugged, "she had to do it. Think of the scandal."

I knew we must return to the party. "Are you doing it with this Richard Lucas?"

"Of course. He's in the Navy, so I don't see him that often, but I'm in love. Anyway, I *think* I'm in love." A silence fell between us. We lay satiated with supper and a few glasses of wine. "Maybe," Charlotte said slowly, "maybe I'm in love with love."

"I'm not," I said. "I'm *definitely* in love with Patrick. Let's get back. My mother must be wondering where I am." I didn't tell Charlotte that my mother would have had a fit if she'd found us together.

We joined the tide of women ebbing and flowing down the stairs, secrets shared over powder compacts, moist lipstick, borrowed lunches, teas, discreet suppers. And the knowledge in their eyes shone like so many miners' lamps in deep subterranean tunnels, shone around me while my feeble candle fluttered. The music of a waltz rose to greet us and the library doors stayed firmly closed to Taiwan whose howls were drowned to everyone except me, and finally even to me, as I found Patrick's arms and we danced on clouds over Paris and whispered to each other, while his ring lay cloistered in my secret place both in my room and in my heart.

Late, very late, I let Taiwan out of the library. If he had made a mess I could surreptitiously clean the carpet and absolve him. He was overjoyed to see me, so overjoyed he forgot himself and a wet pool appeared beneath him. I went to the kitchen and on the way I saw my mother's box of chocolates sitting plump and complacent in her chair. Suddenly a huge uncontrollable urge came over me to put one of her chocolates into my mouth. These were liquor-chocolates, dark bitter chocolates filled with the different tastes of monasteries. But I scolded myself. No one touched my mother's chocolates. Even my father knew not to ask. The chocolates were sacrosanct, some ritual from her dim uncertain curtained past.

I returned from the kitchen with the cloth and the urge became stronger. I stood, with Taiwan dancing at my feet, and I listened. The house was silent, slumbering, a deep-breathing animal spent and exhausted after housing so many people. I took the lid off the box and looked at the silent rows of covered chocolates. Yellow-wrapped chocolate or deep red? The yellow chocolates, I knew, had curaçao enclosed in their bittersweet grip. There were three empty holes gaptoothed. Now mine would be the fourth. Would she notice?

I took the chocolate, unwrapped it, put the wrapper down the front of my dress, bit into it and smiled. I extracted a morsel for Taiwan and then I bit down hard and the liquor squirted down my throat, burning slightly. Never before had I been attracted to sweets or chocolates, but somehow the illicit knowledge that these were my mother's forbidden chocolates, and here I stood alone with my guilty secret shared only by Taiwan, made me feel a merging with the sweetness in my mouth. I picked up Taiwan and left the library. The box of chocolates neatly closed, raped, my fingers would not tell. Taiwan was certainly my ally. The wrapper, somewhere in the sewers of Paris. My secret lay silent. I slept peacefully dreaming of my new life.

Chapter 34

Before I began my "new" life I had two major things to do. One was to go to say goodbye to Jacques and Mademoiselle. The other was to go back to school, take eight O-levels, and say goodbye to Miss Standish.

Phoebe, after loud arguments with Bridie, agreed to attend Mont St Sebastian, the finishing school my mother had chosen for me. "Why should I go to a finishing school?" I also argued.

"Because," my mother said sharply, "you need to be finished." We were sitting at the dining table. My mother, three days after her birthday party, was still litanizing and itemizing the whole event. My father sat nodding his head and murmuring "yes, dear". Now, with the hint of dissension in the air, he put down *The Times* and looked at me.

"I just want to marry Patrick," I said. "I don't want to go to a finishing school. And neither does Phoebe. She wants to breed horses. What's that got to do with being finished?"

My mother sighed. "Mary," she said. "Sometimes life is not what it seems." I stopped. There was a soft look in her eyes, as if she were looking backwards over many years. "No, dear," she said quietly. "You might be surprised at what life has in store for you. This is only a year out of your life. At Mont St Sebastian you'll learn to cook properly and to sew. Anyway, you're too young to marry, Mary. To even understand what marriage is really about. You've always been a romantic. Besides, it'll be a big wedding and will take a year to arrange. Run along now. I have to meet Mrs Biddle for lunch."

My father leaned back in his chair. "Your mother's quite right. I don't want to lose my Pumpkin yet. A year at Mont St Sebastian will make a lady out of you yet." He smiled at me.

Maybe, I felt as I sat there in the cool quiet dining room, maybe one day my mother and I could be friends. On my way upstairs I felt an unfamiliar sense of warmth and then I felt guilty about my mother's chocolate. "I won't do that again," I told Taiwan as he followed me closely up the stairs, his little blonde head bobbing beside me. He looked at me, turning his big brown eyes in my direction and smiling his black leather-lipped smile.

"Do you really think I'm dreadfully romantic, Mademoiselle?" We were in her kitchen, her dear well-remembered kitchen. Baby Marie sat plumply on the floor. Mademoiselle stood stirring a large orange pot of beans. We were waiting for Jacques to arrive home for lunch.

Mademoiselle did not smile, and I suddenly felt I'd been oblivious and selfish. The flurry of my arrival had distracted me from noticing that the little kitchen did not sparkle with cleanliness as it did before. There was a layer of grease on the cooker. The floor under Marie was unclean. The geraniums, while still green, were long and leggy. Mademoiselle had not cut them back this year. A sorrow, a feeling of neglect, filled the room.

"What is wrong, Mademoiselle?" I asked.

"Ah, my child," she said. "Marriage is not a romantic business. For a while, maybe. But when the children come and the bills, they press . . . Romance leaves by the window."

Children, I thought. And then I looked down at Mademoiselle's stomach. Indeed I saw the slight thickening at her waist. "You're pregnant again," I exclaimed.

"Yes," Mademoiselle said. "An accident. We cannot afford another child."

"Didn't you take precautions?" I said. "I know because Phoebe told me . . ."

Mademoiselle smiled a dull, wan grimace. "Jacques didn't want this baby. He works hard as it is. Too hard for too little money. But I am a Catholic."

"I see." And I did see. For me, my faith in God was eternal and I understood so clearly what Mademoiselle was saying. Indeed, it was her passion for life that first had drawn me to her.

"No, Mary," she continued. "This is not an easy time for us. I am always tired and a little sick." She picked up Marie who then sat contentedly on her lap. "We will survive these years, Jacques and I. We will survive because we took the vows . . . Also for Jacques, he is disillusioned. For all his ideas and values, he sees those of his friends who also shared his thoughts slowly become the *bourgeoisie* he so hates." She did smile then. "You see, *chérie*, women are so much more practical than men. For us, it is food-shopping, cleaning . . . Jacques and his friends dreamed of changing the world. I make the food and worry about the butcher's bill. Ah, I hear Jacques on the stairs."

I was appalled when I saw Jacques. He had aged ten years. His once long hair was closely cropped and instead of a large hat and flowing cloak, he wore an ill-fitting brown jacket. His bicycle-clips clung to his thin calves. "Jacques," I said hugging him. "You've lost so much weight."

Jacques held me fiercely. "I know," he said. "It's beans, beans, beans. And more beans."

"Never mind, darling," Mademoiselle said, kissing her husband's cheek. "Today we have your favorite: fresh tomato soup."

The soup was delicious as always. I felt, as I sipped the thick red juice, that I imagined the hours spent by

Mademoiselle making this soup to alleviate somehow the pain in Jacques's thin body, the despair he felt that he could not properly support his wife and his child. And now there would be another child finally to cripple and shackle him to a university he hated and to students who no longer dreamed of a revolution where everyone would have an equal opportunity to share in the wealth. I sat there and felt dreadful. I was a child of plenty. Never for one moment did I contemplate anything less than abundance. I heard myself apologetically explaining that I was going to a school in Switzerland. I explained that I was going to learn to cook.

Both Mademoiselle and Jacques loved me far too much to make fun of me. Before I left and kissed both goodbye, I reached into my bag and took out a big stone jar of black truffles. "I thought you might like this," I stammered. I remembered the empty space in the well-stocked pantry off our kitchen.

Mademoiselle smiled at me. "How we love truffles!" she said. "Thank you, Mary. A treasured treat."

"You will come to my wedding?" I said anxiously and then blushed. "We'll have it in England, at my grandparents' house, but I'll send tickets. I really couldn't get married without you being there. Please," I said. "Please."

Jacques's eyes relented. "Of course," he said. "We'll be there. All four of us." His voice softened and he looked at Mademoiselle. "Monique?" he said, taking her hand. He turned it over and kissed her palm. "Of course, we couldn't miss Mary's wedding. Could we?"

I felt tears rise and a lump in my throat, as the two of them gazed at each other and I knew that they had a bond forged in steel between them that time and circumstance would never break. If only, I thought on the way home, if only Patrick and I could feel the same way about each other. Maybe we did, but I wasn't sure.

Chapter 35

They say when you drown your whole life passes before your eyes. That's how I felt in my last term at school. It was a hot early summer and I had a pretty flowered dress, a present from my grandmother. She wrote, in her incredibly beautiful handwriting:

Dear Mary,

I have been working hard in the garden. I enclose a phial of roses for your bath. I steep rose leaves in mineral oil for three weeks and then I strain the oil and put a few drops in my bath at night. I do hope you never get into that dreadful American habit of shower-taking. The dress, I saw in town and thought of you immediately. Do see that you handwash it. The colors might run.

Mrs Harding tells me that she feels she must retire and take care of her family, all of whom seem to breed without benefit of husbands or the church. Goodness knows why. We have a perfectly run clinic here for that sort of thing, but nobody attends. I know because I do volunteer work. Grandpa gets furious about taxes, and he proposed that all women who are irresponsible in this way should be spayed. The vicar's wife (who is a thoroughly vulgar, modern, little woman) was most upset.

Our other news is that the Lovels are leaving, thank goodness. I think Grandpa's Churchill speeches got them down. Your grandfather is a very determined man. He spent the summer evenings sitting on the lawn with his gramophone playing all his favourites. If it rained, he still sat there holding his London brolly over his head, and dear Ned ran in and out with whiskey sodas. Finally, I think, the Lovels became unnerved. Grandpa did have a bad habit of looming in the bushes with his old Army binoculars. "Just a recce," he explained.

Well, dear, I do know your grandfather very well, but

*I suppose it is difficult for Communists or pinkos to under-
stand our very British way of life. Anyway, they're going
and I do hope this time we get nice neighbors. I am looking forward to half-term and your visit.*

All my love,
Grandmother
PS (Grandfather says to enclose ten shillings and a hug.)

I loved my grandmother's letters nearly as much as I
loved Patrick's. His were usually short. He was in London. A year ahead of me, he had passed all his exams,
except chemistry, and now was working for the London office of the British Oriental Bank (called *the Bob*,
he told me, by its employees).

*. . . By the time I'm finished here you will be a respectable
finished young lady. Then I'll have to mind my P's and
Q's. If you get cross with me, you can talk German and
I'll not understand. But you will never be cross with me
because I'll give you no cause.*

*Oh, Mary. We will be so happy together. I'm longing to
live with you every day of my life, to get up with you in
the morning, and to hold you and kiss you whenever we
like. I love you, Mary. I must stop though. I have stacks
of books to read, loads of Banking Information. And
however hard and dull it is, you make it all worthwhile.*

SWALK
Patrick

Letters like this increased the sense of drowning.
What was I doing, learning all these useless facts? Why
should I care if a triangle wished to isoscelize itself or
have an acute problem with any angle? Let them fight
it out together and leave me in my watery grave, lying
on my back like poor Ophelia, clutching my flowers
and gazing heavy-lidded up and up until I saw the

trees and the grass and the faces of my childhood:
Sam, Max, Françoise, my mother and father, John . . .
And then I surfaced and came back to earth again.

"About bloody time, too," Phoebe grumbled.
"You've been mooning about again. One of these days
you'll go off forever."

I smiled. Indeed my mooning was a source of great
irritation to most of the teachers at Sherwood Park.
I'd sit at the back of the class, my eyes rolled to the
top of my head, and I'd be gone. Far away, to my real
world inhabited by my people. Only Miss Standish could keep me in this world. I was too frightened of
her to disappear. "I am jolly pleased with you, Mary,"
Miss Standish said in the last week of term. "Jolly
pleased. I see both your parents—"(she emphasized
the "both")"—are coming to the fête."

"Yes." And I scuffed my shoes and gazed at them
as they stood to attention. My left shoe-lace was full
of knots. By comparison, my right shoe was quite respectable. All this observation kept my mind from
dealing with the unpalatable fact that within a week
my mother would be here and my Golgotha, my sta-
tions of the Cross, would begin. "Please," I had written to my father, "please get mummy to wear sensible
shoes and ask her not to wear a Paris hat . . ."

"Mary, do sit down." Miss Standish's sympathetic
hand took mine. She had a warm, plump, comforting
hand, and I sat. And then I became enveloped in the
smell of Tiptree's strawberry jam and then (Oh great
answer to prayer!) a Fuller's walnut cake. For me, a
bite of Fuller's walnut cake was far more erotic than
all the sex and the smut the girls discussed in dark corners. Phoebe and I, on pocket-money day, as a special
treat always bought a Fuller's walnut cake. And here
it was without Phoebe, so I could eat it slowly and
enjoy the magic moment when the cake and the walnut
melt into your mouth like the trickle of happiness with

a promise at the end of the bite of more to come. But first, of course, we had brown slices of bread and butter and the Tiptree jam, and the little pips lodged neatly between my teeth. "I'm awfully pleased to tell you," said Miss Standish, "that you have won the Hawthorne-Davies prize for literature." I glowed. For once, my mother would be proud of me. "You know, Mary," Miss Standish continued, "you really could become a writer if you wanted to."

"Really?" I sat up. "My father writes, but I never really thought about a career. I've always wanted to get married to Patrick and have six children and maybe do some writing on the side."

Miss Standish laughed. "Really, Mary," she said. "You are an old-fashioned child. Well, maybe you're right. There's nothing wrong with loving a man and having his children. You know," she said, "long ago I loved a man, but he was killed at the end of the War. I could never contemplate marriage to another man. A part of me died, too."

So, I thought, that was the picture of a handsome young naval officer on her desk.

Miss Standish paused and then looked at me. "*Gels* like you are my reward, and I want you to promise that you will keep in touch with me. I have a special fondness for you." I was touched, deeply touched, because I knew that was true. "Especially," Miss Standish continued, "if you are in any trouble."

I smiled. "I'll be fine, Miss Standish. I'll always be happy. Phoebe and I go off to finishing school, but then you must come to my wedding."

"I'd love to." And we sat together with the early evening sun drawing pinks and blues from the garden into the room. Silently and companionably we ate our cake and I left after giving Miss Standish a longer-than-usual kiss on her soft-skinned cheek.

Maximillian was in a good mood later that evening. "Well," I said, shaking the lettuce in a large muslin bag. "I have to go to finishing school . . ."

"Have you picked the lettuce over?" Maximillian interrupted. "Last time there was a great green caterpillar crawling about the salad bowl on number seven table. Miss Morgan screamed and insulted me in French. *'Oh, là! Mon petit fromage,'* I said, but she was wild." Maximillian sniffed. "Women." He stuck his nose in the air and put his hand on his waist and pranced up and down the kitchen.

"We're not all like that," I said.

"Ohhhh, getting ratty, are we?"

"Where are you going for half-term?" I asked wickedly, knowing the answer.

"My mum's, of course."

"Precisely," I said. "Your mum's." We stared at each other, Maximillian and I. For the years I'd known Maximillian, his one sure topic of conversation was his mum. Everything he did or said rested on his mum's shoulders. I could see the trap she set for him. No other woman would ever come close to the fierce passionate love she had for her only son. That was Maximillian's sadness. These were the lines in his ageing face. Some days his perverse sense of humor kept me in stitches of laughter, but there were other days when he was morose and silent. Today, though, was a jubilantly perverse day. "I really do have to go to Mont St Sebastian," I moaned.

"Well," Maximillian was practical, "I know the chef there. He's very good and very famous. Not our kind, if you get what I mean, but he is a good cook. Learn all you can from him. You know, if you're ever broke you can always cook for a living. Not that any of you spoilt little brats are ever going to be broke. Do it anyway. You'll get through the year faster."

"I suppose so. Do you need any vegetables picked?"

"Yes. Get me a basket of green beans. I snapped one yesterday and they are absolutely ready. Perfection," he said.

I left for the kitchen garden to pick the green beans as they hung in sentinel rows on their obedient vines. Oh why, I thought as I picked, can't people live so calmly? As each bean fell into the basket I thought of my mother's approaching visit. However she looked, my father would gaze at her adoringly and following her little determined figure around the classrooms and into the gym where I, wearing the hugest of navy blue knickers, would have to attempt to jump the horrible mountainous object called "the horse."

The day arrived. I met my parents at the train. After a morning of sitting in town at a tea shop and drinking cups of awful English coffee with skin floating about the cup, we left to drive to the school for lunch and for the fête which marked the end of my life at an English public school. My suitcase was packed, my linen and China again in the tuck box. My luggage stood forlornly by my bed. George and Spice were already back in Ireland, their equine noses wet with my tears.

John MacAllister and his friends worked all week putting up the stalls and laying the matting on the ground for the coconut shy. The local fête was John MacAllister's yearly masterpiece. Once a year John's face beamed from the front page of the local newspaper. But for me, it was nightmare revisited because I had to face the dreaded vaulting horse.

I could feel my mother's eyes on my back. Phoebe always went in front of me. She never had any trouble with this sort of thing. She was so tall, she just lumbered up and sailed over. I saw Bridie out of the corner of my eye and she nodded encouragingly. I started on the long run across the gym. It went on forever. And then I jumped into the air and hit the horse right in the middle. There was an awful silence as the gym mistress gave a rather audible sigh. "Come on, Mary," she said. "Try again."

"Must I?" I pleaded.

"If at first you don't succeed, try, try again."

I walked back to the far end of the gym and tried again. I prayed to God and all His saints to get me over. I soared. I flew. I flopped onto the mat. But I was over. A polite smattering of applause greeted my ears as I slid into my seat next to Phoebe. "Bloody elephant," she whispered.

"Well, at least I got over," I whispered back.

"You may well win a literary prize, Mary," my mother said later in her slightly drawling voice, "but dear me, you did make a spectacle of yourself in the gym."

I hung my head. This time I was wearing my indoor shoes. The webbing made an interesting pattern on my feet. I wished I was wearing nylons because here I was about to leave school and my legs were encased in white kneesocks. Most of the other girls had graduated into nylons and lipstick. Only Phoebe refused both. At least that was her choice. Bridie didn't mind.

"How wonderful!" Bridie said. "Both girls will be able to keep each other company. Mont St Sebastian is an awfully good school."

I could see my mother's eyes glaze over. We were sitting on the great lawn surrounded by other parents. My mother looked madly conspicuous in her latest Paris suit. She had a whirlwind of a hat, black and yellow. I thought every other mother must be looking at us. Most of the mothers wore sensible light tweed skirts with Oxford brogues. Not my mother. She teetered about the three-hundred-year-old lawn on the highest of spiked heels. I was puzzled, because my mother—the arbitrator of fashion and correct living—must have known that it was completely beyond the pale to carve up a lovely lawn with heels like hers. John, I knew, would be furious. I just hoped he was too busy to see us.

The various tents stood puffed out in the mid-summer wind. The grass was stained with the raw hand of the approaching summer's heat. The smell of the beechnuts forming on their trees scented the air. The heavy horse chestnuts nodded their approval. Fathers, including mine, sat back in their chairs. They wore a uniform suit with old school ties: a murmur of years gone past, spent as boys together and then as young men. Addis Ababa, Singapore, Freetown, Elder Dempster. Ships, far places, names that to me were dots on a map but to them meant clubs, cherished seedy bars in Saigon. The feel of books fly-blown, but recording a world now lost. Graham Greene, Somerset Maugham, J. B. Priestley, and Bertie Wooster, my father's favorite character . . .

As fathers sat, mothers swapped notes on recipes or discussed the local flower show. I realized how isolated my mother was. Bridie was exchanging ideas on horse-breeding with Phoebe. "Julius II covered Amy. Do you remember Amy, darling? She was the little Arab mare with a patch over her eye. Beautiful foal. I had to get Joe and Charlie to hold her. The foal got stuck very high up. Had to put their arm up, but we got him out. Nice little stallion."

I didn't need to look at my mother to know her face would be carved from stone. Any sort of biological detail horrified her. I talked to my father about my prize. Oddly enough, Miss Standish gave me a first edition of Oscar Wilde's *Ballad of Reading Gaol*, that agonizing cry from a man who, by now I realized, offended the English establishment and was made to die for it. Maximillian first explained the terrible story to me in the kitchen. I listened in installments as I helped with the cooking. "Na," Maximillian had said. "If you upset the rich in this country, you have to go into exile. Look at poor old D. H. Lawrence. Best bloody writer we got. But he's buried in Yankieland. They won't have him back. Bloody conservatives got memories and bottoms like elephants."

My father, when I asked him about this, agreed rather surprisingly. "England is infamous for hating successful people," he said in that quiet voice of his. "I signed the protest when Priestley was exiled. All he did was to give a few harmless lectures when France fell. He did it to ensure the safety of his family." My father shook his head. "That was a bad business. Very bad. Don't ever become a writer, Pumpkin."

"Actually, Miss Standish said I could be a very good writer."

My father smiled. "You be a good wife and mother, like mummy here." He gazed at her so fondly, she had to smile.

"Well," she said. "Shall we go and see what is happening at the fête?" She said the word *fête* with a French accent. That also made me wince. We were all taught it was extremely non-U to use French words, which were rather suspect things anyway, when good, plain, trustworthy English words were to hand. For all her talk of "lavatories" and "drawing rooms," my mother had an unBritish habit of throwing in the odd French word here or there.

Reluctantly I said goodbye to Phoebe and Bridie, and left their animated discussion and trailed after my mother and father dejectedly.

Fortunately my father was quite good at the coconut shy. He was short and he ran low to the ground. His first ball knocked most of the coconuts off their perches and his second cleared the lot. "I say, old chap. Well done." A beefy Major with a loud blazer stood beside us.

I saw John MacAllister's face. He stood with two of

his friends on the far side of the tent. They had pints in their hands. The Major carried a glass of champagne in one hand and a cigar in the other. "Marvelous day, old fellow," he was muttering. "Perfectly marvelous day." He wandered off into the distance talking to himself.

I could hear John and his friends laughing, and I felt they were laughing at us. Suspended for a moment from the day, I looked down at ourselves. Splendidly earnest parents with clean-cut girls, all standing around a collection of tents: the Women's Institute tent with piles of books, secondhand games, gaudy crocheted mats; the flower tent stuffed with various arrangements . . . All over England at this time of the year, the great British Middle Classes made an attempt to mix with the natives. The great British Middle Classes tried hard, but the natives would have none of it. Except for my father. He took his place in society as his natural right. "John," he said as the laughter died down, "how's the poaching this year?"

"As bad as ever, sir," John replied. He walked over to my father. "We 'ave Irish tinkers this year. They're 'ard to catch."

My mother's nose wrinkled. She was not used to the smell of sweat. She moved away and I looked at her as if through a prism. She alone stood out. Without her world in the Foreign Office, she was the Consul General's wife, a position that had a hierarchical shelf to stand on, a refuge from normal everyday life. The real-world life of Jacques and Mademoiselle. Everyday life: a life where hands were plunged into hot water, raw meat cut by a sharp knife, children bathed, hair washed, meals cooked, worries, bills, sickness, death. None of these things touched my mother. All such things were handled by the servants provided for my mother abroad by the Foreign Office.

Here in England the middle class women were beginning to lose their servants. These women, with a minimum of help, were pitching in and running their big houses and gardens themselves. While John Mac-Allister would never graduate from a cup of tea at a kitchen table, he at least had his territory. But my mother, I realized, had nowhere.

She came from no known family. Maybe my mother was a princess with a tragic background. If she was, no one was telling. But for now the women who attended the fête treated her like a glamorous magpie that had flown into a flock of sparrows by mistake. They ignored her in a very British way. In France, they stared unashamed. In Italy, I was told, they talked volubly. But in England, you simply did not exist. I felt sorry for my mother and spent the rest of the day catching up with news from Paris.

Later, when the stars were out, we took the night train to London. By now Scotland felt like a completely different country. Yorkshire, a place of its own. And then down to the grim towns and cities on the way to London. I fell asleep after a last look at Scotland by moonlight, and I suffered the sadness of leaving such a beautiful country. I missed Phoebe. I missed my friends Miss Standish and Maximillian. "Goodbye, miss," John had said as I left.

"Goodbye, John," I said. "I'll never forget you." And I meant it.

I dreamed of drowning again, deep dark water with lily pads and large monstrous African toads blinking at me with their yellow searchlight eyes and their thick toes gripping, gripping the fleshy lily pads, the yellow flowers beckoning, promising a narcotic death. I felt them pulling and sucking and I remembered no more.

Chapter 36

I sat on the train that took us so efficiently from London to Paris. I wore my Sunday uniform for the last time. In our first class compartment my mother sat in front of me, her legs properly crossed at the ankles. Her brown crocodile hand-made shoes matched her crocodile bag. Each shiny shingle of skin shone rich and satisfied. I swore I could see a cold crocodile eye submerged in the depth of the belly of the bag, but then I was feeling guilty because I had the beginning of a plan forming in my head.

While I waited for the train to puff and pant into the Gare du Nord I wrote a poem. If I was to be a writer at all, I would prefer to be a poet. After all, if I was to be married with children, writing a novel on the corner of a kitchen table was not my idea of a literary life. I vowed that I would never have servants. I would take care of my husband and my children myself. A poem or two written in the early hours of the morning seemed about right. Anyway, I wished to write to Aunt Mary, so I thought I'd enclose the poem, and once I was back in Paris I would telephone her when my mother was out. I was feeling doubly guilty because I hadn't telephoned or written her during the term.

I looked at my father and felt even worse. My plan, I knew, would break his heart. In the dormitory at night all the girls talked constantly about saving ourselves for our husbands. Georgina and Liz were both getting married after they spent a year at St James's Secretarial College. Everyone was green with envy, because Georgina had managed to nab a wealthy farmer. To make matters even more jealous-making, he had a rowing blue from Cambridge. Sandy and Jenny weren't worried because Kenya teemed with a vast amount of eligible bachelors. Jenny had her eye on a district commissioner and Sandy fancied a game warden.

I wasn't jealous at all, because I had Patrick. But I did wonder at the advisability of leaving Patrick on his own for a year. His last letter talked of bottle parties. He said he and the three other chaps who shared his cottage in Drayson Mews had just had a party of their own. "Of course, darling," he said, "even though I danced the night away, I thought only of you." Something stirred in me when I got the letter. I'd never believed smelly Ruth's warnings about other women, nor had I paid any attention to Marian Pool who was going back to Weymouth to be a nurse, God help her patients. Both of them issued evil warnings of what Patrick could get up to after a year in London on his own.

My limited knowledge of sex was mostly thanks to Marian's horrid descriptions. Often I had been kept awake at night listening to the other girls talking about sex. Usually I felt so revolted I lay sleepless, but occasionally I felt a very strange pull and a restlessness between my legs that sent me guiltily to my torch and a textbook. I was sure my excellent performance in exams was a result of not touching myself "there," but putting all that energy into studying and riding horses.

I day-dreamed all the way home with my parents rocking to the rhythm of the train-carriage and the Channel ferry's lilt.

As the car swung into the drive and scrunched that satisfying rich wheel-deep scrunch, I was reminded of the huge gap between the rich and the poor: the rich had money to spend on millions of little white stones that prepared the way from the gates to the massive front door. Barzon the butler took over from the chauffeur, and into the house went my mother's Gucci suitcases and my own tuck-box that looked so crude and innocent beside the elegant suitcases. Aunt Mary and I, I remembered, had jumped off the platform of a big red London bus. She had pushed open her little picket front gate and I had followed her up a narrow bald path to her front door. The house had slumbered until Aunt Mary got the fire going and the lamps lit. Our house was different. Huge bowls of flowers stood about the marble hall. My suitcase and box disappeared up the stairs to my room.

"A sherry, I think," my father said. "Well, Pumpkin, you're with us for a few weeks then off to stay with Lady Carpenter. She will chaperone you for your visit to London. A little treat for you before you go to Mont St Sebastian. Also," he raised his glass, "to a little time with Patrick."

I gazed solemnly at the sherry glass and picked up my own. My mother was drinking Perrier with ice and a twist of lemon. She raised her eyebrows. "I do trust Robert and Vanessa to look after you. They have a wonderful flat in Eaton Gardens. You will be in by eleven every night, won't you, Mary?" I nodded, mesmerized by the color of the pale Spanish sherry. The taste was very very dry. Lunch was about to be served. While we were away the house and servants had a pace of their own, but now we were back there was an electricity and tension in the air. Armand the cook came into the library and handed my mother the menu. "Good," she nodded. "*Carré d' agneau* with *pommes frites.* What shall we drink, dear?"

My father smiled. "A little Perrier-Jouet, I think," he said, "to celebrate Mary's prize."

I was amazed. My mother nodded amiably. "All right," she said.

We sat in the dining room and I felt dreadful. To all intents and purposes we now were a devoted family. During the soup course, my mind flew to the ceiling and gazed down at us. The three of us sat around the table, the daughter and the two people on this earth who claimed to love me. I had begun by now to understand that, for all her swift temper, my mother did love me in her own peculiar way. It was not a way that could be easily understood. She was not a woman that would ever pat a dog or stroke a cat. Babies made her nervous and pregnant women revolted her.

I hadn't even confided my plan to Phoebe. I was just a telephone call away from completing my illicit tryst. All I had to do was to wait for my mother to go out.

I returned my thoughts to the table and told myself I was seventeen and old enough to do as I wished. If I needed to give Lady Carpenter the slip, I just had to telephone Liz who had a flat in Kensington and ask to stay the night. Lady Carpenter, wife of the English Ambassador to France, would never guess at my duplicity. There were many deb balls to attend, and Liz was one of the most famous debs of her year. I could go with Patrick, make an appearance, and then sneak off, arrange to meet Myles Carpenter for lunch at the Savoy River Room, and then saunter back to Eaton Gardens on his arm. No one need know except Patrick and myself.

Later that evening, as I lay in the bath before dressing for dinner, I took stock of myself. Here I was, a virgin. I was not intending ever to sleep with anyone but Patrick, of course. But I was leaving my future husband for a whole year in London, which was a very wicked city. Maybe I should secure my position as Patrick's fiancée and give myself to him before I left. A man never forgets the first woman he sleeps with, Marian Pool told us. "Then you must have a string of men who'll never forget you," said Phoebe. I remember Marian Pool's look of satisfaction. "Yes," she said. "Many of them will lie by their wives for the rest of their lives and always wish they were with me." I felt very envious of Marian. She was awfully good at it.

Anyway, after the bath and a reread of his last letter, I decided it would have to be done. Rather like an end-of-term paper, or swallowing castor oil: the thing to do was to hold your nose and swallow. Well, this principle could easily be applied to Patrick. As to whether I might get pregnant or not, I'd have to let Patrick worry about that. All I had to do was to get him to take me out to dinner then back to Liz's flat and seduce him.

Chapter 37

My plan, to my surprise, worked. Liz was most agreeable. She was away that week, but she said she would leave the key in the geranium pot and I was to make myself at home. We had our flat for the night. Patrick was delighted with the idea that we appear at the Dorchester and then sneak off together for dinner. I didn't explain the seduction bit to him. That had to be my secret. After all, he had to feel he seduced me and took my most precious possession: my virginity. I felt quite magnanimous about all this. At the end of the day, I reasoned, you can only give it away once. A bit like a Christmas card. On Christmas day it's there; by the day after Christmas it's gone.

Anyway, I was longing to see what it was all about, to understand why Hemingway felt the earth move, why D. H. Lawrence carried on like a man possessed. As for *Gone with the Wind* . . . Well, soon I'd be a different Mary Freeland. I would have carnal knowledge. That did sound exciting.

As soon as I arrived in London I posted my letter to Aunt Mary.

Dear Aunt Mary,
I will pop in to see you before I leave for Switzerland.
I am here for a week, staying in London, saying goodbye
to my friends. I wrote a poem because I won a prize for
literature at school, and I decided I want to be a poet.
Here it is. I don't like the end much, but some of it is
quite good.

THE END OF CHILDHOOD

Seen backwards and down long tunnels
of green bracken, unrolling fingertips
touch my body from adolescent years,

Silken ropes of bougainvillea seen
as my eyes first opened in Africa.
Dark shadows stain my memories.
Raised voices, the crack of a hand
on my stinging face, the shriek
and a lonely sob, all fade away
as I look forward to life ahead.

Marriage beckons, its beautiful
bridal veil of mystery.
Children will beam at my table,
my husband not yet known
but grown into perfect love.
All my childhood years
slip down the byways of life.

I see with my eyes awake
the jewelled road, emerald inlaid with pearls,
my future secure, a love for me
for my sake.

You can see the end is a mess, but I am so really happy,
Aunt Mary. Expect a call from me by the end of the week.
Then I go back to Paris to pack and I'm off to be a proper
lady. There is little hope for me, but none at all for
Phoebe.

Love,
Mary

I posted the letter at Victoria Station and caught a taxi.
I had always very much liked my hostess, Lady Carpenter, and Myles was fun. I didn't see much of Sir
Robert. He seemed to be fairly permanently at his
club. Their flat in Eaton Gardens was marvelously
comfortable. One took a lift to the top floor of what
must have been an amazing mansion. At the back of
the drawing room was a balcony that looked over the
greenest green lawn. There we had supper served by
Chinese servants. Myles was in a teasing mood. "So,
you've come all the way to London to see old Patrick,
huh? Well, you needn't worry, mother. I shall chaperone Mary the whole week. Stick to her like a burr. He
shan't get his dastardly fingers on an inch of her white
body. I'll see to that."

"Myles," I said, "stop it."

"All right. I will."

Trying to change the subject, I joked, "Whatever
happened to your existential angst?"

"Gave it all up," Myles laughed. "Existentialism,
bohemianism, the whole lot. Gets rather depressing
after a while, you know."

"I've been meaning to ask," I said, turning my attention to his mother. "Lady Carpenter, may I stay a
night with my friend from school?"

"Who is she?" Lady Carpenter had big blue trusting
eyes.

"Her name is Wentworth. Elizabeth Wentworth."

"Who are her people?"

"Uh, they live in Dorset at Yollop Farm."

"Oh yes, of course. I know her mother. She's doing the season, isn't she?"

"Yes," I nodded, heaving a relieved sigh.

Myles snorted. "Good thing she didn't say 'bad blood.' Then you'd have had it. Mother's like a blood hound, you know. One sniff, and if it doesn't smell right, out with *Who's Who*. She prefers Debrett's, of course, and it's gallop all the way down the pedigree." He sighed. "I've lost some nice willing little fillies that way. Want to go to the Blue Angel after dinner?"

"No," I said. "But thank you. I'm afraid I'm rather tired. I'm meeting Patrick in Earls Court. We're going to a spaghetti house. I've never been to one before."

Both Lady Carpenter and Myles looked amused. "What about champagne and caviar?" asked Myles.

I frowned. "We are going to be married in a year, and Patrick is saving like mad. We have to be careful. Will Wednesday be all right?" I asked Lady Carpenter.

"Of course, dear."

"And, Myles," I said. "Sorry I can't go out tonight, but how about lunch at the Savoy on Thursday? I'll pay."

"Certainly not." Myles looked at me. "You're not going to be one of those awful modern women who want equality with men and all that tosh, are you? Dreadful creatures. They all end up taking shorthand and then die old maids."

I laughed. "You're right, you know."

"I'd love to have lunch on Thursday."

Dinner with Patrick on Tuesday night was a pleasure. I wore a navy blue shirt-waister with a big black tight belt. I had two petticoats, one black with a red ribbon through the bottom, and underneath that a white petticoat that frothed like a spray of plume sea on the shore. My white heeled shoes, carefully polished, contained my feet in nylon stockings, and my suspender belt clung around my waist. I also had on my silk French knickers with lace around the thighs. For once in my life I felt beautiful. My hair was now shoulder length. I gazed at myself in the mirror. Here was a Mary I no longer knew. I brushed my eyelashes with a little black brush. I painted my mouth with bright pink lipstick, and I prayed it would stay on my lips for the evening. I finished my dressing by putting a dab of perfume behind each ear. I decided I would save putting perfume behind my knees for Wednesday night, and I wondered where my knees would be. The thought made my stomach feel all watery. "The colly-wobbles," my grandmother would say.

Quite how I would face her at the weekend to say goodbye, having betrayed her and the entire family honor so dreadfully, I didn't know. All I knew was that if Grandfather ever found out, he'd horsewhip Patrick or get out his double-barrelled shotgun. By Thursday I would no longer be a virgin but a loose woman. And Patrick would be a cad who took advantage of me . . . I soon forgot all my worries in the happiness of Patrick's company.

Other things and people might change, but not Patrick. We found a crowded dark spaghetti house in Earls Court and we sat in a booth, our knees touching each other. I put my chin on my left hand so that everyone who passed would see my engagement ring and know that I was engaged to be married to Patrick Johnson. Patrick's eyes were alight with love. I felt swept away in his smile. He had perfect teeth and he was so handsome I thought I'd burst.

For dinner I had a risotto. Patrick told me all about the bank and how much he loved working there. He was learning all about banking in England. "And then after we're married, darling," he said, "we'll have a flat in Hong Kong right on top of the Peak. Can you imagine," he said, "what it will be like? I'll come home from work, we'll have a drink on the veranda, and we'll see the lights of Hong Kong glittering below us. We'll give dinner parties for our friends."

"But, Patrick. I don't like dinner parties," I interrupted.

"Yes, you do, darling. You'll have a cook and an amah."

"No, I won't. I don't ever want servants. Maybe a washing amah who comes to take our clothes away, but I really don't want to share the rest of our lives with servants. You know, I'm going to do a *cordon bleu* cooking course. I'll be the best cook in Hong Kong. You'll see."

"Okay, okay. Where do you want to go for now?"

"The Blue Angel," I said nonchalantly, as if I'd been going there all my life.

"All right. Finish your coffee and we're off."

Patrick drove a diminutive Morris Minor which he called Morris, a dear little car. It was a warm English summer evening, and we drove along the streets that lead to Berkeley Square. There were no nightingales to greet us in the square, but inside the Blue Angel there was an obnoxious group of naval officers with an equally obnoxious group of debutantes. Patrick and I sat by the entertainer, a nice-looking young man who played his guitar and made up impromptu songs about the people in the Blue Angel. He made up a song about me in my blue dress, and I blushed. Patrick leaned forward and kissed me. I kissed him back very warmly. I saw beads of sweat on his brow. Then we danced very closely. I knew Patrick was excited because I could feel it, so I danced closer still. "I say," Patrick glanced at his watch. "I'd better get you back. It's nearly eleven."

After five minutes of heavy necking in the car outside Lady Carpenter's house, I knew seducing Patrick was not going to be difficult at all. "I'll see you tomorrow then," I said. "At Liz's flat. I'm cooking dinner." Patrick looked as if he were drowning in great pain, which wasn't very flattering. "Are you all right?" I said.

He nodded and shot off down the road. The moon was saying hello to Eaton Gardens. The beneficent white rays blessed the inhabitants, but as for me I was not blessed but in a state of venial sin about to become mortal.

If this is sin, I thought sitting up in bed and filling in my diary, no wonder everyone enjoys it so. In Tuesday's entry I wrote, "BV. Before Virginity." And on Thursday I wrote "AV. After Virginity." Tomorrow morning I planned to go to Bayswater. Moscow Road, to be exact, where according to Marian you could buy little wispy sexy dresses with matching bras. The sort of clothes Harrods would never stock or your mother approve of.

❧ *Chapter 38* ❧

I bought myself a little wispy black dress. It was cut too low to wear a brassière, but it had an enchanting skirt, a bell stiffened so it swayed as I walked. Not that I intended to do much walking. I took a taxi straight to Liz's flat. It was the basement of a very imposing house in Palace Gardens Terrace, not far from Patrick's flat which was in Drayson Mews. I let myself in and looked around.

There was a long hall leading to the kitchen, a small drawing room, and part of the hall held a good Sheraton dining table with four chairs. Over the dining table hung a small crystal chandelier. I pushed open the bedroom door and looked at Liz's bed. It was covered with a white candlewick bedspread. I stood there. My heart suddenly decided to have an independent life of its own. Boom, boom. How awful, I thought, if I were to be found dead on the floor with a heart attack and still a virgin. What a waste of an awful lot of equipment. I wondered if that sort of equipment could go rusty with age. What happened to nuns or spinsters?

I wandered off to the kitchen to get a glass of water. A pretty little kitchen: yellow floor, matching yellow curtains, a small fridge, and an electric cooker. I realized I must hurry to buy the food. I had my Harrods card.

I walked past the bedroom again and then I realized I could not possibly use Liz's bed. If I did, I could never look Liz in the eye again. I would feel awful if anything went wrong. Marian had fearful stories of young girls haemorrhaging to death after the deed was done. Even worse, she had a story of a friend of hers, Vanessa, who developed an unfortunate cramp and was clamped to her lover and had to be carried by ambulance to the hospital. How the ambulance men could possibly get the stretcher down the stairs to Liz's flat would be a mystery, but then to load me with Patrick on top would be a miracle. Did they snigger, I wondered, or laugh behind their hands? At least I'd be covered by Patrick. Poor Patrick. Everyone would have a ringside view of his bottom.

The drawing room was the answer. I'd move the table and chairs into the drawing room for dinner. We could use the sofa. The sofa was a splendid large piece of furniture covered in a dark brown twill. A charming Victorian fireplace supported a large elaborate mirror. Thick brown curtains hid the room from passersby, and the carpet was the palest shade of robin-egg blue. I stood by the sofa and thought. I was the sort of girl who always liked to have everything prepared in advance. I had seen a French film in which everybody made love not only on the bed but also on the floor. So I slid as gracefully as possible, imagining I was feeling terribly turgid lust, to the floor. That was a mistake and it hurt. The carpet obviously concealed concrete. So this time, I tried again, clutching the brown matching bolster, pretending it was Patrick. I did a rather magnificent swoon onto the sofa. Pleased with myself, I left for Harrods.

As my mother ordered most of her specialities from Harrods, we were rather well-known to the staff. They all seemed to love her imperious ways. Her usual style was to sit regally in whatever department from which she desired to purchase clothes, food, or furniture, with me wiggling with embarrassment, and snap orders while a vast array of stuff was brought before her.

Today, however, all that past humiliation paid off. Mr. Jenks, who ran the fish department, said he had just received a fine shipment of oysters from Colchester. Max had taught me how to shuck oysters, and oysters, Marian had said, were good for sex. Next I approached the meat counter. Mr Turner suggested fillet of steak. I could do that, sit them on a little raft of toast, a dab of pâté, a little parsley butter, new potatoes, and tiny green peas. To finish, as we were about to exert ourselves, nothing too heavy. Not cheese. That might give us smelly breath. But two perfect peaches in red wine.

Liz was obviously on one of her many diets: there was little in the way of food in the flat. So I bought eggs, bacon, and sausages, good Colombian coffee, and toast and Rose's Lime Marmalade. Sex, I had been told by Marian, was supposed to make you dreadfully hungry, and I rather fancied a wifely breakfast with Patrick. I would recreate the moment in the French film when the highly sophisticated woman produced a perfect breakfast—not a hair on her head out of place—and slipped into her seat with a wonderful warm smile, and her lover gazed at her in astonishment. Was this the woman who so recently had held him in a passionate and sensuous embrace? This angel, this creature of domestic delight?

On my way back to the flat, I wondered if after our night of passion I would slip out of bed and go to the bathroom and get the gunge off my face. Or maybe I had better change in the bathroom and wash it off then. The thought of Patrick seeing me first thing in the morning with mascara dripping down my face made my knees go weak. "I saw my wife-to-be with her makeup all over her face, m'Lord." "Quite," the Judge would say. "Quite right, young man." Oh bother, I thought. Go away. I'm just going to have to risk it. If after dinner we were to fall passionately on the sofa, and if I rehearsed the evening any further, I might get stale. Better to let things take their course.

Patrick was bringing the wine, and back at the flat I set to work. After I had everything ready to go, I put my sexy black satin nightdress on the top of the case. The brown sofa, I discovered, also served as a guest bed, so that left Liz's room safe. I lugged the table and chairs into the drawing room and laid it with Liz's pretty Victorian china dinner service. When I'd finished I was proud of myself. The table really did look nice. The oysters were open on a bed of ice. The steaks lay on a plate in the kitchen all ready to go, and the peaches sat in pudding plates awash with good red wine and brown sugar. They smelled wonderful. A pretty green salad, strewn with olives and anchovies, awaited our gastronomic pleasure on the bottom shelf of the fridge. The coffee beans in the mill awaited a last minute whirl just before Patrick's arrival. The aroma of the coffee beans would waft to the front door to welcome him. Phoebe taught me this trick. When Bridie was too poor to buy coffee beans for her guests, she always kept a few beans back and then, after a prolonged amount of noise, the beans smelling as only fresh coffee beans can, she served Nescafé Instant.

Now that everything was done, my mind wandered back to my mother and father, to my grandmother, to Phoebe who said she never would . . . Maybe I was making a mistake, I thought. Maybe I should wait. But it was time to take a bath and to change out of my sensible tweed skirt and my silk shirt and become the other me. The Mata Hari with a rose between my teeth. Or maybe more of a breathless Marilyn Monroe.

I looked in the mirror in the bathroom while the tub was filling the room with steam. I saw my face through the mist. Not bad, I thought. Not bad at all. I lay in the bath, the warm flannel between my legs. This is your last virginal bath, I thought as I floated about in the lilac-scented water. On the basin there stood my favorite bottle of scent, Apple Blossom. Whether $E = mc^2$, or 196,000 miles per second was the speed of light seemed pretty small potatoes when one was preparing to get seduced, because obviously Patrick must always believe I had given myself to him because he asked me to. Aunt Mary's soot and butter pills might cure her chickens when they were egg-bound, but never in a million years must Patrick think that I seduced him. That was Rule Number One in Marian Pool's rule-book.

I looked down while I was drying myself. My poor patch of hair looked a little forlorn. I felt insecure again. Still, losing my virginity was something that had to be done. Afterwards, I would belong to Patrick forever. So it was my duty, I felt, to make this sacrifice for my husband to give him memories of his night of passion with me and to keep him faithful and away from "other women."

By the time I heard his step, whizzed the coffee, and ran to the front door with a welcoming smile on my face, the play was set. The deed was done. The play had to go on.

Patrick looked shy. His face, behind a huge bunch of roses, appeared younger than the face I'd seen the day before. In his other hand he held a bottle of Chianti. The familiar warm shape of the straw that surrounded the bottle comforted me. "Hello, darling," he said and he followed me down the corridor. "You do look lovely," he said as I walked with a little wiggle *à la* Françoise style. She would have been proud of me.

In the kitchen time stood still. The coffee smell intensified and Patrick took me in his arms and kissed me passionately, more passionately than he ever had before. I felt a strange sensation, a pulsing throb that sped from my legs up my body and caused both my nipples to feel like bullets. I loved being kissed and I loved being held by Patrick, so solid and so reassuring. He smelled clean and I inhaled his Old Spice aftershave. Patrick paused for more air. "Hang on," I said. "Let's put the roses in water." I found a large Victorian flower pot and filled it to the brim with water. Expertly I slit the stems of the purple passionate roses and arranged them in the pot. "Here," I said. "You carry the roses into the sitting room. Second door on the left. And I'll follow with the oysters."

"Oh dear," Patrick remarked. "I got red wine."

"Never mind," I comforted him. "Red wine will do fine. We have steak next." The oysters lay sullen on the plate. I had opened them too early, and their juice leaked onto the plate. Their plump gray bodies looked defeated. Dear me, I thought. I do hope we aren't discovered in each other's arms dead from a poisoned oyster. How awful it would look in *The Times.* Or worse still, Aunt Mary would read all about it in the *News of the World,* the newspaper that no nice girl ever read.

"What a lovely room," Patrick exclaimed. He

looked around and then he went over to the curtains and drew them shut.

Suddenly we were really alone for the first time in our lives. Alone, unchaperoned, and unobserved. I felt very frightened and I wished I had never got myself into this mess. I wished I were back in Africa sitting on my window ledge listening to the jungle and reading Andrew Lang's *Blue Fairy Tale* book, vicariously reliving a time when princes kissed princesses' fingers and all the grown-up genital business never happened. Why, I thought, did God have to design sex this way? Was He joking?

Patrick looked happily across the table into my face. "Darling," he said, "in a year's time I'll come home every night and we will have dinner together and I will read my bank books and you can read, or listen to music, if you want to. Only us, darling." He took my hand. "The oysters look marvelous," he said.

I squeezed the lemon juice very carefully on my oysters. I made sure every one of them winced, and then I swallowed, wishing I'd chosen a less sexual course for what was about to come.

We talked of this and that. Patrick helped clear the dishes, and then we ate the fillet steak. I was pleased with the fillet steak. It turned out well. The parsley butter slid in the most delightful way across the top of the meat. Then I wondered what would happen if I was too dry. Marian said that this was a virgin's curse. There were apparently special bottles of stuff to use. "We use vaseline on the brood mares," I remembered Phoebe offering. I wondered if Liz had vaseline in the bathroom cupboard. I would have to check.

Meanwhile, through a haze of confusion, I was attempting to make intelligent conversation with Patrick. We both drank an awful lot of wine. I, who never drank more than a glass or two in my life, already had downed four glasses and was on my fifth by the time

I unsteadily retired to get the pudding. "It's funny," I said as I re-entered the sitting room. "I'm a little squiffy."

"So am I," said Patrick. He started to giggle. "Someone put something in the wine."

"Yes," I said. "They certainly did."

We ate our peaches in an absorbed silence and then, as if by mutual magic, we both headed for the sofa. Patrick underneath and I on top, we began to kiss with a certain hysterical intensity. Patrick stood up and took off his clothes. Of course, I had seen Patrick in his swimming suit, but I had never seen an erect penis before. I sat there and just stared at it. All that plumbing, I thought. Good heavens. What an amazing sight. "Undress quickly, my love. Hurry up, darling." Patrick's voice was choked and rushed. "Do hurry up. I love you." His hands were on my dress. He helped me pull off my knickers and then the awful thing happened.

Patrick seemed beside himself. He kissed me and moaned, but he kept prodding me with that thing. "Where is it?" he said desperately. "I can't find it."

Suddenly my whole world took on a shock of clarity. There was the dinner table littered with food. The Chianti bottle stood empty. The lights low, I was giving my virgin body to Patrick and he couldn't find it. My plan was now ruined. This was a detail that had escaped me like a recalcitrant rodent. "Hang on," I said in my most practical voice. "Let me hold it." I took the thing in my hand and firmly positioned it in the right place. Patrick bucked and cavorted like a horse with a thorn under the saddle. My word, I thought. There's nothing erotic about this. I felt as if I was being steam-rolled by a bus.

Abruptly Patrick stopped and fell into a slump on top of me. "That was marvelous," he said. "Did you like it, darling?"

"Of course," I said. "You were wonderful, Patrick."

"Good," he said and rolled over. "I feel like a sleep."

We got up, went into the bedroom, and pulled off the bedcover. Patrick slipped into the sheets and fell asleep immediately. I headed for the bathroom. Liz did have some vaseline. I sat on the loo and gazed between my legs. Nothing looked different. No blood. Still, I reminded myself, I was no longer a virgin. And I went back to the bedroom and cuddled up to Patrick and I slept soundly.

❧ *Chapter 39* ❧

The next morning I had to wake Patrick up for the office. He woke up with a start. "Good lord," he said. "I'm late. By the way, Mary, you did use something, didn't you?"

I looked at him. "No," I said. "Everyone says that's a man's responsibility. I thought you'd have one of those rubber things." Patrick groaned and put his head in his hands. I watched his erection wilt like a flower deprived of water.

He frowned. "We'll probably be all right. Anyway, if you are pregnant, we'll just get married right away." I wished at that moment I was pregnant. Patrick really loved me.

We kissed finally on the doorstep. The morning red buses thundered by, full of gray people on their way to gray offices, but for me the world was golden. I now belonged, in every sense of the word, to Patrick. I saw him turn and wave at the top of the stairs. I returned to the flat to clean and wash and restore my oasis back to its original, calm, tranquil state, so that I would join

Myles for lunch at the Savoy and Liz would push her front door open to a space that kept its secrets.

"Aha!" Myles was at his most irritating. "Shall I 'phone the *Daily Mail* gossip column? Are we still pure and unsullied?"

I felt myself blush. "Shut up, Myles," I said.

"You're supposed to match before you hatch," he laughed.

"Myles, I do not wish to discuss my private life with you. Anyway, I hear you have another little waitress in tow."

"Oh yes. I sneak her past Ma late at night and then I decant her before the milkman calls. You know, it's the oddest thing. Once I've had a girl, I never want to see her again." I had a momentary twinge of worry. I hoped Patrick didn't feel the same way. Myles was looking really sad.

"The roast beef is very good today, sir." The chef pulled the large silver trolley towards us.

"Oh, all right, Thomas. I'd love a plate."

I looked at the slightly pink rawness of the beef: a little too reminiscent of the hours before. "I think, Myles, I would prefer a plain piece of chicken."

"Okay." He ordered for me. "Some wine perhaps?"

I smiled. "I drank a little too much last night," I said, and I sat at the Savoy feeling very much a woman of the world.

"Did you have a nice time?" Lady Carpenter asked.

"Lovely," I said and I smiled at myself in the pier-glass that hung over the mantelpiece. A woman named Mary Freeland stared back at me.

Upstairs in my anonymous bedroom I felt the anonymity. The room was now a guest bedroom but once had been a servant's quarter, I imagined. The furniture was chosen by the housekeeper. Around me were the trappings of a middle class family's life. The chairs were round and pink candystriped. The curtains matched and had gold tassels to allow the Eaton Gardens morning light to peer into the room. I sat up and stared out of the window. Why, I thought, does Eaton Gardens look so different this morning?

I was used to walking through the broad streets, watching the trees in the fine gardens change with the seasons. Spring was always a favourite season. Now the yellow dust of long ago midsummer filtered into the room, the rays falling on my bed, a Peter Jones walnut headboard. My pillows were plump European pillows, fat with goose down, not the more lean and lumpy English version of pillows, ever mindful of Sherwood Park. Just thinking of Sherwood Park suddenly made me sad. How long ago it was that I played with Phoebe, the night we rode our restless horses thundering through the countryside? How could the rapturous joy of that night, the tumescent thrust of the horse between my legs, be compared with what happened with Patrick? Why did I miss a sense of longing to be overpowered, to be carried away in a maze of feelings, from the thunder of my blood to the high whine of ecstasy, the closest I had ever felt that night under the pregnant moon? Why did I now feel a little astonished at myself, a little lost and a little lonely?

I still felt sore and stretched, but for what? Miss Standish's disappointed face rose to reprimand me and I got up to wash away the memories I had created with such considerable premeditation. In the bathroom mirror I saw for a moment my guilty eyes and then I saw a look on my face I had seen on my mother's face so many years before when I had seen her in bed with my father. Red talons clutched at Patrick. He was mine and I would fight to keep what I knew to be my future, my man and my marriage. This fierce feeling, so akin to the roar of an African tigress, surprised me, but strangely it did not frighten me.

I sat down totally naked on one of the plump chairs and took stock yet again of where I was. Well, I was no longer a virgin. That was a fact. I was engaged to be married. After visiting Aunt Mary, I was to take the train to say goodbye to my grandparents and then back to Paris to pack and say goodbye to my parents. I was aware for the first time in my life that I was really looking forward to seeing my mother. Maybe in time we could love each other without hesitation. But for now I realized that my mother had a gambler's instinct: the ability to survive in this world. So far I had been protected by my position, by the affluence of my life, by my place that was automatically procured for me. But after this coming year at finishing school, I would be really on my own. Living in Hong Kong and being a mere housewife would entitle me to nothing more than a place at a dinner party surrounded by people I must get to know on their terms. Patrick was very firm about that. "Entertaining the bank," he said, "is the way ahead. And of course, with your training you should be ace." I'll do, I thought, my best.

Getting dressed hurriedly, I was in time for breakfast. I found I was hungry and the kedgeree comforted me. There is always food, I thought and I caught a bus for Ealing and Aunt Mary's.

"How are you, Aunt Mary?"

She stood in the doorway, her hands clasped and the inevitable cigarette hung out of the corner of her mouth. "Mustn't grumble," she said. " 'ow are you?"

"Okay." I hugged her thin gaunt shoulders. Immediately the contents of an ashtray raced up my nostrils, but it was a good smell, not anonymous, not furniture polish. Just Aunt Mary's habit and she felt real.

"Come on in," she said and I followed her into the

sitting room and sat down on a big overstuffed Edwardian armchair. "What's been happening?" She looked at me with a grin. "I see," she said and my heart sank. She probably did see. Aunt Mary had eyes like radar beams.

"Well," I said, "I am engaged."

"Yes," she agreed. "And now you're a woman, you'll have to behave, won't you?" She grinned. Her face scrunched up into a winter hazelnut smile. "Patrick's a lucky fellow. You'll do well. I've got to go shopping, love. Do you want to come along?"

"No," I said. "I'm tired. Can I stay here and read?"

"All right. I won't be long. What do you want for tea tonight? Lamb chops?" I nodded and waited for her to leave.

Once I heard the gate click and saw her straw hat disappear up the road, I went into the dining room and pulled out the dog-eared books full of pictures. Here I found pictures of my mother, at about the age of ten I guessed, with Aunt Mary in—I could tell by the forested backgrounds of the pictures and by the onyx black faces of the other people in the pictures—South Africa. My mother looked well-dressed but not affluent. Her shoes, I noticed, were not the dreaded brown sandals clamped to preserve the great English feet from the clutches of foreign shoes. Her shoes were patent black and shiny, the kind I longed for when I was her age. Her dresses with Peter Pan collars were homemade in sensible looking patterned cotton. Behind her were bungalows, long and low but unexceptional. No other children were in any of the pictures. There were no pictures of her school or birthday party pictures, just a collection of pictures of her growing up from year to year until a final picture of my mother looking very young and lovely with my father. They were smiling into the camera and she held a bunch of flowers. Around her neck hung a necklace brilliantly shining with many diamonds.

Did they look very much in love? My father did. He looked at her with a blissful smile on his face, but she looked at him almost as if she had something to ask him but didn't dare. They still looked like this today, and the thought crossed my mind that maybe she had loved someone else. Somehow my father in that old picture appeared so sure of himself, his arm around her waist in a protective and possessive clasp. But she, I could see, was pulling slightly away as a flower pulls away from a commanding clump.

She looked isolated in the pictures and I had felt isolated with Patrick, neither of us sure of what we were doing but both of us bulldozed into a path that is offered to those of us who are the dispossessed. I knew I was always teased by Phoebe for thinking too much, for feeling feelings other people didn't feel. "Two skins too few," Phoebe always used to snort when I had shared some worry or sorrow with her. My mother obviously had learned to protect herself from showing missing skins.

I was lost for what seemed to be a long time in those books: browning brittle pictures of China, a place called Macau, and the Peak in Hong Kong. At least I had these pictures, and once in Hong Kong I might find some answers . . .

"Thought you would, you little bleeder." Aunt Mary was back. She had crept up the path and opened the door silently. "Wot did you find out? Not much, eh?"

"No," I said. "But enough to know that my mother didn't tell me much of what happened to her as a child."

Aunt Mary headed for the kitchen. She carried a large string-bag full of parcels. "Come on," she said. "Time for lunch. Sit at the table and I'll get it ready."

Lunch was pork-pie, pink and gelatinous. She added vinegar to the mustard powder and the heat blew a hole in my nose and I sniffed loudly. Aunt Mary found that terribly funny. "All that education and you can still sniff?" I nodded, my eyes watering. "Here," she said. "Have a hankie."

"Why won't you tell me about my mother?" I asked through a veil of tears.

"Well," she said, "it isn't really my business, is it? I 'ave been thinking, though, and I can tell you that when you are married you will get something I have been holding for you for many years and your Grandma gave me instructions to give you an income of your own. The last instructions I ever 'ad from her. She said you were never to be dependent on a man. She's left you a yearly income for life, starting from when you come of age. Your mother knows about this and she knows I can tell you, about the money, I mean, but she doesn't want to discuss any of this with you or anyone else."

"My grandmother? My mother's mother?"

Aunt Mary nodded.

"Who was she? Oh, please tell me, Aunt Mary. No one has ever told me anything about who my grandmother was. My mother's never breathed a word. And now you say I'm to come into some money she left for me, but she never knew me, and I've no idea who she was."

"And you'll not get any more out of me." Aunt Mary's voice was resolute.

"Why?" I said. "But why must there be such a mystery?"

Aunt Mary looked at me very seriously. "Sometimes," she said, "a family has a secret. Maybe if the secret is told it will make the whole family suffer. So there are lies. Not bad lies, but lies that protect and keep the family from falling apart. In those days, way back when, so many people were driven from their homes. Or they had to make lives for themselves, to eat . . . They had to survive." I saw that Aunt Mary had regressed back to the old days and her face seemed, in the dark little kitchen, to lose years. She spoke in a youthful joyous way. Lines flattened out in her face and her hands, normally clawed and clasped, loosened around her cup of tea. She inhaled the tea, both hands cupping the vessel much as if she were drinking Chinese tea.

"Ah," she said. "Those were the magic days. The days when you could be anyone. I remember the Bund in Shang-hai. I pushed your mother along those grand streets with the sea laying ahead of us. Your mother spoke German and Mandarin. We lived in the German quarters. We lived like kings. She was born in a palace, you know, your grandmum. And then when she had your mum . . ."

"Really?" I said. "You mean my mother was the daughter of a princess?"

"Yes." Aunt Mary nodded sideways. "You could say that. But, then, there were lots of princesses from 'ere and there about in those days. But yes. She came from a good family, a Royal Family." She paused. A brick wall came down. I so much wanted to know more. Which Royal Family? A princess of where? But it was too late. I could see that Aunt Mary regretted she had said that much. Her mood changed and she looked across at me. "You know," she said sadly, "Mary, you should try to understand your mother, not fight with her. Your mother only wants what's best for you. Goodness knows she had little enough for herself. She has me, of course, but I stay out of the way. She has her own life now and I'm not part of it."

"But you are, Aunt Mary," I said. "You are. I don't see much of you, but I feel you are my family. I love Grandma and Grandpa, but their life is so closed off.

If something happened to me that was awful, I couldn't tell them but I could tell you. I know you'd understand. Anyway I want to tell you something, something I can't tell anyone else." I found my face burning a deep uncomfortable red. "Two days ago . . ." I said. "Um, well, a couple of nights ago . . ." I found my nose almost resting on my teacup. "I . . . ah . . . slept with Patrick."

I felt Aunt Mary's fingers under my chin. "Oh dear, child," she said, gently lifting my eyes to hers.

I grimaced and then began to cry. Why, I thought furiously, am I doing this? I am a grown woman, I've made love to a man, and here I am bawling like a baby. I put my head down on the table and I howled and howled. I could hear my sobbing hit the walls of the kitchen and rush into the sitting room, up the stairs to my small safe bedroom with its purple quilt, and into the cupboard where on my last visit my clothes had hung in virginal solitude.

I hadn't realized that innocence was a thing that could be lost. I knew all about innocence—the innocence of children, the innocence of a rosy dawn, a thing untouched, undisturbed—but now I realized I had experienced a loss of my own, deeply personal and deeply felt. I had always loved Mamie in Peter Pan, her little house with the outflung arm that Peter built around her to preserve her from the cold and also from himself. Why, oh why, I thought, had I so calculatingly given away that which could never be returned?

Aunt Mary waited until I was reduced to shuddering sighs and then she said quietly, "A good cry never hurt. Don't worry, ducky. You're not the first to claim your own. You're going away and there's many a flighty thing that would want to get her hands on a man like Patrick." She looked at me sideways. Aunt Mary had a sideways look that was both dignified and knowledgeable. "I wanted to ask you," she said, "seeing as I don't know this Patrick of yours, are you sure in your 'eart of 'earts that you really want to marry him?"

"Oh, Aunt Mary!" I was staggered by this remark. I had always wanted to marry Patrick. The idea of not marrying Patrick had not entered my head. I felt about Patrick the way I felt about Mademoiselle and Jacques. They had always been together and always would be, as permanent as the Eiffel Tower. In my world everything was certain. Unlike other girls, I never gossiped and giggled about boys. I didn't need to: Patrick was an eternal fixture in my life. Except for Quentin on the ship from Africa, who had so badly wounded me and betrayed me, I had no experience with any other boy. I think that raw moment when I stood at the gang plank waiting for us to run away together scarred my self-confidence for life. Although now I realize it was a perfectly ridiculous plan for two children, the event awakened me to the possibility of betrayal. And even if Myles and I shared moments of a sort of hilarity I could never share with Patrick, the one thing I knew and trusted in Patrick was that he would never betray me. Now Aunt Mary was shaking the pillars of my very existence. "Of course," I said, "I want to marry Patrick."

A disloyal thought crept upon me unawares as I gazed back at my teacup. A tall man with black hair and green Mediterranean eyes walked towards me. His smile curled his warm mouth and his hair hung in a forelock over his wide brow. He looked at me with a twinkle in his smile. A gone-with-the-wind-over-the-mountains-into-a-dark-cave-full-of-secrets-and-excitements smile...

I shook myself and said crossly, "Don't be silly, Aunt Mary. I'm in love with Patrick."

Aunt Mary picked up the teapot and turned to the

sink. "Ah yes," she said. "You're in love. Well, my dear, there are men for marrying and then there are men for loving. Don't mix the two."

"What do you mean?" I said, scandalized and suddenly, defensively, cross. "Anyway, what do you know about this sort of thing?"

Aunt Mary turned her back against the sink and said sharply, "Mary, don't be rude. I've lived a long time and I'll tell you once more. There are two kinds of men. There's men for marrying and then there's men for loving. Love is calm. Love is quiet. But the other sort is all emotion and passion. No calm, no quiet center. Those men are not for marrying."

"I'm sorry. Have you had a man for loving?" I asked, ashamed of my outburst.

"Yes," Aunt Mary said. "I did a long time ago in Africa." She shook her head. "Those kind of men are only for loving, and I did all the loving and, in the end, the losing. He was one of a kind and I have my memories."

"Did you ever want to get married?"

"Nah." Aunt Mary shook her head again. "'e was one of a kind. Anyone else would be second best, and I don't take second best. Come on now, child. Too much talking's no good. Let's go and see a film."

We amiably sauntered up Acton High Road. On a Saturday afternoon the roads were crowded. Immigrants from all over the British Empire had recently arrived and I felt at home. Pakistani shops advertised curry powders and the familiar spices from the Far East tickled my nose. West Africans walked in huge families up and down the roads talking to each other. African women in brilliant cotton wraps sailed along the pavement with their children clinging to their vast forms. Immigrants gave life to what had once been dull quiet streets interrupted only by a few people racing through the grime to the pub for a pint. The tall disapproving houses hung over the streets. Houses built for aspiring merchants now whirred in a flurry of moving vans to get away. Behind them, as they fled, the immigrants moved in, believing not only that the streets were paved with gold but also that their children would receive the finest of English educations. To all this Aunt Mary lectured me as she trotted up the street. "Streets of gold indeed," she said. "They've been called over to empty the bedpans and to sweep the bleeding streets . . . Education? Huh. See what they done? They get rid of the grammar, and these kids will sink to the bottom. There'll be trouble, mark my words. There'll be trouble. We'll stop 'ere. They're showing a Peter Sellers. Funny wog, 'e is."

I didn't protest. If Aunt Mary thought Peter Sellers was a wog, who was I to correct her? Her views were so foreign to what my father taught me, I said nothing. For my father, any attempt to educate children together was an excellent idea. He felt that Commonwealth children would indeed benefit from a common English education. Not that he would send his daughter to a grammar school or even entertain the idea of a comprehensive school. It was different. I was a Consul General's daughter, and as long as such a position existed, I had duties to perform . . .

Chapter 40

I sat in my high purple swatched bed in Ealing, failing to fall asleep. Too much had happened too quickly. I felt I was on a train that was out of control, carrying me up mountains and down gorges, with me hanging on to the roof while everyone sat safely inside eating amiably and chatting to each other. Over their heads I clung screaming and screaming. Every so often someone would look up and nod smilingly at me. I did finally slide into sleep, but then the faces became those of the people I had left behind me. Max, Saul, my banished nanny Bertha, Taiwan as a puppy. Then Mrs Biddle, Mme Derlanger, the assembly of crows all smiling at me and laughing, my mother standing on the boat that took us from Africa watching me with puzzled eyes.

"Maybe," Aunt Mary said as she kissed me goodnight, "maybe you should think about the fact that you are very like your mother and that is why you fight with her."

I was again surprised by Aunt Mary's sagacity. "You really do love my mother, don't you?" I said, kissing her back.

"Yes, I really do. She needs all the love she can get. You see, she doesn't have family. Just me . . . I'm not much in 'er life, but I love her all the same. What we talk about is between you and me. Your mother knows I love her, and when she's ready she'll tell you what she wants you to 'ear. There are shadows in 'er life, big shadows, but she 'as the right to tell as much as she wants."

"Can you tell me why grandma won't have her picture in her house? Nobody ever talks about my mother."

"I know," Aunt Mary said. "I know. One day, when you're older, you'll understand."

"I hope so," I said.

In the nightmare I felt sorry for my mother and I wanted to hug her. I woke up in the morning with tears in my eyes, but then I heard the sizzle of bacon and sausages. The smell was so exhilarating that I soon forgot my dreams and headed downstairs. The walk across the garden to the outhouse was refreshing. The morning air was cool and scented from the roses. The wind blessed my face, cold from the water in the pitcher, and I walked back feeling very confined and safe in this little row of houses in the middle of the sprawling suburbs of London.

" 'urry up," said Aunt Mary. "You've got to catch the train." I beamed at her fondly, and even more fondly at the station where she cantered after the train hurling instructions. "Don't talk to any strange men!" she hollered. "Do you 'ear me?"

"Yes, I do!" I yelled back and then I settled down to read *Middlemarch.* My new book obsession was George Eliot. I wanted to be a writer like her. I sat back and observed the people in my first class compartment like a writer is supposed to do. I got bored: one old lady with a felt hat and a fussy wool suit, two gentlemen. One looked like a banker with a solid black bowler attached to his head, no doubt put there to keep his brains in. He had a very pink face and he read the *Telegraph.* The other was more interesting. He wore a pair of check plus-fours and a yellow shirt with a red knotted scarf. He had canary yellow hair and pale blue eyes. He crossed his legs like women do and his hands, which were long and thin, caressed a novel. He obviously enjoyed the novel because he had a curious smile on his face. His lips were small and very bright red. I longed to talk to him, but Aunt Mary's face popped up and said "no" very firmly. I dived into *Middlemarch* and thought how like my grandparents' life, how little had changed, and what a genius the woman was in her ability to describe people's lives with a few words.

The train pulled into Taunton station. The old lady fussed and fumed. The bowler hat pulled her suitcase off the rack and handed it to her with a courtly bow. They left together. The canary-haired gentleman slowly, sinuously, stood up and unwrapped his legs.

He stretched and he looked at me sideways. "Well, dear, do you recognize one when you see one?"

"I have no idea," I said. "What do you mean?" A huge flush came over me and I could feel my cheeks going red.

"Well, well," he said, sliding past me. "My, my. We are a little innocent, aren't we?" I got out of the train and then he looked at me through the open door. "Stay that way," he said, suddenly urgent. Then he walked off.

I took my suitcase off the rack and stood on the platform. That awful feeling came back over me, that loss of innocence feeling. What had that man done that was so dreadful? He looked like Faust once his soul belonged to the Devil. Had I sold my soul for all eternity? Is there a strict law that says anyone who violates another's innocence is doomed to hell? In my case I had violated my own innocence and Patrick's innocence. Was I damned forever twice over? Would I look like that man, his face contorted with memories that obviously haunted him? When he spoke suddenly and so earnestly, I saw behind the youthful mask the face of a very old man hung with grim wrinkles, the yellow hair sparse on a pink balding skull: retribution for his sins in lonely old age, surrounded by books, novels to transport him from his place in hell . . .

"Hello, Pumpkin." Grandpa's reassuring voice reached out to me and led me kindly away from my gloomy thoughts. He hugged me and lifted me off my feet. I smelled his pipe and his warm male smell. I always thought of haystacks when I thought of the smell of my grandfather. My grandmother smelled of tea roses at dusk when the dew falls. "Ned is waiting for us. I'll take your case. Your grandmother is cooking pheasant for us, so we'll hurry back."

I settled in the car and watched the back of Ned's head. What a safe world it is, I thought. I watched the hedgerows flash by. I looked at the fields and the cows. Today there must be rain coming because all but one cow were hugging the earth preparing a warm spot for themselves. This one cow, a big Friesian with a vast udder, stood contemptuously in the field looking around her. Maybe, I thought, maybe that was my problem: I couldn't lie down with the others. But then, neither could my mother. I felt hopeful then. When I went back to Paris to pack, I could try to understand her more because if I could understand her better maybe I could understand myself, what it was in her that was like me and which bits of me weren't like her. But it was all right to have both parts.

I stopped analysing myself as we drew up to the door. "Quiet today, aren't you?" My grandfather's thick eyebrows registered surprise.

"I'm just a bit tired," I said. "Can I ring Patrick before lunch?"

"All right, dear. But remember the telephone bill." Grandpa went off to the kitchen to taste the gravy. Gravy and Grandpa went together. If Grandpa's gravy wasn't quite right, he was miserable.

I telephoned Patrick. "How are you?" I said nervously, as I had betrayed his innocence.

"Fine," Patrick said heartily. For one whose innocence had been betrayed, he seemed remarkably cheerful.

"You're not sorry about the other night?"

"Sorry?" he laughed. "Silly coot. Of course I'm not sorry. I can't wait to do it again. Gosh, Mary, that was a wonderful evening. Just think, when we're married, we can have evenings like that all the time."

"Yes," I said. "We can. Patrick, I really love you."

"Of course you do, darling. And I love you."

"I must get off the telephone because my grandfather doesn't like people making trunk calls, but I'll write to you this evening. I promise. And I'll call you from Paris when I get home. I love you," I said, and the word *love . . . love . . . love . . .* reverberated from Taunton up the line to Kensington, London, where all the pretty girls were waiting to attach themselves to my Patrick.

"Goodbye, darling." Patrick's voice was faint.

"Goodbye," I said and sent a kiss fluttering down the phone.

"Come along, dear," Grandma called. "Have you washed your hands?"

"Not yet." And I fled to the bathroom. I watched the water gush over my betraying hands. Somehow Aunt Mary's place seemed safer. I could tell Aunt Mary things that I could never tell my grandparents.

We sat for lunch in the dining room. Mrs Smyth-Jones was serving and Ned poured the wine. The room was shiny and the air smelled of furniture polish, the same smell from the time before. At Aunt Mary's the room always smelled of cooking. The breakfast bacon and eggs clung to the faded chenille curtains, refusing to let go until the smell of a small piece of roast beef tore the eggs and bacon away. Now the smell of roast pheasant wafted out of my grandmother's windows. It did not stay, as if it knew it was forbidden to stay in a household such as this. Any smells would be chased by Mrs Harding fast with her mop and her broom. Still the pheasant was delicious. Grandpa beamed because the sauce was just right. The butter and the red wine caused a glaze that caressed the new potatoes and drowned the fresh little garden peas. "Ahh," I sighed. "Home-grown vegetables. Grandma, how wonderful."

My grandmother smiled. "Yes, darling," she said. "You and I have several days work pickling and jamming. We have the autumn fête before you leave, and I am determined to come first in the flower-arranging.

I don't mind a second or a third in pickling, but my plum jam has never failed yet. The vicar says he will pick the winning flowers to go into the church.''

My grandfather paused. "Of course you'll win, darling," he said. "Who else has such magnificent flowers."

"That awful Rogers woman has been growing huge vulgar dahlias. That's the competition these days. Dahlias," she said with disgust in her voice. "Only the working classes grow dahlias. In my day, they wouldn't be allowed in the church. Awful things. I have been told that the Rogers woman is not above buying flowers from the florist to add to her arrangement. But I have my ways," she said sharply. "When Ned takes me shopping, we always pass her garden and I know what she has growing there. Any cheating and I shall be on to her." My grandmother looked fierce when she said those words.

We sat politely asking each other to pass things up and down the table until we reached the gooseberry course. The berries lay green and content in the bottom of my crystal bowl. Aunt Mary had glass bowls that didn't sparkle and shine like my grandmother's cut crystal bowls. Aunt Mary's bowls were smooth and heavy. These bowls had deep indentations. I supposed it was a little like the rich with their scrunchy pebbles. Poor people had glass bowls and the rich had crystal. I felt confused because I liked the crystal bowls very much, but I also liked Aunt Mary's glass bowls. Aunt Mary and I chattered all the time. I knew everybody's private life up and down her street. The man on the train would have been a source of a whole evening's conversation with Aunt Mary, but now I knew for certain I could not say a word to my grandparents. I would hurt and embarrass them. Horrid uncomfortable things had no place in their lives. They lived insulated and away from anything not considered normal.

Losing your virginity before marriage was unthinkable to my grandparents.

After lunch we moved into the library for my grandfather to have his cup of coffee. Grandpa picked up the *Radio Times* and looked for a good concert on Radio Three. He very rarely stayed awake through the first movement, but we sat and listened. Once his first vast snore shook the books on the library shelves, my grandmother smiled at me and we sneaked off. My grandmother knew she had half an hour to herself to potter about in the kitchen before my grandfather awoke.

"What, what?" Grandpa would snort upon waking up. "Wasn't that wonderful, darling?" This he said opening his eyes. "Marvelous music. Don't write like that nowadays, do they?"

"Of course not," his darling would say, sitting in her chair. My grandmother and I smiled at each other, in perfect complicity.

Learning to pickle and make jam was going to be a lot of fun, I decided. Then I thought about my father in Paris. Maybe this kind of life, where nothing was discussed ever, was what made him seem so remote at times from his feelings. Thinking about it, I could see that he put all his feelings into my mother and she translated what he should feel and then he was happy again. No wonder he was so dependent on her.

The huge house was hushed and content. No bills lay in drawers unpaid. No air of anxiety stirred the trees outside and the moon shone complacently upon Milton Park and I slept without dreaming.

Chapter 41

My grandmother—who had seen the fall of China, stared lions in the face on safari, and watched the Gurkhas charge against the Indian rebels—was worried about the flower show. How on earth, I wondered as I lay in bed the next morning, could she worry about Mrs Rogers? Or Vera, as she was known to the village. I was very used to the silent unwritten code that surrounded my grandparents with unspoken shorthand. If at the pub (called by my grandfather "The Spotted Dick" after a famous club in the Far East), the Eldridges would immediately follow his drift. *Sate Empat Jala* meant "one for the road," and my grandparents always smiled a nostalgic far-away smile for their world that was rapidly crumbling around them. As I dressed, I realized that perhaps my grandmother's way of keeping her world alive was to see that the Mrs Rogerses of this world did not win flower shows. Maybe that was the source of my grandmother's intense wish to win.

I looked about onto the lawn and then I wandered out through the conservatory and I stood in a light drizzle of rain. Early autumn rain in Somerset is a special rain, gentle and caressing. The Somerset women have marvelous soft rained-on skin. Their cheeks are crab-apple red and their hands are curled softly from fruit-picking, the soil so dark and loamy, unlike the red of Devon soil but just as fertile. I breathed in a long draft of autumn smells: burning leaves, of course, but also the soporific smell of things going to bed, the musky smell of the gamely badgers rooting about in their dens, clawing the thick earth for their winter blanket of sleep, worms digging deeper, meeting with midnight moles, the earth preparing itself for the long cold months ahead. I could see a robin on an apple tree, its breast bright red, a good summer's hunting in the hedgerows to see him through the lean months. He churped and waggled his tail and then the gong went for breakfast and I ran in.

Like my father, my grandfather was always able to be busy. His devotion to his library meant that he drove his car many miles to antiquarian book shops. Today we were to stay behind to pickle the cucumbers. Not onions, because they were considered common. Mrs Harding could eat pickled onions, but not us. Aunt Mary let me eat pickled onions until I belched loudly. "Choke up, chicken," Aunt Mary always said and patted me on the back.

I seemed to exist in several worlds at once. Phoebe didn't, though she lived with her mother or at school just the way it always was. Her life was staid in that she did not bother with boys or getting married, nor did she have anyone like Aunt Mary in her life. In some ways she was lucky, but in others I felt I learned so much more, particularly from Aunt Mary. If Aunt Mary was right, and my problems with my mother were partly of my own making, then I had something to think about. I was always happy when I had something intense to think about. "You're a worry-wart," Phoebe always said. Yes, that was true. But then, if I wanted to be a writer and a poet, understanding people was an absolute necessity.

For now I was content to think about my grandmother's flower patch and pickling. Both those things, gardening and pickling, would make me a better wife and mother. "Being married," said my grandmother, "is a profession for women." While she helped Mrs Harding carry in the big sterilizing tub, I washed and dried the glass jars that had been filled with pickles for the last fifty years. These jars were not English jars; they were from all over the world. Sometimes they were filled with mangoes or curries or chutneys or spices, but today they were to be filled with the green thick-skinned cucumbers dangling from the vines in the kitchen garden. Also we had picked and cleaned a glowing pile of chokecherry apples to be made into jam for breakfast. "You see," my grandmother said as we decanted the apples onto the kitchen table, "always cook the whole apple with the pips. The pips contain pectin and will naturally set the jelly. None of this awful modern stuff. Gelatine," she shuddered. "How they can do it? I can't think." Gelatine was obviously a dreadful thing.

Grandma was always dropping calves' feet or pigs' trotters into her soups and stews. Mrs Harding hated those amputated feet. "Disgusting," she sniffed, as yet another pair of pigs' trotters landed in our beef casserole. " 'orrid, Mrs Freeland. Don't see 'ow Mr Freeland can eat that kind of muck."

"Well, Mrs Harding, if you fed your children a few more pigs' trotters instead of buying your food from the fish and chip shop, they'd be a lot healthier." Mrs Harding and my grandmother always bickered when they worked together. Mrs Harding didn't believe in the old ways. She lived in a council house and was very modern in her views.

The water in the sterilizing pan was steaming and bright droplets of steam rose into the air. "Huh," my grandmother snorted. "I'll give you some pickles to take home with you for the children."

"Thanks. That'll do nicely. Goes well with fish and chips, don't it?" Mrs Harding roared with laughter and looked at my grandmother. "So what are you going to do about that Vera? She's aiming to win, you know. My old man is running a book on you two. 'e's got ten bob on you to win."

"What are the odds?"

"Two to one that Vera'll pull a stunt and walk off with it."

"Really?" My grandmother looked surprised. "That high against me?"

Mrs Harding nodded. " 'fraid so," she said. "Them that know reckon Vera's got a flower or two up her sleeve. Know what I mean?"

"I do," said my grandmother. "Indeed I do." She shook her head. "The world has come to something when people cheat at flower shows."

Carefully we filled the jars with unpeeled cucumbers. Then we sprinkled dill seeds and other spices over the vegetables and poured in the white vinegar. I liked very sour cucumbers, but Mrs Harding liked them sweeter, so we added a little sugar for her. While the jars stewed on the stove we went to inspect the flower garden.

This year my grandmother was right to be inordinately pleased with her flowers. For her a flower was not just a thing of beauty; it was like a child that had been conceived in the January cold. Discovered in a catalogue of flowers and then ordered as if by God to be planted tenderly into His soil, and then watched as anxiously as a pregnancy. This year the lupins were magnificent. My grandmother pottered about with her secateurs, talking to each plant. One particularly dense blue plant had obviously had a difficult time in the spring. "Yes, darling," my grandmother said with a croon in her voice. "You poor, poor thing. But you're all right now. Just a little extra mulch and manure, and you came through beautifully." The borders, lined with cheeky marigolds, got a telling off. "And you," she said, looking at a rather busy gaggle of marigolds, "you do your hair every morning. Tut, tut, tut. What a mess!" Snip, snip, snip, went the secateurs. Soon I was as involved as she was.

The days went unbelievably fast. In Paris I had

hours to read and sit and dream, but with my grand-mother and my grandfather I was too busy to read my beloved books. Grandpa loved to read to me. He had a volume of Greek poems and he read well. His voice was deeper than my father's. My grandmother loved to listen with me. I saw how women in my grandmoth-er's day kept busy through all the seasons. The idea of buying, instead of making, a Christmas pudding never entered my grandmother's head. I wondered if I would ever be as good a housewife as my grand-mother. My mother ran an excellent establishment, but she was unable to cook. I so much wanted to be like my grandmother. When we went shopping in the village, everybody knew her. The men always took off their caps and bowed slightly. The fishmonger kept the best fish for her and sometimes, when he had a lit-tle illegal venison, he handed her an already wrapped parcel with a wink. "Probably one of our deer," my grandfather said.

The village had a multi-layered life of its own. Se-crets zoomed from ear to ear, brushing past pint-pots full of Whitbread or Guinness from Dublin. Still, out among the flowers, life was innocent. "I think," my grandmother said, deep in a reverie of her own, "I think this year I'll submit my arrangement in all colors of blue. The delphinia behind, then rows of purple iris, and to fill out the front we'll put a fan of cornflow-ers. I think the innocence of the cornflowers will set off the iris. What do you think?"

I looked carefully at the irises. They looked a little like chorus girls wrapped in green dresses exposing purple-blue breasts. If we waited until midnight I would see them leap from their restraining sheaths and dance wild and naked on the lawn. Indeed the cornflowers, with their blue kitten faces, were inno-cent compared with the irises. And the delphinia, bluer and tall, resembled disapproving older sisters.

I could imagine them stomping off after their naked sibling sybarites and attempting to regiment them back into their flower arrangement. I hoped the vicar would be fast asleep in his bed the night they spent at the show. "I think that will look wonderful," I said.

"Oh good. Then that's settled. Tonight I'll get Ned to water them deeply. Come along. Let's finish the pickling."

Next week arrived with a bang. All day I could hear the sound of the hammers beating down the tent pegs that pulled the guys taut. Then, after much shouting from the green, a huge tent stood stiffly to attention. The day of the show dawned and we were off. Why I felt it was all a little like a horse race, I shall never know. Maybe the tension in the house reminded me of the excitement of a race track in Chantilly where my parents sometimes took a box and took me with them. However, it was one thing to share the excitement of the beautiful Arabs pulling to win, and another to be among the supposed peace and tranquility of a flower show. Our arrangement—for my grandmother and I shared the task of arranging the flowers—looked superb. Sitting on the long trestle tables, our delphinia and the other flowers glowed blue in a shivering contrast to the bright green of the grass outside the tent. Many of the other arrangements lost much of their color because the whiteness of the tent bleached their faces, but our blue thrived against the white and I was sure we would win.

As soon as we were set up, we scouted the other tables for Mrs Rogers's effort. Indeed she had overdone the dahlias. My grandmother put her hand to her throat, which was one of her gestures for when she was upset. In the middle of the bunch of multicolored flowers, which reminded me of the hideous patterns on the carpet of her house, squatted three flowers.

"Birds of paradise," my grandmother said faintly. "She can't have grown those."

"Perhaps she has a greenhouse," I suggested.

"Perhaps she has," my grandmother said distractedly.

Nobody else had anything as exotic a flower as those evil-looking pointy objects. I knew that, and I knew that this year the flowers were not to be judged by the vicar, who was a gardening enthusiast and a purist. No, after much ructions in the gardening committee, the matter of adjudicator had been democratically put to a vote and Mr Hillcrest, a local vintner, was elected. "That's what you get when you let commies in," my grandfather had snorted when he heard the verdict.

Today Mr Hillcrest looked a little bewildered and a little frightened. He had just given an interview to the local paper and now he was surrounded by forty females in various assorted carefully chosen dresses, some with hats and gloves. Whether he was to judge the multifloral dresses or the flowers themselves was a question much on his mind. He knew that whatever decision he made that day, thirty-nine of those dresses would possess furious disappointed faces, and his name in thirty-nine different households would be mud. Worse than that, would they boycott his shop? Would they cut his wife in the streets and his children in the playground? He wished he had left the whole thing in the hands of the good vicar, who always had God as his judge, and all the women would be kneeling in the church, win or lose. Besides, one can't hate the vicar. I saw Mr Hillcrest heave a great sigh and I felt sorry for him. Men really were no match for women.

He gazed and he paused here and there. He inclined an ear to a soft female pluck at his sleeve. He did stop in front of our arrangement for a very long time. I prayed and prayed he'd choose us, and then I prayed a slightly delinquent prayer that he would not choose Mrs Rogers, even when he lingered there looking at the woman's awful display.

Mrs Rogers simpered and twisted her lips into an ingratiating smile. "He supplies her with all her alcohol," my grandmother whispered. "I do hope that doesn't tempt him."

We stood for what seemed like hours, and then the moment came for Mr Hillcrest to do his stuff. "Ah hem," he said, shuffling his feet. "I have decided that the third prize should go to Mrs Garner. A mass of roses . . . tea. The smell excellent . . ." He was stumbling over his words and he blushed a bright red.

But suddenly we began to hear little shrieks, suppressed at first and then shrill. "Oh, how awful! Ahhh!" By now people were vacating the tent. I looked across the tables. There stood Mrs Rogers's colossal bunch of dahlias vomiting earwigs: big, dark, shiny, pincered earwigs. They had been disturbed from their evil sleep by the warmth of the arc lights and they were abandoning ship as fast as they could. Other entrants had grabbed their exhibits and left, but I stood fascinated. Suddenly the flowers looked obscene. The three birds of paradise, their brightly colored noses in the air, took on a menace. I could almost hear jungle drums as the flow of fat earwigs crashed to the ground and spread. They rose up out of the mouths of the flowers like bile, black and bitter.

Poor Mr Hillcrest hurriedly awarded the next two prizes to an almost empty tent. We got a second, but that didn't matter. My grandmother and I returned to the car where my grandfather sat waiting. "Well, darling," grandmother said, "we got a second. But what is much more important is that that awful woman didn't win anything at all." Guiltily I remembered my prayer. The Lord, I thought, works in strange ways indeed.

All the way home my grandmother sat next to my grandfather and regaled him with the day's events. Just as they turned into the drive, I saw him put his hand gently over hers and give it a squeeze. Then she looked at him with such love I felt tears in my eyes. I felt an aching homesickness for my mother, who never looked at my father like that, but then maybe if I really tried to understand her she would one day look at me like that. And above all, I promised myself before going to sleep that night, above all I hoped in the days of our marriage Patrick and I could always look at each other with such love.

What my grandmother and grandfather had was a bridge they shared together. Not a huge lumbering thing, but a finely crafted shimmering bridge that held them both forever together, indissoluble and eternal. I wanted that for myself.

❧ *Chapter 42* ❧

I got back to Paris and good news. My O-level results had come in. My father was still at the office but my mother was pleased. I had passed all eight O-levels and I did particularly well in maths. "Well done, darling," she said and she kissed me a tiny feathery kiss on the cheek. I had trouble with the glass that kept me from the real world, but the wall between my mother and myself seemed to be made of glass bricks and the first one just fell out. Through it I could see my mother's face. This time there was a kindly look on that face that so used to frighten me.

Also, after I so calculatingly made love to Patrick, I realized that life was not really a series of me trying to be perfect and hating myself when I failed. I had read *The Pilgrim's Progress* many years ago and I now realized I had taken the whole journey too much to heart. God would and did forgive me if I was less than perfect, just as he loved and forgave my mother. I also realized that I needed to try far harder to get on with her on her terms. Shopping for clothes and her social life may not be my cup of Aunt Mary's Lipton tea, but that was what she enjoyed, and I as her daughter could learn to enjoy those things. After all, Patrick wanted me to be a good social wife and my mother had much to teach me.

"Tomorrow," my mother said, "we must go off and buy your wardrobe for finishing school."

I saw the hesitation in her eyes, wary, waiting for my ungracious response. "That will be wonderful, mother," I said and I smiled.

The hesitation turned to surprise. "Really, Mary," she said. "You usually make such a fuss."

"I've grown up," I said. "Really I have."

My mother telephoned for tea. "Let's have tea in my study," she said.

I followed her feeling warm and sunny. She really did love me. We sat down together and Madame Charpentier brought in the tea-tray. "I 'ope you 'ave 'ad a good summer, mademoiselle," she said in her heavily accented English.

"Oh, I have. I really have."

My mother looked sharply at me. "You have grown up, haven't you?"

I could see she saw the change in me. "Yes," I said and I waited. There was a long pause between us while I stared at the spout of the teapot and tried not to remember. The tea ran loudly into the cup.

My mother was waiting but without anger. I knew her so well. "You did sleep with Patrick?" she said, quite gently.

I sighed a long sigh. "I'm afraid I did, Mother."

"Well," said my mother, business-like as ever, "we must not tell your father. He would be broken-hearted."

"Aren't you?"

"I should be," she said, "but then I've always been a little different from other women." I felt her history rustle the pages of the past. I knew now was not the time to ask. My mother smiled a funny little smile. "Most women do seduce their men before marriage. Did you enjoy it?"

I made a face. "Not much," I said. "I do hope it gets better."

"Well, it might and then it might not." I saw from the toss of her head that for her it had not. I hoped, as I suddenly felt so much my mother's daughter, it would improve for me.

Father came home and we sat at dinner as usual. We ate the same type of meal that we three had shared since I was old enough to sit at the table. Now there was a profound difference among the three of us. I understood what happened all those years ago in Africa when I saw my father lying in my mother's arms. I had done the same thing with Patrick as he lay sleeping so vulnerably beside me. Gone forever was the jealous furious little girl in open competition with my mother. I was now bound, by my guilty secret of lost innocence, to my mother. Both of us were adult women keeping a secret from a male. Male innocence appeared somehow so much simpler than anything women think up. My grandmother and I had sneaked off while my grandfather slept his way through his symphonies. No words spoken, both females simply knowing that one need not sit bored through the music, but also that grandfather was comforted in our company, so we were back when he awoke. A lie perhaps, but white. Now my mother and I both protected my father.

"Good night, Pumpkin," he said and kissed my betraying cheek.

My mother was in the library just finishing her last stitches of embroidery. "Here," she said as I walked in carrying an exuberant Taiwan. "Have a chocolate." She handed me the forbidden box. Had she ever discovered the chocolate I had stolen years ago? If she had, she'd kept her discovery to herself. "Tomorrow," she said, smiling as I eagerly accepted a curaçao chocolate, "we go shopping. I'm very much looking forward to this."

I wandered off to bed a little euphoric from our time together. "You know," I said to Taiwan's mop of blonde hair, "I'm very much looking forward to it, too. How surprising." Taiwan turned his little face upside down to look at me. His ancient Chinese eyes stared. I knew Taiwan wasn't surprised by anything. And just to prove it, he stood on his head, burrowed into the carpet, and then did a lion dance down to my room. Tomorrow was going to be fun.

"Do you think that I might buy my clothes at *Bon Marché?*" I held my breath. The thought of Madame Gio's hot sticky hands fumbling about my breasts made me blush with embarrassment. Also I resented the exquisitely made clothes, so different from the other girls' English clothes. I wanted to wear cashmere jerseys from Harrods and skirts from Marks and Spencer's. *Bon Marché* was the closest I could get to the dowdy but practical English look.

My mother laughed. "Your father will be pleased," she said without rancour. "He'll appreciate the savings."

"Well, I am glad for that," I said. "I know I don't

usually pay much attention to my clothes, but I will try to find things that we both like."

Off we went in the Daimler. I remember the day with affection. The streets of Paris were thrumming with people. Unlike Ealing where the white people walked sullenly in their overrun streets, the Parisians and the Algerians mixed happily together. Calls and shouts swung in the air. "Half-past three," my mother said to the chauffeur and her elegant diminutive figure swept into the shop with me following behind. When she walked her feet hit the ground like a machine gun rattle. I had to run to keep up with her. She had such amazing charisma that all the sales ladies on the ground floor leaned over their counters awaiting her orders. I was used to this, of course, but rarely if ever would my mother enter a *Bon Marché*, so the sight of this hummingbird with a jewel at her throat was breathtaking. How, ever, if ever, could I be like her? Would I ever light up the darkness and the dingy shops like she could? "Come," she said and we caught the lift to the dress floor. "Have whatever you like, darling," she said. "I won't interfere."

"But please," I said. "You must tell me what to wear. I've no idea."

"All right," she said. "Let's go for a smart black cocktail dress with a small hat and veil. I gather from the headmistress Fridays are open night at Mont St Sebastian. They entertain boys from a local military academy. Not, of course, that that would be of any interest to you?"

I looked at her face which held a sly *femme-à-femme* smile. "Of course not," I said, returning her smile. "But I can still look nice."

We did buy a lovely dress, cut on the cross and falling from a Roman bustline in folds to midcalf. The hat was tiny and perched lightly on my fair hair which was growing quite long now. And as a last minute present my mother brought me a pair of black wrist gloves. I was really pleased with myself. I looked much older, no longer a shy young thing and awkward. "Let's have lunch and then buy the boring stuff," my mother said over her shoulder as she strode purposefully through the store.

One thing I noticed in these early days of our new relationship, my mother was full of life, and never defeated. If something occurred that would bore me to mouth-splitting yawns, my mother took it all in her stride and made a huge party out of the event. For instance, on the few occasions we had a blackout due to a storm, we did not huddle around the open fires or run about grasping candles. My mother simply ordered a tray of food for our knees, and then we popped corn or hung plump marshmallows on the end of toasting forks and then dropped them into our coffee laced with brandy. Once I told her that Balzac made his own coffee with a mixture of Bourbon beans, Martinique beans, and Mocha. She didn't seem much interested, but then a few days later I complimented her on the coffee and it was exactly as he had made it.

Now as we rushed to lunch I remembered her habit of packing picnics. I was quite young for the first one. We had broken down on the Route 19, that treacherous road, and the chauffeur disappeared in a farm truck that kindly stopped to help. We were left, my father forlorn and cross. He hated anything to happen to his cars. "Never mind," said my mother. "Darling, go to the boot and we will have a picnic." There was ice, a bottle of Taitinger, some very light smoked salmon on Melba toast sprinkled with a few fat gray spheres of Beluga caviar looking like rain drops, and then peaches. Out of season, but delicious, for all that . . .

Why did I suddenly remember good times, when

before I felt my life an unyielding battle of attrition with her? I didn't know. Why did she seem positively glad, for the first time ever, to be spending time with me? Was it because she had detected a change, a maturity, in me?

I had very much missed the good French cooking that can be found only in France. I ordered jugged hare and then *crème brûlée*. The salad dressing tasted familiar and refreshing. How I missed olive oil, crushed garlic, and the sting of vinegar. "What will the food be like in Switzerland?" I asked.

My mother laughed. "The Swiss are not known for their food. Mostly cuckoo clocks and chocolate."

I sighed. "Phoebe will be happy. She adores chocolate. She says she'd always rather go to bed with a good box of chocolates than a man." Was I pushing our new-found confidence too far?

My mother raised her eyebrows. "She has a point there," she said.

"Mother," I ventured, "do you like being married?"

She finished her mouthful of grilled sole. "You must understand, darling. In our day we didn't have choices. You either married and looked after your husband and his career, or you were a spinster. I was one of the lucky ones. I married. And I married well. Believe me, I have every reason to be enormously grateful to your father for marrying me."

"I've always wanted to ask you a question," I said. "Did you know your mother? I mean, you never talk about her . . ."

My mother's eyes clouded over and a sombre almost haunted look came into her eyes. I felt I had pushed her onto a precipice and I felt guilty. Then I looked again and I saw tears well in her lustrous, very beautiful eyes. She fished in her handbag and brought out a minute lace handkerchief. "I can't talk about that part of my life, Mary," she said. "You mustn't ask. But

I will tell you that you did or maybe still do have a grandmother in the Far East. She was a wonderful brave good woman and she loved me but had to leave me. I can't bear to think about it. It is far too painful, but your father understands and he loves me anyway. One day, perhaps, I will be able to tell you my story, but for now let us bury the past. I want to see you happily married and then," she smiled, "I want grandchildren. I think I'd be a much better grandmother than I was a mother. I think you make all your mistakes on your children and then God gives you a second chance to get it right."

I smiled, too. "I'll do my best."

We spent the rest of the day flying around Paris buying wonderful clothes. We finished with an elegant trunk and a hatbox. "As yet," my mother said, "you won't need a jewel box. But I do have a special present for you when you are married."

"What is it?" The familiar cloud came up in her face. "Never mind," I said. "I can wait."

We arrived home in time for sherry. I changed into my chic new black dress to show my father. "My word," he said. "I'd better stop calling you Pumpkin."

"Oh no, Daddy. Don't ever," I said, rent apart at the idea he might not always be there as my father. "You must always call me Pumpkin."

He laughed and hugged me.

The few weeks left flew by. I talked to Patrick and he seemed busy and happy. I wished he would say that he missed me more, but then Patrick was always very abrupt on the telephone. I talked at great length to Phoebe who was not at all pleased to be going to the finishing school. "Bloody awful waste of time!" she yelled over the thin wires stretched between Ireland and Paris. "Waste of a whole year. Rotten old Jeremy's bunked Oxford and is off to breed horses in Chantilly.

Mum says she'll do fine without us, because Joe and Charlie are living with her for good. So I'd much rather go to Chantilly with Jeremy, but Mum insists on a year of that awful crap in Switzerland."

"But, Phoebe," I reasoned. "It's only a year and you can learn all those things that one has to learn. Anyway, maybe one day you'll want to get married."

Loud snort from Phoebe. "Listen, Mary. Once you've seen horses doing it, it puts you off for life."

I didn't have much to say to that, so I wished her goodbye and arranged to meet at Mount St Sebastian.

Last of all I called Mademoiselle. "Our little boy's doing fine," she said. "Would you believe it? Jacques is totally infatuated with him."

I laughed. "After all that complaining."

"I know," Mademoiselle giggled. I was glad to hear the old happiness in her voice. "He is always picking him up and I have to remind him I did the giving birth. Have a good time, my little one, and leave me your address. I will send you army rations. Switzerland, *oh là!*"

"Yes, *Oh là,* indeed. Still, it's only a year." And then I remembered a year is a very long time indeed.

❦ *Chapter 43* ❧

We had finished dinner. This was a celebration for my going to Switzerland the next morning. Upstairs my suitcase lay bulging with my new clothes. The meal had been light-hearted and my mother at her best. My father sat twinkling at both of us and then the accident happened.

Taiwan wandered into the room and squatted down to pee. I jumped to my feet to grab him, but it was too late. A damp patch of moisture stained the graceful Persian carpet. Had I been naïve to think that my mother had changed? With a shriek she lunged at Taiwan. I yelled, "I'll clear it up!" and raced for the kitchen with Taiwan in my arms. I pushed him into the cook's arms and grabbed a cloth and a bottle of disinfectant.

On the way back I could hear my mother shouting. "We must get rid of that damn dog! Do you hear me? I won't have that untrained brute in my house."

My father was making useless soothing noises. I flung myself on my knees and scrubbed furiously. My mother by now was standing over me, her hands on her hips. I stood up. "It's all clean," I said, aware that Taiwan would be miserably whining in the kitchen and that Armand our cook had little sympathy with dogs. If only Max were here instead of in Africa.

"It's time that your stupid dog had learned to be housetrained. I won't have a dog that can't behave." She pointed at the carpet. "This is an extremely valuable carpet. Priceless, in fact."

I tried to head her off. "Yes, I know. I remember when we got it from that Arab bedouin tent outside Morocco." On one of her many foraging trips, we went to Morocco to buy carpets. The first time I saw this carpet it was in a huge tent covered with food, chickens, even a goat, only I knew this was no time to remember that. Try rather and seduce her into the memory of her buying sprees. It worked.

She smiled at my father. "Do you remember the sheeps' eyes?"

"Yes, I do," my father chuckled.

The dangerous moment over, I kissed them both goodnight and left to collect Taiwan. I lectured him on the way to my bedroom. Soon he was asleep at the foot of my bed snoring loudly. Sleepless myself, I lay in bed and thought. Part of her rage had nothing to do with me or with Taiwan. It must come from her mysterious past. Somewhere deep down, so much damage lay like a submerged submarine, dark and drifting. Maybe day to day things occurred that caused the drifting submarine to move and to hurt her: a wet patch on a carpet takes on a sinister message. That was what I was determined to find out. No longer was I prepared to take her anger personally. We had now shared enough time together to know that she did love me and I loved her. But the dreadful glass wall had to come down. I fell asleep dreaming of Africa my beloved.

Leaving days are always full of excitement. Unlike Phoebe, who moaned all the way to a new adventure, I couldn't wait to leave. Putting my last few things away, I smiled at my old garter belts. Awful rubber roll-on things had come into the fashion, but I eschewed (such a lovely word) fashion and continued to wear my suspenders, those given to me by Jacques and Mademoiselle. I flew down to breakfast and, as I had thought, my mother's eyes were as clear as a summer beach. My father left for the office, pressing a hundred francs into my hand. "For the journey," he said, "Pumpkin. Goodbye and be good." I nodded and hugged him.

Then my mother and I said goodbye. "You know, Mary," she said, "you have a whole year to yourself before you get married. I want you to be absolutely sure about this marriage. If you don't feel that marrying Patrick is the only thing in your life, don't do it, will you?"

"Oh, mother, we've been through this before."

"I know. But you have never been married. For a man, marriage can be a thing apart. For a woman, it's her whole life. Don't listen to modern women who say you can have both marriage and a career. That really is not true. For us, our relationship with a man is our whole life. It has to be, because little else is important to us. Look at the women of my age who aren't married. Do you think they're happy?"

I thought of the few career women I knew. They were lonely, always seated at the ends of tables and considered troublesome by the hostess because they had to be found male partners and were likely to try and pinch someone else's husband. "I know I can love Patrick," I said defensively. "I know I can."

"But with passion?"

I stared at her. What did she know about passion, I wondered.

She hugged me. "Go," she said, "or you will be late. But take this opportunity to have fun. And take risks. You're only young once." I felt her small body stiffen, as if she had given away a sad memory.

I felt, as I sat in the Daimler, that my mother had never been able to be young. I felt my mother had never had any choices, that events had determined her choices. Here she was, giving me a year for myself. It was her present to me. The thought of that was exhilarating.

Then I was flying, cuddled into a blue wool blanket, spoiled by the first class stewardess. I ate my cold salmon mousse and sipped a glass of *Fleur du Champagne*. The man in the chair beside me was good-looking with yellow eyes and dark black hair. He smiled at me over the rim of his glass. I ostentatiously raised my hand so he could see my engagement ring. It deterred him not at all.

Before we landed, he asked me to go out to dinner, but I was able to tell him that we were locked away for our year at Mont St Sebastian. "I see, mademoiselle." He bowed and kissed my hand at the airport. "We shall see." He had a strange accent, a mixture of

French and German. His hair was *en brosse,* silky. I wondered if it felt like a black velvet pin-cushion.

Then I scolded myself in the taxi. "You have no right to think like that," I reminded myself. "You are engaged to Patrick." But then Reimer (as he had introduced himself) would never see me again.

I lay back and watched the taxi puff up the neat Swiss roads, full of clean smiling people. The fields looked like a quilt had been sewn. Tiny dazzlingly white sheep ate bright green grass. Small cows moved slowly in the fields. Birds sung sweetly, not raucously like the London birds. No large pigeons, in dirty shades of gray, lived here. Of course I had read *Heidi* when I was a child, and had gobbled up the version of the perfect pink-cheeked little girl who herded goats and sang so prettily up the mountainsides and never caught a cold in her life.

The taxi drew up to an immense Teutonic castle. Other taxis were drawing up and disgorging various girls with their piles of luggage. My suitcases looked quite modest and shabby sitting beside the Louis Vuitton owned, it seemed, by everyone else. No sign, of course, of Phoebe. "This way, Mademoiselle Freeland." A small plump maid signaled a bellboy to carry my suitcases to my room. "You are sharing with Mademoiselle Balfor," she said. "And you will share with Princess Obona. She is from Ghana. Our *directrice,* Madame Ferneux, knows that you have lived in Africa and that you will take care of the Princess."

"Wonderful," I said. "I'd like to do that." Our room was in a turret that had a panoramic view of the mountains. We had three virginal beds with white covers. Mine should be scarlet, I thought. Suzette, as she introduced herself, began to unpack my suitcase into a large cupboard. In the room where two very comfortable, overstuffed, cabbage-rose-encrusted armchairs. I watched Suzette unpack and I wondered if she resented me. Here I was, all of seventeen, sitting watching a young married woman unpacking clothes that she would never own, or if she did, they would be hand-me-downs from people like me. "Do you have any children?" I asked.

"Yes, mademoiselle," she said. "I have two children, one of six and the other ten."

"Good heavens," I said. "You don't look old enough."

Suzette giggled. "It is the good clean air we have in Switzerland."

There arrived the unmistakeable sounds of Phoebe's large feet pounding up the corridor. "Thank goodness you're here," Phoebe panted. Behind her a porter struggled with her luggage. Phoebe's big suitcase was tied with a very old piece of rope and her hand luggage consisted of two battered suitcases and a cardboard box. "Ran out of money," she said by way of explanation.

I didn't think the porter had ever before carried a cardboard box into this elegant establishment and he glared at it distastefully. "Tip him, Phoebe," I said.

"Can't. I've run out of money."

I pulled out some francs.

He went off smirking and Suzette smiled cheerfully. "Good day, Mademoiselle Balfor. Shall I help you unpack?"

"I shouldn't, if I were you," Phoebe laughed. "I didn't have time to wash half the stuff and you risk a nasty disease."

"Don't worry, Suzette. I'll help her unpack and sort out the washing." This was not the first time that Phoebe arrived in chaos and I was used to it.

"I will ring for the laundry to be collected before dinner," Suzette offered, leaving us alone.

"Indeed," I said firmly. There was no way that I wanted an African Princess to arrive from a strange country and witness a huge pile of unsavoury laundry heaped about her room. "Come on, Phoebe. Let's get started."

We learned that our Princess wasn't due to arrive until the next day, so Phoebe and I changed for dinner and went down the ornate oak staircase and followed the noise of several hundred girls chattering into a huge dining room. "Goodness." Phoebe stood in the doorway blinking. I blinked. I was more used to elegant dining rooms than Phoebe, but this was sumptuous. The small tables sat six girls. Each table had a *Lalique* table lamp in the middle throwing out soft shadows over the elaborate silver settings. The room was mirrored, making the tables multiply into infinity, and the faces of the girls circled the room. From the room came the smell of money, lots of it. This smell was a clean fresh perfume. Some might say a ten-franc note smells no different to a crisp fifty-franc note; I could smell the difference myself. I was reminded of the two deliciously scented fifty-franc notes in my handbag.

I was glad I had chosen to wear my black dress with my row of pearls. Phoebe wore a dress created by Bridie. The only other handmade dresses in this room were made by Chanel or Worth; though it was Chanel who was all the rage among the young. Lanvin dressed their mothers.

"Good evening." A bent haggard woman with a rictus of a smile came up to us. "I am Madame Rosen. I am here to teach you literature, but tonight I must take you to see our *directrice*, Madame Ferneux." She led us, with a shuffling foot dragging behind her, to a table across the room.

Our *directrice* looked nothing like our previous headmistress, Miss Standish at Sherwood Park. Miss Standish you knew was a highly literate woman and not interested in much outside books and music. Madame

Ferneux resembled a Christmas tree fairy, every day the 25 December. She was surrounded by a group of women dressed in evening gowns, who looked like Christmas parcels set around the tree. Reds and golds sat softly on their shapely shoulders. Madame Ferneux out-preened them all. She was tall, at least six feet, and her black hair was bound up in a stern chignon. Her face was severe, but, as my mother would say, she was *jolie laide:* ugly, but by dint of the ugliness, she was beautiful. Her great hooked nose hung over a wide mouth of large white teeth. Her eyes were big, heavy-lidded and full of antique wisdom. She reminded me of an Eve, wiser than the serpent. Madame Ferneux sat back in her chair and looked at us with a smile. "Ah," she said. "The two little English girls, *les petites anglaises.*" I felt horribly gauche. Phoebe just hopped from foot to foot. "Well, my dears, we will make women of you yet." She had the most lived in face I'd ever seen.

Madame Rosen also smiled. "I hear you are interested in writing?"

"Yes," I said. "Very."

"And you, Mademoiselle Balfor? What interests you?"

"Horses," Phoebe said. "Only horses."

"Ah." Madame Rosen gave a little sigh. "Maybe we will discuss the role of the horse in literature." We followed Madame Rosen back across the room and she ushered us to a table with two other girls. "Relax after your journey and enjoy your dinner."

We did. Both the other girls were German: Frieda and Gretchen. They came from Aschaffenburg and were jolly and laughing. The table wine was excellent and so was the meal. "They must have a French chef," I whispered to Phoebe.

"I guess," she said disconsolately. "Look at all that yuk sauce. I like my food plain."

I knew Phoebe was feeling dreadfully homesick. "How are George and Spice?" I asked, knowing that talking about her horses would comfort her.

Phoebe broke into a torrent of detail until Gretchen stopped her. "Why are you here?" she inquired in a direct German manner.

I shrugged. "My mother wanted to give me a year here to sort of get polished off."

"I'll be polished off in six months," Phoebe said gloomily. "You'll have to accompany my body home for the funeral." She turned to Gretchen and Frieda. "Either of you any good at keening?" she asked.

Our German tablemates didn't know what to say. "Don't be silly, Phoebe," I laughed. "And what are you here for, Gretchen?"

"Ho!" Frieda laughed. She was fat with wild yellow hair and huge blue eyes. "We're here to get married!"

"Get married! How?"

"Every Friday night we have a cocktail and then dinner with the young men from the military academy. We are the only young girls of their age and class, so we have ripe pickings. Yes?"

I laughed. "There you are, Phoebe. That's what you can do: chase military men."

"Only if they have horses," Phoebe smiled. Good, she was feeling better.

We finished our meal and wandered up the stairs. All around the house groups of girls were standing together or leaning against each other. It struck me how the rich always looked beautiful. The hair, rinsed and immaculate, spoke of hours at the hairdresser. I remembered, with a pang, the tired pregnant body and the lined face of Mademoiselle in Paris. Her hair was washed at home with cheap shampoo, and lack of good food stripped her normally beautiful hair down to rat-tails. Most of the girls had never known want in their lives any more than I had. Phoebe certainly had, but even then, poverty in a castle is not quite the same.

Both our beds were neatly turned down, inviting us for a good night's sleep. Just before she went to sleep, Phoebe put out her hand and took mine. "Good night, idiot," she said. "We'll get through this year in one piece, I suppose. At least the grub's good."

"It is," I said thankfully, and fell asleep dreaming of a tall man with a menacing look in his eye, and my engagement ring someone lost.

&❧ *Chapter 44* ❧&

I slept fitfully. Maybe it was the strangeness of the room, or maybe it was the all-knowing smile on Madame Ferneux's face. I awoke about one o'clock. I had just had a terrifying dream. Traces of it still remained: Madame Ferneux's face distorted and frightening, and then the face of the man on the airplane. I leaned my head against the cold window pane and gazed out into the darkness. A mad murderous moon glared harshly back at me. The rays illuminated the nothingness of the countryside. I felt alone and very frightened. What was going to happen to me in this country so far from home? Why did I feel an undercurrent of evil? Was it the vaults in Zurich, not far away, full of gold? In the wind, which was loud around the portcullis of the house, I thought I heard the howling of many devils. "Dear God," I prayed, "take care of me."

Then in the moonlight I saw *his* face again and I shut my eyes. I remembered the words I would rather forget, as he left the airport. "You won't run away, little chicken. I have you under my wing." His smile was smug and he saw into the dark recess of my heart where one thinks things that will never be said in the open. Why did that part of myself exist? I didn't know. I was sure though that Phoebe had no dark places. Certainly I always thought Geneviève, the French Ambassador's daughter, had caves. I saw them in her eyes and in her smile.

I felt a great fear, but also a shivering excitement that I never felt with Patrick. I wanted to draw the man's face through the glass and rest his lips on my breast . . .

I shook my head and said, "Don't be silly. Too much reading." My favorite book of all time was *Journey into the Mind's Eye* by Leslie Blanche. In it the heroine had her Traveler. I had found my traveler, or rather he had found me. Does one necessarily have to go down into a hell of one's own making to know a traveller? I was not sure. Certainly, in *Journey into the Mind's Eye* the heroine never recovers from her obsession with her traveler. Would I with mine? He'll never find me, I thought. He doesn't even know my name. I climbed back into bed and slept badly.

The first day was spent in meetings with our various teachers. I wanted to do the *cordon bleu* cooking course, and Phoebe didn't want to do anything at all. Eventually I got her with a good heart to agree to share my classes. By mid-afternoon our Princess turned up. "Princess Obona Doctoti Amali Sekoto." Suzette announced her as if she announced African Princesses every day.

"Do call me Hattie," this tall elegant girl said, smiling. Phoebe looked at her suspiciously and Hattie laughed. "No," she said. "No bone in my nose, and I left my lion-skin at home in the ceremonial hut." She turned to me. "Madame Ferneux tells me you've lived in Africa."

"Yes," I said. "And I loved every minute of it."

Hattie sighed. "So do I. I get so homesick for our own way of life." She frowned. "I just have to do this damned year and then I can go back. Which courses are you doing?" I told her and then the gong went.

We had our second dinner, and apart from Madame Ferneux wandering up and down the dining room sticking her talons into our backs if we dared to slouch, it was excellent. The night went by dreamlessly and the days slipped away on gossamer wings.

Most of the courses were good fun. I learned to make dishes such as avocados layered with fresh crab, more avocado, more crab, white wine, topped off with a layer of the pinkest, most luscious morsel of smoked salmon, and then to finish a slice of lime and a sprinkle of caviar. The kitchen carried both Russian and Persian caviar. I preferred the Persian. Later that day I wrote down the recipe for my mother and a long letter about my life.

Hattie didn't write letters. She lay on her bed talking to any of her many friends across the world. I envied her. I only telephoned Aunt Mary. " 'ow you doing?" she said when I rang a week later.

"Very well, Aunt Mary. I'm learning *cordon bleu* cooking."

"Ah, that'll keep Patrick a happy man. A man needs his food more than he needs sex."

"Aunt Mary!" I said, hoping Hattie hadn't heard my Aunt's loud voice. She had, and she was grinning. "I'll speak to you again soon," I said, promising myself I would only ring my Aunt if I was alone in our room.

"I heard. Don't worry." Hattie was laughing. "Your Aunt knows a lot about men, doesn't she?"

I nodded. "She's full of good information, but always at the top of her voice."

Hattie looked across at Phoebe who was slumped over the table writing a letter to Jeremy. "In Africa the number one wife always knows how to keep her husband. She puts a powerful spell on him and then she cooks better than the other wives."

"What sort of spell?" Phoebe was still rather nervous of Hattie, who was indeed exotic but not dangerous.

"Oh, nothing much. She just slips a few drops of her menstrual blood into his drink and then he's hers forever."

"Don't wonder," Phoebe said. "Who'd want him after that? "Mmm. Pass me some of that menstrual blood . . .' "

"Hattie, is that true?"

"Indeed it is," she said. "We African women spoil our men. Fortunately, I'm engaged to a modern man and won't have to share him with any other women." She gazed vaguely into the middle distance. "His name is Richard. He's a lawyer."

"Oh good." Phoebe was relieved.

The Friday night cocktails and dances were simply pure and unashamed fun. All of us spent ages putting on makeup and our party frocks. I had a deep blue dress with a plunging neckline, not that there was much to plunge about. Phoebe looked attractive in a white dress, and Hattie looked utterly stunning in her designer dress. "Cost my father both of his legs, this one did," she said twirling around. "But then, I'm his favorite daughter, so I can do anything I like." Anything she liked included a very large hamper from Simpsons stocked full of pâté and other delightful comestibles, plus an unlimited account at Harrods. "You used to be able to order elephants from Harrods," Hattie said mournfully. "When I was in our house in Belgravia, I ordered chickens because I was homesick for the sound of the rooster. They came round very promptly with a dozen hens and a delightful rooster.

I called the rooster "Stalin." He got up every morning to call the sun, not very successfully, I'm afraid. Some neighbor strangled him. Such barbarians, the British. My great-grandfather would have cooked anybody that did that at home. Shame how times have changed." I agreed with her. I liked Hattie, and in time Phoebe did too.

We had fun on Friday nights. The young soldiers from the academy were eager to dance with us and to fight for our favors. All three of us were good dancers and I was learning to flirt. Hattie was definitely the star attraction, and was pursued with dances, chocolates, and little notes. Usually our room had a bunch of fresh flowers from some swain or other, and the telephone burred constantly for Hattie.

But one day, three months after I had been at Mont St Sebastian, the telephone burred for me. It was my father. "Pumpkin," he said, "I have something to tell you that will hurt you very much."

I felt my face drain of all life. "What?" I said. "Is it Taiwan?" How did I know? Taiwan was my oldest and dearest friend and companion, the only creature on this earth who loved me unreservedly.

"Yes," my father said. "You know, he's been incontinent for some while. You remember his little accident on the carpet? Well, that was the first of many. We called in the vet and the vet said he had a cancer that was incurable. So your mother and I decided the kindest thing was to put him to sleep."

"Oh, no! You can't do that! I haven't said goodbye to him . . . I don't believe you could be so cruel as not to wait for me to get home first." I was sobbing incoherently.

I felt Phoebe take the phone from my hand. "I'll talk to her," she said into the telephone as she hung up.

I could hardly hear what Phoebe was saying. I was in too much pain. I had betrayed Taiwan: I hadn't

been there to explain to him. He was my dog. And if
the vet did have to put him to sleep, I should have
been there.

Much of that dreadful night Phoebe sat beside me
and Hattie made endless cups of coffee laced with
brandy. Finally I passed out and awoke the next morning with an aching head and a parched mouth. The
pain was still there and it remained for weeks and
months. I felt betrayed by both my parents. Now I was
ready for anything, and the mood of the school allowed for anything.

In town, I had learned, there lived a discreet abor-
tionist. Many a wealthy parent would have been
shocked to know that their innocent daughters were
in bed with the boys from the military school in between deportment classes where we walked up and
down the corridors with heavy books on our heads.
Hattie had no problems, but Phoebe and I rarely made
the stairs. I was reprimanded because I slouched. I was
so miserable, I didn't care.

Then one Friday everything changed forever.

He stood at the far end of the dining room talking to
Madame Ferneux. Madame Rosen was sitting with me
at our table. We were discussing Jean Brodie. "I see
myself a little like that," she said, her face over her
plate, her back hunched, and her left foot lying on the
floor as if unattached to her leg.

I knew by now that she had been married, but she
was from Auschwitz, where her husband and all her
family were tortured and killed. I felt a deep love and
respect for her. But tonight I was hardly engaged in
our conversation. From the moment I saw the black
hair and the nape of his neck, I was frozen. A cobra
with his mantle extended, he stood talking. I watched
helplessly. Madame Rosen looked up and saw my en-
tranced stare. Then she searched the room. "Oh, no,"

she whispered. "Not that man, my dear. Any man but that man." She stared at me earnestly. "There are public concentration camps, and there are private concentration camps. Please," she said. "Please, Mary. Don't get involved with him."

I shook myself free from the back of his head and I heard myself say, "Of course not, Madame Rosen. I'm already engaged to be married."

But women like Madame Rosen are not fooled. She just looked at me. "We all have a choice in life, and if you do this thing, you will experience your own private hell."

Oh dear, I thought. Why does it all have to sound so grim? I'm sure he could be fun, and dinner out of here would be nice. Just the company of an attractive man, I reasoned. But inside me, my heart was jumping and bursting. He walked panther-like. Why did I always think of a panther when I thought of him? Probably because I considered the panther one of the most beautiful animals on this earth, and his eyes were wide and yellow. I'd never seen yellow eyes on a man before. Large golden and heavy lashed. And he was standing next to me.

"Mademoiselle," he said clicking his heels together. He kissed Madame Rosen's hand expertly. "We meet again," he said to me and he laid his right hand on my left shoulder for a brief moment. The heat of his hand seared my body.

"Yes. We do meet again," I said lamely.

"A dance?" he said.

I nodded and then, watched by several hundred pairs of eyes, we danced by ourselves. A slow intimate waltz. In his arms I became a veritable ballerina. His finger in my back guided me into twists and turns I didn't know existed.

As we moved in larger and larger circles, I saw Madame Ferneux smiling at me and nodding. Her command was to do all and everything. "Don't die," she told us, "until you have lived as fully as you can." To her mind there was no evil, just an absence of innocence, which she took for granted. I often wondered if two world wars, so much loss, so much damage and suffering, had created women like Madame Ferneux: amoral, because she was incapable of understanding sin.

She smiled at me that night, and I don't remember much else except that this man was in control of me and my life. Ahead was a great yawning abyss. Both of us in a boat that had no oars, and huge white-water waves crashed about us. Snarling rocks bared their teeth and he, only he, could save me.

"What did he say?" Hattie and Phoebe were perched on their beds.

"He looks dreadfully dangerous," Hattie said. "Don't you think, Phoebe?"

"Oh, he's not dangerous," I laughed. "His name is Reimer Walter. You pronounce his surname with a *v:* Valter. He's from a Prussian family and he teaches some courses at the military school. Anyway, I met him on the plane coming here, so we aren't exactly strangers."

"Ohhhh, you do keep secrets! *Reimer,*" Phoebe practiced. "How can you possibly call him Reimer? What sort of a name is that? You'll have to call him Rye, I suppose, if he'll let you. Has he got a sense of humor?"

"I don't know," I said dreamily, "but he dances wonderfully. And he's going to ask me out to dinner."

"He's frightfully old, don't you think?"

"Really, Phoebe," I said. "He's only about forty, and he is a mercenary. Imagine. Leslie Blanche had her traveler, but I have my mercenary. Isn't it wonderful?"

"You also have a fiancé," Phoebe, the voice of reason, said seriously.

"Don't worry," I laughed lightheartedly. "Adventurers and mercenaries are only for dreaming. Patrick has nothing to worry about."

I slept well that night. Something in me had come home. Even Taiwan, for the first time in weeks, didn't disturb my sleep.

❧ *Chapter 45* ❧

Who was this creature I had become? Phoebe called Reimer a "cove" and a "cad." "He should wear two-toned shoes," she added, furious with me.

Hattie was more sympathetic. "You're in lust," she diagnosed. "Awful condition. I've seen women die from it. I had an aunt who rushed off into the bush and got eaten by a lion."

I felt as if I was on fire but dry ice flowed through my veins. I felt as if the whole world was haloed in a golden glow. My body felt light, full of helium, and I could not stop thinking by day of Reimer and dreaming by night of Reimer. I saw every feature: the backs of his hands, his fine nose and black hair, above all his eyes, his baleful yellow enchanting eyes, always watching me.

Of course, I realized, he was not as obsessed with me as I with him . . . But then two days later his flowers arrived and a box of Italian *Baci* chocolates. "At least the man has taste," Hattie observed. "Will you give yourself to him?"

I gazed at her horrified. "Of course not. I'm engaged to Patrick."

Hattie smiled an enigmatic smile. "Is Patrick a virgin?"

"No, he's not."

"Well, that's a relief. You won't have to put up with all that fumbling. If he were, I'd suggest you have a roll in the hay with your Prussian. At least one of you would know what it is all about."

"Hattie," I said, half-scandalized, half-relieved that I might not be alone in my sin after all. "You haven't . . ."

"Oh yes I have. Lots of times. I'm having fun while there's still time. My poor mother had sixteen children and never enjoyed the whole business ever. I'm engaged to Richard, but we have a pact that we tell each other nothing of our private lives. When we marry, I'll be faithful. But for now, my advice to you is: go ahead, have a last fling."

I shook my head. "I don't think that sort of thing is for me." But I didn't believe my own words.

I had to wait a week for his invitation to dinner. The school had no better pupil than myself. I obediently walked the corridors and dropped no books. I sat straight as a ramrod and I cooked my meals with a fierce enthusiasm. Everything I did I did for him. My chocolate soufflé *au Grand Marnier* came out puffed with pride at its achievement. My literature classes with Madame Rosen were intensely occupied with the death of Ophelia. "I can understand how she wanted to die," I said passionately in the middle of a tutorial.

Madame Rosen gave me her sly turtle look. "My dear Mary," she said. "Ophelia was the strongest character in that play. Who remembers much of it, but her dying figure in the water with her hands full of flowers? You must neither think of her as mad or as a victim. She was absolutely sane, but very vengeful."

I was aghast.

Madame Rosen smiled. "One is not a victim of other people's behavior; we are victims of our own. Remember," she said quite sharply, "you have choices, Mary. Use them wisely."

On the evening that Reimer was to collect me for dinner I was called into Madame Ferneux's library. There, in the walled splendour of her private retreat, she sat. Elegant, remote, but quivering with life. Remote from a world I knew and understood, but fascinatingly alive. I felt like a mouse confronted by a mongoose. "Sit, sit. Would you like a sherry?" she asked in her sibilantly silky voice. She held onto her S's, so the words poured from her red lips in a slight lisp.

"Yes," I said. "Thank you very much." I was used to elegant women but I was not at all used to a woman like Madame Ferneux. She gave evil a different dimension. I felt that she had lived a life that contained happenings I would never experience. Her smile seemed unclean. She gazed at me as if she knew me carnally, and it made me unsure of myself.

"So, my little one. Sit down and enjoy your sherry." She poured a good Amontillado.

The sherry stung my tongue, it was so dry . . .

"I gather you are dining with Herr Walter tonight. I have given him permission. But remember, little one. You are still very young. Don't play with fire."

"I don't intend to," I said. "He was kind enough to ask me to dinner."

Madame Ferneux smiled. "I hardly think Reimer Walter is ever *kind.*"

"Oh, madame. People misunderstand him. I think they're jealous because he's so good-looking. We met on the airplane on my way here. He made no advances." I blushed because that was not quite true. "I think he feels sorry for me. He knows how much I miss Paris." I heard the scrunch of wheels on the stones outside the library. I knew it was Reimer, but I sat quietly, and slowly sipped my sherry.

"*Herr Walter est arrivé,*" said the majestic butler whose name was Mason.

"*Enchanté, madame.*" Reimer glided through the long room and bent his head over Madame Ferneux's hand.

His lips brushed the back of her hand and I tingled. I didn't know, until I met Reimer, that one's body had a will all of its own, and I had lost control of mine.

"Ah," he smiled. "*Ma petite Parisienne.* Or are we English today?"

I laughed. "Today I'm English."

"I have a surprise for you. Come along. Finish the sherry and we will leave." He turned to Madame Ferneux. "How are things with you, Felice? As for me, I have some news. Our late lamented Father Augustine has left behind a legacy of wine. I am to inherit a cave full of fine beaujolais. I was most pleased. What a good way to be remembered."

"Ah, yes," sighed Madame Ferneux. "But who will take confessions like Father Augustine? Not, of course, that I had much to confess." I saw a look in her eyes that belied her words.

Reimer's yellow eyes blazed with laughter. "Of course, Felice. You were always the saint, and I the sinner."

"Indeed," she said. "You are taking the child to dinner?"

I resented the word *child,* but he took my hand and I felt the strength in the holding.

"I'll take care of her and bring her back unharmed," Reimer said with an ostentatiously gallant bow.

"See that you do," said Madame.

Mason saw us out of the house.

"Have a good evening," Mason said kindly.

"Thank you," I replied. "We will."

I was surprised to find myself telling Reimer all about Taiwan. I had almost forgotten how upset I was about his death. My eyes were full of tears.

Reimer took out a snowy white handkerchief and handed it to me. "Dry your eyes, *chou chou*. Crying won't help and it will ruin your food."

I felt embarrassed that I had betrayed so much emotion. I whispered, "I got carried away." I looked down at the plate of langoustine in front of me. "They're delicious," I said. "I'm sorry to burden you with my troubles. But you are such a good listener." He was. He listened to my stories about Phoebe and about Hattie in Africa and he laughed a lot, a good deep laugh.

"Tell me more," he said as we ate our way through a perfectly cooked Beef Wellington. The pâté, wine, and steak combined into a celestial harmony of tastes. The pastry was so light as to merely bind the juices in the mouth. "Compliment the chef" was Reimer's comment to the waiter. The wine he chose was a *premier grand cru* Gevrey Chambertin, heady and full. My head felt full of fumes, but I managed my *crème brûlée* and a slice of brie with coffee. "A liqueur," he said, "before I get you back for the curfew?"

"No, thank you," I said. "I won't be able to walk."

"Then I'll carry you," and he was true to his word.

"You haven't paid the bill," I protested as he lifted me off my chair and began to walk towards the restaurant door. I was aware that there were other people in the room for the first time that night. I had been cocooned in our own special world. No one took much notice of us. They were all very Swiss and minded their own business like their bank accounts. I lay with my head pressed to his chest and I felt very safe.

"Good night," my hero said as we left the restaurant.

The headwaiter grinned. He obviously knew Reimer

very well. "Good night, Herr Walter," he said. "We will see you soon again."

"Of course. Next week both of us will dine. Until then."

How wonderful, I thought. There is going to be a next week.

Reimer slid me into his Jaguar and we roared into the black night. The sleek car growled up the hills and I wished, oh, how I wished! that the noise of the engine was Reimer, that somehow we could find a quiet corner of this earth for him to make love to me for ever and ever, only pausing to eat glorious meals and bathe in a bottomless bath full of milk and honey and I could lick his skin clean for him.

The shadow of the school loomed and we drew up at exactly two minutes before 10:30. I could see the time on the car clock. "The same time next week?" he said.

I nodded. "I'd love to."

"Good." He leaned across me and opened the door. I was aware of the deep animal smell of him. Patrick didn't really smell, but Reimer smelled of musk. He turned his head to me, as he reached for the door, and he put his mouth on mine. His lips were full but sure, and the tip of his tongue asked permission. I was drawn into his mouth; there I remained, locked in delight. His arms were about my shoulders and I melted into a pool of sensuous feeling. He paused and then he smiled. "Off you go, *chérie*," he said. "Otherwise you'll be late and I will be in trouble with Felice. And I would not want that, would I?"

"No," I smiled back. "She can be very fierce." I left the car and swam into the house.

Mason opened the door. "Did you enjoy your evening?" he said, his old brown eyes showing concern.

"Oh yes, Mason. I had a wonderful time."

I hoped Phoebe and Hattie were asleep or elsewhere. I really didn't want to talk about Reimer. He was too precious. Neither was in the room and I undressed quickly and fell into bed. I still had his handkerchief and I fell asleep clutching it.

Week after week Reimer took me out to dinner. Occasionally he telephoned me to ask how I was. He seemed genuinely interested in my doings, which seemed so childish compared to his life. Of his own life he said very little, except that he traveled a lot. He had fought in Africa and loved Africa as much as I did. He knew other parts of the world, but he observed once that a soldier of fortune by necessity is secretive. I guarded my tongue after that.

As the months went by, spring joyfully arrived and the fields were full of wild flowers. I was getting a little impatient with Reimer. Here was I, quite willing to be seduced, and my seducer seemed to have no inclination to do so. When we kissed, he often disentangled himself from my passionate embrace with the words "Not now, *chérie*" or "Not yet." When he offered to take me on a picnic, I was ecstatic. This must be the time, I thought, alone and on a rug.

I floated among the other girls at the school like a stranger. Phoebe and Hattie, of course, I talked to, and occasionally to a Chinese girl from Macau named Kim Pedalto, but largely I kept company with my fantasies.

One day I sat crosslegged on my bed, took off my engagement ring, and tied a piece of string to the ring. This was an old trick, a piece of magic Bertha, my first Nanny, taught me. If the ring swung back and forwards, the answer was no; if it swung around and around, the answer was yes. This time the ring swung back and forth vehemently. Damn, I thought. Anyway, it's only a trick.

I was hardly aware of the world around me. Madame

Rosen even got cross. "*Tiens,* Mary," she said. "Pay attention to your lessons." She was telling us about Keats, who reached into Byron's half burnt body to take out his heart to give to his horrified wife. Apparently the impractical group of poets who met to burn Byron got the logistics wrong and Byron did not burn too well, any more than Trotsky, whose coffin exploded and his wife saw the gruesome sight of her husband cremated in front of her. In spite of my wandering mind, these details did keep me alert.

I prayed passionately to God for a good day for the picnic. God let me down. Probably he was cross with me for my impure thoughts. All the same, I felt aggrieved and angry. No matter that the rain poured down the windows of the school or that Phoebe and Hattie giggled like the useless loons that they were, I bathed and dressed myself carefully.

I spent an hour and ten minutes in the bath submerged in sweet-smelling water. These days I bought Worth's *Je Reviens* hoping that he would again and again. No longer did I smell like an appletree in full blossom; I was a mature woman with my lover coming to call. I lay back in the bath to contemplate my pale stomach, glad that I had sufficient pubic hair. For a long time it had refused to grow and I had felt bare and childlike. The hair under my arms I shaved, and my legs, but my pubic hair grew soft and curly. I didn't much like my ankles and feet. My ankles were slightly thick and my feet rather broad. Quite unlike my mother's, my two feet looked as if they belonged in some Eastern land standing in paddy fields in China, or perhaps a deep wadi in India. These were the feet and legs that would presumably meet each other in a sensual embrace around his back in a moment of passion that had been described in Baroness Orczy's many books that burnt holes in the bookcases of our school library. Her heroes tapped their boots with whips, their eyes barely ever not burning with impatience to tear their beloved from the arms of her boring family and ride into the night with her body across the saddle into caves where she was always thrown onto mink blankets and her sweet red lips went white from the pressure of the kisses . . . "Hurry up!" Phoebe yelled.

"Go somewhere else, Phoebe."

"You're hogging the bathroom again, Mary! This just isn't fair."

"I know," I said. "But isn't it wonderful?"

"For you, perhaps, but not for us. *Hurry up.*"

Sighing, I raised myself out of the dripping water and stood in front of the washbasin. I brushed my teeth for the second time that day to be sure that my breath was clean. Then I poured a little perfume into my hand and applied it not only behind my ears and at my throat but quickly also behind both knees. I had never done that before.

"He's here!" shrieked Hattie. "I can see the car."

Within ten minutes I was downstairs. "The weather," I said, "is *awful.*"

Reimer grinned. His teeth looked very white in the gloom of the hall. "Don't worry, *chérie,*" he said. "I have a plan. Soldiers of fortune always have plans." When he said that, I felt a familiar goose walk up and down my spine. "Come. Let's make the most of the day."

The plan was perfect. We both lay naked in front of a huge fire. We were in Reimer's shooting lodge, a small house tucked away in the forest. Lunch lay beside us. Reimer's cook packed a cold venison pie and salad. Two Bavarian crystal glasses sat beside us. "Jaboulet Vercherre *Châteauneuf du Pape*" announced the label which faced me. I lay comfortably on Reimer's chest. Waiting. Reimer gently rubbed my breasts. Occasionally he rolled over me and took my nipples between his lips and then fell back gazing into the fire.

"Be patient," he said quietly. "Just relax and I will show you something." He turned downwards and I felt his tongue gently probing. A slow surge of ever-quickening lust made me wriggle and moan. And then, to my astonishment, I heard myself begging and pleading for him not to stop. Half of me was watching from the ceiling, and the other half was exploding. I lost all sense of time and consciousness.

When I came to, he was smiling at me, leaning on one arm. "Did you like that?" he said.

"Yes, I did."

"Now," he said, "we sleep." He lay back and closed his eyes. Too tired to ask any questions, I also closed my eyes.

The dying fire woke us. I pulled the big bearskin around me and sat up. Reimer was already up and dressed. "Come along," he said. "I'll take you back."

On the way to the school I was silent. I was not sure of what to say. Did he want to make love to me or not? Had he been trying just to please me? Maybe he didn't want to make me pregnant. He had been excited by caressing me, I knew.

Reimer chatted happily all the way back to Mont St Sebastian. I decided to keep a check on my tongue and said nothing. "I will telephone you in two days," he said, "and I will see you next week."

When I got to the bedroom, Phoebe was sitting on her bed. "Well?" she asked.

"Almost," I said. "But you're too young to know about such things." I threw my pillow at her and we had a pillow fight.

Chapter 46

My memories of Somerset Maugham's novels were surrounded by his themes of drumming rain and fever. Dengue fever, typhoid fever, black fever. Water lying brackish and swarming with mosquitoes whose long proboscises could inject a shot of illness that made you shake and your very bones stiffen with ague. What a horrible word *ague* was. A non-word, but full of dreadful meaning. I had ague. I had been touched by something from a marsh, a swamp, and I would never be the same person I was before.

There always had been momentous times in my life, times when I reconsidered myself: when I left Africa, when I was betrayed by Quentin, when I left Paris for school with my garter belt and my stockings. There had been years when I was ready for love and found it in Patrick, times when my body knew heat and lust but found its own private expression. Now my soul had been seared and left naked in front of another human being. I felt his hair and his head in my hands. At night I remembered his tongue finding me and turning me into a wanton. During the day I dreamed of him, tall and proud in his dashing clothes. I walked up and down the corridors smelling his smell. I sat in Madame Rosen's classes and pitied poor Poe who fought for his writing and wrote his matchless poetry. *The Raven* especially thrilled me. What a glossy merciless bird with such a bright knowing eye. Reimer's golden eyes were bright.

I tried to explain this to Phoebe. "Once you fall in love like this, you feel powerless and rather ridiculous."

"You certainly look ridiculous." Phoebe was cross. "Hattie and I think you are being very boring and not much fun."

"Oh, Phoebe," laughed Hattie. "It's just calf-love. She'll get over it. Wait 'til he farts or burps at the wrong time and she realizes he is just like the rest of the human race." I was mortally hurt and offended. Reimer would do neither of those things. He was the most perfect man I had ever met. "You will marry Patrick." Hattie grew serious. "Won't you?"

I sighed. "Of course I will marry Patrick." But secretly I longed to elope with Reimer. I believed he might put his cape around me and we would roar into the night in his fast car. We would hide somewhere in the mountains and I would cook breakfast for him every morning. "Madame Ferneux," he said down the telephone of my dreams, "Madame, I have spirited my beloved to my mountain castle. I wish to marry her in our chapel. The priest is ready. Instruct her parents of this fact . . . No, no, Madame. Nothing you can say will change my mind. Ours is a love for all eternity. We were made for each other . . ." That last line was tacky.

"Mary," Madame Ferneux said with a deep smile, a smile that reminded me of a barracuda I had once followed under water. As I swam behind the fish, I heard the gentle clicking of its savage teeth. "Ah, Mary," she said. "I've been looking for you." She glanced at her small gold watch, the face of which was set with tiny emeralds and seed pearls. "Let us both go to my study and have a cup of tea."

I nodded, feeling a blush of embarrassment in my cheeks. I trailed along after Madame's tall elegant figure and I wished I was taller, more slender, had narrow feet and flower-petal hands . . .

"Voilà," she said. "Here we are, chérie. Do sit down, please. I have been wanting to talk to you." I took up my position on the opposite side of her desk. She leaned back in her winged armed chair and the light above her illuminated her head. She looked old but ageless. Her skin stuck like white parchment to her bones. Her long nose threw a shadow beside her mouth and her deeply stained crimson lips tried to smile; her prominent teeth turned the smile into a grimace. "You have been seeing Herr Walter regularly."

"Oh, yes. He is very good to me." I hoped to sound very innocent.

"I see." Madame Ferneux probably saw far more than I wanted her to see. "You do realize that Herr Walter has a certain reputation."

"No," I shrugged. "I don't know anything about his private life. We mostly talk about Africa and myself."

Madame Ferneux smiled again. This time there was a hint of amusement in her eyes that made me feel very young and a little foolish. "Do you not think that Herr Walter might well be playing with you?"

"No, I don't. We have a good time together and he would never do anything to hurt me."

I could hear Madame take a deep breath and then she leaned across the table and took my small hand in her own slender long-fingered hand. Her touch was ethereal and for a moment I was pulled into her body. I was mesmerized by her voice. Low and clearly she said, "My darling, there are men in this world—men of adventure, travelers, gypsies—who ask you to run away with them. Only a certain kind of woman can live with a man like that. You are not that sort of woman. You will be harmed for the rest of your life if you try. You will be his forever if you allow him to take you into his arms and you surrender to him."

I knew what she meant and a cold wretched wind blew through my heart. I would not tell her it was too late, that already I had fatally compromised myself. I would not admit that he had invaded me, that the bones of my head were enmeshed in the memory of him, that my thighs ached for him and my breasts tingled and awaited his touch. I *could* have told her because I knew she understood. I knew that she was fore-telling me my future because she, too, had been touched forever by some adventurer who had abandoned her.

We were interrupted by the tea-tray. Suzette, that sweet happy girl, bustled in and the moment between us was blown away like a spider's web in a fresh wind. Madame laughed. "Tsk tsk," she said. "My little one, you are so sincere, so passionate. Do tell me, what are your wedding plans?"

"Well, I'm to be married in England when I've finished here. We have a family chapel. My mother and father decided that it would make my grandmother and my grandfather very happy if we married there, though my mother and grandmother don't see eye to eye. I mean . . ." I faltered.

Madame Ferneux nodded. "That often happens. Once the old order broke down after the First World War, all sorts of liaisons occurred that would never have been tolerated before. I remember talking to your mother before you arrived here. She would be considered an *arriviste*, someone who married above her class. But then, she has done well. She has that precious gift: *le style*. It is of the greatest importance, style. Without it you can do nothing and go nowhere. Chanel, our own French Coco Chanel, has it. This is what I try to teach you, all of you. There is a way of doing everything with style. You English," she said, "don't have it. But your mother, I don't know where she discovered such style, but I admire her."

I nodded shamefully, aware of my own lack of *style*. "I do try to be like her, but there are great clouds between us."

"Of course." Madame was very matter-of-fact. "Some of us are women with secrets in our past. These days, everyone is very vulgar. Everyone tells all they know. Very boring. A woman *should* have her secrets."

She passed me a cup of scented tea. "Lapsang Sou-chong," she said. "Very calming for the nerves and for the liver. Too much passion can bring on an attack of the nerves. After all, I am here to look after you and to protect you, my dear. Even if he is the most hand-some man in the world. Or so you think."

"I do," I said. "I really do. We are going out for din-ner tomorrow."

"Well, I must ask you to daydream less in class. Your percentages are not as good as they were. I don't want you to disappoint your family. These are all things you will need to know when you are the wife of a banker. Who knows? Your Patrick might end up the head of the British Oriental Bank, and then you will really need to know your protocol. Most of the girls here will marry well and into good families. And even those that don't—I knew she was thinking of Gretchen, naughty loud lewd Gretchen—"will, if they become mistresses, still know how to dress and to be-have and run a good table."

I laughed. I imagined Gretchen as a mistress. That was what she always said she wanted to be. "Yes, Ma-dame," I said. "I do understand, and I will try harder." I rose to my feet and put the cup on the table. It was possible to feel a terrible loneliness in the warmth and safety of this glamorous room, and I felt it.

"The world," Madame remarked, "is a very danger-ous place. If you choose to allow that danger into your life, then you take the consequences. You cannot blame others for your actions. Only you, and you alone, can decide."

I nodded and I walked out of her room. After I closed the door, I paused. "Get me Herr Walter. Im-mediately," I could hear her voice through the door. I stayed to listen. The hall was empty and the air was hushed. "Ah," she said, her voice bright and jagged. "I have just been talking to my little Mary. We had a very interesting conversation. I trust you will not do anything I might make you regret, Reimer." A silence while she listened. "I see . . . Good. That's a promise? I would ask you to cross your heart, but then," and she laughed, "you don't have one, do you?"

I left the door and walked up the stairs. I thought, that's the end of ecstacy. The old cow.

Gretchen and the crew were all holed up in our bedroom. Gretchen loved a gossip, and word was round the school that I'd been called into Madame's office. "Ha!" Gretchen exclaimed. "Did you confess and tell her all?"

I smiled. "No. She just gave me a wigging for not working hard enough. I have to concentrate more and all that." I shook myself. Here I was with my friends, sitting, drinking coffee, and eating Hattie's chocolate biscuits just after having a very serious conversation with Madame Ferneux. I was also getting married, and Patrick's letters were full of plans, as were mine. And then I had a letter from my mother telling me that Geneviève Derlanger had asked me to her wedding to that awful Rollo. And my grandmother sent news that the unspeakable Angela Rogers (Mrs Rogers's daughter) had married the local Master of the Fox Hounds. Marriage must be like 'flu, I thought. Very catching.

Was I to be the only one with a hopeless love? Did Geneviève hide a secret? I doubted if Angela had a secret. The village saw to that. But here I sat among my friends. Gretchen didn't have secrets. She just had a lot of sex with a lot of the men from the military academy. Jonathan was her latest. Gretchen's candid sexual explanations embarrassed me, but there was also a marked fascination to be with a woman who had no sense of modesty.

Then, in the midst of the girls talking and laughing, I made my decision. I must not see Reimer again. Reimer was a fantasy I could not afford. I went to the phone. "Herr Walter is not in," his butler told me. "Who shall I say is calling?"

"Never mind," I said. "I'll telephone later. When do you expect him?"

"About eleven o'clock," the butler said. His voice was reedy and tired.

Poor old man, I thought as I went to the library. He had to stay awake for Reimer to come home before he could go to bed.

I telephoned at half past eleven. Reimer sounded surprised. "Is anything wrong?" he said.

"No." I was nervous but determined. "I just think we should not see each other again, Reimer. After all, I am going to be married in a few months' time. It doesn't seem right."

Reimer laughed a quiet amused laugh. "Come along, *ma petite.* You have been listening to Felice. She is like a hawk with her chickens. I won't hurt you, I promise. Only dinner. How about that? Only the restaurant."

"No kisses," I said firmly.

"Of course not. I never kiss a woman against her will."

Oh, well. Only a few more weeks, and he did promise. "All right," I said. "I'll see you tomorrow at half past seven."

"Good night, *chérie,*" he said.

I put down the phone and my heart did a jig for joy. He called me a woman! I, Mary Jane Freeland, was officially acknowledged a woman.

All the same, I spent a sleepless night. For so long now I had kept Reimer and Patrick in two separate compartments. Reimer was such a passion in my life that there was not much room for little invading tentacles of guilt about Patrick. If I did have pangs of guilt, I ignored them or reasoned them away. Patrick stood on a safe shore somewhere in another country. For now I was alive and burning with life. For now I wanted time to pass slowly and languorously, to slip like snakeskin through my hands.

The most frightening aspect of this experience was that it was so totally enveloping. Here I was, behaving in a way that I knew my parents and my grandparents would not believe possible. Aunt Mary might understand, but even Phoebe and Hattie, as much as they teased, did not realize the depths to which I had sunk.

I had never seen myself as craven, but the last dinner before I took the train to Paris turned out to be an abysmal experience. "So," Reimer said. "This is goodbye." We were sitting in the comfortable depths of his car. The leather had the rich polished smell of a handmade vehicle. The wooden dashboard gleamed softly. Reimer had just eased the top off a bottle of Perrier-Jouet *Fleur de Champagne*, our favorite drink for the moment. I held my glass in my hand. I—who had always been proud of my ability to contain myself— broke down. "Oh, Reimer!" I cried, heavy embarrassing tears sliding down my cheeks. "I can't bear it."

Reimer smiled. "All good things must come to an end," he said. It was unlike Reimer to speak in clichés. I looked at him and he was still smiling.

"I suppose I am a joke to you." I was very angry. "Just a little girl you picked up from a finishing school and thought you could amuse yourself with. Is that it?"

Reimer put his head back and drank a long slow mouthful of champagne. I saw the powerful muscles of his neck relax under the gentle swallow of the champagne. He sighed. "Mary, I did nothing to you that you did not ask for. Women must be responsible for what they do. Far too many women I loved lost my respect when they asked to make love and then whined when it came to an end. You are not going to whine are you?"

"Certainly not." I finished my glass of champagne rapidly. "I'll have another for old times' sake." Two of us could speak in clichés. Maybe clichés were invented to get people through hard emotional times when there was so much to say that one dared not. How could I say, "Reimer, I have made an awful mistake. I don't want to marry Patrick. I don't want to be a banker's wife. I want to go off with you and do all the dangerous and suspicious things that you do. I know I would be awfully good in the jungles of Africa and on large boats in the Amazon. If what you were doing was illegal or immoral, I wouldn't even ask. I would be your woman, and where you went I would go, without complaint . . ."? All those words were spoken in my heart, but I sipped the cold champagne and I kept silent.

"Good night, my dear," said Reimer.

"Please kiss me goodbye," I said, my head swimming with sorrow and loss.

"You told me on the telephone not to kiss you, and I have been faithful to your wish."

"I know." I felt debased and craven again. "But now I'm asking you."

Reimer took my glass and put both glasses into the bar. He closed the door and then he took me in his arms. He kissed me deeply and passionately and I knew, with a tiny glow of triumph, he would miss me. Me, a seventeen-year-old girl, and Reimer the more experienced man of the world. It comforted me to think that he would miss me.

"Goodbye," I whispered. "Goodbye." I ran towards the school and then looked back. I could see the tip of Reimer's cigarette glowing inside the car and I could just make out the profile of his face. He waited until I was inside the building, then I heard his powerful engine growl and the tires squeal. He was gone. The sound of his car filled the valley. I ran upstairs and leaned out of my window and watched the lights caress the trees and the fields and I remembered his hands on my body. I lay my hot face against the exquisite coldness of the glass and I cried for myself and for my lost innocence.

Chapter 47

The last week of the year ended in a flurry of activity. Of course my wedding lists had been placed in Harrods several months before. Aunt Mary made repeated journeys to see the presents we had and I got a list from her of all the items that were crossed off. Our side had not too many relations, but Patrick's family was vast with elderly aunts and uncles who were in trade in a rich North Yorkshire way. They were all digging in their attics and producing massive amounts of the silver that no longer graced their dining rooms; they could not afford the underfootmen to clean it, and their butlers—the new upstart butlers—refused. Aunt Mary's letter read:

Dear Mary,
I write to you from the end of a busy day. Now summer is here, have to clean out the coal hole and see that all my roses are pruned back. My neighbors don't believe in pruning until next year, but I say prune them back hard and you'll have a wonderful show.
Anyway you're doing well on your list at Harrods and you should have a good show on your wedding day. Don't be sorry I shan't be there. Your mum knows best as always and you'll look as good as she did on her wedding day.

I enclose a picture of your mum I kept for just this moment. Don't she look lovely?

Yours affectionately,
Aunt Mary

Yes, she did, I thought. I looked down at the yellowing document. The picture must have been taken with an old Kodak. There was the familiar ruffled edge and the patina of time that always separated those years of the English colonial life from now. All so far gone, so far away. My slim mother stood beside my father in the same wedding picture I had clandestinely seen before in Ealing when my Aunt Mary had stepped out. My father looked at her with such tenderness and love. She, I now saw, did not look happy. If I had not experienced the joy of loving Reimer, I would not have picked up the slightly lost look in her eyes. Her mouth was smiling, but her eyes were haunted. Maybe those who have another love, an all-abiding love, always spend the rest of their lives haunted. I shivered. I wanted so much to hug my mother and say I was sorry for so many years of misunderstanding. I now understand. Who was it that had bewitched her all those years ago, and what happened to make her so sad? One day she would tell me, just as I would confide in her. But for now I had to pack and to say my goodbyes.

Madame Ferneux was surprisingly gentle. *"Hélas,"* she said, "you have said goodbye to your friend Reimer Walter?" On the word *friend* she looked at me suspiciously.

I smiled back. "Yes, Madame. He was a good friend and a confidant. I shall miss him."

"Humph." Madame allowed herself a peasant sniff. "Just as well. He is a heartbreaker and no good for a girl of good family. Marry Patrick and send me a photo of the wedding. I have a big book for my good girls."

Then she smiled. "And also I have one for my naughty ones. Some of them have done quite well for themselves. Run along now. The cars are leaving for the station."

Phoebe had already gone with Hattie, both back to Paris. Hattie was extending her stay in Europe before returning to Africa. She and Phoebe were joining Jeremy in Chantilly. Jeremy had inherited a large sum of money from his father's estate kept in trust until his coming of age. Bridie refused to give up the castle, but encouraged Jeremy to open a breeding stable. Much to Bridie's sorrow, Phoebe decided she was also going to breed horses. Bridie wanted grandchildren and she wrote long letters, loudly bewailing the fact that little colts hardly counted. But she said she'd be fine running the castle with Charlie and Joe and she was happy for Phoebe to live wherever she wanted.

Phoebe hugged me before leaving. "I'll see you at the wedding. And there's no getting out of it now. It's not every day I get to be chief bridesmaid."

I nodded. "Phoebe, do wear something nice, won't you?"

"I'll see she does," Hattie laughed. "I'll drag her off to Chanel. Chanel will do something with her."

They left so blithely and so innocently I was nonplussed.

The train didn't leave the station until six o'clock, so I left the house later than the other girls I wandered up and down the stairs remembering the sounds of all the others up and down the huge school. I trailed my hands on the dark mahogany railings and I listened to the astounding silence. I had always been aware that each silence carried its own sounds. Echoing in this silence were my tears in my pillow, my feet running or lagging on the stairs, the faint echoes of my talks with Madame Ferneux, my lectures with Madame

Rosen whose faint trailing foot was still heard on the floor, whose soft and gentle all-understanding eyes followed me as I came into her classroom and read Stendhal, Mallarmé, Flaubert, the Russian writers and the Romantic English poets. "We all suffer," she said, "in unspoken words. Literature is the history of suffering. To fail to suffer is to fail to create. To refuse to feel is the inheritance of the people who live all their lives the lives of the dying. If you must die, then die for something. Don't die for nothing."

I knew what she was saying and I stood and I listened as the wind moaned outside the windows. Then I ran upstairs. I saw my taxi panting its way up the hill and I was glad to be gone. It was good to hear and smell the familiar sounds and scents of a railway station. I had with me an excellent hamper of food and a bottle of white wine. A very different girl from the one who had come to Switzerland a short year before, I was going back to Paris.

Chapter 48

I sat with my window open. My *wagon lit* was fitted out in pale blue. I had a small washing basin lined in brass and my bunk was thick and comfortable. I sat with my book on Swinburne's poetry flat on the table. The little reading lamp cast a warm yellow glow over the pages. All about me I heard the flushing of steam, the roaring of the engine, soon to pull us for so many miles up and down green mountains and through fertile valleys. I loved the sound of an engine about to leave. The first hoot warned visitors to leave and the sound trembled in the air.

I suddenly felt I was being watched. And then I

smelled something else, not the steam and the engine, but the distinct smell of a well-known cigarette. "Reimer?" I gasped.

"Ah, well, *chérie*. I could not let you go without coming to say goodbye again, now could I? It so happens I am on my way back and our paths and our trains crossed, so here I am. Do you want me to come in for a minute?"

My heart panicked. I had spent the whole week resolutely not thinking of Reimer, so many hours lecturing myself on my folly, so many days on my knees begging God to forgive me. I was completely confused by his reappearance. Faust sold his soul to the Devil. Juliet stabbed herself. And here I was, smiling and obediently letting him into my *wagon lit* and my life. "All right," I said. "We're off in a minute."

Reimer slipped into the chair on the other side of my reading table. "Very comfortable," he remarked. "Very comfortable indeed." His tall figure filled the compartment. He removed his broad velvet hat and stretched out. His long fine boots hugged his legs. His velveteen trousers would have looked ridiculous on anybody except Reimer. He could wear anything and look magnificent. The second whistle shook the train. I felt the sound moan and whine through my body. I must ask him to go. I must. But my mouth stayed silent. "Shall I stay?" he said simply and my Judas neck nodded.

"Yes," I heard myself say. "You can stay."

"Oh good." Reimer was like a child. He stood up and stretched. "You know," he said, "I have always loved trains."

There, again, I thought. He's done it. Yet again we shared a common passion: I for trains, and he, no doubt, for engines. He took off his coat and threw it on the upper bunk. We were pulling out of the station, *clackity click clackity click*, it began to pick up speed. I watched Reimer. Lazily he pulled down the blinds. The first one clicked into place, blocking out vision from the corridor. Then he moved to the second. We were in our own compartment with a cocoon of light that held us both in its arms, as gently and tenderly as a mother with her children. "Now," Reimer said, "now let's have dinner. Just see what I have with me."

I had to laugh. While I had been thinking about sex, Reimer had been thinking of food. We were both laughing, he with the knowledge that I was not cross. I couldn't ever be cross with Reimer for long. His life was like gossamer. It shimmered and glowed.

Reimer had his suitcase packed to the brim with good things from Italy. My cold chicken was a thing of the past. Out poured a torrent of green and black olives, salamis, some pink and gentle, others filled with spices and green peppercorns, small jars of sun-dried tomatoes. Reimer rang the bell and handed the astonished train porter a packet of fettuccini. "Take it away and have it cooked for no longer than eight minutes. *Al dente.* Tell the cook *al dente.*"

The porter was used to the Reimers of this world and he arrived back exactly nine minutes later with a steaming heap of pasta. "Good, good," muttered Reimer. He mixed in the sun-dried tomatoes and then carefully the olives and a fine green olive oil. Slowly the olive oil seeped into the pasta and the black olives winked at me. "Shred the salami into little bits," Reimer ordered. I felt I was in an atelier watching an artist give birth to a great work of art.

When he was finished he beamed at me and reached into the depth of his carpet bag. "Here," he said. "For our journey." He flourished a large bottle of Chianti. "The best," he said. "The very best for our journey."

Fortunately no one would be meeting me at the station. The thought of our chauffeur politely sitting in our Daimler witnessing my arrival with Reimer was too much to imagine.

For now I had to suspend judgment. I could not go on living in two spheres: the person who was here with Reimer and the woman who was sitting on my shoulder, like Madame Ferneux, disapproving. "What do you think Madame Ferneux would say?" I asked.

"Pouff," Reimer laughed. "Brush her away. No one exists but us for this moment." He stood over me and pulled me into his arms. "Now," he said, "I am going to kiss you," and he did. He pushed me breathless into my chair and then he heaped my plate full of pasta. "Eat, eat," he said. "The night is still young and we have hours to ourselves."

I knew from his eyes that we would make love and I ate ravenously. By the time we had finished, the table was full of discarded bottles and the plate of pasta was empty. We both drank much of the hot red-peppery Chianti. I took off my clothes as if a ballet was being performed. He lay back on the bed and I, as if I had made love all my life, set to to arouse him.

Kissing his body was a pleasure. Slowly he too came to life. He rolled me over expertly, as he had all those weeks ago. This time he entered me without pain or hurry. If before I had been exultant, now I was beyond words. We flew alongside the train. The clackity clack of the rails echoed the motions of our entwined bodies. Unhurriedly, and then more rapidly, we entered the valleys and then the mountains, reaching the moment that the engine raced up the sides of the Alps, and we both lost ourselves in the pine ridges of the windy forests. Reimer subsided and then took my face in his hands. "Sublime," he said.

"You sound as if you're discussing a bottle of wine," I said. I felt exhausted. I had no idea that making love could be so strenuous.

"A little out of condition perhaps, but *premier grand*

cru all the same," Reimer teased. "You travel marvelously, and I expect you should age well."

"I shan't age at all, if you insist on bursting into my life like this."

"Ah, dear one," he said, stretching his long cat-like stretch. "Let us sleep."

I was tired and also a little bewildered. Here was a man I had banished from my life, back again as if he had never left. But I was too tired and too replete not to fall into his arms and sleep, my head tucked into his neck and his breath mingling with mine. I fell into a deep dreamless sleep and the train went on and on through tunnels and over plains while we lay together.

☙ *Chapter 49* ☙

I sat in the Daimler on the way to my home and I made a vow, this one not to be broken. I would not—absolutely not—think about Reimer again. He promised before he left the train that he would not intrude in my life ever again. "I love you but I am marrying Patrick and that is the end of it," I resolutely told him. I watched him pull on his trousers, as if we had been married for years.

"My dear," he said with mock severity. "I always do what you say, don't I?"

I smiled. "But this time I mean it."

"Of course, *chérie.* I will disappear like Tinkerbell. Only, if you need me, clap your hands and I will come."

"I shan't need you," I answered.

I did feel very self-sufficient as we arrived at the house. My mother and father were waiting to greet me. Behind them were piles of wrapped presents waiting to leave for Somerset. A wedding was going to take place—mine. I had much to do and not much time to do it in.

Being in the house again, I missed my Taiwan, my true friend from childhood. My room seemed so quiet without his perennial panting and dancing and snoring. Taiwan would have understood everything I told him. Instead, a crow of guilt sat there, one wing on the floor, croaking.

The day of the wedding began with the sounds of women getting organized. I was staying with my grandmother at Milton Park, but my parents stayed in a hotel in Taunton. My mother and my grandmother were very civil to each other. Both women knew how to play the game by using diplomatic rules; still, it made me sad because I loved them both in very different ways.

My mother had been wonderful the first few days I was home. She concentrated on all the lists and all the arrangements and she treated me a little like an invalid. She didn't even mind when I said that Patrick and I would like to miss the reception. I did try to talk to her about Reimer, but she surprised me by reiterating what Madame Ferneux had said. "Darling, hush. Don't tell all your secrets. There is too much telling and not much silence these days. Whatever happened happened. Learn from it. Remorse is a useless emotion because you cannot relive the event or blot it out. Live with it with courage, darling."

"Like you do?" I said hesitantly.

"Yes," she said simply. "Like I, and many more, do. Women are much more complicated than men, you know. Men like to think they are complicated, but they are not. Let them think they are wise and in control. That is the secret of a happy marriage. Feed Patrick well, and love him, and he'll give you his heart in return."

But do I have a heart to give? I wondered. Mine was already given, miles away somewhere in Switzerland, if he had not already taken off to China or Turkey on one of his endless adventures.

My mother shrugged. She knew me well. "Come on," she said. "We have to get you married."

Today it was going to happen and nothing I could do would change that fact. And this was my doing. The moment when I said "I do" I was condemned to live the rest of my life with a man whom, I realized with a panicked intensity, I was not sure I loved enough or in the right way. No point lying in bed. The hours went by and the minutes ticked away, whether I lay and ruminated or got on with the day. I jumped out of bed and went down to the kitchen.

"Well, Mary." Mrs Harding was pink with excitement. She had her best wool suit on and thick stockings. Her church hat hung on the edge of the kitchen chair. "Excited, are we? Where are you having your honeymoon?"

I shrugged. "We'll just go to Hong King. I want to go to Florence, on the way, to look at the Uffizi gallery."

"I didn't know Patrick was interested in painting," my grandmother interjected. She was stirring scrambled eggs at the stove.

"He isn't. He'll learn." The sentence sounded much flatter than I intended it to be. I quite frightened myself: it sounded more like something my mother would say. So I laughed a queer strangled laugh and said, "I'm just nervous, Grandma. Once it's all over, I'll be fine."

I always have disliked services of any sort in a church. Jesus would have married us beside Galilee in a cool breeze with a few words. Here his emissary, the vicar, pleased at such a huge society wedding, was pink in the face and on his best sermon. "Dearly beloved . . ." he said. I groaned. I knew his Dearly Beloveds of old, and his sermon could run from the German attack in the First World War to the odds on the rugger field at Twickenham. Anything was grist to his mill.

The chapel was slightly chilly. I looked around me, hoping at the last minute to see the friendly faces of Mademoiselle and Jacques or Miss Standish; I knew they would not be here. They had all made perfectly reasonable excuses for their intended absence, sending on congratulations in their stead. Why wouldn't they come? Was it an omen? Were they reluctant to lend their presence to a ceremony they felt should not take place? My father, with his consummate tact and grace, walked me beautifully up the aisle. How I got there, I shall never know. I was in a vacuum. I walked the length of the chapel until I reached Patrick who was waiting for me. He looked so young and so frightened. I wished I could have whispered into his ear "Let's not do this." I looked at him instead and sensed he was as frightened and as unwilling as I was, but we were trapped by the people who crowded behind us, waiting for the vows and the promises we made to each other that day. "I do," I said.

"I will," Patrick said. We would love, honor, and obey, and in sickness and in health . . . Did Patrick say those words to *me*, or did he have an adventuress in his life who had gone off with his heart? I saw Reimer's eyes staring at me. When I said "I do," I saw Reimer. He nodded and then he smiled. Phoebe, my chief bridesmaid, helped me pull back my veil and I kissed Patrick, his lips soft and anxious, and then we faced the congregation.

The organ swelled out Mendelssohn's bridal march and my mother and father beamed at me. Everybody seemed happy. Even Patrick, his palm sweaty with effort, was happy. The pictures took forever, and then we changed and got into Patrick's little car. The tin cans bounced behind us and *JUST MARRIED* had been painted by a delighted Hattie across the back of the car. We drove to London to spend our first night in the Savoy bridal suite, a present from the Johnsons. And now, I kept reminding myself with astonishment, I was *Mrs Patrick Johnson*, no longer Mary Jane Freeland.

I was glad of the suite. While Patrick slept the satisfied sleep of a satiated bridegroom, I leaned out of the window and gazed at the River Thames. I promised God that I would make Patrick a good wife and a good mother, and then I went to bed.

❧ *Chapter 50* ❧

Patrick went on to Hong Kong ahead of me. We stayed at the Savoy for a week and I wondered, if I had not known Reimer and his love-making, might Patrick and I have had a better chance at happiness? Certainly Patrick was sweet and kind. I reminded myself that I had been to finishing school and introduced to life by a much older, self-assured man. Patrick was a little older than I, but self-assurance was hopefully something that would grow with time. His skin was very fair and, as he ordered dinner in the River Room, he flushed and mumbled. He wasn't naturally graceful like Reimer.

We came from very different lives. His was rich but casual, mine rich but laden with ceremony; his family loud, glamorous and careless, mine quiet, thoughtful and withdrawn. We used ceremony to make up for lack of feeling. The Johnsons had little ceremony and yelled and bellowed with a refreshing lack of pretension. Patrick's three sisters, Anthea, Joanna, and Lucy, were all married. Lucy was childless and intended to stay that way, but the other two were permanently fecund.

Lucy took me out to dinner the night before I was to catch the airplane from Heathrow to Hong Kong. We dined at Waltons in the little mews row of cottages that once housed servants and now served millionaires. Lucy was blonde like Patrick, but sharp. She had a cutting edge he did not. She wore a yellow silk dress that gave her eyes summer, even though the weather outside was bleak and cold. "I envy you," she said. "Imagine, Hong Kong instead of this awful climate." I smiled. I had two suitcases full of clothes for hot weather and already my mother had shipped linen and china, plus various large amounts of silver for the flat. "You'll be living on the Peak, you lucky thing." Lucy picked at her dinner. I chose duck, a lovely concoction of marmalade-glazed pink-fleshed duck, tiny peas and potatoes, and a salad. Lucy picked at a sole truffled and drowned in a *sauterne.* I felt she was unhappy. "You've only been married a week or so, so you have an excuse." I was surprised. Lucy, who was known to me largely from Patrick's stories, was not one to confide in a virtual stranger. Her hand quivered. "You will think this is silly, but you have no idea how much pressure I've been getting from my family *and,*" she emphasized bitterly, "from my husband to have a child."

I paused. She was right. The thought of having children or not having children was not one that had ever really preoccupied me. Of course I'd have children. Hopefully two: one boy and one girl. Really, it was rather like ordering bacon and eggs. You ordered these items and they arrived. "I see," I said rather absently. I did so much want to enjoy my duck. All this marital tension and giving of birth was a little barnlike. I rather sided with Phoebe on this one. Women should give birth unseen and unheard. I was all for harems. I had resented both Anthea and Joanna swaying into the church like camels with beatific smiles on their faces, when what they had done to resemble these animals was to indulge in some carnal lust, the results of which could be seen all over the church. I lost count of how many offspring the two had between them. The husbands stood limply beside these two pagans looking worn-out, muttering "Stop it, Tristan," or "Mallory" or other such names. Lucy I felt should go against the grain and remain childless. I nodded. "You've got a whole battalion of children in your family. Why, you have a cricket team at least. Do you want children?"

Lucy looked at her plate. "I don't," she said, very controlled. "No, I don't. Do you?"

"Oh. Yes, of course I do." Disloyalty gripped my throat. I saw my boy with dark hair and yellow eyes, but, of course, any child I had would have Patrick's blond hair and our blue eyes. "Yes," I said. "I would like children. Not now, of course, but later, when Patrick is older and we have a little more money. I inherit, I've been told, when I turn twenty-one. I don't know the details, except that there will be enough to buy a house. Then it will be a good time to have a baby."

Lucy shook her head. "All I really want to do is to go on working for my magazine. I've been married for the last two years. You haven't had time to see our flat, but I love it. James comes home from the office. He sells wine so we have a good stock. When I arrive, we have a civilized drink before dinner and then we sit down and we talk. I know this is awfully selfish, talking about me, so I'll try to explain.

"I always wanted a career. I watched my mother with all four of us working like a loon. We had servants in Paris, but my father lost almost all his money due to a partner's crash. Suddenly we were no longer the gay fashionable Johnsons, and I saw my mother struggle to keep up. She was wonderful. No one ever really knew we were just about bankrupt and couldn't pay the school fees. You see, Daddy made it on his own. When times were hard, there was no family to lean back on. His family lived in small houses in the north of England and he supported them. They were good people, but they had nothing to give but encouragement."

"Patrick's never said anything about this to me."

She paused. The memories must have been very bitter because her face was sad. "Patrick was very little, so he never knew about this part of our lives. Then I met James, and to me James was everything my family was not. He was quiet and calm. He took a first from Oxford. I went to a minor public school, and then along came this man who opened the door into another world. We'd had classical music at home, but mostly romantic. We had books, but none of the great French writers, because we only needed French to get by if we were in Paris."

Her face began to flush and her eyes to glow. The sharp hard Lucy changed and the soft gentle light made her beautiful. I felt a pang of envy. Lucy had her adventurer, an intellectual wayfarer, and she was married to him. "I can see why you don't want to spoil what you have."

"Do you really?" she said.

I felt a surge of compassion for her. "You know, I have always been envious of you because you all seemed to be such a big happy family."

Lucy nodded bitterly. "Yes, you're right. But then, that is all there is: *The Family.* I feel suffocated and stifled living in London. Well, maybe James can ship wine somewhere else. There is the whole of the Far East, you know. Jardine Matheson, Dewar's all have offices in Hong Kong. That would be fun." Lucy finally brightened up. "Maybe we'll join you."

"Maybe," I said.

"You'll be very happy with Patrick," Lucy remarked as we got into the taxi for the Savoy. "He's a dear boy, even if he is my brother."

"I know," I said. "Goodbye, Lucy. I'll write to you."

"Everything all right, Madam?" Fred, the Savoy doorman, opened the door.

"Yes, Fred." I saw the taxi bowling away into the rush and the hubbub of London. The bells tolled out the measured night and I slept my last night in London.

The journey was long but untiring. I pulled the First Class blue blanket up to my chin and prepared to sleep. Behind me the Economy Class of the plane recorded the cries of tired children and exhausted mothers. They, too, were on their way to Hong Kong. Some, newly married, like myself bore that pale green look of bodies denied the sun. We stood out like worms against the old Far East hands who looked brown and healthy. My wardrobe, chosen with the help of my mother, was fashionable and suitable. But many of the tourist passengers had no idea of the heat that awaited us. They dressed in nylon stockings, tight-fitting high-heeled shoes, belted dresses, and thick cardigans. I felt sorry for them, for by now we had been a day in the air and had come down in Bombay. We had a very aggressive man blind us with insect spray, as if the insects needed protection from the raving hordes of Imperialists. And then were ordered to disembark.

The heat and the stench were oddly familiar to me,

but Judith, a quiet girl sitting next to me, was unprepared for it. "Breathe hard," I said, "and breathe deeply. You'll get used to it."

"No, I won't." She sounded near to tears. "I'll never get used to this."

"Come on. I'll get you something to drink." I found myself more forceful than usual. I asked for an iced drink. "We don't serve drinks now that the flight is terminated. You will have to wait." The stewardess was obsequious but determined.

"Get me a drink, please. My friend is feeling unwell."

"Madame," she said, glancing at my wedding ring and noticing an absence of diamonds on my fingers, "we are not allowed."

"Do it," I said. There was such a note of authority in my voice, I was shaken.

Judith was grateful. She swallowed the water in great gulps. We walked together down the front of the airplane and we were transported by bus in air-conditioned comfort to a First Class hotel.

"Don't, whatever you do, order curry," I said. "Don't drink the water unless it's been boiled. So don't order a drink with ice in it, or you can come down with an awful stomach ache."

Judith was very impressed, so was I. "I don't think I'm going to cope," she said miserably.

"You will," I said cheerfully. "I'll be there. Hong Kong is a very small place, you know. If you're marrying a Navy man, we'll probably be at the same parties."

Judith looked even more miserable. "I don't like parties," she said. "Bill does though. He says the way up is to get to know everybody, and then if he works hard he'll become a Chief Petty Officer. And then, of course, there's my money." She looked at me. "My dad has a shoe factory in Nottingham. We're somebody in Nottingham. Here I'm nobody."

I laughed. "That makes two of us. I was the Consul General's daughter, and today I'm just a junior banker's wife. Let's make a pact. We'll stick together, and when we get back to the plane, we'll eat as much lobster as we can and get squiffy on the champagne. Junior bankers' wives don't go First Class, any more than junior Petty Officers', so this could be the last time for a very long while. Let's have fun."

Judith smiled. When she smiled she was rather pretty. Something had to be done about her wispy hair. I liked her.

I lay at my window, watching us fly into a huge red dawn, and hoped and prayed that I could settle into my new life and my new beginning finally without regrets. A new start. Beside me little Judith lay sleeping trustfully. I had a little sister, someone to protect. I pulled the blanket under her chin and I watched the red sun rise.

Book Two

Chapter 51

I woke up as the pressure in the airplane changed and my ears popped. Judith was awake. "I am going to miss my mum," she said. "I've only been away for holidays before."

I was surprised. Of course I'd been away from home for long periods of time, and I did miss both my parents, but I heard real anguish in her voice. "Never mind," I said. "I'll look after you. We'll have such a good time, you won't notice the time fly by. Look, here's breakfast." I was hungry and the coffee steamed my face. The bacon was properly fried to a sizzle and the omelette was tucked like a hospital blanket onto the plate, a pale yellow. Outside the sky was a hazy blue and we slowly felt the plane dropping height. The stewardesses must have been behind schedule because they were whisking around the cabin like terriers.

The plane came out of the sky, big and heavy. I saw little boats weaving in and out of the harbor. Hong Kong appeared so much an island, and Kowloon sprawled back into China, ancient and enduring. Little Hong Kong looked like an impudent toe stuck out in the water. The plane crept down past the jagged peaks, the Peak where I was going to live. We tried to look for the naval base where Bob and Judith had a flat, but we couldn't see it. Then, with a final lurch, we were down and the engines reversed and we came to a screaming halt.

I felt exhalted, happy, and rather frightened. Here was a whole new world. For the first time, it was my new world. I could do with it what I wanted. My success or failure did not depend on my parents paying fees, or my grandparents' kindly concern.

Patrick was standing at the barrier staring straight at me. He looked so young and so vulnerable, my heart went out to him. I felt a wave of love for his kind patient nature. I really will try and be a good wife and a good lover, I promised. Maybe the best kind of love came after a time of knowing each other and building a relationship that was permanent.

I saw Judith rush past me and throw herself into her Bob's arms. He had on the uniform of a Petty Officer. he looked considerably older than she and I didn't much like his face. It was pink and raw. He was smiling. I hugged Patrick and then pulled him over to meet Judith. "Here's Patrick," I said.

"Pleased to meet you," Judith answered. "This is Bob."

Bob nodded his head and shook Patrick's hand. "Pleased to meet you, sir," he said.

"Bye, Judith," I called as we left to collect my luggage. "I have your address. I'll phone in the next few days." Judith didn't hear me. She was hanging on to Bob, gazing at him adoringly, the sort of look that a woman gives a man when he is her whole world. Disgusting, as Phoebe would say. I did miss old Phoebe. She said she wouldn't visit me in Hong Kong because the Chinese were all too short. Typically Phoebe, but then we had leave coming up after a year and we could visit her in Chantilly with her inevitable horses. *We*, again. How odd to think in terms of *we*. I was always *I*, with *my* plans, my ideas. Now it was *our* plans and *our* ideas . . .

Patrick was full of news. "I've missed you so much," he said. "I hope you like the flat. I have a cook called Su Wei, and an amah as well. She's your age and her name is Ah Lim. We are now members of the Dogwood Club, so if you want to swim or play tennis, there's no problem."

"I'd love that, and I'll invite Judith. She is very homesick and will need company. Anyway, I'm very fond of her . . ." I felt a sudden silence. "Anything wrong, darling?" I asked.

"No. I mean, not exactly." Patrick always hated to contradict me, but I knew him well enough to know he was uncomfortable.

"Go on," I said. "What is it?"

"Well, Mary, you see, Bob is a Petty Officer."

"I know. He's hoping to make it into the officer ranks."

"Yes, I see that. But for the moment, he is other ranks, isn't he?"

"Yes."

Patrick was still uneasy. "You can do what you like, because we're banking people, but Judith could get into trouble. She would be *fraternizing*, as it's called. Other ranks are not meant to fraternize with people outside. The officers and their wives swim in their own pool, and the other ranks have a separate pool. I must say, it's a much bigger and nicer one, but that's not the point. It's all a matter of discipline. I know it's different in the Foreign Office."

Yes, it is, I thought. Of course, there were ranks and unspoken territory, but the Ambassador's wife shared the same water as the most junior wife at the Embassy. The big joke was always that the chauffeur was likely to be the most senior member of the community, because he was probably the head of M16. All Embassy children played together. There were certainly individual snobs, but not an imposed system. "Well," I said, leaning back in Patrick's arms. "They can have their rules, but I have mine. Don't worry, darling, I'll be careful."

"I'm sure you will." Patrick pulled me to him and kissed me hard. We were in a taxi climbing up the long vertical road to the Peak.

"There," he said, pointing to a large building, "is the Helena May, known as the 'virgin's retreat' or 'menopause mansion.' See the little fellow selling jade in the doorway? He's an interesting fellow. During the War, the woman who runs the Helena May was interned in Changi Jail with the other women and children. He used to crawl up to the wire and give her fruit and bits of rice. That's how she survived. Now, as repayment, he gets to sell jade outside."

"I don't understand. Why isn't he living inside? After all, he did save her life."

Patrick smiled benevolently. "You wouldn't understand. You've only just arrived."

I decided to say nothing, and looked instead at the scenery.

Patrick sat back and we both looked out of the windows to the beauty and magic that was Hong Kong. "We are going to be very happy here, aren't we?"

I smiled. "We'll be ecstatic. I can't wait to explore."

That night I lay in Patrick's arms. Feeling an urgent need to give him all I had, and feeling so grateful that he should love me, I was able to climax with him. Patrick hugged me close and whispered, "I never knew love-making could be so good, so much like a religious expression of our love."

"Neither did I," I said, and that was true. What I had with Patrick was a calm peaceful existence. I slept.

And then I woke. It was early morning and a fleet of cockerels were extolling the beauty of the new day. Patrick was still sleeping. I got up and looked out of my third floor window. We overlooked the city of

Hong Kong. Way down below I could see the water. The pale recently risen sun touched the glass of the sky-scrapers. The light was rosy, and the sea deep blue. I quietly walked across the white marble floor to the sitting room. I could hear someone in the kitchen.

I had met Ah Lim, the amah, the night before. She had served us dinner. Now I met Su Wei, our cook. He was a young man with many gold teeth. "We have breakfast at eight o'clock, madame," he said. "Master done go office eight forty-five."

"All right," I said. "I'm just too excited to sleep. I want to go out to the markets and see Hong Kong."

Su Wei smiled. "I take you," he said. "I go to get meat today."

I was pleased. I felt that I could arrange my own menus, like my mother, run my own life. Our packing cases had arrived a few weeks before and I wandered about the flat opening drawers and I was thrilled. There lay piles and piles of sheets and pillow cases, napkins and tablecloths. In the lined pantry table, I had my box of silver knives and forks, and there in pride of place were the Russian Orthodox silver servers, beautifully carved, the grooves carefully hand-chiselled. I traced the groove with my finger. Under the slight pressure of my finger, I felt the hollow, the ravine that bit into the knife. Further on there was a passionate swirl that ended the design. My finger was pulled invisibly into the swirl as if some huge fish had leapt out of the water and then sucked me down into the blue Hong Kong sea. My body, remembering the night before, disloyally remembered other nights.

I walked back into the bedroom and woke Patrick up with a nuzzled kiss. "Make love to me," said my faithful brain, but my body had no intention of behaving itself. We made love slowly and passionately.

But I sighed. Why can't I be like Judith?

"I must get up, darling," Patrick said.

I watched his now familiar body rise from the bed-clothes to walk naked to the bathroom. His body was young and fair. There were no mats of hair on his chest or his arms. His penis hung flaccid, all excite-ment spent, and he smiled the blazing smile of a man in love. I did love him, I felt sure. I had always loved him since I was a young girl. Contentment will come, I whispered to myself. It will just take time. "I'm going off with Su Wei to buy you a very large steak."

Patrick smiled. "That's my wife," he said. "Always thinking of my stomach." We sat down for breakfast. I had tea and toast. Patrick had bacon and eggs.

I stepped onto the balcony and savored the day. Hong Kong buzzed like a bright blue-bottle fly. It was a hard city and metallic. The sounds of Hong Kong clipped and clopped. The smell was quite different from anywhere else in the world: a smell of dried fish overlayed with jasmine perhaps, stewed duck and straw. Overall the smell was sweet. Under the smell there was decay; not a rotting, more a decay into a re-newal, that which decayed going back into the dust to be born again . . . "Bye, darling," and Patrick was gone. "I'll see you at six. We'll go for a swim."

I looked over the railing of the balcony that ran be-side our flat and I smiled as I saw his blond head disap-pear down to the station where the cable cars would soon be full of men in dark suits. Thank goodness I did not have to work. The whole city lay before me, a vast wonderful playground. And I intended to play.

Chapter 52

Su Wei was delighted to take me shopping, partly because we took a taxi and he did not have to carry large parcels back home. I remembered little of the African markets, just blurs and colors. Here, as we raced through the crowded streets, I despaired of us ever buying anything that looked clean or even edible. Su Wei was an indefatigable shopper. Once up a very busy side street, he pounced on what looked like a tortured pig's foot. "Oh no, Su Wei." I shook my head. "We can't eat that."

"Of course you can eat," he said cheerfully. "Master loves this eat."

I supposed *master* had very little idea of what went into his food. Patrick was never one to be fascinated by what was put in front of him. But he did like his pig's thinkers (brains, I understood) and his family, I knew, positively revelled in kidneys and offal. Perhaps, I reflected, I must concentrate on my wifely duties and learn to cook slightly more basic menus. My *cordon bleu* cooking course certainly did not allow for pig's feet, cow's stomach, or rhinoceros horn. The rhinoceros horn label directed my attention to the fact that, should I find my sexual urges wanting, a quick pull at the bottle would put me back on the right course. "Come along, Madam. We got to get fruit."

I was very happy that first day in Hong Kong. Not far away the sea glittered, and there was a constant chorus of little boats talking to each other. Some had high pitched screams, others were mellow and rumbled. The beat of the great heart of that city was faster and more furious than any other city I had ever lived in. It had not the quiet lacy green of dignified London, nor the sombre gray of Paris, but an energetic pulse that never stopped.

This was a Saturday morning, and the children were

in the shops helping parents or spilling out onto the streets, their natural home. Some played games with sticks. Others laughed and teased each other. So many hundreds of thousands of people! All outside, all milling and piling about the roads. The cars ran a hazardous course between the human bodies, but all was laughter and all was joy. Not like the furious Paris drivers brandishing angry fists out of the car windows. I was pleased to feel so quickly at home; I had been somewhat afraid to come so far away from all that I cared about. I had worried that I couldn't or wouldn't fit in.

Fitting in sounds an odd idea, until you realize that for certain cities different kinds of people do fit in. My mother fitted into Paris. In Paris she looked like an English woman in the height of fashion. Other French women certainly saw her as a model. However, in England, for my wedding, she did not fit in. Whatever indescribable ambiance it was, that made for an English country woman, did not belong to my mother. But Paris, like Rome, did not demand a city persona and a country persona. England was quite different. The *soignée* elegant woman of a London drawing room could and did turn into a dreadful old drear in her baggy gardening skirt in the country. But now I felt I would fit in here in this busy city.

We chose fruit and I remembered the heavy sensuous smell of a ripe mango, the juice of which had to be sucked from the husk of the round pendulous pip. Astringent papaya, bright black caviar seeds on the bright pink flesh, a little squeeze of lime and a dusting of ginger for breakfast. All available in abundant baskets. Then home to my new flat and my new way of life.

The first two weeks passed extraordinarily quickly. By day I was out by myself exploring the streets, watching the wood-carvers carving their chests, the wood peeling from the chisel and falling in loops onto the ground, giving off that unmistakeable smell of cedar. With equal fascination I watched the glass-blowers and the china-sellers. I bought bowls with a big fish on the bottom and I bought chopsticks.

"Come on, Patrick," I said after the first two weeks. "Tonight I'm going to cook and we are going to learn." Both servants had the night off and I began to prepare *red fish* in the wok. Su Wei was teaching me to cook. *Red* cooking was when you cooked the fish for a long time in soy and other sauces. I put the whole fish in with slices of ginger and onion and was proud to produce it for the table a few hours later. I lifted the skin below the eye and carefully took out the oyster for Patrick. Bowing, I said, "See? I can be a good Chinese wife as well." We drank rice wine, slightly heated and very scented. Patrick laughed and we sat in our flat on the Peak, delighted with life and with each other.

As the days faded into nights, I felt more and more at ease with Patrick. We shared a love of traveling. We both swam happily together. There was a boundless innocence and a willingness on Patrick's part to let me be myself. Maybe, I thought as the fumes of the rice reached my brain, maybe Reimer would have expected me to be a creature of his fashioning. We had lived a sort of hysterical drama, but what I now found with Patrick was a serene love and friendship. We knew each other so well that we could predict the end of each other's sentences.

"Let's leave the washing up." I was still covered in the fumes of fish. "Let's have a bath," I said. "I'm hot."

Patrick seized the bottle of rice wine, and I a couple of mangoes with a knife. Our bath was a modern one, large and square. We filled it to the top and then got in. Knee to knee we sat, with the water lapping around our shoulders. The rice wine added a recklessness to our laughter. I inexpertly peeled my mango and handed Patrick a slice. "Hmmm," he said. We exchanged slices until just the huge pip was left, and then we slid under the water.

"I've never tried it in a bath," I remarked coming up for air. I caught myself, feeling I had almost let something slip.

"I tried the sea once. Too much sand."

"I don't remember that," I said with mock-hurt in my voice.

"That's because you weren't there."

"You mean there've been others?" Of course, I knew there had been.

"Ancient history," Patrick said with a strikingly warm and sincere smile that removed any hint of insecurity from my heart. "And never to be repeated. It's only you forevermore." He threw his head back and the water hurled from his head onto the floor.

"Poor Ah Lim. She won't know what's happened," I said as the water fell onto the floor.

As Patrick rolled and twisted and I moved to greet him, the water continued to run out of the bath, but neither of us heard it or minded. The satin feel of the water, the lightness of our bodies, and the fulfillment of our need for communion, bound us in a moment of happiness, the joy of which was shared safe and secure in each other.

Then Patrick took my hand and we wandered naked into our bedroom. We lay slightly shivering on the sheets. We were wet, but the hot Hong Kong night air dried us gently with scented fingers. We slept more in unison than ever before. I hoped that this night would cement our happy marriage forever.

Patrick and I were happy enough, but Judith was having a bad time. She telephoned me a week later and asked me to visit her. I had to have a car, though I was a rotten driver. Patrick—who used the Peak tram—and

I picked out a small Morris Minor with an inexhaustible appetite for petrol. Several things were wrong with the engine, but she had such an engaging personality, I couldn't resist her. "Let's call her Emma," I said. Patrick looked less than enthusiastic, but agreed, and I was the proud owner of my Emma, my companion and fellow adventurer in Hong Kong.

I took off for the Royal Naval Base. Once there, I asked for directions and found myself in a block of flats. Judith and Bob lived on the top floor. Bob wasn't home. He was away for several months on his submarine and Judith was quite on her own. "Most of the other women have children," she said, "and I don't. So I . . . They have very little to do with me."

"Well, what do you do all day?" I asked.

"We have a lieutenant's wife and a few of her friends who organize games for us."

"Organize games, for grown women?"

"Yes," Judith nodded her head miserably. "Games like *Beetle*. You know, you add a leg for each letter you get right. Or we have a quiz, like 'In which country do you find Trafalgar Square?' " She made a face. "The woman is a fool, and she gets cross if I get the answer right. There is, of course, the dance. We all get invitations to attend dances when the ships are in."

"But you're married. You can't go out with other men."

"I don't go, but I'm just about the only one except for Ginny, and she's a Bible-thumper."

I was aghast. "Come on," I said. "Let's get going. If we don't get out of here, we're both going to end up grease puddles on the floor. It's far too hot and there's no wind." We climbed into my car Emma and set off down the road. "Do you use the swimming pool?"

Judith shrugged. "I do, but then it's full of children and babies. And the mothers who have young children can only talk about their children." I thought of Lucy.

"Look, Judith," I said as we drove out of the gates of the naval base. "Don't let all those other mothers get to you. Half of their problem is envy. They produce like rabbits to compete with their friends, and now they're stuck with it. We've joined the Dogwood Club. Let's go swimming and have lunch there. Damn, I didn't tell you to bring a swimsuit. Never mind. We'll go to the flat and get a spare."

"My!" Judith was amazed. "You have a wonderful flat." She gazed out of the window that looked down on the harbor boats. The Colawan ferry, that hauled hundreds of people a day between the island of Hong Kong and the port of Colawan, screamed its rapturous message: *I'm off, just see me go!* We were too far away to see the departure in detail, but close to the ferry landing we watched last minute passengers throw themselves across the ever-widening water and land precariously on the deck. Judith was very still for a while and then she said quietly, "You know, Bob has changed since I arrived here."

"We've only been here a few weeks," I said. I really didn't want to hear anyone else's troubles, because I had worked so hard on finding my feet, being a good wife, and loving Patrick. I knew I must not be selfish, and I knew what Judith had to say. I saw her face the day she threw herself into Bob's arms. I waited.

"He's different. I don't understand him. When we were home and courting, he was loving and kind. We always did everything together. He swore he never loved another woman like me. He'd had a bad childhood. His father was a terror, and Bob said in our marriage he would make up for all the bad things he suffered when he was little. But now he gets so angry over little things. Just before he left one night I burned the dinner. It actually wasn't all that much burned, but Bob got so angry I was frightened."

I shrugged. "Maybe it's just the strain of the new

job. Maybe when he gets back he'll have calmed down. Do you have an amah?"

"No, and I do need someone to help. It's not the work; it's the heat. I just can't wash all the clothes, cook, and clean like I can at home."

"Judith, you *can* afford an amah. Come on, we both can. You come from a wealthy family. Get an amah, and then you can get out and we can explore, swim, play tennis, enjoy ourselves before we have babies and join the ranks of the multiparous."

"Perish the thought." Judith smiled her sweet smile. "Mary, where I come from, you clean for yourself. Doesn't matter how rich you are, unless you're a mill-owner. Then you put gold on your taps and on your car doors and everybody sniggers."

"So let them snigger," I said. "I'll ask Ah Lim if she knows somebody. Anyway, while Bob is away, you need another soul about the place."

I picked up the swimsuits and we headed for the Dogwood Club. Architecturally the Club was beautifully designed. Old, square, and gracious it sat in the heart of Hong Kong surrounded by tall green welcoming trees. Usually Patrick and I swam after he returned from work. We had a drink and then went home. But today the hot sun reflected the blue pool, and only four women lay on their backs in the long deck chairs, observing us through their dark glasses. More crows, I thought to myself, remembering my mother's mahjong-playing friends. The crows here were slightly younger, but definitely the crow variety. "Come on, Judith," I said. "Let's get changed."

We both still looked pale green against the tans of these older women. "Not long," I said, "and we'll be as brown as anybody else. It makes Ah Lim dreadfully cross. She thinks I'm crazy to sunbathe. A white skin is a great mark of distinction among the Chinese. It means you are rich and don't have to work all day in the sun." I plunged in and swam a length. The water slid between my legs and sucked under my arms. I have always loved water. For a moment I forgot poor Judith and lay with only my nose just jutting out. High above me arched palm trees and great many-branched other trees crisscrossed with vine leaves, all pulling together for so many hundred years.

I still found it difficult to really believe I had slid so easily from one way of life to another. Letters lay in my desk to answer, but for now I left them: strings to the past, not to be ignored, but to be put aside until the past and the present were truly unentwined. I was searching for an unshakeable feeling of going forward and leaving behind a past that could now be left safely.

I turned and watched Judith diligently swimming laps. "I can do thirty laps now," she said.

I laughed. "I can do two, then I need a gin and tonic. When you finish, we'll have lunch. Are you feeling better?" Judith nodded. "Good. Let's swim and play tennis regularly. By the way, I got a message from a girl I knew in finishing school. Well, half-knew really. We were more acquaintances than friends. Her name is Kim Pedalto. Anyway, her family live in Macau. They're awfully rich, and she wants to meet me in a couple of days. Want to come?"

Judith's face was very relaxed and she smiled and I felt less ashamed. I may not be able to do much about Bob, but at least we could have a good time while he was away. My applecart was safe and I felt quite pleased with myself. Tonight I was to have a couple from the bank to dinner and I spent the afternoon organizing this event in my mind.

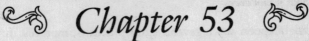

Chapter 53

My social life was falling into place. I had Patrick and the Club and, of course, Judith, but something rather awful had happened with Judith. Just before we were leaving the Club after our swim, a woman in the changing room came up to Judith and said, "You must be Judith Ericson. Your husband is a Petty Officer on my husband's ship." Judith nodded but looked rather frightened.

"Don't be silly," I said on the way home. "She's just another interfering old naval bitch wearing her husband's rank." I was wrong.

I got a call from a very upset Judith. Bob had been called into his Captain's office and told off. "Told off?" I said. "For what? For your swimming in the same pool as that old toad?"

"I'm afraid so," she said. "And Bob was really put out. We can't go again."

I was outraged, but I kept it to myself. Judith was afraid enough and I wasn't going to add to her troubles. "We'll find other things to do," I said. "I'll ring you next week."

"Good luck with your dinner," Judith said.

"Thanks." I put down the phone and stared into space. Why, I thought, do humans have to behave like hierarchical apes? Because, I reminded myself, we *are* hierarchical apes, only the apes know who they are and get on with it. If the good Captain had bared his hairless English chest and beaten his bosom with huge growls and howls, then Bob could have responded no doubt with even louder growls and more effective howls. The result of this scene in nature would have been the advent of the Captain's wife presenting her withered bottom to Bob while her vanquished husband wept and grumbled on the sidelines. What made this all improbable in human terms was the fact that the Captain wore several gold pieces of material on his body while Bob wore none. The small pieces of material prevented both of them behaving normally. Civilized it might be to human minds, but underneath it all stalked two men in a rage. No doubt, a rage that boiled over when Bob went home to vent his anger on Judith. No doubt, the Captain recounted his scene of victory to his wrinkled wife and hoped beyond hope that he would have his reward after dinner when, awash with wine and a chota peg of whiskey, they fell into bed and she wrapped her skinny legs about him, well-suntanned from the Club, and he was blasted into oblivion until the next day when he must smile at her in an embarrassed fashion over Lipton's tea and toast . . . Perish all those beastly thoughts. I used to get into trouble with Madame Rosen. "Mary," she'd said in that soft voice of hers, "you are too cynical, not sympathetic enough. People will not like you." Ah, I thought in a deep dark shadow, do I care?

But today was my first dinner-party day and I wanted my guests, Frances and Julian, to like me very much indeed. Julian was Patrick's best friend. He was English, and Frances was American. I hoped she was nice. By *nice* I meant unlike the other ladies at the Club. Most of them were much older than I. Most of them were Navy wives who felt they could throw their weight about. We of the British Oriental Bank were considered infra dig, but even lower than ourselves (because we were about money) came the Air Force wives. They sort of crept into the water or joined a swimming club in Kowloon where the Chinese had membership.

I was pleased when Frances arrived. She was tall and blonde. She had a snub nose and protruding teeth, a good warm smile and she was dressed in sari material, a shimmering gold and cream. I wore a dark green taffeta short frock. Both men wore white shirts with open necks and long trousers. We took our drinks out to the verandah where Ah Lim had set a table for dinner. The candles flickered and waved to me in the soft breath of wind. Above us the top of the Peak twinkled in hundreds of little lights. Up there the gardens would be illuminated by tiny jewelled fairy lights, chains of them competing with the fireflies while the very rich celebrated another day of deals, money, houses, ships, art from museums. How busy they must be, with all that responsibility for spending money. I didn't envy them.

I had enjoyed today with Su Wei in the market. We had picked over a mound of firm plum shrimps, choosing the best for our curry. We shook a coconut, the liquid reverberating in my ear. "Good one," Su Wei said and he put it in his string bag. Here and there we hovered and I listened to Su Wei barter. His voice was sing-song and hypnotic, a fusillade of bargaining, and then money changed hands. If the deal was good, Su Wei smiled and ho-ho-hoed to the shopkeeper. If the deal was no good, Su Wei hissed through his teeth like a very cross camping lamp and generally behaved as if a favourite aunt had died. "Don't worry, Su Wei." I trotted behind him. "We can afford it."

Now in the cool evening the whole day came together. The feeling of my house, my possession, my husband, and my ability to take care of him as I vowed I would, made me proud of myself. The curry was perfect. Julian's verdict was the most important. He had lived in India and was generally agreed to be the expert on curry. "Very good," he said. "Very very good indeed."

I blushed with pride and Patrick glanced at me and smiled. I sat satiated with wifehood, and then my secret Crow sat on my shoulder and whispered, "Who ever thought Mary would sit and blush like a bride? Whatever happened to the other Mary?"

"She's dead," I silently snapped. "Go away." He

fled heavily from the verandah, out into the night he had just spoiled . . .

"Mary?" Frances called me.

"Oh, I am sorry. I must have been daydreaming again."

"Don't apologize," Frances laughed kindly. "For the first year I was here, I was so homesick I was always taking a magic carpet back to Minnesota."

"Are there many Americans here?" I asked.

"No, not at the moment." Frances sighed. "I find life here dreadfully difficult. You see . . . well, I don't really want to be rude . . ."

"Don't worry," I said, grimly thinking of Judith. Frances looked surprised. "I just had a run-in," I explained, "or rather, I just caused a run-in with a Navy wife. My friend got told off."

Frances wrinkled her very short nose. "Well, well," she said. "I thought it was only us Americans who were discriminated against."

"No, but I promise you this is all new to me. We have snobs in the Foreign Office, but I've never seen anything like this. The wives usually all get on together."

"Anyway," Frances smiled, "we're going out in the boat tomorrow. Ask Patrick if you can both spend the day with us. You'll meet some Americans and you don't have to be on your best behavior." I liked the idea of a day on a boat.

Patrick and I went to bed. I was too tired to make love, and Patrick lay beside me, his soft breath against my ear. "Well done, darling," he said as he fell asleep.

"Tomorrow," I said mostly to myself, "before we leave on the boat, I must telephone Kim Pedalto."

All day on a boat. I wondered if it would be like the company boat that Patrick's father kept on the Seine. I remembered his birthday party and how we kissed. I hugged him gently and fell asleep. *Macau* a neon sign flashed. *Macau.* That was where Kim lived.

Chapter 54

I was excited and pleased to be taking a boat trip, my first in Hong Kong. The boat belonged to Ian and Isla Campbell. Ian was *in* Jardine Matheson. Everybody in Hong Kong was *in* something. Not *in* love or *in* as in feeling, but *in* as in a business. Goodness knows what one said if asked and one was not *in* the Bank or *in* the Navy/Army/Air Force or married to it. Isla was considered the island's reigning queen. She was known as "The Princess" and she was very beautiful indeed. She came from the Isle of Skye and even her origins were romantic. I felt awkward and ugly.

The boat rocked as I tried clumsily to board. Isla laughed gaily and floated over the side and settled onto the deck like a leaf blown in the wind. She was a glossy brown color, her hair chestnut and shining, her eyes large and brown with huge enviable eyelashes, the sort that permanently dropped onto her cheeks. She was tanned and it looked suspiciously as if she sunbathed naked. I had the usual swimming strapmarks, striped like a lemur, atop the shoulders and at the top of my legs. I also had the regulation sunburned nose and a few strips of burnt flesh on my back. I was dressed in my Swan and Edgar's swimsuit, nicely cut and extremely demure.

I was introduced to Cindy and Norris Goden from New York. I realized that all three women—Frances, Isla, and Cindy—were wearing bikinis. Isla smiled at me. "You get used to boats here. We all take off most weekends to get away from Hong Kong. It's so small. Still, we're away for Christmas back to London." I was amazed: to want to be in London, when one had the whole of the Far East at one's disposal! I didn't say anything. These were Patrick's friends and I so much wanted to make a good impression.

It was a clear hot day without humidity, and the air

was bright and the waves sparkled. We nosed out of the harbor and quickly put to sea. Behind us the junks were rocking on the waves, their huge furled brown sails flapping in the wind. As we passed, some of the children leaned over the edges, their hands outstretched. "Give us money!" they yelled. "White lady, give us money!" I reached down to find some coins.

"No," Isla said flatly, "don't do that. If you do, we'll be surrounded by children swimming to us and demanding money."

I remembered children in the sea a long time ago. It must have been on the boat out of Africa. They looked so happy, leaping like otters from the water and splashing back, a glint of silver in their hands. I remembered envying them . . . But Isla knew best. Isla knew everything and everybody in Hong Kong. Patrick said she was very famous at Cambridge. A man had written a book about her. She had jilted him and he had died of a broken heart. Her husband Ian looked the typical strong dour Scot. He was at the helm, and Patrick ran about the boat jibbing and tacking and doing all those nautical things you are supposed to do on a boat. He did it very efficiently. I was proud of him.

We pulled away from the last of the junks and I felt like a chick who had lost its mother hen. Here we were, a bunch of strangers, sailing to goodness knows where. At least the junks were home to hundreds and thousands of families in Hong Kong. I missed the sound of the creaking, and then we turned and I could see the naval ships, rows of them, anchored out at sea. Bad weather was perhaps expected in the next few days. They were out there riding the coming of a possible typhoon. Lean and mean as whippets they strained, and seemed ready for war with anyone. We moved on, rolling up and down in the boat.

I sat on the edge with my bare feet holding me steady. The movement of the boat was hypnotic, and

I had little to add to the talk among the others: Isla evidently had been arranging a dinner dance; somebody had behaved very badly with someone else's husband; Cindy and Norris were preparing to go back to New York for six months . . . Did I want their amah? This question was thrown at me and fortunately I was concentrating. "No, thank you," I said. "I have an amah. Her name is Ah Lim." I began to list her virtues. I saw Patrick look at me quizzically.

He had done whatever it was he had to do, and for the past ten minutes we had been sitting on the foredeck listening to the talking. I realized that Isla's eyes were glazed with boredom, but Frances—my friend from last night—intervened. "We all felt like that about our amahs when we first arrived," she said. "Trusting and unsuspecting, I mean. But wait until your Ah Lim steals your silver and the bed linen. I do hope you keep a count. If you don't, you won't have any evidence. Anyway, Cindy, I'll take your amah for six months. Does she wash?"

I was silent. This was not my world. Does she wash *what*? Herself? Other people? Clothes? Of course I knew Cindy meant clothes. Maybe this was just a shorthand that one learned in time.

The sun was overhead and by now the sea shimmered rather than sparkled. The sun was hot and I was thirsty. Isla, Cindy, and Frances disappeared below to organize lunch. I was left with Norris. He looked at me very suspiciously. I felt the same about him, but decided to try my mother's technique: always get them to talk about themselves, she urged. All right then, I would. "How long have you been here?" I asked.

"Two years."

"Do you like it here?"

"No."

"I see," I said, sounding interested. "Then why do you stay?"

"For the money."

"Oh. Of course. Uh . . . What do you do?"

"Journalist."

"How wonderful." (I tried not to over-enthuse.) "What do you write?"

"About the Commies."

"Really. How interesting. Are there many of them?"

"All over the place. Look." He pointed a massive finger at the horizon. "See that boat? I'd betcha they're following us."

He was right. There was a small boat not too far away. The thought of it being chock-a-block with Communists—all watching us, insect-eyed binoculars around their necks—seemed fascinating. Definitely something, I noted to myself, to write to Grandpa about. He was always difficult to write to, but a whole piece about Communists would give him an electric charge for a day at least. "How extraordinary!" I said. "What do they follow us for?"

"Information." Norris must have been, I figured, originally from the American Southwest, given the economy of his words. His wife might well have been a native of New York, or so Patrick said. She was small, rather a hedgerow bird. She hopped and she talked with a deep nasal twang. The twang was either New York, or she had a bad case of sinus. Norris on the other hand was unusually tall. His lack of vocabulary must mean that much of his life had been spent on a horse. And he obviously did not appreciate being made to vacate his horse to record the finer points of Chinese Communism for his readers.

Patrick was up at the helm and I felt an awful failure. I was with the only other passenger available for conversation, and I couldn't even keep a decent discussion going. Isla appeared on deck and smiled at Norris who beamed back. She knew how to handle him. Behind her, Frances carried two large Thermos flasks and Cindy had a tray. On the tray a stack of lobsters lay, split end to end. In the middle of the tray was a bowl of mayonnaise. "Pimms, everybody!" Isla shouted.

A little way away I saw the leeward end of an island. We were going to pull in and anchor for lunch. What an idyllic paradise! I hoped Patrick and I would have a chance to go off and swim by ourselves.

Within a few minutes the anchor had been secured and the boat tugged gently and amiably at its mooring. We all sat cross-legged on deck and pulled apart our lobsters. Patrick sat next to me and we grunted at each other. The Pimms was cold and fresh and thirst-quenching. I still had little to add to the talk. Everybody spoke in a shorthand that I was sure I would learn over the coming months. Still, I was more interested in looking around me at this paradise than in the conversation. I drank until I was dreamily aware that the meal was over. "Come on, Patrick," I said. "Let's go for a swim."

"Don't you think you ought to help clear away?"

"No," I said, rather cross because none of the women had bothered to talk to me. They behaved as if I had purloined one of their favorite bachelors. The Pimms inside me loosened my tongue and betrayed a mind still somewhat irked. "They can borrow my amah," I said, perhaps a bit more sarcastically than I intended. "That is, if she doesn't steal the lobster picks. They'd better count them first, just to be sure." Patrick looked at me with alarm in his eyes. He said nothing. We lowered ourselves over the side and swam away towards the island.

It was a little knoll or, I suppose, a castaway atoll in the middle of the sea. When we stepped onto the beach, small land crabs scuttled nervously away and shot down their holes, only to reappear disapprovingly. How dare we invade their sanctum? Many rounded bulbous eyes waved furiously at us. We laughed and strolled hand in hand, the clean sand scrunching under our feet. "Isn't this marvelous?" I sighed.

"Yes, it is." Patrick laughed. "Last one into the water is a monkey," and he shot ahead of me and threw himself into the sea. I wandered to the edge and watched him rolling about like a porpoise. He made a face and then put his hand down to his submerged foot. He pulled out his hand and in it was a huge red starfish. Its five limbs were swollen and purple and the crown looked dangerous. "Ugh, how disgusting!" and Patrick lobbed the starfish as far as he could throw it over my head.

I ducked and laughed. "Serves you right for wanting to be first." We swam some more and then went back to the boat.

Norris was asleep and the three women were talking. How they could talk, those women. *Woman's talk*, I suppose. "Are you going to join the bridge team?" Isla asked. "I need a partner."

"I'm afraid I'm not much good at bridge."

"How about canasta?" Cindy asked.

"No." I shook my head. "Not canasta."

"Do you play tennis?"

"Yes," I said, "but I really am bad at it."

"What do you do then?" Cindy sounded quite cross.

"Well, I read a lot. I sort of swim, and I like to listen to music. And I love to cook . . ." Slowly I felt the air round me grow cold. All three of them, I knew, felt they had tried and I had failed the test. I had very little to offer them. These were professional *women*. My mother had learned to become one of them. I now realized what a huge effort my mother must have made. It does require an effort to put that much time into dressing immaculately, learning to play all socially acceptable games to a reasonable standard, remembering that if the wife of Shell Oil loses at bridge, Shell Oil loses at bridge. If the British Embassy Canasta Team in Paris won canasta, then the British Embassy won and their victory would be followed by a triumphal cocktail party. The women were extensions of their husbands' jobs and the husbands themselves were extensions of corporate monoliths. I feared I was not a very good bank representative.

Patrick seemed not to notice. I was very tired as we sailed back. The wind had risen and the sails bellied out. We raced back towards Hong Kong and tacked our way through the junks that were crowding in to harbor. A weather report had upgraded the storm. Soon it began to rain in big plump drops. I felt myself grow cold and sweaty. "I'm afraid I'm going to be sick," I said desperately.

"Oh no." Isla was not pleased. "Go in there," she said pointing to the head. "Try not to make a mess." I could see from her face that *making a mess* was a cardinal sin.

I knelt on the wooden floor, the bilges rolling with dirty water under me, and I was sick. Dreadfully, dreadfully sick. I held onto the lavatory and swore at myself. How could I be so stupid and so useless? I couldn't even go sailing without messing everything up. When I had finally stopped retching, I flushed the lever and got dizzily to my feet. We were in calmer waters now. I closed the door behind me; the others pretended not to notice that anything had happened. Patrick was aloft helping Ian to maneuver the boat into her berth. I collected our towels and put them into my swimming bag.

"I do hope you enjoyed yourself," Isla said as we left the boat.

"Thank you very much," I said. "We did."

"I'll see ya when we're back from home," Cindy added.

They all waved us off and I felt sure, once we were out of sight, they would get out the pitcher, pour another round of drinks, and proclaim me the failure I was. Poor old Patrick . . .

"Are you all right now?" Patrick was most solicitous when we were safely back in the flat.

"Yes, I'm all right," I said. "I just need to clean my teeth. I'm awfully sorry. I do hate being sick."

"Too much lobster and too much Pimms."

"Don't pontificate, Patrick," I said. "I made a fool of myself in front of all those people. I feel bad enough as it is."

"Oh, they don't mind. Really. Aren't they nice? I can't get over how friendly people are here."

I sighed. "Yes, they are." There was no point in arguing. These were Patrick's people. I did wish I could speak to my mother. Now again I realized that in her own quiet way she had been warning me about these people. It was all very well for me to say I'd play by my own rules, though I knew of a woman who managed to do just that: eccentric old Mrs Balderstone. She lived out on the Point and was the talk of Hong Kong. She dressed in an accumulation of once expensive rags. She wore hideous hats and veils. She insisted on hoisting the Union Jack every time a naval boat went through, which meant that the whole ship had to stand to attention and salute the flag every time they steamed out of Hong Kong. She did indeed break every rule and was politely ignored and snubbed by everyone . . . I was sixty years younger than she. Did I really want to endure such ostracism?

I didn't know, but I was going to Macau to visit Kim Pedalto, and maybe I should practice my tennis with Judith.

Chapter 55

Kim Pedalto telephoned me on several occasions about my trip to Macau. I hardly remembered *exactly* which one of the many Chinese students at Mont St Sebastian she was. Her voice was hurried and nervous over the telephone, but I did understand her need to talk to someone who had shared the same experiences. "You see," she said in her very English well-educated voice, "there are so few young women in Macau. They all leave. Besides, I have to trail round with my bodyguards and it makes me so conspicuous. I thought about you in Hong Kong, and I wondered if you would like to visit with me." I was delighted. We had been in Hong Kong for several months now and I felt I could do with a break from the never ending Club, swimming, tennis, and parties. More and more I dislikes the parties and those who attended them.

Judith remained the one person I could really talk to. *What is the matter with me?* I asked my mirror. Why am I so different? Judith felt very much the same way. All the other young wives seemed to be having a wonderful time. They had amahs to take care of their children, and parties to go to whether their husbands were there or not. There was a huge dearth of women and an enormous pool of available men. Judith was absolutely faithful to Bob, even though he had a frightful imagination and regularly accused her of being unfaithful. "I sometimes wish I was. It's all so unfair," Judith said. "There are those little tarts, handing it around like biscuits, and I'm home reading or sewing, and he accuses *me.*"

Anyway, Judith was all for the idea of my going to Macau, this time with Patrick. I did hope Kim had decent friends who didn't talk about bridge or makeup. Hopefully her men-friends didn't sidle off to talk about "serious" things where dizzy silly women could not follow. I usually followed and got glared at.

"Really, darling," Patrick frowned the morning after a dinner party during which I had entered a political conversation. "You must try and be more tactful."

"But my father always talked politics in front of me and so did his friends. I probably know more about politics than most of your friends."

That made Patrick very cross. He stomped off to the bank. I therefore was not terribly surprised when he phoned up and said he couldn't make the Friday night ferry to Macau. But I was rather surprised by my own reaction. "Oh dear, how awful," I said. "Never mind, I'll catch the ferry and you can come over on Saturday."

"You mean you're not going to cancel the trip? The ferry takes all day to get there, and then we'd be coming back on Sunday. It isn't worth my while."

"I know, darling," I said consolingly, "but I'm all packed and Kim is expecting us. I'll tell her you can't come. I'm sure she will understand. After all, an audit can happen at any time. Can't be helped." I knew Patrick by now and knew he was upset. His methods of retribution were to withdraw and leave me feeling guilty. This time I was determined not to be guilty. I had been his perfect but failing wife ever since we arrived in Hong Kong and I needed a break, if not from Hong Kong, then at least a few days away from Patrick and his eternal concern over what other people thought, might think, or would think in the future.

I telephoned Judith. "Do you think I can leave Patrick for a weekend after only a few months of marriage and not feel guilty?"

"I don't know." Judith was sounding rather sad. "I can't leave Bob for twenty-four hours without feeling an awful physical pain. It's like surgery. The first few days he's away at sea are agony. I feel someone has tied a rope around my heart and is tugging and pulling. But you should go anyway, and see how you feel. Macau, everyone says, is a grand place to visit. Can you believe this heat?"

"No, I can't," I said. "But after England, I don't mind. Besides, if you think this is hot, try Africa."

"No thanks," Judith said, "I'd melt."

Friday was a big market day for me. Now that I knew where the markets were, I went by myself, much to Su Wei's disgust. When he was cross he sucked his teeth. When I told him that I was going to Macau without Patrick, he sucked his teeth and shook his head. "No good, Missie. Must stay with husband or husband find other woman." I laughed. The idea of Patrick with another woman was ludicrous. Ah Lim took the news very seriously. She also sucked her teeth. So, with both of them united in their disapproval, I took off for the vegetable market.

In among the fruits I thought about going off to Macau. I tried very hard to choose good things for Patrick to eat while I was away. Why didn't I cancel the trip? After all, it was not as if I knew the girl. If it had been an arrangement with Phoebe or Hattie, I would have owed them loyalty. But surely I had no business leaving Patrick. He was my husband . . . as hard as I tried, I simply couldn't feel very guilty. I had a bubble in my veins, a bubble of excitement. I loved to travel and I was interested in people. We knew no Chinese except for Ah Lim and Su Wei, both of them so built into my life now that I hardly imagined a time when I didn't know them. But Hong Kong was like that: a small enchanted bubble in the middle of the China Seas. I had to remind myself again and again that there were other worlds, other people.

Recently I had written to Miss Standish, just to remind myself that other people approved of me and thought me clever and worth bothering with. Here in this colony I was like an iguana plonked down on a dinner table in Bournemouth. Most people regarded me with horror as I tried desperately to talk about anything other than the new Yardley shipment of face cream. Or suffer the long and tedious stories of other people's misdoings. Not that Judith and I did not enjoy a juicy bit of salacious gossip. Not at all. If I had a piece worth telling, Judith and I met for lunch, where the fact that Mr Johnson from the bank had made a pass at his secretary took several minutes in the telling. But an even more interesting fact was that Mrs Johnson had just taken a job in a department store, no doubt to help pay for all the silver ashtrays and cigarette boxes that littered her flat. I was forced to endure this snob because her husband Mr. Johnson was Patrick's boss and, because they had the same surname, he decided that Patrick was the son he never had. Needless to say, I didn't get this sort of gossip from Patrick. He would have considered it "frightfully low" to gossip, but then he was a man . . .

I ended up day-dreaming around the streets and took a taxi back to the Peak, my basket full of good intentions for Patrick, but my soul doing a samba, not because I was leaving Patrick behind, but because I was going to travel.

I had to leave before Patrick came home, so I left a note with a list of things I'd asked Su Wei to prepare for him. Patrick was easy to cater for, as he really was a meat and potatoes man. I had steak organized for tonight, and for Saturday night I ordered his favorite steak-and-kidney pie.

The ferry was crowded on the lower deck, but the First Class lounge was quiet. I had booked an overnight cabin. I pushed open the door and just stood there looking at the bunk with quiet contentment. I loved boats. Not Hong Kong gin-palaces such as the boat I was on with Patrick, but real boats that smelled of tar and deck oil. This boat, the *Fat Shan*, was built a long time ago. She was squat and wonderfully ugly. She rolled even in the harbor, but the hull was massive and safe. The decks were surrounded with thick wire netting and the Captain's quarters were cut off from the passengers with extra netting. "Pirates," the cabin-boy offered when I asked why.

"Oh," I said, faintly alarmed.

"No worry, Missie," he said grinning. "We have guns. Pow! Pow! Captain asks you for drinks. Six o'clock. Half an hour time, okay?"

"Okay," I said. In fact, the idea of being chased by pirates did sound alarming. A drink with the captain might well be in order. I was getting awfully good at drinking these days. Several gulps and even the most boring banker looked a little less awful.

I washed my sweaty face and hands and wondered how the Chinese always managed to look so cool and impervious to the heat. Su Wei never sweated, neither did Ah Lim. I felt so awful as I daily struggled into the flat like a flounder without water. I lived in the shower. This evening, anyway, I had twenty minutes to get ready and get up to the Captain's cabin.

What I saw at first was not dreadfully reassuring. "Captain Moses at your command." He was huge with ears that sprouted the most amazing amounts of hairs. His belly hung over his vast trousers and there were patches of sweat under his arms. He took my out-stretched hand reverently and put it to his lips. For a man so rough, he had a surprisingly gentle grip. "Come," he said, and we walked from the deck into the control room. "What'd you drink?"

"Anything," I said hopefully. "What about wine?"

"Nah," he informed me. "Don't usually carry the stuff up here, but I'll get some up for you from below. Any particular color?"

"White," I said. "But only if you have it."

"Jo Jo!" he bellowed down a brass tube. "Bring the lady white wine! *Juldee!*"

"You're from India," I said, laughing.

"How can you tell?"

"The way you said *'juldee.'* In India, women were called *memsahib* if they were married. Here I'm called *Missie* whether I'm married or not."

Captain Moses pointed to a canvas chair. "Take the weight off the old plates," he said. "Jo Jo will be right up. We've been together a long time, Jo Jo and me. From the old days when India was India. We tried settling in Blighty, but there was nothing for us. An out of work soldier and a wog—no one wanted us. So we came out here and made a life for ourselves. He's a good fellow, old Jo Jo. Except when there's women, then he slinks off like a dog. I leave him to it and he comes back, tail between his legs. Never found a woman who could hold him, has Jo Jo."

I looked around during this monologue. The control room was clean and polished. Contrary to his appearance, Captain Moses obviously loved his ship. "What is this about pirates?" I asked.

"Oh, *them,*" he said contemptuously. "Don't mind them. We had a raid two years ago. A junk came out from one of the islands. Armed to the teeth, they were. Climbed on board like rats. I had to shoot one off the rigging. Little bastard clung like the devil. Had to shoot him twice. The women were all screaming at the top of their lungs. Don't know what for. Them bandits ain't interested in women. They wanted money. I had the money up here, locked away. Anyway, after a time, most of 'em were dead. But the shipping line decided to fence us in. Don't worry your head. I'm captain here and nobody boards my ship unless I say so. Huh, Jo Jo?"

Jo Jo came in with a bottle of white wine and a glass. He was small with intelligent black eyes. He nodded. "The Captain is an excellent shot, Madam," he said. He put the glass on a round table beside me. "Let me introduce myself. I am John Joseph McLaren. Almost a lawyer, from Bombay. I say "almost" because the war intervened and I had to look after the Captain here."

"I see," I said, feeling foolish.

"Is your husband with you?" Captain Moses inquired.

"Well, no," I said. "At the last minute he had to stay at the bank for an audit."

"I see." I was rather afraid that Captain Moses did indeed see far too well for my liking. He had drowned eyes, the sort of eyes you only see occasionally on a fisherman or a sea captain, as if they were born to go to sea. I looked at him and his eyes were fathomless. I felt I could throw an anchor out to him and his eyes would take the anchor and find a rock in his massive frame and the anchor would hold through the good times and the bad. "I see," he said again.

I smiled a self-conscious smile and sipped my wine. Jo Jo had thoughtfully added some ice and I thanked him. "Not at all, not at all," Jo Jo replied. "Will you stay with us for dinner?"

"I would love to," I said and I realized that I really meant it.

"All righty," said Captain Moses. "Dinner is at eight sharp, in my cabin. Don't be late."

And I wasn't.

Chapter 56

I returned to my cabin to change. The air was hot and very humid. Drops of sweat stuck to my nose and slid off down my chin. In the cabin the fan cooled me off and I watched the gray clouds float across the sea. Long lean tendrils of rain were coming towards us. I looked forward to the rain. Patrick, I knew, would not at all approve of this dinner invitation.

Upstairs in the First Class lounge there was a restaurant for the First Class passengers and each passenger according to rank *should* have his or her place. Mine would be a very lowly place because my husband was a very junior bank official. The Captain *should* sit at the Captain's table but, having met Captain Moses, I could see that he would have none of it. Still I was hungry for adventure and I quickly changed and ran up the gangways until I reached his rooms.

The sign read *Captain Moses* in big brass letters. I knocked and Jo Jo opened the door. We were in a very comfortable sitting room somewhere in Rawalpindi I imagined. There were camel stools to sit on, an actual elephant's foot full of golf clubs and a few umbrellas (some highly carved), scented wooden tables and armchairs covered in swags of chintz flowers. "Surprised?" Jo Jo laughed. "We don't live like swine, we two," he said. He pointed proudly to the pictures hanging on the walls. "These are my art collection, you see. I collect from everywhere." Indeed he had collected a very gentle collection of watercolors from all sorts of countries. "I am looking for a Chinnery in Macau—yet another starving artist painting years ago here, giving away his pictures for food. And now?" He shrugged and held out his palms. "But then, what is money? What is a hundred years or so? The pictures remain, don't they? Now this one," he pointed to a camel gravely walking in an Indian market. "This is a Russell Flint, well worth collecting."

How strange, I thought. Here these two people have a part of the world they have made very much their own. Even if separately they could have lived, Jo Jo in India and Captain Moses in England, they would never have felt at home. Here in this room *I* felt at home, such a funny feeling. I realized, for the first time since I had arrived in Hong Kong, that I had not been at home there. Here in the land of two misfits, I was home. There were books in rows against the walls. It occurred to me that I had given up reading, except for the Hong Kong morning paper. Life had become a buzz of action and reaction. The Johnsons invite us out to dinner, we invite them back with two other friends, who then invite us and the Johnsons, *ad infinitum.* But in this cabin on the boat, nothing much happened except for music. I could see a big Victrola and a pile of records.

Shouts erupted from the door in front of me. Abruptly Captain Moses strode into the room trying to tie a bow tie. "Jo Jo, do something about this thing! It wants to strangle me!"

Jo Jo fluttered about but succeeded in calming Captain Moses down. "Sit, sit, sit," he said soothingly, as to a child. "Let me do it. Look. It takes a few minutes, under like this, over like that, and there we have it." He stood back and we both admired his handiwork.

Captain Moses raised himself and looked at the pier-glass over the small mahogany fireplace. "Very good," he said, pulling at the black satin edges with his thick fingers. "Very good indeed. Don't often have a lady to dinner, so decided to wear black tie."

"Oh, I'm sorry. I didn't realize we were dressing."

"We're not," he grinned. "I am. I like to dress for dinner. And as for you, you look lovely. Quite beautiful." He took my hand and said, "Come. Let's you and I sit down while we ask Jo Jo to order drinks. What can he get you?"

"A gin and tonic, please."

"Of course. Jo Jo, I'll have my usual. And let's have a few bits and pieces to nibble on." Jo Jo silently disappeared. I was left staring at this man whom I had known for two hours at the most but who seemed to be my oldest and best friend. "Don't look so surprised, Mary." Captain Moses glanced at me. "I'm nearly seventy, damned near retiring age, but then I won't retire. No, Jo Jo and I will find a spot for the old boat and live on her until we're ninety."

As he talked I felt my soul tremble. I had so much to say to him, so many doubts and fears, none of which I could articulate yet. *Had I made a dreadful mistake?* was my first great fear. Did I love, or had I ever loved, Patrick? Was Patrick an adolescent dream of my unhappy years when I thought only of escape from my family? An escape into what seemed to be a big, boisterous, happy family? Now, after the wedding and many many letters from my mother-in-law and the sisters, I learned that those letters were full of nothing, except the letters from Lucy who yearned for an escape from the family I had so recently joined. I couldn't believe that Anthea and Joanna could write in such boring detail about their children. Certainly I was glad the children produced teeth, and would have been properly horrified had they remained toothless, but to recount teeth dropped here and there and the whereabouts of the tooth fairy—were such particulars really necessary? My distracted misery and uncertainty did not go unnoticed by Captain Moses.

"I'll tell you a story," he said. He cleared his throat of several years of collected memories. "Hurry up, Jo Jo!" he interrupted his story's beginning.

"Yes, sir." Jo Jo put the drinks down and sat reverently down beside me.

"I was a boy from a big family," he began. "We lived in Hounslow . . ."

"Yes yes yes." Jo Jo had obviously heard this story many times before, but he was perched on the end of his chair, his long slim hands pressed together in a prayer of anticipation. "You listen very carefully, Madam," he said. "This is a very important story."

"Where was I? Ah, yes." Captain Moses had a tankard of beer in front of him. "My father was an alcoholic, as they call it nowadays. In my day we were proud of him, when he wasn't shouting and yelling.

He raced horses when he had money. And when he didn't, the horses pulled coal. My brother Jack, God bless him, was the smallest of us all, and had to ride jockey on the great brutes. When my father was in a good mood and the horses were doing well, he was a good kind man, but when things got too bad or he didn't win at the races, he got drunk. He could pin five men against the wall with one arm. He was built like a brick shithouse, my father was, and he drank. How he could drink! A quart of whiskey a day. I remember dancing on the bar when I was three. I had long golden curls and I danced to entertain the customers in the Black Lion pub he bought out of his winnings one night. But wait," Captain Moses put his hand up. "There is a point to this story. Be patient."

I took a sip of gin and tonic. I was interested. Captain Moses was not a garrulous old bore. He shone with an intensity and an intelligence I had missed all these months. He reminded me very much of my grandfather, whom I missed. Both men had traveled the world. Both roosted in their old age in their own worlds. Would I be that lucky, that I too after years could honestly live and be content with what I had around me? I listened.

"My brothers all went to the local grammar. All of them clever. Jack and Bill were going into the Gas Company. My mother wanted me in the Post Office. I was the youngest of the seventeen and my mother was a saint, but I wasn't going to stay in England. The First World War changed everything. I was given the white feathers by women on buses. I was fourteen and big for my age. But I knew. History was my passion. For all I read, I listened to Churchill. I read everything he wrote, and when he escaped from those Boers in South Africa, I knew I must escape and I did.

"I studied and studied, got out first from the grammar, and then went into the Army, just in time to get in at the end. After the War, off I went to India. I worked there and found JoJo. He was my batman. Then came peace. We were all shipped home and there was nothing for us. Not for the likes of us, I mean. Jo Jo and I didn't fit anywhere. My mum died. My dad was old and on a pension. He lived with my sister and the pub was his life. I looked at life in England and knew it would never be the same. Killed off all the best of them, the War did. Then, years later, they wiped out the next crop of men. But by then I was gone.

"Jo Jo and I travelled on ships all over the world and finally we got here. The *Fat Shan,* my own ship. That's where my heart lies, in this ship." He laughed. "D'you see?" he asked.

"No, not exactly," I said. "I see that you love this ship."

"No, no, no." Captain Moses was amused. "Love is a sentimental word. I don't *love* this ship. *Fat Shan* is my life. I have given my heart to my ship. Not to another woman, which is what men usually do, but to this ship."

Jo Jo nodded. "True," he said. "Very true. Captain Moses never looks at another woman." He looked at the Captain and a perfectly imperceptible joke passed between them. I did not understand the drift of the joke, but then I did see that old friends like that matured like gorgonzola cheese: a slight sniff, and the aficionados can tell you the history of the cheese. Years lay between those two, just as I hoped years would lie between Phoebe and myself and Judith.

"The point, my dear," the Captain continued, "is for you to give your heart to something. So many people go through life giving nothing of themselves away. They take no risks. They marry properly. They have children. A garden shed, a lawn mower. Life passes by quite steadily. The breaking of the garden rake assumes the same proportion of decimation as the declaration of drought in Ethiopia. Both events require some money; both events assume equal proportions."

Jo Jo had disappeared. I hoped he would return with dinner.

"At the end of this weekend," Captain Moses said, "you think about what you really want out of life. I saw your passport when you came onto the boat. You're a Freeland. That was your name before marriage?"

"Yes. That's my maiden name."

"Major Freeland. Well, well, well. It is a small world we live in. Of course, looking at you I can see the man now. We served in India together. He was my senior, of course, but a good brave man. Your father, I remember him as a boy." Captain Moses's face changed. "He married Lavinia . . ." He paused and Jo Jo came through the door with several little plates of spicy hot meats. "Jo Jo, Mary is Major Freeland's granddaughter. I told you she was."

Jo Jo smiled. "Those of us who served in the East share a great fraternity. Your grandfather was a fine soldier."

"But," I said, "you mentioned my mother. What do you know about her?"

Captain Moses sighed and finished his beer. "Nobody these days likes to talk about stock, but whatever you've been told, I can tell you one thing. You come from wandering stock. Lavinia will tell you when she wants to tell you, but listen to my long story. We are outsiders, Jo Jo and I. If you are truly an outsider then you stay outside. Don't try to make a life on the inside. You will fail. Worst of all, you will feel you're a failure, when really you had no chance of success. Many people rush off to foreign parts of the world to prove they are not insiders. They have been reading too much Camus, an insider if there ever was one. What do they do when they get to a foreign exotic climate? They put on their white shorts and their neat little dresses and gloves and go off to the Governor's house to sign his

book and then go to the same cocktail parties they left
behind. They join the library and read air mail editions
of *The Times*. At six o'clock they listen to the BBC
World News and on Sunday they all meet each other
and eat a curry at the Club. Best of all they get to call
other people 'boy' and they feel important.''

The sweet meats were perfect and very filling. I was
tired. Captain Moses gave off such huge surges of energy, I felt I'd been listening all night, not just two
hours. But I had listened very intently. I had to admit
what he said was very true. I really did want to think
about my life. I was not happy. I knew I wasn't happy,
because recently after making love with Patrick, I often
turned my face into the pillow and cried. Not out of
frustration. Making love with Patrick was satisfying
physically. But emotionally I was unfulfilled. Maybe
Captain Moses knew something about me. I was not
surprised he knew my grandfather. He was well known
to almost anyone who served in India or the Far East.
But yet again there was a stone wall where my mother
was concerned . . .

"I think you've had enough of a lecture from an old
codger like me. I'll see you Sunday after you've had
a weekend in Macau. It should feel like home to you.
This is naturally your part of the world," he said enig-
matically.

"You won't explain that, will you?" I said.

"No." Captain Moses shook his head. "sometimes
you destroy a person by telling them what is in their
future or their past. The time will come for you when
you reach out for your destiny. Until then, nothing can
happen. The earth just goes along day by day."

"Does everybody have a destiny?" I asked.

"Of course. We are all called by name before the
earth was formed. You can be called," he said, "but
will you listen? You're a stubborn girl, Mary." He
smiled. "Very stubborn, but you can learn. Now off
with you. We'll land early tomorrow morning."

"Thank you," I said and I shook his hand. "Thank you very much." Jo Jo saw me out of the door and I walked down the long narrow gangways thinking of the sermon I had just heard. I would have to think about it.

❧ *Chapter 57* ❧

I awoke to the smell of the mud-flats. The last time I remembered mud like this was in Africa on safari. That was clean, sweet-smelling mud; this mud stank of the effluence of a city that did its washing and ablutions in the sea. We were tied up at the jetty and I sat up and looked out of the window. Not very different to Hong Kong, except for the Portuguese gunboats. They hung their washing on lines slung between their guns. Knickers and sheets flapped gaily in the breeze. Macau felt lawless, unlike Hong Kong which suffered under a heavy British bureaucracy. Macau was run by the Portuguese who left the Chinese population severely alone, Kim had said.

Before I left the ship, I ran in to Captain Moses. "Have a good time," he said. "And don't forget to gamble. Fan-Tan, guess three." I had no idea what he meant, but I promised and took off to find Kim.

Kim's car was waiting by the ferry. Her driver and his companion looked unhappily into space. Neither smiled. Both wore thick black suits and had what I imagined were guns under their bulging armpits. We were not introduced, but the driver got out and took my suitcase which he put in the back of the car. They both made me nervous. Kim shook her head. "Don't worry," she said. "You'll get used to them. I'd be a lot more nervous without them. Anyone who's prominent here has to have bodyguards. The last British Consul was shot. The bullet went right through his hat. It wasn't even meant for him. He just got in the way. You see there?" she pointed to a perfectly innocuous tree. "Last year the firecracker king was shot dead right under that tree. Bang, and he was gone." She sighed. "He was such a nice man."

"Why do you live here if it's so dangerous?"

Kim laughed. "I'm in love," she said.

Oh well, this trip looked as if it was going to be interesting, but I did hope that Kim wouldn't spend all her time talking about her man. "Can we go gambling?" I asked.

"Of course." We pulled into a narrow drive and climbed almost vertically up to a large house that hung out from a huge rock. The house must have been carved out of the stone.

We walked through a small courtyard into a cool spacious hall and then into a large long room spanned by a green verandah. The floors inside the house were white marble. The verandah was made of green, almost jade-like, marble. The graceful arches delineated the pagodas that topped each end of the verandah, and dragons and small dogs of Fo stood guard. The view was panoramic. "There," Kim said. "Look across there. China." She had sadness in her voice. "I have never been to my home," she said. "I was conceived in Tsingtao. We left on the last boat out of China. At least my mother left with my father and my grandmother. I was born here in this house. But sometimes I wish so hard that I had known China. We can see the Communist gunboats from up here. They patrol up and down." I could see them. Gray, like mosquitoes. "They don't trouble us. They follow us if we take our boat out to Collowan. We'll do that tomorrow. For now I'll show you your room."

Upstairs she ushered me into a big room with two single beds. It too had a sweeping verandah and a white marble bathroom with one of those deep Victorian baths. I immediately felt at home. Patrick's and my flat was so small and cloistered. I always loved large square rooms. In the flat I felt defeated; the rooms were tall. But here in Kim's house, Michelangelo may very well have dictated the proportions.

Kim lived on her own. Next door was her mother's compound. We were to dine there that night but first, after a cup of coffee and some fruit, we were off to see Macau. Kim's mother had married again. Her father, she said, had made his second fortune once he got here. "Mostly trading with Hong Kong. My father was a big man here, much liked. He died in mysterious circumstances though."

"I'm sorry," I said, not quite knowing what I should say.

"I was very little," Kim continued. "Those days were hard times for people who arrived with nothing. The boat stopped in Hong Kong and then went on to South Africa with hostages. My parents were lucky. They survived the beatings. Others did not. But we were lucky. My mother married again to Papa Pedalto. He is a Eurasian, half-Portuguese and half-Chinese. He is a good man and a good father."

We were driving very slowly up the road running parallel to the sea. Around us were sweating rickshaw coolies, their swollen legs near bursting in their calves. These rickshaws were powered by bicycles, not by cars like Hong Kong. Here, as we turned into one of the long main roads that ran through the city, I felt that everybody knew everything. Of course it was a tiny population and they would know each other well. But more than that, I felt, there were secrets, deep dark secrets, to do with money, sex, and power. "What do you do for a social life here?" I asked.

Kim shrugged. "There's always the Navy. We have a small Officer's Club. The British Consul entertains when the ships come in to call. He gets all dressed up in his white outfit and his hat with feathers, and they blow whistles. Then our men play the ship's football team. The Consul usually loses his temper if his men don't win. Last time he kept screaming 'Foul!' until I thought our Governor was going to create a diplomatic incident." I laughed. I imagined Grandpa in that situation. He too would declare fouls in a loud voice. I liked Kim. We had never really talked to each other at any length at Mont St Sebastian, now she made me feel as if I'd known her for ages. "Besides," she grinned, "I'm in love."

"Good or bad?" I asked, remembering Reimer out of my guilty past.

"Awful," she said. "Just awful. And he's married."

"Oh no," I was horrified. "How could you, Kim? A married man?"

"I know," she sighed, and we forgot the view or that we were sightseeing.

"Where does he live?" I asked.

"Hong Kong. He's a professor at the university. I met him when I took classes there in philosophy."

"He was your tutor?"

"Yes. Banal, isn't it?"

"It's never banal. It hurts too much. Will he leave his wife?"

Kim shook her head. "He says he will, but so far it's been all promises. Look." She pointed at a huge arch. "This is the British Cemetery." We walked around the old carefully tended tombs.

"A Churchill is buried here," I remarked. Various priests and other functionaries lay peacefully in the clay of Macau. I still felt as if somewhere in unhallowed ground there lay the real freebooters of Macau, those that ran the boats full of whiskey, the junks loaded with opium. "What happens to the gunrunners here?"

Kim smiled. "If they catch them . . ." She put her neck up and ran her hand across her throat. "Then they throw them into the mud."

"Oh," I said. "Not exactly British Justice."

"Justice! There won't be any justice anywhere until men stop lying to women."

"Oh, Kim," I said. "Don't be so bitter. Not all men lie. My father adores my mother, and my grandfather would never lie to my grandmother. There are happy marriages in the world. Really there are."

"What about you, Mary? Are you happily married?" She looked earnestly at me and I had to reply.

I didn't know this girl very well, but I felt that I could talk to her. Judith was my only other friend. Phoebe never answered letters. And anyway, Phoebe would not be interested in talking about feelings, unless the feelings belonged to one of her horses. "Honestly? I don't know, Kim. I think I need to think, if you know what I mean."

Kim laughed. "I do know what you mean. I can't stop thinking about *him*. His name is Tony McGuire. He's Irish and you should hear him talk. He has a voice like a honey bee." Poor Kim, I thought. But she smiled at me. "Don't pity me," she said. "You English women will never understand an Oriental mind. To die for love is our heritage. Look at how we bound our feet. Such horror, such pain. All for a man. Look at Madame Butterfly, never to be forgotten in her watery grave. Anyway," she was getting back into the car. "Let's have lunch. I shall win him over in the end, precisely because I am an Oriental."

"What's his wife like?" I asked.

"Typically British. Neighs like a horse and wears ankle socks."

"How do you know?"

"I watch them play tennis at the university. I wear my cheongsam and dark glasses, and he sees me watching and gets terribly scared. But she doesn't know it's me, so it's all rather fun. If I want to, all I have to do is telephone the President of the university and my dear Professor McGuire would be out of a job."

"You wouldn't do that," I said, aghast.

"I might."

"If that is Oriental thinking, you *are* different to us. We would call that 'sneaking,' or 'not playing fair.'"

"But then, you also say 'All is fair in love and war,' don't you?"

"I suppose so." I was uncomfortably reminded of the lengths I imagined I might take to track down Reimer, the phone calls when he was late, the fevered imaginings that there might be another woman. I didn't envy Kim her obsession. Or did I?

When we got back to Kim's house, I telephoned Patrick. He wasn't in. Probably at the Club, I decided. I didn't try there, promising myself instead I would telephone in the evening before we went out to dinner.

The moon was rising when we arrived at Kim's parents' house. The great doors that guarded the house swung open. The chauffeur and the bodyguard parked the car. "Wait here," Kim said to them. "We will go to the gambling houses after dinner."

Inside the courtyard there were several other courtyards made from hedges. The main courtyard to the house featured a pond with large pink and white lilies. The night was scented with hot frangipani smells. Mrs. Pedalto looked like Kim. Both of them were small and had long dark hair. Kim wore her hair to her waist. Tonight Mrs Pedalto had hers in a bun. Mr Pedalto was tall. He combined the best of both the Orient and the Occident. His face appeared carved out of ivory. His features were Chinese, but his eyes round. Kim's parents escorted us into the house.

I was amazed. I had seen beautiful European houses. Even my grandparents' house had a certain turn-of-the-century beauty about it. But this was unrestrained magnificence. Walls of jade were ornamented with clusters of oriental sculpture. In the dining room I saw pictures of ethereal valleys and crags hovering in mists. There were wall-scrolls inked to show ancestral temples. And on the tables stood birds, big brilliantly colored birds, carved out of ivory and malachite. Some of the bowls around the room deserved hours of staring. Blue-green cerulean bowls. White Ming vases. They sat on intricately carved small tables. Was Kim really going to give all this up and go off with an Irish professor?

For the moment Kim was chattering away to her mother and step-father. We sat down and the serving began. Some of what I ate was new to me. Mr. Pedalto served me the best bits from his plate or from a bowl. I knew enough to eat all that he gave me, but I found the constant toasting difficult. We were drinking small bowls of hot rice wine. The wine filled my nasal passages and my head with a delicious sense of unbalance. The meal was long and fascinating. Mr Pedalto told me of some of the origins of the founders of the Portuguese colony in Macau. "Still," he said, laughing, "we do business ourselves with the Chinese. We understand them and they understand us, you see. The English are hopeless. They think a few boxes of chocolates at Christmas, or a Stilton from Fortnum and Mason, will get them the things they want." He smiled at me. "I don't mean people like your parents, the old China hands. They were different. Your grandfather must have been sent up the Yangtze to live with a Chinese family to learn his thousand characters. These present people they send from London can't speak Chinese. How can you do business if you don't speak the language?"

"I don't know," I said, feeling foolish. "I'm afraid I can't speak Chinese. Neither can Patrick."

Mr Pedalto frowned. "You learn Mandarin now. Most people speak Cantonese or their own dialects, but Mandarin is a beautiful language and you can read the original poetry and tales of China. The Boxer Rebellion reached all the way to here, you know. The old lady the Empress held her ground though." He looked at Kim. "Chinese women are the toughest in the world. The American women think they are aggressive and get what they want. But a Chinese woman, she'll tie your laces for you on her knees, and you'll never even notice that you tripped."

Dinner came to an end. Mrs Pedalto said very little during the meal. I noticed she concentrated on seeing that her husband was fed and that his bowl of wine was full. Evidently, I thought, I have a lot to learn from Chinese women. We left, Kim and I, with many a bow and a permanent invitation to come and see the Pedaltos whenever I liked.

"They really liked you," Kim said as we climbed into the car. "I'm pleased. Often Europeans don't know how to eat properly with chopsticks. We have to put out those dreadfully messy knives and forks. And Europeans smell really *awful.*"

Dimly, like a strange creature appearing through the depths of a murky sea, a shadowy memory arose, a memory of having had this conversation before. Years ago, as a child in Africa. That's right, I remembered. Madame Yeng told my mother the same thing. My mother had looked horribly put out . . . "Really?" I said. "Europeans smell?"

Kim nodded. "Too much meat," she said. "You all eat so much meat that you smell. Even Tony smells. I have to get him to have a shower before he gets into bed."

I felt as I imagined my mother must have felt. I didn't much like the idea of being a smelly European. I decided to cut down on meat right away. Had my mother considered vowing the same vow? "How do you see him, now you are living in Macau?" I asked, forcing myself to return to the present.

She laughed. "He comes over once a fortnight to

tutor two English girls that are due to go back to England next year. We have three days together, and then he goes back to his boring wife. How he can make love to ankles like that, I shall never know. But never mind. He promises me he thinks of me when he's with her and he only makes love when she insists, which isn't often. She prefers tennis to sex, and probably other women. Don't you find English women rather sexless?"

We were on our way through the bright jazzy streets to the gambling club. I was still ruminating about the strange echoed discussion from my childhood, and about the fact that Mr and Mrs Pedalto liked me. I hadn't really felt liked, except by Judith, for a long time . . . Kim was going too fast. She sat perched beside me like a small gold-beaked oriole. "I don't think we're sexless," I said defensively. "I think it's English men. They're not taught to think about sex as a pastime. Sex to them is something you do after a shower and before bed. Sort of another form of athletics." I thought guiltily of Patrick. "It's all rather gung-ho. One never discusses it with one's mother or really, come to think of it, with one's friends." I blushed, thinking of Reimer. "Then, of course, there are the others . . . Men, I mean."

"Yes, there are," Kim breathed. "There's Tony. To tell you the truth, at first he was awful at making love, but now he's getting much better. I am teaching him Oriental ways, you see."

I had forgotten to telephone Patrick. When we arrived at the Club I asked for a telephone. Patrick was still out. It was ten o'clock at night, so I was a bit perturbed. The least he could do was suffer a little and eat a meal by himself. The few nights Patrick was late at the bank I did just that. Sometimes, if Bob was away, I would eat with Judith. But on my own I wasn't considered worth inviting to dinner: the Odd Wife Out syndrome. Here was Patrick, and I'd bet he has had masses of invitations: the Poor Abandoned Husband, I thought.

The gambling took place in an old hotel. Both the chauffeur and the bodyguard came with us. I felt squashed with these huge men beside me but very safe. We pushed our way through a crowd of Chinese. Here and there we saw a European face, but the clientele were mainly Chinese. "Look!" I took Kim's arm. "Over there."

Kim laughed. "Those are the prostitutes."

"Why do they have to be prostitutes? They are all so beautiful."

"Can you guess which ones are men dressed like women?" she asked.

I, somewhat shocked, could not. The girls mingled with the people on the floor. They looked like the petals on an enormous flower. They wore cheongsams of black, gold, and silver. As we walked the people fell back, brushed aside by the two guards. Money was the dominating factor in this huge hall. I looked up to the circular balcony of the mezzanine above me and saw rows and rows of faces. Tier upon tier, hands dangled ropes tied to little bamboo baskets. Hundreds were lowered down onto the tables. Some were stuffed with paper money, others with only a few coins, but the expressions of the gamblers were the same, betraying the passion to gamble and the desire to win, the lust for money.

We reached the table of Kim's choice. "I always gamble here," she said, her eyes shining. "I'm lucky here." The hall was not air-conditioned. It was hot and smelled of the poor and the unwashed. Beside me jostled a woman in blue pajamas. She could have been one of the boat women or maybe a shopkeeper, but she had her money clutched tightly in her hand.

The dealer had a long wooden rod. He pulled a pile of little buttons to him and swished the bowl about calling loudly for bets. Pandemonium broke loose as everybody around us clamoured to place their bets. I suddenly understood what Captain Moses had said. "Three!" I shouted. "I bet three!"

Kim bet two. The woman next to me smiled. "I follow you," she said. "Yellow hair lucky."

The dealer looked up at the crowded faces hanging over him and we all waited while he took his rod and cleared away any remaining buttons. Now the only buttons that remained were held captive under his bowl. He lifted the bowl. Slowly he counted in Chinese and divided the pile of buttons into four even divisions. The excitement increased. I felt and heard sighs of disappointment but I knew I was going to win. Captain Moses was indomitable. I did win. After the dealer had divided all the counters by four, three counters remained. Three was the winning number. I got back a sheaf of notes for my ten dollars I had put in. The woman next to me was crying with excitement.

Kim laughed. "A winning streak," she said. "Come on. Let's roll some dice."

I'd never rolled dice before. The dice tables were on another floor. This was a much calmer area. "The Americans brought in dice during the war," Kim explained. "The Chinese people don't really like to play dice." We joined a more European crowd around the table. Here the men wore tuxedos and black ties. "Shoot!" someone cried slightly hysterically. The voice came from a heavily made up woman. She was emaciated and her lipstick stuck to her teeth. She wore too much rouge on skin that was white and cracked like an old jug. "Who's that?" I asked.

"That's Lady Janner, or so she says. She has a house here and is always gambling. And she usually loses, but she seems to have endless money. Her crowd are a bad crowd." Kim looked around her and frowned. "And they're all here tonight. Maybe we should go home."

"Oh no, Kim. I've never played dice before. It looks

fun. At least let me lose my winnings." Kim stood irresolute. Both guards seemed anxious to get us out of there, but I hadn't had any kind of excitement for ages, so I pushed my way in using my elbows and my best British *I beg your pardon* voice. The others followed and I ended up next to the woman I had seen.

"You're a new face in these parts," she croaked.

I smiled. "I'm on a weekend from Hong Kong," I said pleasantly.

"Take the dice," she said, handing me those she had in her hands. "Let's see you throw."

"I've never thrown dice before."

"A virgin!" Lady Janner's eyebrows, scant as they were, lifted. "Then I'll double my bet."

I saw a hand with a cigarette in the mist of the people crowding around me. It was not Reimer's hand. This hand was smaller, but the tilt of the head reminded me of him and all of a sudden I felt wicked. If they were the bad set, well, then I would show them . . . I threw the dice inexpertly but my throw of eleven was greeted with a round of applause.

"Try again," Lady Janner said. I felt the man with the cigarette moving in behind me. Would the guards let him through? I rolled the dice with a prayer for God to forgive me. Apparently I threw well. Kim was bouncing up and down beside me. "Seven! Well done!" she shouted. "Do it again." Well, I thought, third time lucky.

I could smell his *eau de cologne* through the smells that surrounded me. From Paris, I could tell. That unmistakable smell of a very rich man whose suits are made in London, his table linen and *eau de cologne* made personally for him in Paris, and all his leather in Italy. As I threw, he reached the table. Both guards moved back to accommodate him. "Kim," he said. "I haven't seen you for a long time." His voice was quick with only the slight hesitation of a man who knew many languages. His hair was fair but fine, not tousled like Patrick's which grew in tufts on his head. This man's hair was golden and it lay flat and obediently on his head. The unusual thing about him was that he had one green eye and the other was blue. He smiled at us both. "Well done," he said. "A run of three. Come. You must be thirsty. I'll buy you both champagne." Flanked by the guards, I followed him with Kim beside me.

"Who is he?" I whispered.

"Philippe de Lacroix. He's supposed to be descended from the French Royal Family. Do be careful, Mary. He has an awful reputation."

"I'm married," I said firmly.

"I know," she said. "He prefers them married."

We walked to the bar at the back of the room. Philippe's back was turned to us. He was ordering the champagne. His gestures were curiously fluid. He ordered as if he were orchestrating a particularly beautiful piece of music. I stood behind him, my heart racing.

✎ *Chapter 58* ✎

I stood mesmerized. I felt a very deep stirring, a very far away memory from my childhood. "He wants you," the little voice inside me whispered. The accent was unmistakably French and then I remembered. That voice—it belonged to Françoise, the maker of my dreams and fantasies, the teller of my secrets. I thought she had gone. "He's dishy to look at," the voice whispered. "Shut up," I replied. "I'm married. He's just a friend of Kim's. He's bored and needs a couple of drinking companions . . ." I did so wish I could get to a mirror to check that my hair and makeup were in order.

Philippe turned to us and pointed to a table. "Here," he said. "We can celebrate your winnings. Do introduce me to your friend."

"This is Mary Johnson," Kim introduced.

"Mrs Mary Johnson," I added.

"*Enchanté, Madame.* In that case I may kiss your hand."

At the other end of the room Lady Janner was hopping up and down, her long claw-like hands pulling at shoulders. The crowd around the dice all seemed to know each other with an intimacy that seemed indecent. I felt as if they shared secrets and pastimes among themselves that gave them the right to make private jokes that bound them into a separate world. Was Philippe part of that world? I looked at him from under my eyelashes. He sat, politely leaning forward in his chair, talking to Kim. He was teasing her. "Clearly another hopeless case of unrequited passion," he said laughing.

Kim blushed. "Really, Philippe. You mustn't say that. Tony loves me very much."

"Kim, Kim, Kim." Philippe put his hand up. "How many English professors fall in love with little Oriental girls? You tell me that."

"None that I know of," Kim retorted. "Anyway, you're one to talk. How about your celebrated affair with the doctor's wife?"

"Ah, you have me there." Philippe leaned back in the chair. "But it was such fun, and the doctor was so exquisitely cross. He left, by the way. Did you know that?" He shrugged as if innocent. "Now we have a new doctor."

"A bachelor, I hope." Kim was caustic.

"Unfortunately, yes." Then Philippe smiled at me. "And how is *Mrs* Johnson? Are you enjoying this champagne? It's a rather good Lanson. Quite nice for this time of the evening. I prefer Taitinger for breakfast though, don't you?"

I felt myself blush. "I don't drink champagne for breakfast. Patrick has to go to work."

"I see. And, pray, what does this Patrick of yours do?"

"He works in the British Oriental Bank. What do you do?" I tried to reverse the questioning. I felt like a small schoolgirl being inspected by a teacher.

"Do? Ah. Well, I don't exactly *do* anything, I suppose. I look after several châteaux. We have vineyards in Bordeaux. And then a place in London. All very tiring. But one really doesn't *do* anything, does one?"

"Real people do," I said crossly. "Real people get up in the morning, go to work, and worry about their bills."

"So I've heard." Philippe's voice was faint. "But then, I am not much interested in *real* people, Madame. I have my world, and they make theirs. *N' est-ce pas?*"

I said, "Everybody should work at something."

Merde, alors, Françoise interrupted. What is this *bêtise?* I ignored her and frowned at Philippe.

"Madame is cross." Philippe smiled at me. "So young," he said. "And so virtuous. So unobtainably married, so sad. A little adventure does you good, you know. Brings back the sparkle into your eyes. Improves the skin." He leaned towards me. I could feel a tingling current of electricity leap from his body to mine. I felt all the hairs on my skin stand up and I had to laugh. "She laughs! All is all right for Philippe," he said. "*Hélas,* Kim, I have a new conquest. A new reason to live. Without love," Philippe said, "I do not exist. I am dead to the world. Indifferent to the songs of birds . . ."

"For Heaven's sake, Philippe," Kim said, rolling her eyes. "Save all this Gallic charm for one of your other women."

"I have no other woman, save Mrs Mary."

"Don't be silly, Monsieur de Lacroix," I said finishing my champagne. "I live in Hong Kong with my husband and I leave tomorrow."

Philippe shrugged. "You can leave any time you like," he said. "But look." He held out his small neat hands. "There, in the middle. Can you see it?"

"No," I said, "what is it?"

"I have your heart in my hand, Mrs Mary," he said. "And I will never let it go." The word *never* reverberated down a corridor of silence. *Never, never, never.*

We looked at each other. Philippe saw me as I really was. Not the Mary Johnson, or the Mary Freeland, but the Mary that took risks, the Françoise side of myself that had been buried for so long. He knew the side of me that was dark and frightened me. I knew his dark side. Reimer had a dark side, but in Reimer I had found there was nothing to fear. His dark side carried no danger to me. Philippe, however, could be a different matter. Maybe that was why I was so intrigued. I said. "This is ridiculous. It is late and we must be going."

Kim got up quickly. "Yes," she said. "Come on."

Philippe did not get up out of his chair. He sat back and looked at me. "I need you, Mary," he said. "Only you."

I shook my head. "No, Philippe."

"You'll see," he said.

I was quiet on the way home. So was Kim. As we entered the house, the chauffeur and the bodyguard said goodnight and left for their quarters. Kim and I went into the drawing room for a final drink. "I'll have a Cointreau, please," I said. I needed the sweetness to remove the slightly acid taste remaining from the champagne.

"Oh dear," Kim said. "You seem to have made a deep impression on Philippe tonight. He isn't usually that direct. It's not his style."

"Here we sit," I said, looking out over the balcony at the moored junks in the river in front of the house.

"You have your lover in Hong Kong and I'm going back to Hong Kong, to Patrick, who is not my lover." We sipped our drinks in silence and quietly we went off to bed.

Kim's lips brushed my cheek. "Why does life have to be so difficult?" she sighed.

"I don't know," I said. "Maybe we like it that way. Maybe if we didn't have dreams and obsessions, we would just fade away like shadows on the grass."

"Good night, Mary. Sleep well." Kim glided away up the corridor leaving me in my room.

Tonight there was just a thin sliver of a moon. New and proud she sat, promising rain.

Nothing, of course, would come of that conversation with Philippe, I told myself as I undressed and got ready for bed. I slipped into the sheets and sat up, my arms hugging my knees. I'll forget him. I lay back and turned out the light. He will be easy to forget. But at least it was nice to know that a man found me attractive enough to flirt with. I'll forget, I thought. tomorrow I'll see Patrick, I promised myself. The heavy flapping of junk sails sent me off to sleep.

♦ꙮ *Chapter 59* ꙮ♦

The trip back to Hong Kong was diabolically hot. Sweat trickled down my face and made embarrassing splotches under my arms. Captain Moses was busy this trip—he had some senior men from his shipping line on board—but not too busy to stop by my cabin and enquire if I'd used his number at fan-tan. "I did," I said, "and I won. By the way," I asked as casually as possible, "Captain Moses, do you know anyone by the name of Philippe de Lacroix?"

Captain Moses's eyes, always unfathomable, became bottomless. "Yes," he said. "I do know him. Why?"

"I met him yesterday," I said, "when we were gambling. What is he like?"

The Captain shook his great shaggy head. "He's Jekyll and Hyde, that one. Jo Jo knows him better than I do, but I hear he's a devil with the ladies. Has he taken your fancy then?" There was a teasing tone in Captain Moses's voice.

I tried to respond lightly. "Of course not, Captain. I'm a married woman."

"That's the problem right there." He looked very sternly at me. "You're married all right, but in name only. Anyone can see that." I felt a horrible red stain sweep across my face. Was it that obvious? "Come, come. I didn't mean to shock you, Mary. But you don't have the glow of a happily married woman."

We were standing on the deck. The boat was running before a strong wind and ploughing her way through the waves that parted before her powerful thrust. "I know," I confessed to the man I hardly knew but had known from all time. "I don't know what happiness is, at least not in marriage. I know how to be happy with books, friends, dogs and horses. Gardens make me happy. So does wind and the weather, or ships like this one. But being married seems so static. Really the problem is that I don't fit in with Patrick or his friends. I don't fit in with the idea of doing the same thing for the rest of your life. I don't see why Patrick and I don't buy a boat and sail around the world and write a book. He likes taking photographs and I could write the text, but he got furious when I suggested it to him. As for his friends . . . They're impossible. Except for Judith, but she's really *my* friend— nothing to do with the bank—and we have to sneak about in case we get accused of fraternizing."

Captain Moses sighed. He must have heard all this before from other unhappy young wives who had come out to Hong Kong. "Your problem," he said, "is that you're an outsider trying to behave like an insider."

Well, at least my predicament had a name. "An outsider? What's that?"

"Someone who is born not to fit." Moses's eyes lit up. "When I was a kid," he said, "living in the grimy streets of Hounslow, I swore I'd run away to sea. It took a long time to escape, but the day I was eighteen, I ran away. It was much easier in those days. We had the War, and a big lad was considered a good hand on deck. Never looked back. Never joined anything. Own no house. Never got married. If tomorrow I die, I leave my ship to Jo Jo, and my books. But I go a happy and contented man. I've seen the world over several times. How many folk can say that, eh?"

"Not many," I said. "Are you an outsider?"

"Oh, aye. Jo Jo and I are both outsiders. We couldn't fit in with ordinary folk. I'd pine away if I had to live nine-to-five with a night out for darts in the pub. Nah. We live our way. And if anyone doesn't like it, to hell with them. Here," he said. "I'll get you a book. It was just what I needed once. Maybe it will help you."

The book was Herman Hesse's *Steppenwolf*. I had tried to read it a few years ago but it meant nothing to me, just a stilted portrait of a disturbed young man. But now, as I sat reading in my cabin, I became absorbed in the young man who stared at the circus that went on in front of him. Slowly the clowns became Patrick and his friends. I felt cold and isolated: the smell of the grease paint on their faces, the rouge used by Isla and Cindy quickly became chilling drops of blood. White powder spread a revolting sickly smell as it fell from their hands and legs. I closed my eyes and realized that I had made an awful mistake. I knew it was my mistake, not Patrick's. Aunt Mary had seen the mistake. In her own way my mother had tried to warn me, but I was too headstrong. To get married had been my only ambition. It was the state of marriage I looked for, not the marriage itself. Patrick's family, who years ago had looked so happy and full of fun, actually turned out to be very conventional. Being married to Patrick was boring, I admitted to myself, and I was stuck with it.

It occurred to me that my mother was largely bored with her life in the Foreign Office, but she long ago decided to stick with it and play the game. What toll her decision had taken on her I would never know, but in her eyes I now recognized that there often hung a heavy look of defeat. But she was an excellent actress. I was no such actress. I yearned for adventure, for other countries and other people who lived with a danger and felt a passion. Philippe was one of those other people.

I suddenly found myself crying, sobbing in fear. I was trapped. I had trapped myself. I had made my mistake and would I now have to live with my wrong choice for the rest of my life? I felt alone, afraid, and completely helpless. I lay on my berth and rocked myself, my own arms hugging my body. How could I live with this pain? I knew I did not want to hurt Patrick, but how could I spend the rest of my life trying to be something I was not? How could I pretend to delight in the company of his friends and his banking crowd? On the other hand, how could I tell him how terrified I was of living forever a meaningless monotonous life? How could I do that to him?

Somehow, I resolved, I must get out of my marriage. Then I would be free to dream.

I left the boat without saying goodbye to Captain Moses. I would see him again, because Macau was my escape from Hong Kong and from my husband. This seemed a dreadfully disloyal thing to think, but now that the unadmitted truth had surfaced, I felt a kind of relief.

I was unhappily married. Unfortunately to a very nice man who was a good husband. If I were Judith, married to that ogre Bob, I could walk out with impunity. "He was a violent man and he beat me," I could tell the judge. But what was there to say about Patrick? "He was kind but unadventurous, my lord." My lord would probably lean out of his seat and say, "But so are most men." I had to smile. Certainly Julian, Norris, and Ian wouldn't win prizes for originality, but then their wives seemed happy. Maybe Captain Moses was right. I was an outsider. The other Hong Kong couples wanted certain things in marriage and they already had what they wanted. Houses, boats, servants. None of them had children. They all intended to wait until they were at least thirty. They all met for lunch, went shopping, swam, played tennis at the Club: all things that I could enjoy occasionally, but not as a way of life.

The taxi was climbing up the Peak. I did love this drive. Higher and higher we chugged, the engine rasping and gasping. Away fell the streets, and as we passed the halfway mark I could look out and see the ferry lights. Evening was softly embracing the island. Night-time began with the smell of food everywhere, pots of spicy pork, baskets of *dim sun,* steaming bowls of soup and rice, white fluffy rice, with dribbles of dark strong-smelling soy. If I had to be unhappy at least I had picked a good spot. No one could be really unhappy in Hong Kong. The great natural beauty that surrounded Hong Kong seemed a lasting reminder that I would cease to exist in a twinkling of an eyelid, but the Peak would remain, only older and stronger.

My return home to the flat wasn't as difficult as I feared. Once I walked inside the door, Patrick was there to greet me. He hugged me tightly and said "I missed you" into my neck. His muffled voice confused me. Here was the familiar smell of a man I had loved and wanted to marry for all those years. And he did love me, even if he didn't understand me. Eagerly he pulled me towards the sitting room. Patrick had purchased an enormous bunch of mixed spring flowers.

"Oh, darling," I said. "How lovely." To me my voice sounded hollow.

"Did you have a good time?"

I nodded. Ah Lim was unpacking my clothes into my cupboard, and Su Wei called us for supper. He had made Peking duck—his speciality—for me, as Su Wei knew I had a passion for the crispy skin wrapped in pancakes, a sprig of onion and a sauce I could never replicate. "Delicious," I said, suddenly pleased to be back with my self-made little family. "Simply delicious."

Later that night, as I lay in Patrick's arms, I thought of the book I had just read. It wasn't poor Patrick's fault he had married an outsider. Perhaps, because I was an only child, I had never been able to conform. Certainly I did on the surface: my mother had seen to that. Maybe she was so violent in those early years because she realized that, if I followed the same dreams she must have had as a girl, I would be an outsider and never fit into the life that the rest of the world considered "normal."

If I had never known Reimer, never been loved by Reimer, would I have been happy with Patrick? I let the question hang in the night air and then I knew the answer. Oddly enough, Captain Moses filled the room with his presence. Maybe, like a visitor from outer space, he gave me the keys to my freedom. That book, now by my bed, confirmed what he said. The man who wrote it was an outsider. Whether I had known Reimer or not, my marriage with Patrick would never have been a success, he with his different interests, his normal need for companionship and I with my need for solitude and my books, my lack of interest in crowds and dislike of social occasions. We were a mismatch. That was all. There was no one to blame.

I felt sleepy but more comforted. My discontent now had a shape and form. I would consult with Judith in the morning. I fell asleep dreaming I was safe in the *Fat Shan* sailing away for an adventure.

Chapter 60

"Wow," Judith said. "You've had a busy weekend." She was looking pale and ill.

"You don't look well." I felt guilty for babbling on about myself. We were in the Dairy Queen having an ice cream.

"I'm all right," she said, "but I'm pregnant. And Bob doesn't want children." She made a face. "He took it quite well, but I'm worried. He's waiting for promotion and he's drinking a lot. He gets very angry when he's drunk. Still, I expect he'll get used to the baby."

"And are you happy?"

Judith nodded but I was not convinced. "I'm going home to have the baby," she said. "I think I'll need my mother. She's thrilled and so are Bob's people." Thank goodness my mother never asked personal questions. "Maybe," Judith said, "your marriage would be better if you settle down and have a child." I was startled by this suggestion and resolved to think about it later.

"I do understand about insiders and outsiders, Mary, but I can also see it from Patrick's point of view. He married you in good faith. You took vows to love him and honor him and all that. After all, being a good wife does mean entertaining for him. I have to entertain other Petty Officers' wives. I don't like them all, but I do it for Bob's sake. And I suppose I'm rewarded by the smile on his face when I've done well. We both are married, for better or worse." She shivered. "Why do I feel a goose go over my grave when I say those words?"

"Because," I said, rather crossly, "even if you do love him, you're afraid of him." I was nearly at the bottom of my ice cream. I could see Isla and Cindy bearing down on us. If they had to join us, I would console myself with another huge ice cream float.

"Mary!" Cindy's nasal scream could be heard across the room. Isla trotted after her. Both were carrying bags from expensive boutiques. Cindy hit her chair first and stuck out her legs. "Gee, it's hot out here," she said. Isla smiled at Judith. They had met before. "I'm Cindy," Cindy introduced herself and then she narrowed her eyes. "You drive that little red Kharmen Ghia, don't you?"

"I'm the one." Judith's eyes sparkled.

"Well, I *love* it," whinnied Cindy.

The conversation between Judith and me interrupted, we spent the rest of the hour gossiping.

"Judith is pregnant," I informed Patrick at dinner.

"Is she?" He looked surprised. "She looks such a sad little thing."

"Bob has a filthy temper," I said. "But he can be very kind and nice when he's not upset. I hope the baby will help matters."

Twenty-four hours away from Macau and life felt back to normal. After dinner I wrote letters, one responding to Aunt Mary's letter and one to my parents. An unexpected letter from Phoebe reported that she was fine and they were expecting six foals. Hattie, Phoebe told me, had fallen so in love with Chantilly and with horse-breeding that her plans to return to Africa and marry her fiancé seemed to be permanently on hold. Phoebe's brother Jeremy apparently was fearfully pleased with the world because he had won some major race in Chantilly, and when was I coming to see them all? When, indeed. Aunt Mary's news was brief as usual. She was cold. Her arthritis hurt. The price of food was lamentable, but she "mustn't grumble."

When Patrick and I were in our bedroom I asked if he wanted a baby. I was sitting at my dressing table looking at the brush given to me by my mother. It had a matching silver-backed mirror. Both the brush and the mirror had belonged to my mother's mother. My mother gave them to me the evening before I was married. We were in my father's parents' house in Somerset. "I can't take those," I said. "They've been with you all your life."

"No, take them," my mother insisted. "These are the presents I've always promised for your wedding. You take them. I promised my mother I'd give them to her granddaughter. And I want you to promise you will give them to your daughter, my granddaughter."

"Of course," I said and I kissed her.

Now I remembered my promise and now I vowed to forget the past and to concentrate on the future, being a good wife and mother. After all, Captain Moses could afford to be an outsider. He made his choice many years ago. Jo Jo too had no one but himself to report to, but for me to spread my wings and go, I would leave behind many damaged hearts, not the least, my parents'. I had a strange feeling my mother would be the only one who might understand. My grandparents would not, any more than Patrick's family. Above all, I would break all my marriage vows to God. Judith had cause enough to leave. Occasionally I did not see her for a while and I knew now to leave her alone. She was waiting for the worst of the bruising to go away. When I did see her again, I could see the telltale yellowing bruise, but to the oblivious eye nothing showed. If Judith could keep her vows, who was I to complain when Patrick did everything he could to keep me happy?

Patrick came up behind me. "I thought you'd never ask," he said. "I'd love a baby. Or maybe even twins. You can stop taking those pills every night and we can have fun."

Actually making babies was fun. There was a purpose for sex. I was surprised, though: I thought I'd become pregnant immediately. The first few months I didn't fret, but by the sixth month of trying I was seriously worried. Now I was nervous. Judith was showing and I was barren. "Maybe I can't have babies," I said bitterly. "Maybe I'm a failure at that, too."

Judith consoled me. "Here." She gave me yet another of the myriad of books she had on childbirth. "Don't panic. Sometimes it takes a year or two."

"A year or two? Of making love every night and twice when your temperature's up? I'll die. 'Here Lies Mary. Loved to Death.' Oh no, Judith. It can't take that long."

Patrick was saved an embarrassing visit to the specialist by the announcement that I was a week overdue. This time it looked like we'd done it. Through the last six months we had been close. The idea of a baby gave us an interest in common. I felt much more committed. When the test showed positive I was ecstatic. At last I had done something that made me a success. I was pregnant and proud of myself and of Patrick. Although I was only newly pregnant, I went out and bought myself some maternity clothes. I loved the way the dresses billowed out in front of me and I walked with my stomach stuck out as far as I could. I read omnivorously every baby book that I could get. Cindy and Isla laughed at me, but then they were sad creatures: they didn't have children. Above all they did not understand what it was like to stand naked in front of a mirror and stare at my belly and think of the little life that grew every day inside me. Mary Johnson, a mother-to-be. What a miracle.

Patrick was a very attentive father-to-be. We went to lessons on pregnancy and childbirth given by a Miss Wordsworth. Apparently she was distantly related to the poet. At least she had inherited a beard. She was a spinster with large feet and cold blue eyes but she loved childbirth. "Feel your baby," she crooned at me lying on the floor next to other sweating mothers. It was too early for me to feel anything, but Patrick obediently knelt beside me looking rather nervous. Around us other bellies heaved and strained as we mimicked various stages of childbirth. Sometimes a voluminous mother would be missing from the class and we all knew that she had gone off to do it in real life. Soon the details of the birth would be triumphantly repeated by Miss Wordsworth. "A boy. Nine pounds, ten ounces. Good chap, just like his father." She made it sound as if she had ordered the baby and the event herself. Maybe she had.

In our lives Miss Wordsworth was a king. She knew how to get through childbirth and what to do with heartburn, which plagued me, and she said it was all right to eat pickles with boiled eggs. I had a small problem with blood pressure, but nothing, I was assured, serious. I had to rest in the afternoons, but most evenings after Patrick came back from the office we swam at the Club.

"You both look so sweet," Frances said. She and Julian were eating a plate of freshly fried chips. The chips were a speciality of the Club. I was forbidden to eat them by Miss Wordsworth because she had a phobia about putting on weight. Weight had never been a problem for me and now the chips sat there tempting me. The chef at the Club had a clever way of making chips that were fat and crisp. He also made a tomato sauce with a bite, like the nip of a crab on a bare toe.

The combination was unbeatable. I sat with Patrick, my belly now clearly outlined under my maternity swimsuit, and I thought: yes, Frances is right. Patrick and I are a sweet couple. For the first time in our marriage I was really happy with him. In the past, I had sat at dinner at the other end of the table and looked at Patrick. I had stared at him and wondered how anybody could be that uncomplicated. As long as he was well-fed and had sex he was happy. He sang in the shower and hummed about the flat. He was never really cross and if I was tense he went out of his way to please me. Now I was pregnant, he treated me as if I were Dresden china. I felt loved and special.

My mother wrote to say she was glad I was pregnant, if that was what I really wanted. A most peculiar attitude. Patrick's parents were delighted and Aunt Mary wrote as if unmoved and nonchalant. I knew she was pleased though. She sent me ten shillings "to get a little something special" for myself. Phoebe said, in reproving tones, that she thought there was a lot to be said for foals, but Hattie and Jeremy were thrilled.

Judith went back to England. It was a sad gray day when she left and I had a feeling she wouldn't be coming back, although she didn't say anything. Bob was at sea. I saw a look in her eyes. There was a lot of pain there, but also resolution. "Goodbye," she said when I took her to the airport. "Take care of yourself, Mary."

"I will," I said. "*You* take care."

"I am taking care of myself and my baby," she said very forcefully. "I really am." It was the way she said *my* baby that made me feel she had had enough of Bob's bad temper.

If Judith left Bob because she couldn't expose the baby to his rages, it would be a relief. I had spent a lot of time worrying about her. I couldn't discuss Bob with her because she was too embarrassed about his temper, but when she was missing for days or didn't answer the phone, I worried. My mother had mellowed with the years, but I did not forget the fear of her I had felt as a young stubborn and defiant child. I recognized that I had a difficult nature, but Judith was not difficult or obstinate nor did she have my dangerous need for a grand passion. Maybe it was true that men lived for their work in life but women lived for a relationship with a man. Now I was pregnant with Patrick's child, maybe some biological trigger kicked off and I belonged to him in a biological way that lay so deep one didn't realize the force.

For now, eating chips by the side of the pool made me happy, and when I was happy so was Patrick. If I could learn that life didn't have to be a grand drama, if I could learn that happiness existed as a permanent force in life, not as a fleeting moment of grand passion, then I could feel better about myself. For now I was content.

Chapter 61

What was an idyllic time came to an abrupt halt. Sunday night I was in pain. I had been decorating the Christmas tree. I reached up to put the fairy on the topmost branch. I was standing on a dining room chair and I fell. "Oh no," I moaned as I hit the floor. "My baby." Ah Lim rushed in and pulled me to my feet. She helped me to get into bed, and I lay there praying I had done no damage to my child. Sickeningly I felt an oozing between my legs. I checked. It was blood. Amah telephoned Patrick and he rushed home pale and anxious. Together we drove to the hospital. "You'll be all right," he said in the car. "I know you will." I didn't say anything. I was in too much pain.

Lying in the hospital bed I looked at my neighbors.

All the other women in the ward were about to give birth or had already given birth. I felt alone—a pariah. I couldn't control the flow of blood. Miss Wordsworth would be furious with me. She took all pregnancies personally. Miscarrying, which was what I was doing, was strictly against her code of ethics. Born dead was one thing, and she considered that a tragedy, but to lose a baby? She saw it as a mother's personal failure. No doubt she would blame it on my indulgence of chips at the Club. I lay and wept.

The doctor was young and not very sympathetic. "You're young," he said. "You can always have more children."

"You don't understand," I cried. "This is my child."

"Oh come now," he said in his best awful bedside manner. "Don't let's make a fuss. Think of it as a practice run, one of nature's mistakes."

"It isn't an *it*. You are talking about my baby." He didn't understand.

During the week I was there nobody really understood. After three days the doctor decided I had truly lost the baby. I was nearly five months pregnant and the familiar flutter of my baby was gone. Patrick arrived every night with flowers and fruit, but it was no use. A world I was beginning to love had gone. I looked at Patrick and he was a stranger. A nice kind stranger, but there was no longer anything between us. Nothing was left except an anxious man with a shock of fair hair.

Guilt returned. I turned on my pillow and stared at the whitewashed wall. My marriage was over. I was no longer a good little pregnant housewife. I had tried, and I really and honestly had tried. Maybe I was never intended to be a housewife.

I telephoned Kim from the hospital. I felt strangely cold and yet exhilarated. "I've had a miscarriage," I said. "Can I come and stay with you for a while? Patrick can't leave the office. I just need to get away for a week."

"Of course," she said. "When do you want to arrive?"

"On Monday," I said without hesitation.

"The week before Christmas? Are you all right?" Kim's voice was concerned.

"I'm all right. Maybe it's for the best, Kim. I'll talk to you when I see you." I rang off and began to plan.

Patrick was most understanding. I wished he was more fraught. How could anyone be so nice, so kind and so loving? If only he had faults or gave me reason not to love him, but he didn't. He belonged to a world I could never enter. I was barred from the comfortable space he lived in. I had too many black thoughts and fears. I felt like Prometheus chained to the rock, the taloned eagle of monotony tearing at my flesh. As soon as the eagle gulped down the flesh it grew back again. Now I was empty.

As I wandered the corridors of the hospital, that was what I felt: empty. Empty and hollow. Around me women were feeding babies, holding them, or walking with that proud stomach-protruding walk.

The day before I left I wandered through a long ward. I saw a much older woman sitting in her bed staring at me and I approached her. She was a warm and motherly looking woman. Naturally I looked down into the cot at the foot of her bed. I realized why the woman had such a lost look about her. Her baby had slit eyes and a huge mouth, its tongue perpetually stuck out through thick lips. "Is it a boy or a girl?" I asked.

"A boy," she said, not smiling.

I could think of nothing to say to her. She had her hell at the foot of her bed. Of course in time I expect she would love her baby very much, but for now there was nothing to do or say. Her faith in God must have been as shaken as mine. What had I done to lose my baby? Perhaps my marriage, like this poor woman's baby, had been imperfectly conceived.

I wrote to Judith before I left the hospital and I packed my suitcase and went home in our little car. We parked and Patrick carried my suitcase. Su Wei and Ah Lim were at the door to greet me. They had nothing to say.

We ate our roast chicken in silence. I could tell that Patrick was glad that I was going to Macau for a week. "You have a good rest," he said later that night. I remember hating him. He didn't mention other children, and he didn't try to make love to me. The doctor told both of us to wait a few weeks. "Give it a month or two," he said, "and then try again. If nothing happens, come and see me. We have a new technique that seems to work wonders."

I couldn't imagine spending your life finding new and different ways of encouraging other people to have babies.

Other women left the hospital with their babies wrapped in white shawls. I left with Patrick and a suitcase. The same suitcase I would pack for Macau.

Captain Moses was a comfort. On the way over I had dinner again with Jo Jo in attendance. "You'll get over it," the Captain said.

"I know I will." I didn't mind his prediction as I minded other people's responses to my loss. Isla and Frances were sympathetic but disingenuous. They had never wanted children and had never been pregnant. I felt Captain Moses had suffered in his life sufficiently to acknowledge my grief. Maybe the words were trite, but his eyes were understanding.

Jo Jo tutted and fluttered about the room. He said softly, "So sad."

"Eat your dinner," Captain Moses commanded me. "You lost weight."

"The hospital food was awful."

Jo Jo had made satays. The meat he plaited onto sticks, and the sauce was a mixture of peanuts and soy with a hot chilli. My mouth burnt delightfully, and for the first time since the loss of the baby, I felt comforted. Good companionship and good food.

I borrowed *Far from the Madding Crowd* and I immersed myself in Hardy. I slept dreaming of the rolling Dorset downs. The swell under the boat rocked and soothed me. I wished this journey never to end. I was safe here on the *Fat Shan*. Hung between my past and my future, I had no decisions to make. I was safe, cared for by Captain Moses and Jo Jo. Maybe I should buy a ticket for eternity with them, never leave the boat . . . But then that was not in my stars. If I had a destiny, then I must live it. Tonight was not a night to worry about the future. Sufficient to sleep, and I did.

✖️ *Chapter 62* ✖️

Once in my familiar room in Kim's house I felt safe. Also, I realized, I felt single. The weather was stiflingly hot. In a week I would be celebrating Christmas with Patrick and his friends, but for now I removed the little engagement ring and the gold band from my finger. I was no longer going to pretend that I was truly married to Patrick. Our first year of marriage was also going to be our last. Marriage was not for me. It did suit Patrick, and the sooner I let him free the sooner he could find himself a good wife who would love him and take care of him.

Leaning over the verandah and smelling the mud, I breathed deeply. Apart from Reimer, I had taken no risks with my life. Now it was time to allow for change and to give life a chance to surprise me. Phoebe in her own way was taking a risk. Breeding horses in Chantilly might not be my idea of a good time, but I intended to leave Hong Kong as soon as I could and join Phoebe and Jeremy and Hatti, if they would have me.

I could see the island of Colowan quite clearly. Kim's boat, moored below the house, was waiting to take us for a beach picnic. I put on my black swimsuit and looked at myself in the bathroom mirror. My stomach was flat again and I was glad Philippe was one of the guests. My life with Patrick, my pregnancy, my miscarriage, must now all be put behind me. I had a whole new world waiting for me, one which I very much hoped would include Philippe.

My heart skipped a beat when I saw him. I had forgotten just how handsome he was. There was a hawk-like cast to his face, an expectant look about him. "Mary," he said. "I heard you were coming, so I bullied Kim into letting me take you off for a picnic. She insisted on coming too, but we can ignore her, can't we?"

I laughed.

Kim was wearing a blue *cheong sam*. Her hair hung down her back. Tony McGuire was arriving on the night boat so she was bright with anticipated passion. I envied her. She was very sweetly sensitive and left me very much to myself. "I'm coming on this picnic," she announced, "to keep an eye on Mary." But she noticed that I wore no rings. There was a conspicuous band of white skin where my rings had been. I saw Philippe turn his avian head and look at me. I smiled at him. "Welcome home," he said.

I nodded at his accuracy. "Home is so far from home since father died," I quoted.

Philippe nodded, too. "Some of us have no home," he said. "And then it is a mistake to try and make one."

"Do you really think so?" Kim looked interested.

The boat was underway. I could see the thick hands

of the steward on the wheel. We sat behind the steward and the spray from the prow of the boat rose and sparkled in the air. Philippe lolled, relaxed and very brown, beside me. Kim, perched as always (she never seemed to stay in one place for long), was happy.

We anchored in a deep bay just off the shore. The steward let down the rowing boat and Philippe lifted me off my feet and put me down in the stern of the boat. Philippe rowed the three of us to the shore. His strokes were firm and steady. "You've rowed before," I said.

"I rowed against Cambridge before I left Paris." His back bent under the strain of the heavy oars. The rowing boat was made of old-fashioned teak. "These boats," he said as he pulled. "You could catch a whale, and she'd survive." Certainly the rowing boat was a thing of beauty. Her ribs were polished and she cut through the water towards the shore. Ahead of us lay the island. A few summer houses, but otherwise uninhabited.

We beached and the underside of the boat scrunched on the clear sand. The sound was welcome, but even more welcome was the cool of Philippe's summer house after a walk down the long jetty. The door creaked from lack of use. The verandah was an oasis from the heat of the day. "Please wait a moment," Philippe said and he disappeared into the house.

Kim and I sat on long cane chairs. For a moment I remembered Africa: the rain and my parents sitting in silence, a drink in each hand. How things had changed. How I had changed. I knew I would tell my mother first about the failure of my marriage. I knew, in spite of all our problems and her wish for me to conform, she would understand. For whatever reason she loved my father and was grateful to him, I knew inside her there was passion unassuaged. Surrounded as she always was by adoring men, I also knew she was absolutely faithful to my father. She had lived her life without risking passion. I could not, but I trusted her to understand. My father would not understand, any more than my grandparents. I could hear Aunt Mary snort . . .

"Drinks," Philippe announced. He carried out a silver tray with long frosted glasses beaded with cooling lemonade. "Fresh," he said. "Drink it." He handed Kim a glass and then me. His warm hand touched 'mine. Was it love or was it lust? I honestly didn't know. I wanted to be near the blue of Philippe's eyes and the glint of his blond hair.

We ate our lunch and we teased each other like schoolchildren. Kim said she would wash up, so Philippe and I walked out of the house and down to the beach. I was aware of the steward in the boat, but we walked unselfconsciously holding hands, as if we had been together all our lives. "We two are very much alike," Philippe observed.

I looked at the tideline. Nothing much had floated up from the sea, except for a white dead sea urchin bereft of its spines. I put my foot on it and it crumbled into small shards. No longer would it menace bare feet in an otherwise safe sea. With the crunch of the sea urchin, I also finally came to terms with my failed marriage. "I am going to divorce my husband," I said.

"Yes, I am not surprised. You were not happily married."

"No." I shrugged my shoulders. "I wasn't. But how do you know if you're happily married?"

It was Philippe's turn to shrug. "A woman who is happy has a certain *je ne sais quoi,*" he said. "A glow about her, a way of walking. One knows she is having all her needs met."

He looked at me with heavy-lidded eyes. He was right. Patrick met most of my needs, except that for ecstasy. Reimer had elicited that passion, but I could hope for more, so much more, from Philippe. Reimer was a careless traveler. Philippe traveled carefully. It was evident from the way he had prepared this trip. Everything we had for lunch—the prawns, the fruit, the melon—had been carefully thought about. Reimer had a wild animal passion; Philippe had an air of controlled danger about him. There was a smoothness. He walked carefully. He held himself in check. I moved along beside his graceful form. He made me feel precious and treasured. "I must go back and tell him," I said.

"Of course," he said.

I needed to get back to the house and to Kim. Kim, as Judith had done, kept me sane. I felt as if I was on a high cliff and about to dive. I really wanted to dive like a swan and to gracefully execute a splashless entry into the water. "Let's go back," I said to Philippe. "Kim will be waiting."

Philippe looked at me again. He turned to go back to the house, still holding my hand gently.

I said, "I would have left him whether I'd met you or not. Eventually."

"Good," he said noncommittally. "I can't make love to you until you leave him." We walked back.

Once we were back Kim looked at me with a particularly discerning look. We both moved into the kitchen, the secret place of all women who love. Over the sink, still smelling of fish and the sea and distant love, we talked the talk of women hopelessly in love with a man. "Will he come to the house tonight?" she said simply.

"No," I shook my head. "We won't meet again until I've left Patrick. Kim," I asked anxiously, "afterwards, can I stay with you for a while? When I tell Patrick, I'll move into the Helena May Club while we sort out the details, and then if it's all right with you, I'll come over here."

"You can make plans if you like," she said, "but listen to me. Be oriental, and let Philippe be responsible for what happens. Lesson Number One, Mary. Women civilize men. Let him have all the power he wants. Let him think he's organizing everything, even leaving your husband, but underneath you hold the power."

I laughed. "Sounds wonderful, but how do I do that?"

Kim smiled. I could see she had a particular secret she was thinking about. She glowed quietly in that kitchen.

"Do you know something I don't know?" I asked. For me, sex with Patrick was a really overrated pastime.

"We oriental women," said Kim, "are trained in the ways of love."

"Really?" Kim nodded. "Who taught you?" I asked.

"My grandmother."

"Good heavens." I felt faint. The thought of my grandmother teaching me about sex was a million miles away from learning about the garden and how to cook a cake. Now with Philippe's brooding presence I felt very sure I had a lot to learn and I was willing to learn. "What do you do to keep Tony?"

Kim smiled. "It's all in the feet," she said.

I was about to dare to ask her to be more specific when we were interrupted by Philippe. He put his head round the kitchen door and said, "Are you two girls going to gossip all day long?"

"We're coming," I said.

Philippe didn't say much on the way back. He was a quiet man, almost obsessively so. He lay on his back on the small deck with his arm over his eyes and I wondered what he was thinking. I found myself wanting to kiss the pale underside of his arm. He looked vulnerable, a golden-haired child of nature who needed to be looked after. Patrick didn't have that quality. Patrick was perfectly self-sufficient.

When we arrived back at the jetty, the steward tied up the boat. For me it was like leaving a perfect vivid dream. I liked to think of it as an island, my island, set apart and away from the rest of the world. I didn't want to see Philippe in an everyday world. I wanted our lives to be alone together on a beach.

Kim's cook made me an excellent fish dish. I drank most of a bottle of Pouilly Fuissé, my favorite wine. Kim was spending the night in the Bella Vista Hotel. "So my mother won't know," she explained. "Neither of my parents suspect that I am in love with Tony. If they did, they'd be horrified." She was the golden fairy on top of the Christmas tree.

"How can you be so sure he'll leave his wife and marry you?" I asked.

"Because I'm sure," she said with such certainty I was glad for her.

My head pleasantly swimming with wine, I walked upstairs to my bedroom, already familiar and comfortable. The night air was hot and sweet. I walked from my air-conditioned bedroom out onto the balcony. The heat clung to me. The junks lay heavy in the water and the cicadas called frantically to each other. Lucky insects, I thought. No marriage to worry about, no mothers, fathers, and grandparents.

I leaned on the balcony and looked at the corners of the roof where the various gods carved out of wood smiled at me. One satyr with a gnome-like face had his tongue out. Yes, I thought. I'm heading for trouble, but I'd rather have trouble than the unendurable boredom that I'd lived for the last year. I hated being married to Patrick and I hated running a house. Maybe, I thought, I didn't like the English. Patrick was very English, very controlled and very kind, but he was boring. Before Macau must now be a BM lifetime. AM—After Macau—was my new lifetime. I would have to work diligently, like a black furry mole in his hole, to make my new life, to quarry my way out of the marriage and to escape.

Perhaps Philippe was so fatally attractive because he was French. I, who had been brought up in France, missed her almost as much as I knew I'd miss Philippe. What was it about France? Of course my roots were there. Of course there was Mademoiselle and Jacques, but there was also a certain light, a pale gray sinuous light that one saw in the early evening. The light bathed Paris and hinted of dark mysterious secrets. Passion behind shutters. Parisian eyes told all and said nothing. Philippe looked like that. A novel, a story, all waiting to be told. Who was he? Where did he come from? He told me nothing except that he was happy to hold my hand on a beach, to restrain me from too much kissing. What was there behind the beautiful sculptured face? I had to find out.

As I dreamed and drowsed in the expectant darkness, I saw a small glow through the tree below me. "Good night, my beloved," floated the voice and the glow moved slowly towards the wall. It jumped briefly and was gone. Did I dream that or was it true? Had Philippe been there all this time or was it the wine? I didn't know. I went to bed and I slept deeply. I dreamed of the sea and bottle-nosed dolphins. On the floor of the ocean lay a huge black manta ray with a cruel sting, but the ray looked at me and I prayed it would not hurt me. This was my first prayer—though uttered in a dream—since my baby died. Maybe I could begin to believe again in God.

Chapter 63

I woke up with a sense of joy tinged with despair. What on earth was I doing?

Kim was downstairs for breakfast, her lover by now safely in his office. "What is it with the feet?" I asked her, still curious.

Kim laughed. "It can't be taught," she said, "except by grandmothers."

"Fat chance I'd have," I replied. "After my grandmother's lessons, about all I can teach Philippe is how to graft apples."

"Philippe will teach you," Kim said.

"So, you know?"

"Of course." Kim was in a very oriental mood. She looked down at her scrambled eggs and sighed. "Tony's wife is being very difficult. She won't agree to a divorce. You see, if she divorces him, she is no longer the Professor's wife. She will lose face. She doesn't love him; she just wants to be married. Like so many women. You know, Mary, you will have to change if you're going to have an affair with Philippe."

I stared at her. "What do you mean?"

"Philippe is very much a man of the world. And you, even though you were a Consul General's daughter, you are not very worldly."

"I am very worldly," I said. What on earth did she mean?

"I mean," Kim said, leaning forward, "Philippe is not going to be faithful. He has affairs, lots of them."

"Oh, *that*," I scoffed. "That's because Philippe has never been happy. I'll look after him and care for him and he'll never look at another woman."

Kim shrugged. "Have it your way," she said. "But don't say I didn't warn you."

"I won't," I promised her and I rushed upstairs to write a letter to Judith.

On the boat back to Hong Kong, Captain Moses looked at me. "Happy?" he said.

"Yes," I answered. "Very. I'm leaving Patrick."

"About time, too." Captain Moses knew me so well. "Knew your grandmother," he said.

"My mother's mother?" I was fascinated. "Do tell me about her," I begged. "Please."

Jo Jo came by. "She wants to know about her grandmother!" Captain Moses bellowed.

Jo Jo smiled and shook his head. "You ask your Aunt Mary," he said.

"Do you actually know my Aunt Mary?"

Captain Moses laughed. "We're a very small crew, the old China hands, and we do all know each other. I can't tell you much, except to say that your grandmother was a legend. No one knows exactly what happened to her. She was a White Russian, became famous here in Macau and Hong Kong. Managed to move among the Chinese very well."

At last: a piece fell into place. "A Russian, you say? A White Russian?"

"That's what I say," Captain Moses nodded, "and that's what she was."

"Aunt Mary told me my grandmother was a princess . . . And you say she was a White Russian."

Captain Moses smiled at me. He could see me fitting the secrets together into a mosaic that began to resemble a person. A picture. I had seen her in a picture. A striking occidental woman with searing eyes and long black hair . . . *Moved among the Chinese very well . . .* In the picture she wore a *cheongsam*. A White Russian princess dressed like an Oriental. My grandmother. Captain Moses laughed. "She was known as the Snow Leopard and she wasn't afraid of anything or anyone.

What a woman! You're her granddaughter, so it's no wonder you can't stay married to Patrick."

No wonder my mother was different. No wonder I was different. No wonder I had these mad rebellious genes in my blood that made me soar and dive. I wasn't just a Consul General's daughter. I was the granddaughter of a Russian princess. I was thrilled. More deeply, I was satisfied to have at least a vision, however distant, of the mother of my mother.

I slept the night away on the *Fat Shan* ready to go back and end my marriage.

Patrick met the boat and we went out for dinner at the Peninsula Hotel. If I was going to break the bad news, the Pen was the place to do it, in the beautiful formal dining room overlooking the sea. I told him how I felt. "I was very unfair to you," I said. "I married you for your family. And to get married, because that was what I thought I wanted . . ." Then Patrick completely floored me.

"I know," he said. "I've known for quite a while. And I wanted to tell you that I'm in love with a girl at the bank." He took my frozen and astonished hand. "Please don't be upset. I've been meaning to tell you for ages, but I couldn't because of the baby. You've been through so much, I couldn't burden you with this." I was aghast. *Patrick unfaithful?* My dear kind Patrick? "I'm serious about her," he said. "Her name is Sally." I knew Sally. Little mouse-brown Sally, a secretary.

"And you've slept with her?" I asked, still incredulous.

"I'm afraid so." Patrick hung his head over his roast beef. Of course he was eating roast beef. Here we were at the Pen, with the best food the world could offer, and Patrick was eating roast beef. Fortunately they didn't have Yorkshire pudding and the brussels sprouts looked firm and tender.

"I see," I said, not seeing at all. "Do you want a divorce?"

"I was getting around to that," Patrick said. "I do feel we have always been good friends rather than lovers."

He was right. We were good friends, never lovers. What choked me was the fact that Patrick was capable of having an affair. It proved to me that I did not know Patrick at all. Perhaps we were mirrors for each other. He controlled my wilder self, and he lived more fully through my wilder self. Now I was going to give rein to that wilder self. In his own way he had given me permission. I said, "I'll move out tomorrow."

"No hurry," he said very politely. I felt I was talking to a stranger. His thoughts were elsewhere, with Sally.

Tears, I noticed, were trickling down my face. How embarrassing, I thought, in the middle of the Pen dining room. The tears were not of sorrow, but for what might have been. Any failure in marriage is sad. Even ours, conventional as it was. We had failed, Patrick and I, and we had failed each other.

And we went home and made inevitable, habitual love. I seduced him again, as I had years ago. But it was an empty meaningless orgasm on my part and just a sexual release on his. On the ebb tide of passion not felt lay the detritus of our failed marriage.

Chapter 64

The Helena May was a refuge, a safe harbor of other women. The large friendly woman who ran it asked no questions. She didn't even remark on my ringless finger. My little band of white flesh haunted me. I was no longer Mrs Johnson. There was going to be another Mrs Johnson, Mrs Sally Johnson, same name as his mother.

I telephoned Judith far away in damp England. "I had the baby," she said in a thin wire voice. She sounded as distant as another galaxy. "It's a boy."

"I've left Patrick," I said. "He's in love with another woman."

"Oh no." Judith sounded shocked. "I'm not going back to Bob."

"Oh good," I said. That was one less thing to worry about.

"Are you all right?" Judith asked. I could hear the sound of a baby wailing.

"Yes. I'm all right. I'm going to Macau to stay with Kim." I didn't want to tell her about Philippe. I hadn't told anybody about Philippe. He was my secret and I hugged it to myself.

I had my own room at the Helena May and the few objects I took from the flat sat about me in my dormitory bed. Some rooms were communal, the cheapest ones. I was frightened by them. Some of the women who shared them were in their forties, even fifties, women who had failed to settle down and have a family, or women who had preferred adventure and failed. What was failure? For me failure was to end up sharing a room with four or five other women who had all failed too. Were they happy? In their way. They slept with men in Hong Kong and drank rather a lot. One of them, the most worldly, called Anna, gave me the address of a fortune teller.

The fortune teller was a thin anxious woman. "Your marriage won't last," she said. She could tell that from my finger. "You will marry," she said, "but away in the future."

"What about the man I'm in love with?"

She shook her head. She had sightless blue eyes. She could see, but they were blank like mirrors. "No," she said. "I see dreadful danger." Still, she was only a fortune teller. Nothing could break this need for adventure. I returned to the dear Helena May and I sat down to write to my family.

"Good heavens," Kim said when I told her. "Are there any faithful men in the world? Come and move in with me until you decide what to do." I was more than happy to do that, but I didn't want to tell Kim what I had seen: I was in the Dairy Queen when I saw her Tony with his wife. She was pregnant, very obviously pregnant, and they were very obviously a couple.

I spent the rest of the week in Hong Kong seeing our lawyer and arranging for my personal possessions to be delivered to the *Fat Shan* for my new life in Macau. How long I was going to live there I did not know: it depended on Philippe.

"I left Patrick," I told Philippe over the telephone.

"Good," he said in his soft voice. "Now we can begin our life together."

"We can," I said and my soul rejoiced like a nightingale after the sun has set.

Well, now I had my divorce and I was free. Free to go to Philippe. My mind was miles away. It was goodbye to Francis, Cindy, and Isla. I did not care. I didn't have to pretend I was happy, radiantly, passionately, and wildly happy. Life was an adventure. Dorothy Parker was right. Life *was* a banquet, only few people consented to attend. She took her own life so she got something wrong. I would never do that. Never. Life was precious to me. A mere flick of an eyelash to be lived and enjoyed to the full. Together Philippe and I—for a time at least—would live life to the full, and I thought of soft beaches and coral. I thought of lying in the waves and making love in the sea. Curious fish watching us as we lay naked . . . But always at the edge of the sea lay a thin black line. Maybe it was a rainstorm coming, or a warning. But it was there. Could I control the cloud?

A woman in love can change any man. If Beauty can kiss the Beast, then I could kiss Philippe until whatever was bad in him turned out to be good. He was my knight in shining armor. He rode a white horse and he was waiting for me. I hurried through the week waiting for the moment he was in my arms, my face against him and the smell of him in my nostrils.

Captain Moses was realistic. "It is over?" he said.

I nodded. "He left me for another woman."

Captain Moses smiled. "Just as well," he said. "No guilt."

I laughed. He knew me awfully well. "Am I like my grandmother?"

He nodded. "She always took risks," he said and then I *knew* that he and my grandmother had been lovers. "Your mother," he said, "was the prettiest thing of a girl when I saw her." That was all he would say.

I sat as the deep green waters fell away and I enjoyed my fish steak. Jo Jo cooked it especially for me. I was safe on the *Fat Shan*, safe with both of them. Maybe I could suspend myself again, safe before the adventure: all the excitement to come but none of the risks. I fell asleep lulled and caressed by the big boat. The engines hummed a song of the sea to me.

Other people have written about Macau. George Chinnery left England to paint Macau, loving Macau with a very special love. Macau is a jewel set in China. Not a diamond, because diamond is too hard a stone. More the blue of a perfectly cut aquamarine or maybe the green of an emerald.

The smell of the mud and the island perfumed my nostrils as I awoke. I was Mary Freeland again, no longer Mary Johnson, about to begin a momentous affair. Thanks to Patrick, it would not be an adulterous affair. Philippe was honorable. He refused to make love until I was free to do so. Maybe Kim's worries about him were idle rumor.

But first I would have to tell her about Tony. He was not worth her love. I owed her that.

I did tell her at lunchtime. I began, "I saw Tony and his wife. She was very pregnant."

Kim's mouth went hard and thin. "Thank you for telling me," she said. And she left the room.

She went to her telephone in the hall and I could hear her talking. She came back into the room and waved away her dessert. "I've lost my appetite," she said to the cook.

He nodded. "Missie upset," he said.

She nodded. "I've taken care of him."

"What did you do?" I asked.

"I called the President of the university and told him I was taken advantage of by his professor. The President knows my father. Tony and his precious wife will be on the next airplane to England."

"I'm so sorry."

Kim looked at me very seriously. "This is the best part," she said. "Now I can grieve and mourn for him. I was getting awfully bored with the stories of his wife."

"But you were so sure he would leave her."

"Not really," Kim said. "And I couldn't have married him anyway. He was an awfully proper Englishman. Rather a chinless wonder, really."

We both giggled, I despite myself. "Know what you mean," I laughed.

"Come on," Kim said. "Let's have a drink." We sat in complicit female silence on the afternoon balcony. Philippe was away until tomorrow and she and I gossiped into the night.

"Tomorrow, my love," alone in my bed I whispered to myself. "Tomorrow."

❧ *Chapter 65* ❧

I did not see Philippe for five days. He knew I was arriving but he did not come to see me. He was somewhere on the island but he did not answer the phone. Unlike Kim, I did not appreciate suffering at all. She revelled in her misery. All day long she talked about Tony and how she felt about him. I realized that while she was talking about him to me he still existed for her. When she eventually fell silent, she was depressed and dejected. "How could he?" she kept saying. "How could he do that to me?"

Kim had had her revenge though. Tony had been sent immediately back to England. Not to my England, the gentle Devon, Somerset, and Dorset. Or the wild beauty of Scotland; he was back to his hometown, Leeds, a city in which I found little attraction. While she gloated, Kim also suffered, and I suffered with her. Why had Philippe not contacted me? And then he telephoned.

He sounded slightly petulant. He said he'd been unwell—"only 'flu, nothing to worry about"—and he had been staying with Mrs Wu who was his old nanny. I instantly regretted that I'd been cross. I said, "I understand. How awful for you. Are you better?"

His tone brightened. "I'm well now," he said. "I'll be around tonight to take you out to La Pousade for their famous pigeon."

I dressed studiously that night. Before I left Hong Kong I had bought myself one of those corsets you see the girls wearing in a Toulouse-Lautrec painting. I stood in front of my mirror and looked carefully at myself. I was slim and my breasts had filled out after my miscarriage. I wore a very high heeled pair of black shoes. My hair was long and hung straight over my shoulders and my eyes slanted. Very oriental, I thought and I wondered again what Kim did with her feet.

I found out what Kim did with her feet. Philippe explained it to me by showing me when we were in his bed. He took a long languorous time taking off my corset. While we were making love I didn't have time to think. When he kissed the bottom of my foot I realized that Kim knew what she was doing. I had never thought much about feet until now. I certainly hadn't considered them erotic objects. Now, suddenly, each toe had a different meaning. Philippe's feet were long and graceful. His whole body was like an orchestra and I felt we were both playing the same melody.

This is as close as I can get to communion, I thought as we lay back, spent. What a strange feeling, half-sexual, but half-spiritual, two souls entwined in one. I knew I could never leave him. We were made for each other, until death us do part. "Do you feel we were made for each other?" I asked him that night.

He nodded, his thin hawk-like face for once at peace. "I do," he said. The *I do* reverberated in my mind.

He took me back to Kim's house and kissed me tenderly. "Tomorrow," he said between kisses, "I'll find you a little house to live in."

"Can't I live with you?"

"No," he said. "I can't explain, but it's all part of my job." He was gone as suddenly as he had arrived.

He had this strange ability, like an eagle. He dropped in and out, one moment diving in as if from the sky, the next winging quickly out of sight. "What does Philippe actually do?" I asked Kim.

"Oh, he's in the French Foreign Office. You know, *Our Man in Havana?* Well, he's sort of the French version—Our Man in Macau. All very hush hush."

"I see," I said. In England we called those people "One of the Firm," a network of old boys, like my grandfather.

Philippe's house in Macau was rather grand and ornate. Late Louis XV. The bed we had made love in was a big brass four-poster. I didn't remember much of the restaurant beforehand, but the pigeon was excellent.

I listened as Kim talked about Tony, but apparently a new man had entered her life. She met him playing fan-tan. He was an ex-soldier of fortune. Her brown eyes sparkled with mischief. "But Kim," I said, "you're supposed to be dying of a broken heart."

She burst out laughing. "After tonight," she said, "my heart may well be mended."

I shook my head. I didn't understand her making love without love.

The week passed quickly. By the weekend I was installed in my own little house. The house stood at the end of a narrow dirt road and I fell in love with it.

I spoke on the telephone to Patrick about the divorce the day I moved in. I needed nothing and took nothing from Patrick, as my twenty-first-birthday inheritance had been paid into the bank and I had fifteen thousand a year to live on. The capital was invested in blue chip stocks and shares, and, according to the terms of the trust, was to go to my daughter on my death. I wondered why my Russian grandmother who left the money for me left nothing for a possible boy. I was grateful though: I could live carefully and devote myself to Philippe.

The first three months were idyllic. Philippe was a

wonderful lover. He arrived every night at six o'clock and I cooked for him. I took cooking lessons from the cook at La Pousade. We ate at my little Victorian dining table and I played records of Portuguese *fados* for him. Only for him. The haunting wail of the songs frightened me. Those women who sang sounded as if all the pain for women across the world lay in their smoky husky voices. Philippe liked to listen after dinner with his glass of velvet port. I didn't drink port. "It is not for women. It's a man's drink," Philippe said. "You must be like my mother."

My heart sank. Philippe's mother had died when he was eight and he had never really forgiven her. In a way Philippe had died with her. There was a childish quality about Philippe. I loved that quality in him, but he could be very demanding and a little cruel, but he was always so apologetic, I forgave him.

Once, when he yet again did not turn up for dinner and I was left sitting with the burnt remains, I was cross when he came round to apologize. "I can't use the phone," he said plaintively. "I'm an old-fashioned man and I just don't like telephones. I did mean to let you know, but time slipped by."

I was still cross. "You can't treat people like that," I said. He walked off with his shoulders hunched. He looked so much like a hurt little boy, I ran after him. "Don't go," I said. "I can't bear to see you hurt." He picked me up and carried me upstairs to my bed and we made love. All Philippe had to do was to make love to me and I'd forgive him anything.

The months slipped by smoothly until a year had passed and it was another Christmas. Philippe had to go back to Paris on business in the New Year. "Here's to our first Christmas together," I toasted Philippe. It was the cool season in Macau. The rain dripped down the windowpane. Kim had her new lover ensconced in her house and we were going there for Christmas dinner. Old Lady Janner had been invited and I was just getting ready to go downstairs when Philippe urgently demanded that we make love. I had put my hair up in a *chignon,* but he insisted. So I took out a bottle of champagne.

After we made love we toasted our first year together again. Before we left my house I looked back at it. So much love and laughter passed between those little walls. Now I was going with Philippe to Paris to visit my parents, then to London to visit my grandparents and, of course, Aunt Mary. I left Paris a young married woman and I was going back with a bad reputation. The letters from all sides in response to my news soon ignored the fact that I was living with Philippe. No one mentioned him and he was not asked to visit my parents. He was also going to Burgundy on family business, and after I had finished visiting my family we would meet at his château. I was a little daunted.

Apparently Philippe had no parents, but there were two aunts whom he had looked after. "They will look you over," he said, "and decide if I can marry you. They are very stern women," he added. I was worried. I felt like a horse under starter's orders. Philippe had taught me a lot of things I had never considered before. He was better read than I was. He was a lover of Elizabeth Barrett Browning. He quoted from all sorts of literature and he never misquoted. I, though I loved to read, could never quote accurately and he mocked me for it. Philippe had graduated brilliantly from the Sorbonne. He spoke six languages and was a chess expert. To keep up with him I began to study in earnest. When I wasn't with him I read about antiques. Before going to Burgundy I needed to know all there was to know about Russian icons. Apparently the aunts both collected them, so I learned. I bought a guitar and began to learn classical pieces and I cooked. How I cooked. Thank goodness I'd taken cooking lessons at Mont St Sebastian. Philippe loved to eat. He knew food and could name the wine I used. I was looking forward to having good French wine again. The Portuguese wine was excellent but lacked the clarity of French wine. "You wait," Philippe said many times, "until you taste my wine."

Christmas dinner at Kim's took place at six o'clock. Lady Janner looked like an old moth-eaten carpet, but she had a special smile for me. "So," she said, "you seem to be lasting the course quite well."

"I didn't know there was a course to be lasted," I said pleasantly.

"Be careful, my dear." And she looked around the room anxiously. No one was with us. The men were in the library drinking brandy. The meal was cleared away and Kim was upstairs. "I don't want to sound like a bad fairy," she said, "but do be careful of Philippe."

I nodded knowingly. "I know he has an awful reputation, but he really has changed."

Lady Janner shook her head. "There is nothing more to say, is there? Your mind is made up."

"Yes, it is. I have been so very happy this last year. We love each other very much and he is going to marry me. I hope my family will forgive me when they finally meet him. I shall be meeting his aunts in the New Year. I do so want this marriage to be a success." Lady Janner shrugged and turned away.

Kim came back, happy and laughing. "What's the matter, Mary?" she said. "Has a goose walked over your grave?"

"No, I've just been warned about Philippe by Lady Janner."

"Oh, her," laughed Kim. "Don't listen to her. She

has always picked awful men. She's had five husbands, you know."

"Good heavens," I said. "Then she must know something about it."

My new life with Philippe was totally absorbing. He was a drug. I didn't interfere with his daytime activities, but the few times he was elsewhere at night I hungered for him and the pain did not ease until I saw him again. He also became anxious if I was away and questioned me minutely on where I had been and whom I had met. I supposed it was his Foreign Office training to be thorough. I gladly told him, because I had no secrets from him, except my miscarriage and Reimer. Those were blocked off events in my life and I would share them with no one except my mother. More and more, I was looking forward to seeing her.

Chapter 66

We traveled together on the *Fat Shan*. Philippe and Captain Moses obviously knew each other well, but then the Captain must have known all the ex-patriates in Macau. We caught the airplane in Hong Kong after a night of love in the Peninsula Hotel. As I sat on the airplane demurely covered in my blanket I wondered at the woman I had become.

In a way Kim knew me well. I loved Kim, but she frightened me a little. I knew and was bothered when things were wrong. But Kim had no scruples. She lived like a small cat in the back of a dustbin. Whatever was thrown to her she took. Even when it was not hers to have, if she wanted it she took it. Tony had felt the power of her ruthlessness when crossed. He lost his job and probably would never work again. I didn't have that kind of anger in me or need for revenge. But I was beginning to get a taste for perversity. I began to delight in the malicious gossip that flew around the room. The endless shifting in relationships. In the early days with Philippe I was easily upset. "She really didn't do that," I said. Philippe had an engaging giggle. "She did and she does. Everyone knows about her . . ." I didn't know the woman discussed, but was horrified. "Don't be such a silly goose," Philippe laughed. "Your famous writer, Forster, had an *affaire scandaleuse* with his dog."

Slowly, as I was sucked into Philippe's world, I began to worry less about the content of the things I heard. There was a kind of magic to be had when one suspended worry and disbelief, when one allowed one's mind not to measure everything against a moral yardstick.

We were high in the clouds and I looked across at Philippe. He had fallen instantly asleep and lay slightly curled and vulnerable in his sleep. I loved to look at him. For a man who was about to have his thirtieth birthday, he looked no more than eighteen. I felt very blessed to have Philippe. Our marriage would be a great success because I would make it a success. One failure was quite enough. I escaped the Helena May and for that I was grateful. I was not going to be a displaced woman in a world that had no use for women on their own. For a woman unattended by a man, the world was a lonely and forlorn planet. No amount of politics or rhetoric could wipe the sight of Lady Janner from my mind. She had money and a title, but was just barely tolerated by those couples who invited her into their houses. A lone woman was a nuisance and an obligation.

Still, I had Kim. And Judith, who wrote dismal letters. Dismal because she was unhappy. She lived with her mother and the baby and she was lonely. Poor Judith. But at least she had left Bob. Better to be lonely than beaten . . .

I had the rest of the flight to Paris with Philippe, and then I would be home for a while. I smiled, realizing that I was achingly happy, contented, satiated and satisfied.

Later I slept, and then was groggily awakened as the plane landed in a typical Paris mist. Home, I thought. At last home. As much as I would miss Philippe, for now I wanted nothing more than time alone with my mother.

Philippe and I clung to each other when the time came to say goodbye. "I can't imagine a day without you," I said.

Philippe's lips were soft and warm. "Or I without you."

I watched him go, the soft brown camel of his coat fade into the early morning fog. I saw the gloved hand wave from the taxi and he was gone.

I looked around and saw the chauffeur. "Good morning, Madame," he said as if I had left the day before which, indeed, I may well have. For the chauffeur, life consisted of moving people and things from place to place. He was not a man to know personally. He was the back of a neck that I knew well.

The reassuring scrunch of the driveway reintroduced me to my old life. For me coming home was like swimming under water. My mother had fashioned a very safe life with no risks at all. Standing in the hall I smelled the old childhood smells. The reassuring scent of polish. The calm in the eye of a hurricane. No surprises. "There you are, darling. I've been waiting for you." My mother, unchanged and unchanging. Maybe a touch of silver at the temples, but still beautiful and imperious. "Good heavens! You do look well, Mary."

Never could I recall my mother saying anything favorable about my appearance. "I am," I said gladly. "I'm in love." I had intended to wait, to ask for some time when we could go to her office and sit and talk and maybe have tea together. But love made me impatient. I smiled inwardly as I remembered Kim burbling on about Tony. At least I was not talking of lost love. My love was simply elsewhere but present when I spoke of him.

My mother did not look surprised. "I guessed as much," she said. "From your letters I could tell there was something making you happy, and for a woman to be so happy she must be in love."

"Then you do understand. Don't you?"

My mother looked at me again. I saw the submarine submerged in her depth. "More deeply than you will ever know. But we all have choices and we must live by them. You have chosen to leave your marriage and I assume you are living with this man."

(Did I hear a chill in the way she said *this man?*) "Yes, I am. But we are going to get married. I'm to meet Philippe at his château in Burgundy. He has two aunts I have to impress and then we can set a date. My divorce is through, so I am free to marry. Look." I fumbled in my bag. "Here is a picture of Philippe."

My mother gazed at the photograph. "Lovely looking man. Has he been married before?"

"No, Philippe lost his mother when he was very young. He was brought up by servants and these two aunts. His father died during the war. I know you'll like him. I hope Father understands."

"Yes, he does, Mary." My mother was reassuring. "We both want you to be happy. If Philippe can make you happy, that's wonderful. Only don't make the same mistake you made with Patrick. Marry Philippe because you want to marry Philippe, not someone else's way of life. You've always been impatient, so take your time before you plunge into another marriage."

The gong sounded for lunch. I heard the car arrive at the door and my father was home. Through the door with him came a dear familiar smell of tweed and frost—for the morning was cold and spring was still months away. We talked and we laughed, the three of us. Geneviève, I learned, gave birth to twins. Far away in my past that information gave me a twinge of regret, but then it was for the best. Now I was with Philippe, I could hope again. The idea of his child filled me with pleasure. A child with his eyes and his slick fair hair . . . Melitta, the Australian Ambassador's wife, was in town. My parents and I gossiped like starlings.

My father returned to the office and my mother and I sat at the luncheon table talking while the sands of time ran through the hourglass and the bottom glass globe got fuller and fuller. I told her everything, even about the miscarriage, and she nodded. "It happens," she said, "and you get over it."

"Being away from Philippe is like a physical pain," I said. "Do you feel that way about Father?"

"No," my mother said. "I don't. I did once about a man, but it didn't turn out well. Your father and I share other things, including a deep respect and a calm kind of loving. I would never hurt him, but more than anything else, I owe him my life." I heard a strange sound in my mother's voice. "I had to make a choice," she said. By this time we had moved upstairs to her room and the shadows were beginning to fall across her face. Underneath her face lay the face of a young girl crossed in love.

"I understand," I said. There was so much unsaid between us. Her secrets lay in the shadows and I knew I must not press her.

"I walked away," my mother said. "He was too big a risk. Then your father proposed and I knew I would be loved all my life. I needed to know that," she said urgently. "And he has loved and cared for me and always will." She smiled. "There are men to love and then there are men to marry."

"Surely you can have both," I said.

She nodded. "Yes, if you're very lucky. I hope Philippe is such a man."

"I know he is," I said with confidence. "This time, there's no question."

Philippe did not call for the first few days. I felt desperate. He was moving around visiting friends, so I didn't know where to contact him. When he did call he was apologetic. I was so glad to hear his voice, I didn't care. He was well and he missed me. I missed him deeply. I was amazed at my capacity to feel pain. Without Philippe the world tended to be a dull blur.

Mademoiselle and Jacques were pleased with my news. They had moved into a larger house. Mademoiselle looked marvelous. She had made the house her own. Pots of geraniums stood everywhere and her herbs grew thick and green on her kitchen windowsill. The two children were solemn and shy and stared at me. Jacques, home for the evening, also looked well. They were now a solid bourgeois family, while I the rebel was off on my adventures. I didn't envy them any longer. Jacques was now a very senior professor at his university and Mademoiselle no longer taught but stayed at home, waiting for the children to arrive from school and she supervised their homework. Her life revolved like the sun around her family. It was her world and nothing much from outside intruded. Certainly she was interested in my new life and she laughed ruefully when I told her about Patrick. "We didn't think that marriage of yours would last," she said, "but there was no telling you. You were always so headstrong." We talked the night away.

I was anxious to get to Philippe, but the days were slow and dragging. I bought clothes and endlessly talked to my mother about Philippe. She listened on her way in and out of the house to social engagements. I went with her to some but soon stopped. They were nothing to do with my life. There were the same people saying the same things, drinking the same drinks, obsessively living life safely until they died. "Maybe," my mother said, "some people like the security of sameness."

I was restless and fraught. Philippe's voice soothed me down the telephone. "Not long now," he said, "and we will be together forever. Only two weeks more."

"I know," I said. "Only two weeks. It feels like two years."

"Go and visit friends," he advised.

"I have no friends," I said, guiltily ignoring Geneviève. I knew I couldn't face an evening of Geneviève and her children. Why is it French women can get so completely caught up in their children? Their husbands seem not to exist.

My visit to my grandparents was brief. Grandpa was not in good health. He sat quietly in his chair but he was pleased to see me. My grandmother was anxious. I knew that the idea of outliving my grandfather was abhorrent to her. They had been together for more than fifty years and had never been apart, except for the war years. They were utterly devoted to each other. My grandmother's love was of a different quality than my mother's love for my father. My mother existed in her own right as a person; my grandmother lived for my grandfather. I couldn't imagine her with-

out him. Her face was always turned, listening for him
if he was out. She had an uncanny knack of hearing
the car long before I could, and then she would smile
such a joyful smile. I hoped desperately that Philippe
and I would be that happy.

Aunt Mary was more sanguine. "You're going to
marry that Frog?" she said crossly. "Why can't you
marry one of your own?"

"I love him," I explained.

"Huh." Aunt Mary was not pleased. Her arthritis
had been troubling her. "I don't hold with foreigners," she said. "Far too many in this country without
you marrying one."

"You'll love him, Aunt Mary . . ." Obviously diver-
sionary tactics were necessary. Aunt Mary didn't approve of divorce. "Captain Moses sends you his love,
and so does Jo Jo."

That news mollified her a little. We sat at the table
and ate our salad. I liked Aunt Mary's salads. They
were eternally the same: hardboiled eggs, beetroot,
lettuce, and her own tomatoes. "Captain Moses?" she
said. "Eh. That was a long time ago." She leaned back
in her chair. "He was a lad, was that Captain Moses.
I was a woman on a far journey to a strange land, but
he helped us, he did."

"He says he knew my grandmother."

The lamps hissed disapprovingly. The silence was
icy. "Been talking too much, 'as he?" Aunt Mary shook
her head. "That's your mother's business, not mine,"
she said. Those words, uttered with inarguable final-
ity, closed the conversation. We got back to shallow
water and discussed the Communists who were taking
over Ealing town hall and other familiar subjects.

Miss Standish was the most understanding. "You
know, Mary," she said secure in her booklined library.

"You always looked as if you might go into a career, but I always thought of you as a fragile butterfly with wings of steel." She smiled. "I've read a lot of Victorian novels and you certainly are living your life to the full. Hong Kong, Macau, what wonderful exotic places!"

When I left she handed me a copy of the latest Graham Greene. "He is one of the greatest writers alive today. Study his technique, his fluidity." She smiled again. "God bless you, Mary, and stay in touch with me."

I really relaxed when I visited Phoebe in Chantilly. Hattie was there, as elegant as ever. "Hattie," I said one day, finding her alone in the stables brushing a horse, "can I ask you something? When we were at school together, you always talked about that lawyer—Richard?—you were going to marry once you went back to Africa . . ."

"And took up my rightful position as Princess Obona?" Hattie added with a wry smile.

"Yes," I said. "But you've never gone back, have you? What happened? At first you said you were just staying on with Phoebe for a visit, but that was several years ago."

"I hardly know how to explain," Hattie began. "Well, Richard. Let's start with Richard. I got a letter from my parents, just after we passed out of Mont St Sebastian, saying Richard wasn't too keen on the idea of my going away to school in Switzerland anyway. He found himself a good young virgin to stay home instead."

"I'm sorry, Hattie."

"So was I, I suppose. I mean, when he and I used to talk, he really seemed to want a wife like me who would know the world and want a career of her own. Maybe he was lying. Maybe he just changed his mind.

I don't know." She shook her head. "But that was the problem. I came to know the world. I was sent to school in England and Italy and France and Switzerland, and somehow I was never sure if I wanted to go back to Africa."

I was amazed. How could anyone not want to return to beautiful Africa, to the Africa of my childhood? "But, Hattie . . ."

"But what, Mary?" She stared into my eyes. "But surely I should be dying to go back to everything you think you remember of Africa? We know two different Africas, Mary. Yours was a British bubble in the middle of time. Mine was an entire way of life that now feels foreign. I've seen so much, so many different ways of life. When I was growing up, it was my grandmother who raised me, not my mother. I thought of my mother more as an older sister. But that was the way children were raised. And when I got older . . . It's funny, but *love* isn't a word you hear between married people in my Africa. The couples stay together forever, but there's no mention of love. Love is a very European idea. Richard and I used to talk about love. It was going to be different for us. But it looks like Richard didn't want his life to be different.

"And I've been away for so long, and I've become so *used* to living in Europe, that now I really can't imagine going back. Going back to what? To find another traditional African man to marry and turn myself into a traditional African woman? I'm afraid it's too late for that. I know my father says I've been seduced by the "decadence of Europe." Perhaps he's right. Perhaps I have. But he was the one who sent me here in the first place, and there's no going back now."

I could see the sadness in her dark face. "You and your father used to be so close. Do you still speak with him?"

Hattie shook her head. "He cut me off from the family when I told him I was considering staying in Europe. So it's my younger sister who's the Princess now. I'm just me." She raised her hands and let them flap loosely to her thighs.

"Oh, Hattie." I put my hand on her shoulder.

"There's no need to feel sorry for me, Mary. I have my freedom. Yes, I'm alone for the moment, but that's fine. It will take time to get over the hurt of Richard, but someday I'll be ready to give my heart to another man. Until then, Phoebe's awfully good to me, and I love working with the horses." A cool wind blew through the stables. Hattie shook her head and looked out of the stable door as if clearing her thoughts from a troubling dream. "Sometimes I think, Mary, there are those of us who are meant to be cut loose from our pasts. Exiles, really. Nothing dramatic, like political exile. More of a self-chosen exile from what used to be home."

"You must miss Africa," I said, thinking how much I often missed it.

"Yes. Very much. But I can't, or won't, go back. It's my choice. And now I've the chance to make a home for myself wherever I choose to be. If you really think about it, Mary, could you return to Africa? To live forever, I mean."

I did not answer. My sunlit past in Africa seemed now so very distant. Would I recreate those memories if I could? Perhaps they were better left in the past. Why resurrect the past? That must be why my mother, and everyone from her past, was so doggedly reluctant to speak of those mythic ancient years.

I felt I'd found a new understanding of my mother. The understanding did nothing to allay my yearning to know her history, but at least now I could begin to fathom her need for secrecy.

Was I too a sort of exile like Hattie? Captain Moses certainly was, and Jo Jo. My mother as well, I supposed. But, as Hattie had said, the trick was to make one's *home* someplace new. I knew exactly where I wanted my home: with Philippe. Philippe would be my refuge, my country, my world.

Phoebe didn't care whom I married or why. She had not changed either. Still tall and disheveled, she forbade me to talk about Philippe. "Don't go on about men, Mary. There's far too much talk about men these days. If you had brothers like mine, you'd understand them. Feed them, keep them clean, and ignore them. That way you'll be happily married. Now, about the horses . . ." and off she went into a long list of pedigrees.

We walked interminably around the stables and I did my best to admire fetlocks and hooves. "Good withers," Phoebe said.

Finally, on a particularly chilly day I got fed up with the whole horsey thing. "Phoebe," I said as we sat in her sitting room, "what do you do for sex?"

"I don't."

"Ever?"

"No." Phoebe looked at me quite seriously. "There are some people in this world who don't need it, and I don't. I prefer horses and my friends. Jeremy is always in love with some tart or another and I have to come to the rescue. Such a waste of time and energy."

I must admit that when I saw Phoebe's horses at full gallop in the early mornings I caught some of the exhilaration of her lifestyle. Her racing colors were red and green and her horses were magnificent. I watched them strung out in a long line, their hooves thudding, throwing up clods of thick brown earth. Her stud stallion was a foaming white creature that easily outraced the mares. He stood panting, his tongue hanging out and his eyes alight with the effort of winning.

Then I was back with my parents and the last few days slid slowly by, but at last the day arrived to catch the train to Burgundy, to my beloved. I was nervous because of the aunts, but I was happy. "You look radiant," my mother said as she kissed me goodbye.

My father hugged me. "Look after yourself, Pumpkin."

And I was gone. My pumpkin years were over. No more ill-fitting glass slippers, no more midnights. My knight and my prince was waiting for me.

Chapter 67

I took the train to Dijon. I sat looking out of the window. I liked trains. Airplanes picked you up and put you among strangers. A train pulled you along so that you could see where your journey was going.

And I could think. I had a lot to think about. For the first time in my life I had spent time with my mother and we didn't fight. Why did she accept my disgrace so easily? Maybe she imagined I would come to my senses. Certainly a divorce in the Freeland family was unheard of. And then to live in sin with a man was even worse. But for once my mother had held her fire and listened sympathetically to all I had to say. Perhaps because my mother was a woman of the world, and now I was one too.

The train passed Fontainebleau in the distance. I imagined the life of the huge goldfish blowing contented bubbles at tourists in the pond outside the castle. I saw the green of the Forêt d'Othe, a gentle rainsoaked green, all moist with the spring. My new life awaited me, Philippe in Dijon waiting for me. I very much wanted to put my old life away and begin afresh.

I had behind me Hong Kong, Macau, Paris, where my past lay under a shadow. I would not fail again.

A familiar feeling of excitement invaded my throat. Tonnerre went by. We ran alongside the Burgundy Canal and then I saw Dijon in the distance. Dijon, the city of hot mustards. Philippe's city. And he was there on time, for once. "Darling," he said and he took me in his arms and we kissed. I felt immediately that our world together was complete. Last time I had seen him he was leaving me in the freezing cold in Paris. Would I ever see him again? I kept that thought tightly locked up in the back of my brain. The thought was too close to the train station with Reimer. The thought itched in the mind and plagued me when Philippe did not ring, but here he was, dear and familiar. "Come," he said, taking my two cases.

We pushed our way through the busy station out into the road. His car, a red Kharmen Ghia, sat waiting for us. Like lovers who know each other intimately, we had little to say at first, just both of us happy to be in the same place at the same time. He put his hand on my knee and I felt the heat between us. "Did you miss me?" I asked foolishly.

"Of course," he said, "but I have been very busy." That was the difference. Of course he had been busy. He had buyers and shippers over from America and in the following weeks I would be there to help him with the entertaining.

We took a small winding road up to his château. We passed the little village of Arbrit. The white cafés stood with their doors ajar and the village had a few desultory shops. Philippe was explaining that I must visit with the aunts. I was half listening. I loved the sound of his voice and often I missed his words because I listened to his voice as one listens to the sound of an oboe in an orchestra: oblivious to the main melody the oboe sings its own song. Melancholy underneath the brightness. Was Philippe melancholy? He looked fine. "Do you miss your life in Macau?" I asked.

Philippe sighed. "I must come home. My aunts are too old to go on running the château by themselves, and they have asked me to stay. To tell you the truth, I am happiest in Macau and in the Far East. But this is my inheritance. So what can I do? My aunts will soon die, so I must take over now."

I did not say that he sounded a little cold about the death of his aunts. I knew that Philippe did not accept personal criticism with good grace. I also knew that as a child in L'Hermitage, the lord-and-master child, he was spoiled badly by the servants. Still, if this was his way of showing grief at leaving Macau, then I would accept it. For my part I must think of moving my things out of my little house in Macau and selling it.

Slowly the Château L'Hermitage came into view. It was a beautiful fortified building, not immense and baroque like Loch Hey in Scotland, but round and solidly set in a forest. The road up to it was white and clear. Immense oak trees guarded the way and brown cows walked slowly chewing their cud. I said, "How beautiful!"

"I know." He nodded. "If only the château stood in Macau instead. You have no idea how provincial the people are here."

We passed rows and rows of vine leaves tied onto stakes. Rank upon rank, bare now, but soon to put forth shoots. I felt like the vines, ready to burst green shoots, and then in the hot languor of the autumn to be picked and squeezed dry of all moisture. "Did you really miss me?" I asked again.

"I did," he said and took my hand and gently licked my palm with the tip of his tongue. Deep inside me I felt a surge of excitement. "Soon," he said. "I promise. Soon."

Several servants were outside the house eager to greet me. These days a mistress could enter the château by the front door. What a change from former, stricter times, when a mistress would have had to have been smuggled in. I was here as his lover, not his bride. One day, I hoped, things would be different.

L'Hermitage was too big to take in all at once. We walked through hall after hall. "There has been a de Lacroix here since the middle ages," Philippe announced. "I am the last heir to the title. When my aunts die, there is only me. I don't intend to have any children. This place will become a museum. Others can walk through and see how it once was. I couldn't leave it to a son. Not today, with so much envy and greed around. But I must stay here for the rest of my life just to keep the Paris tax inspectors off my back. We, the château-owners, should be paid by the people of France for looking after their heritage rather than be hounded with bills and taxes."

I nodded. I hadn't known that Philippe intended not to have children. It was true that during this year we were together he took no interest at all in the little Chinese children that played by my door.

We walked to a main staircase and then we climbed. "My goodness," I said. "You have to be fit to get to the bedrooms."

"I have given you the Pompadour suite." He flung open a large pair of double doors. The servant gratefully put down my suitcases and bowed his way out. "We have tonight to ourselves," Philippe said. I walked across the suite's sitting room floor and pushed open a door into the bedroom. There on a dais was a big canopied bed. It must have stood there for centuries. Philippe was behind me. "Like it?"

I could feel his hot breath on my neck and his hands slip around my waist. We moved towards the bed. We climbed the two steps and then we fell together. Our lovemaking was urgent and frenzied. Philippe fell back and lay staring at the ceiling. I dropped into a light sleep beside him.

Soon I stirred. He had gone, slipped away like a lizard down a wall. I felt an ache of disappointment.

I called a maid to unpack my things and then I bathed away the lingering smell of love. I sat in the bath and remembered my own bath in Paris. Mine no longer, because I had left my father's house for the second time for a man. Obviously Philippe and I were not going to share the same bedroom. Somewhere in this massive château he must have his lair. I wondered vaguely if I would ever see it. Or would he keep it a secret as he kept secrets in Macau? I was used to people with secrets. I knew how to walk on the quicksands of their minds, not to put my foot too close to the sucking sand. If he had moods and temper tantrums like my mother, I could cope with those too. I was good for Philippe because I understood him. He was as changeable as the wind. One minute all calm and not a cloud, the next the beginning of a hurricane.

The bathroom was made from white marble. The fittings were gold and the basin was set in a large mahogany counter. I was not spared an ancestor: a rather long-nosed sniffy version of Philippe gazed down at my naked body with disdain. As well she might, I thought, drying myself on a large fluffy towel. Here I am, living in sin with her descendant. If Philippe had his way, the next people she could disapprove of would be tourists. That should make her nostrils curl. But I hadn't taken Philippe's words about children too seriously.

I heard Philippe knock on the door. I knew his knock like I knew his way of clearing his throat. I knew the sound of his shoe on the floor. Philippe loved to watch me put on my makeup, so I sat with my back to him, facing him in the mirror. He lay on a large sofa and looked at me. "Go slowly," he said and I did. Finally I put my hands up to knot my hair. "Come here," he said and I did. Roughly he pushed my head down between his legs. "Finish this for me." His voice was harsh and ugly. Fearfully I looked at him and did as I was told. He came and I brushed my head against his thigh. He had never behaved this way before and the event revolted me.

I looked at him from my position on my knees. "Philippe?" I said. He lay there with his eyes closed, looking very pale and drawn. "What was that all about? That didn't feel like love." He didn't move. I stood up and went to wash my face.

"This house," he said as he got up. "This house is haunted. I do things here I don't like. I'll see you at dinner. Eight o'clock in the dining room." He left, his feet quick and nervous over the carpets.

I was shaken. I had known Philippe for over a year now. I knew he had moods and storms, but this time I felt used. As if I hadn't been there. Still, I thought, maybe the news that he had to come back to France had deeply upset him. Perhaps I should not have excited him with my makeup. I thought we were playing a little game with our eyes, but for him it was not a game. Maybe he could talk about his feelings later on. But I did know that sex was something we *did;* we did not talk about it. I just hoped, as I dressed, that he was over the squall. I finished dressing.

My clothes had been put away by a discreet servant. I hoped she hadn't heard anything, but then there had been nothing to hear.

Just before eight o'clock, I walked down the flights of stairs and asked a footman where the dining room was. He directed me down several corridors and then I found it. The room was large and the dining table long and gleaming. Philippe was seated at the other end.

He got to his feet and he took my hand. "I've had them lay your place next to mine. This way we don't have to shout," he said. This was Philippe, not the stranger of a few hours ago. He smiled at me warmly. "You look lovely, darling," he said. He waved away the footman and pulled my chair out for me. "Let us dine." Maybe the moment had been an aberration. Maybe it hadn't been Philippe at all but a ghost of an ancestor.

I tried to push the incident out of my mind.

Chapter 68

I took deep breaths over dinner, still feeling sick and a little shaken. Philippe, however, seemed full of good spirits and he talked instructively about wine. We were drinking a Louis Jadot *Pouilly Fuissé*. He knew it was my favorite wine, but tonight the taste failed to delight my mouth so recently abused. After dinner he led me to my room and kissed me chastely. "I must go," he said. "I have a lot of work to do. Our guests will be arriving tomorrow. But before that, we lunch with my great aunts."

"I'll be nervous," I said honestly.

"Don't be. They are very formal and old-fashioned. Just be yourself."

I walked across the floor to my bedroom. I felt cold and empty and confused. I put my head against the frame of the casement window and I watched my young self flying innocently through the moonlight on my horse, Phoebe behind me. In those days our only problem had been the rush for second helpings of food. Then we had all lain about and gossiped together. Years away, my childhood years. A golden shroud around them. The next time I remembered having stood like this, comforting myself, was waiting for Reimer, always waiting for him in my room at Mont St Sebastian. Other girls titivated and pranced, but they remained innocent. Or they did not. They cared no more for the boys than the boys for them.

In Reimer I had chosen an adventurer. I had retrieved my heart from him and it was alive and burned, but now it was in another's hands which weren't safe. Why, when I had safe hands around my heart, could I not be content? Why, oh why, when we had read *Wuthering Heights* with Miss Standish, did my soul burn to be carried across the heath?

I rolled my forehead on the glass and I sighed. Will I give up my life in Macau? My little house? Will I give up my friends, all for Philippe? With an awful sense of the inevitable, I knew I would. I had read about women like myself. Fools for love. Phoebe had no such foolishness. Neither did Hattie. Kim was no fool; she controlled her relationships. Judith left Bob, but she did have her baby, so all of him was not gone. But I, oh I, knew that I had no control over what was happening to me. I stood at the door of a burning blazing furnace while Philippe, with his hair on fire and his arms extended, drew me step by step into the inferno. I knew I got no pleasure from pain, so why then was I here?

For a moment I felt I stood in the eye of a storm and could see clearly. For that moment the earth was hushed. All I had to do was to take my two suitcases and go down the stairs out into the open and leave. I saw myself walking down the great stairway, out onto the broad path, my back resolutely set against Philippe and the château . . .

I remembered his eyes. How sad they would look if I, too, abandoned him. His lost mother and dead father stood beside me. Captain Moses also nodded. "You must live your destiny," he had said not so long ago. "It lies ahead of you and you must walk every step of the way. If you turn back, you will find it ahead of you again in a different shape." I squared my shoulders and nodded. Of course I couldn't leave Philippe and run away. Maybe he was just not himself. This house was huge. A mausoleum. Many things must have happened in this house, including murders and shootings, riots and revolts. These walls were no strangers to blood . . . In the morning, I told myself, all would be well.

Chapter 69

I woke and stretched. The room was dappled with sunlight. I had slept for a long time and I had missed breakfast. I telephoned the housekeeper and she laughed. "Monsieur told us to leave you, but he says please be ready for luncheon with his aunts."

"What do I call them?" I asked rather nervously.

"Tante Brigitte and Tante Michelle. They will be here at one o'clock and you will await them in the *petit salon.* Do you wish for some coffee or *brioches?* Maybe an English breakfast?"

"No," I said. "Thank you. I'm not hungry. I'll be down soon." I dressed quickly and ran down the stairs, hoping to catch a glimpse of Philippe, but he was nowhere to be found. I finally discovered the library and looked at the thousands of bound books. Each book had a family plate and they smelled of leather. I picked up a copy of Victor Hugo's *Hernani.* I was delighted to find it was the original French edition. In this library I could spend several delightful years reading.

I wandered on and came to a music room. It was circular with an adorable frieze of cherubim serenading

God in this almost empty room. In the middle of the room was a Steinway grand piano immaculately polished. Beside the piano lay a cello, often enough played, I could see by the rosin on the bow. I sat at the piano and played a long-remembered minuet which brought back Jacques' voice. "Eeyum Tum Tum," he breathed in my ear. It was good to know that he and Mademoiselle were not far away in Paris and that I could visit that oasis of now bourgeois calm. The door to the music room pushed open.

A startled little maid gave a gasp of fear when she saw me. *"Pardon,* mademoiselle," she said. "I didn't realize. I thought her ghost had come back to haunt this room."

"Whose ghost?" I said pleasantly but with interest. "What is your name?" I interrupted myself.

"My name is Lotti. I keep this room clean, but since Madame Rose left, nobody has been here to play the piano." The little girl crossed the floor and touched the piano.

"But you said a ghost."

"Nobody knows . . ." She looked at me. Lotti's face was frightened. "There was a terrible night and then she was gone. We don't know where or why. The next day we packed all her things. She had taken nothing with her."

"How long ago was this?" I asked evenly, a dull thudding in my heart.

"Oh, about two years, I think."

"I see," I said, but I didn't and I was certainly not going to ask any more questions. Perhaps all this was usual servants below-stairs gossip. "Thank you, Lotti," I said. "I'll get on with my piece. I haven't played the piano in years."

Promptly at 12:45 I was in the *petit salon* waiting for Philippe. The minutes ticked by and I became more and more tense. "Where have you been?" I whispered as he slid into the room just as a silver gray Rolls Royce stopped at the bottom of the steps that led into the house.

"None of your business," he snapped.

Oh well, I thought, all his business-people have arrived and now he has to deal with his aunts. I took his hand. "Sorry," I said. "I know you're busy." Philippe smiled at me and my suspicious heart melted. Of course there would be things between us that were not right. Everyone has to work at marriage. God, in whom my faith had returned, would bless us and take care of us.

The door opened and the aunts arrived. Tante Brigitte was tall and grim. She had a hooked nose, a pair of matchsticks for lips, and two hooded-back eyes with no eyelashes or eyebrows. She glared during the day as she must have glared at night. Tante Michelle looked a little softer, but not much. They stood in their Edwardian capes, two white lace bonnets, matched by lace gloves. The housemaid flustered around disrobing them. "A glass of sherry for you both?" Philippe enquired. Both nodded and then looked at me. I felt four eyes and four imaginary stilettos pierce me.

"An English girl?" The tone of Tante Brigitte's voice was less than thrilled.

"Her father is the Consul General in Paris," Philippe explained.

Tante Michelle smiled. "At least she speaks French, I suppose. Do you speak French?" She spoke loudly and carefully.

I nodded. I couldn't speak. Being a Consul General's daughter didn't rate in this house. Nothing less than French Royal Family counted. Anyway, the French hate the English, particularly this sort of French family.

We sat primly on the elegant sofa in this pretty room while Philippe talked charmingly of the vineyards and the buyers who had arrived and were all in town. He talked and the aunts stared sideways at me, like night cats wondering when to pounce. I had nothing to say or to offer. We knew no one in common. Theirs was a life so elevated from mine. Most of their time, I imagined, was spent in church business, working efficiently among the workers of the estate, visiting the sick, tending the dying. Above all their time was devoted to God on their knees in the cathedral at Dijon. If they thought of men, they thought of the Bishop or maybe a lesser abbot who came to dine at their fine table. These details I knew from books. Fortunately my mother trained me well and I did manage at last to chatter about the château and ask questions about the paintings and the ancestors.

After lunch we walked a slow shuffling walk with the two aunts down the picture gallery. I remembered Phoebe's mother's gallery. Down from those ancient gray walls hung pictures of dashing seafaring Irish men, their eyes blue and their mouths full and smiling. Those days when we laughed and ate at the kitchen table with Jeremy and Joe and Charlie . . . I walked along behind the aunts and Philippe. I smelled the slightly sour musty smell of age, of cells disintegrating, and I listened to the stories of Le Comte de This and Le Marquis de That. These men looked miserable, all brown eyes, hooked noses, and disappointed mouths. "Is your father there?" I asked.

Philippe shot me a furious look. "No," he said and there was silence.

I'd made a mistake again. I must not probe: what was past in this house stays in the past. Poor Madame Rose, I thought. I wondered what was said that expelled her forever from this place, leaving only some notes from the piano somewhere in the universe.

We turned and slowly shuffled the other way towards the grand door. After much draping and shaking of hands, Philippe kissed them both on their wrinkled damson cheeks and they were gone. "Ah," he said. *"C'est ça.* That's a relief. Let's go and have another cup of coffee."

Chapter 70

For three months we were very happy. At times Philippe grew irritable, but I knew how to handle those occasions. Once, when we were discussing politics, he lost his temper and asked why I thought women had any business talking politics at all. "My father," I said, "always talked politics with me."

"Your father?" he shouted.

I could tell by the anger in his face that he was going to throw something at me. I watched his right hand tense, and then the motion to throw, and I ducked. The cup went sailing over my shoulder and, after hitting the wall, fell on the ground. "You'll have to get more practice," I said and smiled.

The storm over, Philippe was contrite. "I'm sorry," he said in my bed that night. "I am really sorry. You are so good for me, Mary. With other women I have a horrible temper, but with you I can contain myself." He slept as I held him inside me and hoped he was right.

Hopefully, I thought, looking at the high riding moon, hopefully one day I will learn where all the pain in this man is stored away and then help him unpack it like an old Gladstone bag. Somewhere in a high attic in this house must be the reason why this man was so unhappy.

Now Philippe was either happy and smiling, full of tricks and laughter, or he sat looking out of a window with his eyes like dead oysters. Too many cares, too many responsibilities. Dark owls hooted commands and he was unable to brush them off. But now I was there and willing to help.

Six months later my father telephoned to tell me that my grandfather had died suddenly in the night. My father's usually calm voice was choking. "At least, Pumpkin, he died in his sleep with absolutely no pain. Your grandmother had gone downstairs to fill his hot water bottle, and when she came back up he looked at her and . . ." My father's voice was shaken by sobs. "He said, 'I love you, Caroline. I'll always love you.' And then he died." I, too, was crying by now.

I put the phone down and went to find Philippe. "So, it is sad, *ma chère,*" he said. "How old was your grandfather?"

"He was eighty-three, I think."

"Well then, he must die sometime, mustn't he?"

"Philippe, I loved him very much."

"Of course. Of course. But still you can't mind that he dies. It is only nature."

"I do," I said. I was weeping. We were in a large conservatory where Philippe had one of his many desks. He sat behind it looking at me. "Philippe, I must go to the funeral. All my family will be there."

"What about me?" I heard the warning petulant tone of his voice. He hated me to leave the house, even to go to the village.

"I'll just be two days, and I'll be back."

"Your dead grandfather means more to you than I do?"

"You can come with me, Philippe. The family would be so pleased to meet you."

"I don't want to go to some family graveside. I hate

funerals. No. You can't go. You must stay here. Send a wreath."

Our eyes crossed swords and in the clash I realized that if I disobeyed him, something dreadful would happen to me. Madame Rose must have disobeyed him. I stood my ground and I warned him in my mind that we both knew this was a step back for me, but his feeling of triumph must be tinged with the knowledge that I could always go. So far I had made no attempt to have my house sold in Macau or to ask for my belongings. All I owned were the two dark blue suitcases . . . I lost the ground and stepped back. "All right," I said. "I'll call my mother. I hope she understands."

"No, I *don't* understand," said my mother. "What do you mean you can't come for the funeral?"

"Philippe needs me here." I felt foolish.

"For what?" my mother demanded.

"Well, he's very busy and he needs my help and . . ."

"Mary, your place is with us at this funeral. Your grandparents may not have accepted me, but I shall be there. If you choose to live with this man, that's your business, but you must come home now. We'll meet you at the airport in Paris this evening."

"I can't be there, Mother. I really can't." By now Philippe was behind me with a small triumphant grin on his face. I knew that smile. It was perverse. It arrived when he'd caused conflict. I felt embattled between my mother's anger and his promised fury.

There was an arid silence. Then my mother said, "You're a coward, Mary . . ."

I put the phone down. I didn't want to hear any more. I knew my mother's litanies by heart. But she was right. I was a coward. No man would ever issue orders to my beautiful brilliant jet-jewelled mother. A warning cloud in her eyes, the twitch of a muscle in her cheek, and everyone fell silent. Well, I didn't have any of those qualities. "I just . . ." I started to explain to Philippe.

"Don't worry," he said, giving me a hurried hug. "We can go out to dinner tonight. You have to meet some of my friends. You'll like them. It will take you out of yourself. You need cheering up, locked up with Bluebeard here. Come along. Rush up and change and I'll book. We can go shopping first and then to the restaurant."

I turned without smiling and walked upstairs. So many arguments meant so much *le shopping.* I had never met his friends and doubted they would be much different from his crowd in Macau. I missed our life in Macau. We were lovers then, not quarrellers. Now we quarrelled too much, I as little as possible, but Philippe almost daily. As I changed my clothes and beheld myself in the mirror I realized I'd lost weight. My body was thin and my face strained. What was I doing to myself? Or was he doing it to me?

We went shopping and I came to own yet another pair of earrings and a ridiculously high heeled pair of shoes. Philippe liked high heeled shoes. I didn't, but I tottered obediently into the restaurant, my body clothed in elegant black and my soul in dull grief and despair. My family would now be across the Channel and on their way to Milton Park, my grandparents' (no, now only my grandmother's) house. I was here in this fashionable restaurant reserved for the very rich. We sat on plump banquettes and two other couples arrived. "This is Yvette Samour," Philippe said, bowing low over her hand and kissing it at length. "This is Juno." He shook Juno's hand and then greeted the remaining couple, Maria and Ramon.

We all found our seats at the table and Philippe gave a little laugh. "We are here to cheer up poor Mary.

Her grandfather died last night and I won't let her go to the funeral. Such wretched affairs, funerals."

Yvette looked at me sympathetically. "I am sorry," she said, but then they all began to talk with great financial speculation of *l'héritage*. Ramon, it appeared, did well when his grandfather died and he was awaiting his next fortune when his father died. I was glad they were talking so fast and so furiously. I couldn't be there with my grandmother, but I sat and prayed for her. My mother had shaken my newly built bridges with her. Maybe the answer was to retract the drawbridge and get on with my own life. After all, that was what these people were doing. They were unattached. They had no sentimental ties to anything or anyone. Even each other.

I knew this because before we left Philippe said these people were in and out of each other's beds all the time. "What harm," he mused philosophically, "does a little love do?" He called it love . . .

I looked at him severely. "A lot of harm," I said. "More than you imagine."

"Oh, *ne t'en fait pas.* Don't worry," he said. "I am the faithful type. Not like them. And besides, think of the germs." Philippe hated germs.

I drank a lot of wine. I knew Philippe would want to make love, and for the first time in our relationship sex was the last thing I wanted. I realized, as I lay across the bed in my black slip and my high heeled shoes, that I would have wanted to make love to Philippe if he was capable of loving me and comforting me. Sex for Philippe now had very little room for love. What was happening now was lust. Now, after nearly two years since I'd first lived with him, Philippe could not orgasm easily. I could, and this made him angry. More and more he needed to rely on high heeled shoes, and erotic underwear. And once he tried a vibrator. "For you," he had said. I had laughed and then saw the fury in his eyes. "No, Philippe," I said. "I'm not into that sort of thing." He shoved the object into me and twisted it. I screamed from the pain of it and he ejaculated.

Tonight that cloaked memory came back. Somehow, as he labored and I lay passively, those memories flapped back like lost crows. A year ago the bad memories were few and easily forgiven; now too many and all too awful. He came and rolled off me. Tonight he was going off to his room, a room I'd never seen. In the beginning I had been curious, but I prided myself on giving Philippe the secrecy he so needed. Saturday, he said—the day of my grandfather's funeral—we were going to a party at Ramon's house. "It is a magnificent house," he said, "and they have a lovely pool." He grinned a smile I did not like. When he smiled like that I knew I was to be tested and when he tested me I usually failed.

❦ *Chapter 71* ❦

The rest of the week Philippe was very kind and very loving. Here lay the vortex of the confusion. While he was loving and warm, we shared jokes, silly little childish jokes. We were in my bed when I asked him why I could never see his bedroom. "Because," he said, "I can't sleep with anyone else in my bed. Anyway, I need my private place, somewhere I can go and be alone."

"Even alone from me?"

"Yes." His eyes clouded over.

We had just finished breakfast. I put the tray on the side table next to my bed. "Isn't this wonderful?" I said and I stretched.

Philippe rolled over facing me. "It is. Our life together is perfect. Promise me, Mary, you'll never leave me." I was surprised. There was a tone of supplication in his voice I had never heard before. "I don't know what I'd do without you."

"Philippe," I said. "What on earth is this all about?"

He put his arms around me and hugged me closely. "I've never loved a woman like I've loved you." I could feel the flame burning between us. His legs began to tremble as mine did, the thick impatient moment of desire rising unquenchable. Only Philippe had the capacity to arouse and satiate me, and I was lost, rocked in the depth of the ocean and eternity. We lay moistly clinging together, two orphans alone in this great house.

Philippe was now solely responsible for all the bills and the duties that went with managing a huge vineyard. No wonder he was unable to let me go to my grandfather's funeral and it was kind of him to buy so many white gardenias for my grandfather. I knew nothing would make up for my betrayal of the family, but then they did not know or understand Philippe. Only I understood him. As he lay sleeping lightly in my arms, I thought about this man I loved so much. Reimer was never frightening. He roared and he lived like a lion. Patrick, so simple and kind, was dull. But Philippe was a gadfly. He liked to sting and to hurt. He always teased me. "Pouf," he said. "You're so bourgeois."

"What's wrong with that?" I replied wounded.

"Perversity is the spice of life. Without it everything is flat and boring. A little sin on the side makes confession an event." Philippe's family were old Catholics. "I try to make the priest laugh. He laughs with envy every time I confess. That is, of course, before I met you." I believed him. I knew he lied over little things, but I believed he was faithful to me.

Soon hopefully we would get back to the subject of marriage. When we were in Macau we talked of it often. Perhaps, I thought, I should suggest to Philippe that we go off and find a cottage to rent for a week or so. There we could do normal things together. There I could do the shopping. We could choose thick loamy potatoes, a recently plucked chicken, yellow with sinewy legs from running wild and tasting of the fresh grain and the grit it had pecked from the French farm soil. I could wash Philippe's socks and his underwear in the sink. It had been so long since I had done anything for myself, I felt out of touch with the world. In Philippe's world one lived on a very rare kind of oxygen. I did not even have the duties my mother had. Philippe arranged everything, including the menu, with his housekeeper. All the staff were aged. They had been here before his father died. They knew him and adored him. I was merely a decoration, and sometimes when they looked at me I felt they thought of me as a flower—not a very glamorous flower; one that would wilt and be thrown out to be replaced by another. Perhaps if we could find the easy times we had in Macau in my house, we could recapture some of the untarnished times together.

When he awoke and I explained my plan, he made a face. "I've never seen a plucked chicken," he said. "I don't know if I'd want to. I'm really not good at roughing it, you know. Maybe if we take a hamper or two and you can feed me by a fire lying on one of our bearskins . . ."

"Or two?" I said hopefully.

"We will see," he said. "Now I must go out. I'll be back this evening."

The days were long and by now I was very bored. The gardeners did not want me in the gardens. It was a hot summer. The house was dark and cool and I wandered about the rooms dreaming of our lives together, dreaming of our babies, dreaming of the time I would be his wife, not his mistress, wondering if I should do a little more sewing or maybe a little painting. I had recently read the whole of Trollope again and was now rereading the Brontes. What terrible brooding lives they lived, cut off on the moors in the clutches of their incestuous and alcoholic brother. Poor girls, I thought. Poor, poor girls . . .

I came to a corridor I had not yet explored. How exciting, I thought. The house was full of wonderful things. Maybe a Titian painting? No, today I was in the mood to find a gentle Dutch painting, a woman seated with a little girl at her side, the tiles under their feet warm from the sunshine. I walked past several doors to the end. One door was slightly ajar and I pushed it open. It was as if I had opened Pandora's box.

This must be Philippe's bedroom. I felt dreadful. This was not at all as I imagined Philippe's bedroom to look like. I had always thought of his bedroom as a lair. But in truth Philippe, my sybaritic Philippe, slept on a little white iron cot. His bedcover was red and white checked cloth. On the bed lay a teddy bear. Beside the cot was a small chest of drawers. On the other side of the room stood an old fashioned commode. A white jug sat in a large white basin and then there was the chair. Small for a man, it must have belonged to him in childhood. The chair was hand carved, very carefully and lovingly carved. The seat was of straw, slightly scuffed from the years of giving seat to Philippe. My heart nearly burst with pity. Here was the child in Philippe. At the end of each day, the hurt little one crept away from the grown-up world and slept the sleep of the innocent.

I fled down the corridor and promised myself that

this would have to be another secret from Philippe. This must join the knowledge that I shared with young Lotti about Madame Rose. What had she done for her to disappear? I did not know, but I was going to love and to care for this strange man.

On Friday Philippe announced that he had made an appointment for me at the hairdressers. "I have decided," he said in that infant bullying way he had, "you need a haircut."

"Oh no, Philippe. Please. I dislike my hair enough as it is. It just grows. Besides, I hate hairdressers. They smell awful and all those women . . ."

He put his hand up. "Please, *chérie*, do it for me." I remembered the little bed and I gave in.

By five-thirty that night I had lost most of my hair. "A cap cut," the lady said. *"Très chic."* I had to admit I rather liked the cut. My hair sat close to my face. My eyes looked a lot bigger and I smiled.

"You look marvelous," Philippe said when I returned.

That night we made love again and again. I did not know it was possible to create electricity that could burn and sear and tear. At the moment of orgasm Philippe hit me, hard on my thigh. It was too late to protest. I could not stop the moment, but to my horror the orgasm became a convulsion. The pain and the pleasure entwined and then I exploded out past the edge of the abyss, out past the line known to mortal men and women and far away from what was normal and loving. "Why did you do that?" I asked.

Philippe lay back and grinned. "To show you," he said. "You read books all the time, but you do not practice what you read, you little goose. There are all kinds of pleasure."

"Not for me," I said. "Don't ever do that again."

"Ah, Mary," he said, rolling over. "You're so boring."

He fell asleep and I lay with my eyes wide open. Most of all I felt disgusted with myself. It was pleasure but of a different kind. I had read the sad books of the Marquis de Sade. I knew most of what there was to know about the brilliant genius Oscar Wilde. I had been through a stage of loving the strange dark drawings of Aubrey Beardsley. I had toyed with the dark side of myself, but I put that side of myself very firmly away. Françoise, my dark self, had gone. Tonight she had returned with a sensual smile on her face. Strange to see my mirror image. Strange for her to look at the tears that trickled down my face. "You silly little fool," she said contemptuously. "You stupid idiot. He will never change."

"Go away," I replied. "I won't listen to you."

"Yes, you will," she hissed. "You know it's hopeless, but you're too stubborn to admit it. *Mary, Mary, quite contrary, how does your garden grow?*" she chanted. "Well, you don't have a garden any more. It's ruined."

I groaned. She was right. What had been lovely lawns and tall trees, blossoming heavy with the fruits of hope and desire, now hung broken. The lawn was yellow, not just from the summer sun but from despair. I now knew evil. Maybe that's what evil was: the Devil takes a delight and then transforms it into ecstasy and even deeper pleasure. Into the innocence of love comes lust. Not a lust for natural desire outpoured at the touch of the one you love. This lust reached out across a chasm and as you reached out the chasm got deeper and darker. There were two roads. Both of them straight. One was clear and uncluttered. There were objects on the way but the path was bright. The other was dark and dangerous. There were pitfalls. I reminded myself of Captain

Moses. His face was clearly before me and behind him in the moonlight rode the *Fat Shan*. "You can choose," his voice boomed. "Only you can choose." I nodded and fell deeper into the sleep towards which I already had dreamily drifted.

❧ *Chapter 72* ❧

I sometimes wondered if each new day for Philippe began with the history of yesterday wiped clean. On Saturday, the day of Ramon's party he was animated. "Now," he said at breakfast, "I want you to wear something magnificently *chic*. You are meeting my real friends tonight and I don't want you to let me down." I nodded, still feeling ashamed and disgusted with myself. My head felt naked. My short hair made my nose look larger and I felt unfeminine. But I said nothing. "Whatever you do, don't be a silly goose and embarrass yourself. This is a sophisticated party. People are coming from Paris and London. I don't think you will have been to one of these parties before."

"The French Ambassador's parties were pretty huge."

Philippe laughed. "He won't be at this sort of party. This is *haute monde*, the very rich at play."

I looked at him. "I won't have to do anything I don't want to, will I?"

"No, of course not," he said. "Just enjoy yourself."

I decided that the only way I was going to enjoy this event was to pretend I was a Kodak camera, perhaps my first camera, a little Brownie that pulled out in the front. I would take pictures of what was happening with my eyes and then throw away the roll. It was not like Philippe to issue warnings, so I went feeling like

a small brown skinny calf, a rejected calf not worth sac-
rificing.

We arrived at yet another château with streams of
cars behind us. Our car was taken by a liveried footman, and we were ushered into the vast hall. Our
names bellowed, and I, embarrassed by the fact that
we were not *Monsieur et* Madame *de Lacroix*, arrived at
the reception line blushing. So far so good. An orchestra played and there were fifty or so tables with settings for six each. This was nothing I had not seen before.

However, as I looked about, I realized that many of
the people present were men dressed as women, and
several very masculine women stood talking. Although there were on occasion transvestites at our
parties, this was different. At our parties there was a
polite hum of people talking. Here people didn't seem
to be talking; they were shrieking at each other.

"Bottoms off, bottoms up!" the man next to me
said. I stared at him. I didn't quite know what to say.
"Rotten sport," he muttered and he moved off. I had
lost Philippe. He was gliding about the room like a fish
made out of silver. I stood back against the wall and
watched. *Click*, a picture: a woman (I think) wearing
a dress that allowed her nipples to be seen and a slash
in her dress that meant she was virtually naked. *Click:*
a man dancing in a kilt. A big handsome man. He
twirled and the kilt lifted so his bare buttocks could
be seen. His partner raised his eyebrows. I see, I
thought. *Bottoms up . . .* or whatever had been said. I
looked for someone to talk to, but I saw no one ap-
proachable.

Gradually, as more alcohol was consumed, the party
got rowdier still. After dinner we moved outside and
my heart sank. Of course I'd heard of swimming pool
orgies. Geneviève had been to them as a teenager. Occasionally one heard of them from the girls at Mont

St Sebastian, but I had never imagined it happened amongst adults.

"Are you all right, darling?" Philippe came flashing back for a moment. He smiled. His teeth were white, his eyes electric, but not with love for me. I could see that. He dashed off and I saw him move again among the crowd. He was not going to take his clothes off, was he? Yes, he was. He stood, my naked lover, among all the others who had drinks in their hands, chatting in the huge shallow pool that had been built on the side of the house. Part of the pool jutted out into the dark. As I stood, I saw Philippe talking to a girl with red hair. She, too, had the *chic* look he had made me adopt and they swam slowly out into the night. I stood with my glass in my hands and felt the vessels of my heart tear and break. Blood oozed and clotted in my veins. Iced water dripped behind my eyes and then I knew, as a woman who loves a man knows, that Philippe had not been faithful. Once a man and a woman have shared carnal knowledge of each other, there is a sensual bond that is visible to others. The way they swam together mimicked the way they made love.

I stood with my glass in my hand and I resolved to chat to anyone at all. What I said made no sense to me, but it was the mindless chatter I had learned from my mother. I wished I were my mother. She would have made a scene, stormed and shrieked, ruined the party, made whichever swain she was punishing pale with fear. But this was just me, Mary. I thanked her though for her teaching me such self-control.

I will give him one more try, one more chance, I thought. Just one more. That was my pact with God. If we go away for a few days, maybe I can talk to him, explain that I can't live like this. Certainly not among those people. I would ask him if he had been faithful. And I would ask him about Madame Rose. We could not live with this wall of secrets between us any longer.

Chapter 73

"You were very good last night," Philippe said as we surfaced for lunch.

I had a hangover from far too many brandy Alexanders. I felt white and washed out. "Well," I began, "fair is fair. I went to your party, now I want us to go away for a week on our own."

Philippe made a face. "A whole week?"

"Yes, I need a week away from all this. You don't understand, Philippe. I need to do things for myself. To cook . . ."

"You can cook in the kitchen. Just tell the chef."

"Don't be silly, Philippe. Your chef won't let anybody in his kitchen, not even you."

Philippe laughed. "But he is the best in France."

"I know, but I want to cook for you and look after you. That's what wives . . ." And I stopped. But of course: I was not his wife.

"All right. I will telephone Juno. They have a cottage on the edge of the forest of Fontainebleau. You will like it there. Very small, but pretty. But what shall I do all day? We will have to make love all the time. Otherwise I shall be bored and I *hate* being bored."

Bored he was. We had been in the little cottage for exactly fifteen minutes before he was striding up and down the low-ceilinged sitting room. "We have to do something," he said. "I can't sit still."

"We will walk to the market." I had had the chauffeur drive us to the cottage because I didn't want Philippe zooming off and leaving me for days on end.

"I don't walk," he said. "I never walk."

"Well I do. And we are doing something for my sake this week." I had a big shopping basket on my arm and I set out, if needs be, alone.

"Oh, all right," he grumbled and we walked along the forest road. The end of summer lay before us. Just the tip of autumn showed, but only if you looked carefully at the leaves. A little curl, a slight roll, as they prepared to release their grip on the trees and fall to the ground and crumble to dust. We walked and soon saw the edge of a village. The shops were bright and clean and I loved bargaining. Soon I had my chicken, its dead eyes turned up in horror. Must have been strangled, I thought. Usually they cut off the head. "Ugh." Philippe was not impressed. "I shan't eat it," he insisted like a fussy child.

I piled the basket full of cream and butter. We chose a bottle of *Les Amoureux* and we smiled at each other but Philippe smiled uneasily. Walking around a village, surrounded by villagers who didn't know him, who didn't recognize him and make obeisances, made him nervous. I was in my element. This reminded me of the days I had visited Mademoiselle and Jacques when I was a little girl: the freedom of the road and the shops, the smell of tightly plaited garlands of garlic and onions, the exuberant sight of fresh green peppers, red peppers, and tomatoes. How I loved tomatoes! We walked back slowly and Philippe was very quiet.

That night we did indeed make love. I had brought the bearskin with me. I loved the feel of the fur against my naked skin. I had not lost my fear of Philippe, so I was unable to relax, but I put on a very good performance and was pleased to see him fall asleep, although alone in the second bedroom of the cottage.

During the next days we played cards in the evening and we listened to the radio. Philippe was not happy. He was like a tightly wired spring and I knew no way of helping him uncoil. "What is it?" I said on Thursday night. "We are going home on Sunday. Do you want to go now?"

"No," he said belligerently. "I said I would stay a week, and I'll stay a week."

"We don't have to stay," I said. "I just felt that we needed a few days on our own. Without other people around. I like getting up for breakfast without clothes, without feeling that other people might see us." We were sitting after dinner in front of a small fire. I felt unsure about what I was going to say, but it had to be said. "Philippe," I said. "There is something I want to ask you?"

"What?" His short tone made my question all the more uneasy.

"Have you had affairs while we have been together?" He stared at me and a warning light flickered in his eyes, but I realized that I could not live, or go on living, with Philippe's warning signals. After nearly three years I was trapped like a car in a never-ending traffic light. Green, you can go. Amber, watch out. And red, rage. Then green and tranquil again. "You see, I know a Madame Rose lived at the house before . . ." There was a loud explosion in my head.

I, for a moment, did not know where I was or what had happened. Perhaps the lights had gone out. Perhaps . . . I put my hand up to my nose. I didn't have a handkerchief and my nose was running. The liquid was wet and slippery. Then I opened one eye with difficulty. The other would not open. Philippe, still in the same chair, looked at me. "You hit me," I said. I stood up and walked unsteadily across the sitting room to the bathroom.

"You've been spying!" he screamed.

"No. I haven't." I shook my head. "I tried, Philippe. I really tried. But this is the end." I spoke to the empty air. Philippe had gone and with him went any possibility of our loving each other again.

I lived through the next few days drugged with pain. My face was black and the bruises dripped in yellow stains down to my chin. By Sunday, with makeup, I looked better. Dark glasses hid the black eye.

Where would I go and what would I do? My first thought was that I could not and would not go back to my mother. I felt too raw with pain. Phoebe would be my refuge. Dear Phoebe. I telephoned her. I felt reassured hearing her voice. And Philippe knew nothing of Phoebe, so he would not find me hiding in Chantilly. "Of course you can stay," Phoebe said comfortingly. "Stay as long as you want. That ass Hattie is off with some fellow. What's the matter? You sound awful."

"Philippe hit me, Phoebe." I was close to tears and the car was due. I was going to get the chauffeur to drop me in Paris and then I would disappear. Thank goodness I still had all my things stored. The clothes and the jewelry Philippe had bought for me I would leave. To go back to L'Hermitage to pack would risk seeing Philippe again, and he was a drug I could not afford. Like a heroin-addict must run from his pusher, so I must run from Philippe.

"Are you there?" Phoebe said.

"Yes, I'm here."

"Well, stop dreaming and get here. Anyway, Mary, think of it as falling off a horse. It hurts for a while, then you get up and do it again."

"I'm not getting up and doing it again," I said, crying. "Never."

"I'll see you tonight."

I collected my few things from the cottage and I left the bear rug on the floor in front of the empty grate.

The car arrived and the chauffeur looked at me and my still-bruised face. Another story for the servants. Only they had other stories—other than mine—to tell.

"It's your choice and your destiny, remember," Captain Moses had said.

"I know," I answered. "I know."

 Chapter 74

Philippe's chauffeur dropped me in Paris at the Gare du Nord where I sat for a while on a bench watching people go by. Old people. One very old couple with stringbags full of fresh produce were obviously coming to visit a child in the great city. They had the air of country peasants. The man's blue serge suit was old and frayed at the cuffs. His large scuffed brown leather belt just about contained his stomach, a snug protrusion. The wife had a face like a quince due for picking. She was little and round and reminded me of my grandmother. Both the man and the woman chattered. They must have lived and loved each other for a long time. He carried the bags and she her leather handbag. How I envied them their lives.

Then two lovers passed by, entwined in a characteristically Gallic fashion. No English couple would be seen in such a convoluted embrace. They scurried crab-like across the station, their mouths pressed together. Then there were single people, but all busy, all rushing to something or somewhere.

I sat. I had nowhere of my own to go to. Phoebe waited for me in Chantilly, but I was afraid of being a burden in her busy horse-filled life. I sat cold and lonely and twenty-two years old with nothing to show for those years except a badly broken heart. I felt as if I'd been in a dreadful car accident. At least an ambulance would have come and taken me to a hospital where kind people would have taken care of me.

Friends would visit with flowers and soft whispers. But a broken heart is an embarrassment to other people, particularly your friends who don't endlessly want to hear the details.

I saw a public telephone and an overpowering urge to ring Philippe came over me. What was it about Philippe that made me act as if I were another person? I remembered something I had been taught in my literature class by Madame Rosen, she of the limping leg and haunted eyes. She said that a person in a novel, as in life, never acts out of character, but I knew now that her dictum was not true, at least not in real life. Now, and all the time I was with Philippe, I did often act out of character.

I approached the phone kiosk as if I suffered some mind-destroying curse. Maybe Philippe was my albatross, forever tied to my neck, as I walked the world recounting our dreadful relationship. The pain and the degradation made me realize how accurate the ancient mariner portrayed those of us who were betrayed or abandoned . . . "Monsieur is away. He says to tell his friends he has gone to the Caribbean."

"Where in the Caribbean?" my painfilled heart asked breathlessly.

"To the Tiara Beach Hotel on the Brac."

In character, I thought. This was like Philippe, to take off to the Caribbean and to hide on some beautiful remote island. He knew the islands well. I imagined him sitting at the bar of the hotel, his hair sleek and his smile polished, looking at the women with that lazy look of his. Hotels were anonymous places for sex with itinerant women and I had to realize that was how Philippe wanted his life. Emotionally he was no adventurer like Reimer. Emotionally Philippe was a gypsy, but a dangerous one. The only person who could perhaps cope with Philippe would be another gypsy.

How close I felt to simply walking under the incom-

ing trains. I stood afraid, with my small weekend suitcase in my hand, and I felt again compelled to walk
towards the trains as they came into the station hissing
and panting. I was standing beside the train to Mar-
seille looking at the bright shining rails. One moment
and everything would be over. No pain, no one to
blame me for what I had done. Oblivion . . .

Captain Moses's ever-present face rose up and he
shook his head. "Coward," he said and I knew he was
right. Whatever my destiny, I could not choose this
way out. Abort the difficult experiment of life and you
deny God.

I decided to take a taxi and go back to the church
where I years ago had first knelt beside Patrick, where
we had promised to each other our undying adolescent love, where it had all gone so badly wrong.

Safe inside the little sanctuary I knelt before the Virgin Mary and begged her forgiveness. As a woman she
must understand another woman. She must have
faced scorn and anger when her friends found her
pregnant. Joseph married her, but she knew what it
was to feel an outcast. I felt an outcast. Tomorrow the
world would go round Philippe's friends that I was
gone, and within a month I would be a mere half-
memory. I cried in front of the altar. I cried for myself.
For the day that Patrick and I young and innocent had
whispered vows in the church. I cried for my dead
grandfather whom I had betrayed. And I cried because
I couldn't go home to my mother.

I stayed until the stained glass windows grew darker.
I was alone in the church, until a man came in, knelt
down, and then was driven away by my sobbing. I
heard him behind me nervously shuffling towards the
door. I even drove strangers away. I dimly remembered the prayer, the *De Profundis*. "Out of the depths
have I cried unto thee, O Lord." Hear my prayer! The
depths were unimaginably deep places. I felt I was

drowning and I knew I had to get to Phoebe. Dear, kind, sensible Phoebe in whose house I would be safe from myself, in whose arms I could be held and some of the limitless pain I felt would be assuaged.

I took a taxi for the long journey to Chantilly. I had money in the bank and in my purse. I had spent little enough of my inheritance when I lived with Philippe. I had left behind me a king's ransom in jewelry and clothes, in presents from Philippe.

"Are you all right, Madame?" the taxi driver asked in some concern.

"No, not really," I said.

He looked at me in the driving mirror. His black sharp taxi-driver eyes dredged my face and caught the fading bruises on my cheek. "*Alors,*" he said. "*Le boyfriend.* Tsk tsk tsk." He shook his head. "How they can hit a woman?" He was talking to himself, keeping himself company. I was probably his last fare and he was pleased because it was a good one. Tonight he would tell his wife about me and my face. Nevertheless, the fact that he even noticed and was sorry for me was a type of balm.

Soon the countryside flattened out and the lights of Chantilly could be seen. I was nearly at Phoebe's, as near home as I, being homeless, could get.

⤳ *Chapter 75* ⤶

I was comforted to see once again Phoebe's house, or rather her shooting lodge. The lodge stood in green fields and all around it I could hear the sounds of horses. The air was fragrant with the smell not only of the horses but also of hay and muck. The taxi deposited me and left. "*Bonne chance,*" the driver said as he drove away. How at that moment I would like to have been that taxi driver! How I would have enjoyed his simple unencumbered life. Death and taxes were his worries and that gave him something to grumble about. I knocked on the door and there was Phoebe.

She hadn't changed at all. She was wearing jodhpurs and a roll-necked sweater. I threw myself into her arms and began to cry all over again. "Really, Mary," Phoebe said, hauling me into her sitting room. "All this noise over a man."

"It's not just a man," I wept. "It's Philippe."

"Well, he's a Frenchman, and you know they make dreadful husbands. Why couldn't you just have been content to have an affair with him like Hattie does? She has a perfectly deadly lover at the moment, related to the Sarawak of Borneo, or somebody like that. Awfully rich, but quite deadly. Hattie keeps him under control though."

"I can't keep anyone under control," I wailed. "Oh, Phoebe, I'm a dreadful failure."

"No, you're not, dear," she said. "You're just silly and rather weak. You let . . ." I took off my dark glasses. Phoebe saw my bruises and was aghast. "How could you let him, *anyone,* do this to you? I'd have killed him."

"You don't understand," I said. "I was too frightened of him to fight back."

"Where is the little bastard?" I'd never seen Phoebe so angry. "I'll go and teach him not to hit women." She was rummaging around looking for a riding crop. "I'll whip him until he's senseless."

"Oh, Phoebe, you won't find him," I said, half-laughing and half-hysterical. "He's on a Caribbean island."

Phoebe snorted. "No doubt carrying on with some other little innocent. Really, Mary, you shouldn't have let him get away with this. Why didn't you clobber him with a frying pan?"

"You don't understand," I repeated. "I was afraid of Philippe, especially towards the end. He became so omnipotent, so powerful. I felt helpless and weak and afraid." I was crying again. I knew Phoebe loved me and cared for me, but I also knew she could never understand. Only women who had been in relationships like mine could understand. The fear, the sweating paralyzing fear, that those men could hold over their women. Even now I did not feel safe. It wasn't safe to feel safe. That thought would mean nothing to Phoebe. She lived her rock solid life, full of good relationships. Except for fighting off Jeremy's constant admirers, she lived calmly and happily. I didn't. My life was up and down, like the *Fat Shan* in a storm, only she rolled with the waves. I just sank to the bottom and sat surrounded with seaweed and dead promises.

"You are to stop crying," Phoebe ordered, "and go and get changed for dinner. Come on," she said with a comforting softness, but reassuring firmness, in her voice. "You'll feel better for it." She marched me up to a small room filled with flowers. "I picked them for you, you fool," she said gruffly.

"Thank you, Phoebe. You're so kind."

Phoebe hugged me. "Well, someone's got to look after you, you chump."

My excursion into the high life had left me drowned. If that was how they lived—on the thin line between self-affirming joyous life and the base rasp of the saw, the howl of the torrential wind, and the faces of satyrs—I would leave them alone.

I turned my face away from that world and I changed into my only frock. Tomorrow I must go out and buy some clothes. Tomorrow was another day.

Downstairs, Jeremy was sweetly pleased to see me. "Made an ass of yourself?" he said with typical Irish tact.

"Yes," I smiled and controlled the tears. "I did. An awful ass of myself."

"Have a drink," Jeremy said. "I always find a swig of booze and the pain eases, two and it's gone, three and I've forgotten her."

"Maybe you've forgotten, but the girl certainly hasn't," Phoebe interjected. "I have to deal with her." She turned to me. "They're always called Margaritte, or something beginning with *M* and I get them all mixed up. Really, Jeremy, you will have to settle down. We'll get run out of Chantilly by farmers and shotguns."

Jeremy grinned. "No, we won't. I stay away from those. Married women are a better bet."

"You're impossible."

"I know," said Jeremy with quiet satisfaction. "And I intend to stay that way."

"Don't you ever worry about the pain you cause the women you leave?" I, who was so recently pained, enquired.

Jeremy shrugged his shoulders. "I don't know any women who are faithful to their husbands any more. Seems to have gone out of fashion. At one time it was the men who were out tomcatting. Now, with all these new ideas, you have no idea how pushy women are. Wanting to pay for their own meals . . . As for offering a woman a seat, good heavens! I've stopped all that kind of stuff. If they want to open their own doors, jolly good for them!"

"Will you ever marry, Jeremy?"

Jeremy sighed. "I don't know, Mary. Sometimes I see a sweet young face at the races and I think I might, but she would have to be eighteen or so and really know how to look after me. After all, Phoebe knows me and my ways. Why change anything? These days a man can have anything he wants for free."

"Except love," I said. My voice was bitter.

"True enough, Mary," Jeremy said, "but, really, I didn't mean to be so serious. Maybe the French taste for philosophizing is contagious."

"Look where love got me."

"Don't cry over dinner," Phoebe snapped with persistent firmness. "Didn't they teach you anything at Mont St Sebastian? *Noblesse oblige?* So go ahead and oblige me by forgetting that dreadful little Frog. Stick to Englishmen."

"Or rich princes." Hattie walked into the dining room, immediately lightening up the atmosphere. "Dear, dear, Mary," she said and she crouched down by my chair. "You poor little sparrow. Did he give you a rough time?" I nodded. "Oh dear, you should have told me about it earlier and we could have poisoned him. I have a perfect poison for horrid men. One swig and they're gone. You see," she said earnestly, moving around to her seat at the table. "There is a particular fungus which produces a wonderful poison. Not much taste, but very deadly. Aflatoxin, it's called. Not a trace left behind, and there you are: problem solved."

"We are not going to talk about that rat anymore," Phoebe said. "Death is too good for him. Leave him in the good Lord's hands and something unspeakable will happen. I shall pray for it."

"You can't do that, Phoebe." I was horrified.

"Oh yes I can," she replied, speaking with all the strong Celtic assurance that I years before had heard in her mother's voice. "Hattie might have dibs on African fungi, but I pray. The last man that annoyed me ended up drowned on holiday. Imagine that! Fortunately, the good Lord takes care of His people. 'Vengeance is mine,' said the Lord and He meant it. So leave it up to Him." That thought comforted me.

We finished the meal and I realized I was tired, very tired. "Do you think you will ever get married, Hattie?" I asked.

Hattie wrinkled her nose. "I don't know," she said. "It's difficult for me to find anybody as marvelous as my father. Only a little more open-minded. He was an amazing, wise, and wonderful man. I hope someday I'll find a man like him. And it obviously wasn't meant to be old African Richard, whom, I'm pleased to announce, I feel completely recovered from. I really don't know."

I nodded. "There must be something in between dreadfully violent exciting men and nice ordinary boring men. There must be," I said.

"If there is," Hattie said, "I haven't found him yet."

There must be, I said to myself as I climbed the stairs, because my father is one. He was never boring. I went to sleep crying because I thought of my father as a *was*, in the past tense—because I was cut off from my parents by my own doing.

Phoebe's answer to sorrow was work. I diligently followed her prescribed regime. I put the following few weeks into good use. I went to Paris and bought myself some clothes. Now I was with horses, I bought jodhpurs and riding clothes. I bought grand dresses for the races and ball gowns for the parties after. I knew I would be seen by the Paris élite and that word would filter to Philippe. He would know that I had survived. Not only that I had survived, but that I was happy and dancing. No longer with him, but with others. The days dragged by, and I tried.

After the first two months I could get through the day without thinking of him. I raked stalls and mucked out the horses. I got up in the morning at dawn and galloped away my shameful desire for Philippe's body. There was no physical relief from that tormented desire. I tossed and turned in my bed, remembering the inside of his thighs, the back of his neck, the curve of his foot that he loved to have kissed. Work and only work helped. Work until I fell into bed too exhausted to cry.

Then there were the days at the races. Coming to know the horses individually, it was exciting to watch them race and win. I got caught up in the excitement, but my cheating eyes never ceased to scan the racing crowd. I danced at the balls, but I imagined I was in his arms. Does one die of such love? Maybe not.

I telephoned Kim in Macau when Phoebe was out. I could afford the call and I had to know. It was one of those awful, awful days when the compulsion to go back was at its worst. Kim's voice was faint and far away. "Good heavens!" she said. "I've just answered your letter. How psychic!"

"Have you seen Philippe?" I asked.

"Yes, he was here briefly. He's gone back to his island. He says it's the last paradise and he's buying property."

"Was he with anyone?" I tried so hard to keep my voice steady.

"No, not really," Kim said. "He said you two were over."

I sighed a long sigh that stretched over France and across the seas to Macau. "I told Captain Moses," Kim said, "about you. He was asking."

"What did he say?"

"He said it was something you had to do and to learn from it."

"I learned," I said bitterly. "I learned a hell of a lot." Then I pulled myself together. "What's happening to you, Kim?"

"I've just written to tell you I'm engaged to be married. You'll love him. He's in business in Hong Kong."

"Oh, Kim! How marvelous!" Kim, of all people! Still, I couldn't deny her her happiness. I congratulated her.

"I do hope you can come to the wedding."

"I hope so, too." But I knew I never would. Why not leave the *Fat Shan* where she was: Captain Moses and Jo Jo ferrying across the China Sea, my bad memories laid forever to rest.

By now it was autumn and I had begun to love the mood and the rhythm of the day: riding horses in the morning, then the cleaning of the stables with the stable boys (a clutch of young hopeful jockeys); then lunch; a leisurely nap; and then friends round or a night out in the local restaurants which were excellent. I was known by now to the other residents of Chantilly and several men were asking to take me out. I went, but not because I cared for any of them. I wanted to go to the best and most expensive restaurants so that word was bound to reach him. I also attended the most exclusive parties, particularly at the Jockey Club where he had been a member.

I danced and I dined . . . And then my father telephoned.

His voice was weak and shaken. My mother had had a stroke. My father was with her at St Thomas's Hospital in London. They needed me. "The thing is, Mary, I have to go to Carlton House every day," he explained. "Your mother won't let anyone else touch her. You know how proud she is. She can't speak . . ." My father broke off for a moment while he collected himself. "If you could be here during the day, I can sleep beside her on the cot for the nights."

I stood stunned. My mother was indomitable, invincible. But no, my mother needed me.

I ran to find Phoebe. "I am so sorry," Phoebe said, "but your mother will be all right. She's young and strong. You hurry and get packed and I'll drive you to the airport."

❧ Book Three ❧

Chapter 76

The telephone call ended everything that had been my life. Even Philippe faded into the distance of time. My mother was dying, so my father said. I did not believe him until the moment I walked into her room at the hospital. Her eyes still shone with a fierce eagle light. Indeed that was how she looked: a frail body that could not move, but still indomitable. I took her hand in mine and was horrified at the little talon that lay in my healthy grasp.

The hospital psychologist was American, an easy-going tall Texan. I was prepared to dislike him, but he was sure about my mother and gentle with her. He talked to her as he would have had she been able to answer. "Talk to her all the time," he told me and my stricken father. "Treat her as if she were not ill." All this sensitive psychology sounded strange in his soft Texan drawl. I could tell my mother liked him (her immobile body seemed to relax in his presence) and I was prepared to tolerate him for her sake.

I was angry. How could anything happen to my mother? She was, I now realized, my rock, my focus and my anchor. I could never be indifferent to her. In the intensity and the passion lay possession. I was possessed by my need for her and her approval, and now she lay dumb.

In the weeks that followed the stroke, I was there every day. I washed her and nursed her and gradually I came to realize her strength. Never ever did she even admit, by the shadow of a gesture, that she was ill. She lay in the bed and she looked as if she were merely resting between social engagements. I did her long hair every morning and I made up her face. The face that took her hours to prepare was now in my hands and I didn't let her down.

The psychologist visited her at ten o'clock every morning and she awaited his arrival like a young bride. He teased her and I knew she was laughing, although there were no signs on her mask of a face. I knew, because as the weeks went by, I became intensely sensitive to her needs and I saw her eyes shine.

My father came to the hospital every night. He had aged dreadfully and was thin and tired, but he never failed to stay the night with her. He lay in a roll-away bed and then left for Carlton Terrace in the morning, wearing his business suit and his bowler hat and carrying his umbrella. No one would have guessed that he spent the night in a hospital. That, I realized, was the secret my family kept. *Noblesse oblige.* At first, in early years, I had resented that phrase. I thought it was old-fashioned and snobbish, but now I learned what it meant. "Grace under pressure," Hemingway had said for all America to learn. I felt more French than anything else, but for me it was my father and mother who taught me that discipline—an inner discipline carrying them through life's vicissitudes with valor—was obligatory. I, who bucked and rebelled against all their dicta, could now see the discipline at work.

Above all I felt a tenderness for my mother that had been latent all my life. The tables were turned and I cared for her. Her eyes followed me as I moved around the room. "Your mother," the psychologist said on a coffee break when he came upon me in the lobby, "is a truly remarkable woman."

"I know," I said and I meant it.

"I want to see you with your father this evening. I'll be in my office at six o'clock."

I nodded. Another progress report, another uplifting talk to the possibilities, and my father's face would ease and his shoulders straighten.

That, however, was not the case. "I am sending your mother home, but I think a trip to Paris would be too much for her. What's your situation here in London?"

"We've rented a flat in Chelsea," my father said without emotion, as if sticking to facts would help him hide from what he was afraid to hear. "I've some work to do here with the chaps at Carlton Terrace, so there is the flat. Mary's already settled into one of the bedrooms, and there are enough rooms for Lavinia to have her own . . ."

"I'm sure that will be fine," the psychologist smiled. Then he sat back in his chair and folded his hands. "We had a case conference today." The psychologist was firm but kind. "We looked at her test results. I'm afraid it's not good news. She has survived the stroke, but it was a very serious one. Considerable damage. It could well lead to further damage." He looked seriously at me. "The early days are vital as indicators of recovery." He turned his eyes to my father. "She is not making the progress we hoped she would. To be absolutely honest with you, Mr Freeland, your wife has battled bravely, but . . . She was a wonderful woman." That dreadful word *was,* the *was.* I saw my father cringe. She was going to die. They did not hope for her and they were sending her home.

I wanted to scream in protest, but the neat well-ordered office kept me under control. I was angry with this man. Who was he to play God? What had Texas got to do with London? Why was he here telling us these things? Well, we would take her home and I personally would see that she didn't die. I would take care of her and one day she would be back on her feet, back in Paris standing at the head of the stairs, patronizing Madame Derlanger, and by then I would have done something to make her proud of me. If I saved her life that should be good enough. "All right," I said abruptly. "We will take her home."

As we left the office, the psychologist said almost shyly, "May I visit her once a week? I have become very fond of her, you see." He cleared his throat. "I know it's unusual, but she's a very special person."

I forgave him his intrusion because I knew my mother liked him. "All right," I said. "I'll telephone you when it is convenient for us."

"Thank you," he said and I left.

Chapter 77

I learned how quickly the world can shrink when illness is at its center. Until my mother moved into the flat in Chelsea, I had hardly noticed any of its features. It had been a place for me to collapse exhausted after another day by my mother's side in the hospital. Nothing more. With my father sleeping every night at the hospital, I had remained in the flat for a few oblivious hours, alone and unconscious.

Once my mother arrived by ambulance and was carried up the stairs and to her room on a stretcher, the flat became my entire universe. It was a flat like many others between Chelsea's Kings Road and the River Thames. Mercifully the flat was at the end of its road, so at least from the windows I could catch sight of the reassuring river.

The flat was typical of governmental anonymity. Its furniture, a few Victorian armchairs among mostly Edwardian dark-stained relics, showed no distinct character or history. Many Foreign Office officials, temporarily home from abroad, had stayed in this flat, and many more would after we had gone on. The spine of the flat was its corridor, dark and all but untouched by sunlight. At one end the sitting room overlooked the street. Then the corridor retreated past the kitchen and bathroom and on to the three bedrooms. The bedrooms were neither generously large nor cosily small, their ceilings neither high nor low. They were functional: simply rooms to house bodies. Overall, the flat was not decrepit, nor was it in good repair. It had old flowered wallpaper, but this was beginning to peel in some uppermost corners. It had wooden floors, but these needed fresh polish. It had a few generic oriental carpets, but their colors were dull, their fringes knotted, and some of their patterns worn down to crossthreads. The kitchen's gas cooker and electric refrigerator were chipped and antiquated. The bathroom's taps, like an old man's nose, threatened to drip. These were not the beds to which exuberant freshly married couples would rush to make love. This was not the bathtub in which one could lie, with Mozart playing on the radio, and luxuriate beneath scented bubbles of oil from Paris, a fluted glass of champagne in one hand and a fully ripe peach in the other. The flat was indifferent to the senses, and this was as it should be, for ours was a house of illness.

The irony would have been too great and too cruel if my stricken mother had been brought to lie among a bright and exotic loft, a cache of living plants and spicy treasures from far-off worlds. But, I could not stop myself from wondering, maybe more sensuously and sensually appealing surroundings would have been inspiring for the wilting soul to revive itself.

As it was, what the flat had most of was silence. Not

the silence of the healing, but the silence of the moribund.

My time became regular and unchanging. My time
was spent with my mother. I washed her, changed her,
made up her face, brushed her hair. I tended to her
bed, rolling my mother onto one side and then the
other to put down fresh sheets. I held my mother's
shoulders up with one arm while with my free hand
I plumped her feather pillows. Though she was
speechless, her throat still worked. Her lips had lost
the gift of expression. Chewing was for her next to impossible. But she could swallow. I prepared her food
to be swallowed easily. I made soups for her and ran
the chunks through a blender. As a treat, I cut up solid
foods for her, infinitely small so that she would not
choke. I fed her with a spoon, half teaspoonfuls at a
time. I wiped the corners of her mouth between swallows.

Her eyes were still my mother's eyes. Looking into
them, I could see that my mother's mind had lost none
of its discernment, none of its ability to think, nor its
capacity to watch me and weigh me. In the eyes' scru-
tiny of me as I moved about my mother's room, did
her mind weigh me and find me lacking?

Talk to her, the psychologist had instructed. Talk to
her about what? I honestly did not know what to say.
Days became weeks and my routine afforded me no
exciting events to recount. What can one say of a monotony that promises no certain end? After several
weeks, I found myself—I'm sure I didn't mean to—
talking to my mother as a cheery nurse talks to a patient. "How are you feeling today? Here, let's sit up"
(I slipped my arm beneath her shoulders) "while I fix
your pillows. Better? Here. Here's some nice soup.
Not too much now. All right, one more spoonful and
there's the bowl finished."

My father came home every evening from his work.
He would enter my mother's room first, hold her hand

and kiss her on the top of her head. "Hello, Lavinia." Then he walked up the corridor and sat, while I cooked. I cooked for him and for myself in the kitchen. Real food, though it seemed tasteless, before I cut up the pieces to feed my mother. "How was she today?" my father would ask.

"A little stronger, I think," I would answer on some days, but not really meaning it. Her state remained constant from one day to the next. My father and I sat at the small dining table mostly in silence. Silence can become a power, a force that prides itself in its obstinate will and actively defies violation by its foe, sound.

After our family dinner, my father would take up his chair beside my mother's bed and, obeying the habit of many years together, tell her of his day. "Some trouble over in Kenya. The chaps are quite alarmed." He talked in general terms about declassified information. I, sitting in an armchair against the wall, listened and tried to be interested. Sometimes I would say, "Oh really?" and ask a question. My father eagerly answered my questions with longer explanations than necessary, simply relieved to have the chance to converse.

Then, when he too had run out of things to say, he'd suggest, "Shall we hear some news?" I would walk up the corridor and turn on the radio in the sitting room loud enough to be heard from the bedroom. Radio news seemed granted a dispensation by Silence to enter the flat. It was only a burbled monotone, as sounds went, no real threat to the siege that Silence had placed on us. Music, of course, was a different matter. The flat had a phonograph, but my father never played a record. Somehow the true sounds of Beethoven or Haydn or Byrd understood that they were forbidden to enter Silence's kingdom.

My father, not really listening to the radio, would read his newspaper. From time to time he'd make a noise. He'd laugh out loud and lay the newspaper across the bed as if for my mother to read. "Why, look at that! Old Little's been made a knight. Good heavens. I'd never have imagined! You remember Little. Not a bad old stick."

After a few hours my mother's eyes would shut. Every now and then she'd let out a muffled snore. I cherished those snores, for they were the only sounds to be heard from her lips. My father would fold his newspaper, stand up, kiss my mother's head again, kiss me on the cheek. "Good night, Pumpkin." I would sit back down in my chair. I heard the sounds of his shoes walking up the wooden planks of the corridor. The bathroom door shut and I could hear the taps running as my father washed his face and brushed his teeth. The door would open, the light snapped off with a *click,* and my father went to his room, shutting the door behind him, for a lonely night's sleep. When I was sure my mother was safely and deeply asleep, I'd walk to my own room and lie down, waiting to escape the silence of the day into the silent but blissfully unaware emptiness of sleep.

In the mornings my father and I got up before my mother awoke. This was strange. Never could I remember waking before my mother. During her life (no, I must not say that; she was still alive) during her health, she required very little sleep and was always awake early, bustling through the Paris house and eager to get on with the day's social events. Now my mother slept late in the mornings.

My father would wash, shave, dress, and come to the kitchen where I had hot coffee waiting for him. He hadn't the appetite, he explained, for a breakfast.

Mornings are, by nature, expectant times. Fresh sunlight comes in through kitchen windows around the world and promises a new and interesting day. In the mornings in the flat, I could not help but feel a sort of habitual exhilaration with each day. My father looked fresh, all ready for work, and he smelled of life, the clean smell of a man in the morning. But nothing, I knew, would happen during either of our days. He drank his coffee quickly, wiped his mouth with the corner of his napkin, and rose.

In the mornings my father and I hugged before he left the flat. He held me in his arms and squeezed solace and fatherly reassurance into me. It was not his way to say anything, but through his hugs he conveyed many feelings: worry, hopelessness, but a comforting love nonetheless. Pulling away from our embrace, he would smile and say, "See you this evening, Pumpkin." The door would shut behind him and I'd be left to sit by my mother, waiting for her to wake up, wondering whether or not she would.

Eventually I, like my mother, came to look forward to Monday afternoons. That was when James (the American psychologist. He had a name, I found out. James. James Robertson) visited.

After feeding my mother her lunch on Monday, I'd change her into a particularly pretty blue flowered night-dress. I painted her face with extra care, applying the rouge and the lipstick only lightly, just enough to give her pale skin color, as if natural. I brushed her hair—still miraculously lustrous and alive—and gathered it in her special silver clasp. Then the doorbell would ring. Always the doorbell. He never knocked. And the high-pitched ringing of the bell, like a lark singing out over a desert, promised brightness and joy.

I opened the door and in would come James with his blessedly loud voice. "Hello, Mary. Nice to see you." James was a big man. His hair was the color of shiny polished walnut wood and his eyes were a warm brown. His wide shoulders looked anathema to the London suits they were squeezed into. We walked down the hall together while, in whispers, I'd ask if I could expect any change in my mother's condition and give brief reports as to how she remained the same. James would turn the corner, his hand behind his back, and greet my mother with a broad sincere smile. "Mrs. Freeland! I brought you a little something!" And taking his hand from his back he'd reveal, like a magician, a bouquet of flowers or a box of chocolates. (My mother loved the chocolates. After James had left, I'd cut them into tiny pieces, heat them slightly over the stove to make them soft, and feed them to my mother. She shut her eyes in ecstasy as each piece slid down her throat.) Ignoring the straight-backed chair beside the bed, James would boldly sit right on the bed next to my mother. He held her hand strongly and confidently, not with the shy timidity that both my father and I automatically seemed to use as if her hand might break. "Glad to get away from the hospital," he'd bellow at my mother. "Hospitals can be awfully depressing places, you know," he announced, radiating friendship and happiness. "No, I look forward to my chance to sneak off and spend some time with my two favorite ladies, Lavinia and Mary Freeland." I swear I saw a delighted blush rise through the rouge on my mother's cheeks.

Then, never at a loss for words, James would talk. He talked about Texas, where he was raised, about his uncle's cattle ranch, about the time his horse reared after being spooked by a rattlesnake. Never once did my mother drift into a doze while James sat on her bed telling us his stories. And the stories made me laugh. It was hard for me to believe, but suddenly I would laugh and, as if guiltily, realize what I'd just done.

Inevitably James would have to leave towards the end of Monday afternoon. I think both my mother and I felt sad at his going. I saw him to the door. "I'm worried about you, Mary," he'd say seriously before he left. "You'll go crazy if you stay cooped up too long. Do you ever get the chance to go out?"

"On the weekends, when my father's home, I pop

out to the shops to buy food." Then I said, as if to prove my diligence, "but I'm never gone for long. Not more than half an hour at the most."

"I know it's hard, Mary. But you have to give yourself a break sometimes. There's only so much you can do."

I had no reply. I'd shake his hand at the door and say goodbye until next week. Then I'd walk back to my mother's room and sit in my armchair, my mother and I both quietly holding on to the afterglow of James's warm presence.

One day in the middle of a week I thought I would go mad with boredom and loneliness. I sat in the sitting room and stared at the unused telephone. I stood up, walked on tiptoe to my mother's room: she was asleep. I left her door an inch ajar and padded back to the sitting room, stealthily closing the door. I dialled. "Aunt Mary? This is Mary." I hardly spoke above a whisper.

"Mary! Where are you? You sound so close! And I 'aven't 'eard from you in such a long time."

I explained that I was in London. Choosing my words with care, I told her that my mother had had a stroke and was not recovering. We were living in a flat in Chelsea . . .

Aunt Mary was immediately upset. "Lavinia? When, Mary? When did this 'appen? Nobody tells me nothing." I could hear her flustering with fear and distress. "Lavinia? Your mum? When? 'ow long ago?"

"What month is it now?" I said, shaking my head. "I honestly don't know. Oh, Aunt Mary, it's dreadful." I started to cry. Weeks and months of hidden agony burst out of me. I told my aunt all I could, about my mother, about looking after her, about day after day of her neither living nor dying.

"My poor child," Aunt Mary consoled, her voice growing softer. "Well, there's no doubt about it. You must come and see me. Someone's got to look after you for a change."

"I can't. I can't get away that long. Ealing feels awfully far away, and I'm afraid. Why don't you come and visit here? I'd love to see you, Aunt Mary. And I think it would mean a lot to my mother."

There was a long silence on the other end. "You think that, do you?" Aunt Mary's voice was strange, wary. "I don't know, Mary. I don't know."

"But you must, Aunt Mary. Please."

"It's been years since I've seen your mum, Mary. And it may be better for 'er to count me as past. I mean, I don't want to upset 'er, what with 'er state and all."

"I really think . . ." I began.

"I won't promise nuffing. Maybe I should send some flowers . . ." She paused as if she was holding herself back from becoming uncontrollably upset. "I won't promise nuffing. Look after yourself, Mary." And she put the telephone down in haste.

It was a Saturday and my father was home for the weekend. "I'm just going out to buy some food," I said to my father. "Back in a minute."

"Mary," my father said, stopping me from leaving. "Wait. I know how hard you've worked. I think you deserve some time to yourself. Don't rush to come back. Why don't you have lunch out? Go for a walk. Go to the Tate. Do something for yourself. It will be all right. I'll be here to look after your mother. You don't have to worry. Please, Mary. I think you need it."

"Thank you," I said to him and walked out through the door of the flat. *How can I explain to him?* I thought as I descended the stairs to the street. How could I tell him of my guilt? I walked up to Kings Road and towards the shops.

I walked past the shops. No, I told myself. I won't

go straight back. I'll do what my father said. Lunch, of course, was out of the question. It would keep me from my mother for too long. But I would take myself for a walk, to a flower nursery up the Kings Road to buy something alive and growing. I moved through a Saturday crowd of people on the Kings Road and felt myself invisible, as if I wafted through them in a different dimension. Had I made a point of standing right in front of one of them, I half expected they would walk right through me. I felt like a ghost.

By the time I reached the nursery I was almost overwhelmed by guilt. It was not simply that I felt I should be always at my mother's side. It was not only that I was afraid she might die in my absence. It was a deeper, older guilt. Somehow, I felt, I was the cause of my mother's stroke, of her illness, and of her possible death. I, in my life, had hurt her. Thinking back I had hit her once. When I was twelve. Where did I hit her? Was it in the head? I had struck my mother. Now she was dying. Was it my fault? I remembered with relief that I had hit her across the chest.

I walked through the nursery and picked out a tray of half a dozen young tomato plants, the small green beginnings of tomatoes on several of their stems. I could put them on the little balcony outside the kitchen window and I could help something grow. I paid the cashier for the plants and left the nursery. But I still felt guilt, guilt that my mother and I had not been better friends.

I wanted to run back to the flat, to apologize. But I could not. I had to do the food-shopping first. But I would set things right. I would quell my guilt. I renewed the vow I had whispered while my mother was still in hospital: I would not let my mother die. I had my duty. I alone would keep her alive. My ministrations, my apologies, would restore her.

Quickly I selected and paid for our food. I walked up the street towards the river, towards the flat, my arms weighed down with shopping and tomato plants, my head full of resolve. I had my duty. I would speak to my mother and explain. No longer would I treat her with cheery professional disregard like some impatient nurse condescending to an immobilized patient; I would talk to her and explain. I would find my moment to set things right.

"Mother," I began. It was mid-morning Sunday. My father, I could see at breakfast was restive. I told him that everything would be fine if he wanted to go out for a while. He sat quietly while he ate his breakfast without any appetite. Then he said, "I think, if it's all right with you, I'll go to church." I was glad. I was glad that someone would pray in church for my mother, for our family. I was glad my father would be going out. I was glad, for once, to be left in the lonely flat alone with my mother. "Mother," I said again. I sat not on the chair but on the bed, as James had done. I held her hand not weakly, but strongly as if holding the hand of an able-bodied mother. "Mother, I'd like to talk with you."

Her silent eyes looked into my own. With no choice, she waited.

I hardly know how I started or what my first words were, but once my mouth began to speak, out came a deluge. I explained. I confessed my sins. I told her how awkward and misfitting I felt as a child. I told her how much I thought I loved Patrick. And then we married and I tried so hard to make it work. I really did. I tried to fit in with his friends and his bank and with everything in Hong Kong, but I just couldn't. I failed as a wife. And I tried to be a mother. I tried to have a baby, but I failed at that too. I found myself crying. "That should have been your grandchild," I sobbed, still holding her hand. "But I got it all wrong."

I told her of leaving Patrick and meeting Philippe and hoping that he was the one person in the world meant for me. "But in the end I couldn't be like him or his friends either." I wiped my eyes with my hand and, as an automatic gesture, pushed my hair back over my forehead. But my hair still had not grown to any womanly length since Philippe had had it cut short. I laughed out loud at myself. "You've probably been wondering about my hair, why it's so short. I know it looks terrible. But Philippe didn't like long hair, so it was all cut off. And I did so much love having long hair. Never mind. It will grow back one day." My mother's eyes continued to stare.

"He hit me, you know," I said, as an explanation. Again the tears pressed. "Only once. That's when I left him.

"So you see, Mother," I finally said, feeling that my eyes were empty of tears and my lungs scorched dry by my weeping, "I can't blame you for not loving me. I've been a dreadful daughter to you, absolutely dreadful. And I'm sorry." I shook my head and was silent.

I felt stupid. What could my speechless mother say in response? Had she even heard me? Then my hand clutching hers seemed to be squeezed. A slight tightening, so small that I could not decide whether it was my mother's effort or simply the movement of my own hand. Perhaps it was only my imagination. But I wanted to believe that my mother had squeezed my hand as an answer. Yes, she understood. Yes, she forgave me and loved me.

Tired and spent, I leaned beside my mother. I raised my legs above her bedcoverings and settled them next to her own. I held her hand still and lowered my shoulder until I lay, like a child, facing her. A small child being comforted by a loving mother. Was my mother glad to have me beside her? I couldn't tell. But she shut her eyes when I looked at her, and I too closed my eyes. I lay for many minutes listening to the soft steady in and out of her breathing.

Some time later I arose and saw that my mother was asleep. Quietly I took my hand from hers and left her room, walking towards my own. I could not say for certain, but I felt it was quite possible that while I lay beside my mother I too had slept, the rest of the absolved.

❦ *Chapter 78* ❦

A Saturday or so later, I was getting ready to be taken out by James Robertson. James, during his afternoon visit on the Monday before, had all but insisted that, unless I gave myself some time of my own, I would end up collapsed in a useless heap of exhaustion. "And that wouldn't be good for you or for your mother. The best thing you can do for both of you is to take a day off. Everyone needs a day off, Mary." He had said this in front of my mother, a wise and clever move on his part. James turned towards my mother for a response. Her eyes remained steady. "There, you see?" James said with good cheer. "Your mother wants it for you, too. It's all set then. I'll pick you up on Saturday and you can show me around London." I felt excited by the idea but also slightly railroaded by James and my mother. How was it, I wondered, that my mother from her bed of silence still managed to orchestrate my life? When I held the door of the flat open for James to go, I asked, "Is this the way you treat all your patients? Taking them around London on the weekends?" "For therapeutic reasons only," James laughed. "Of course."

As I prepared, I organized my thoughts with the same care that I had picked out which dress to wear, which shoes and belt to go with it, and which light makeup to apply to my face. My father was home for the day. I did not, I told myself, have any call to feel guilty for leaving my mother in good hands. Perhaps I'd been too diligent, obsessively diligent, in my self-imposed confinement within the limited walls of the flat. And I promised myself I would not let my still lingering twinges of accustomed guilt ruin my afternoon with James.

James, announced, as always, by the bright ringing of the flat's bell, arrived as always with a bouquet of flowers in his hand. "How thoughtful," I said, and turned to take them to my mother.

James put his hand on my shoulder. "Mary, these are for you." He smiled.

I could tell I was blushing. How funny, I thought. I felt as if I were going on what I had heard Americans call an old-fashioned "date." There was something wonderfully innocent and exciting about it all.

I could not say that I had entertained any thoughts about James. Why should I? I didn't know him that well yet. But by the kindness in his eyes I could see that he expected nothing other than a pleasant few hours together and the hope of beginning a friendship. No demands past that. Such a relief. "They're lovely, James," I said, feeling safe and relaxed and innocent, "I'll just say goodbye to my parents and we'll be off."

In my mother's room I put the flowers in the vase by my mother's bed. "James brought these for me and I'd like to give them to you." I said this, absent of competition or envy or any of the other convoluted emotions which the presence of a man had, in past years, stirred up between my mother and myself. I kissed her lightly on the forehead and turned to my father. He kissed my cheek and smiled. "Enjoy yourself, Pumpkin."

"Where would you like to go?" I asked as we walked by each other's side up the Kings Road.

James laughed. "Harrods," he said. "Like any good American in London."

"Oh, James, you've been in London for some years now. Surely you must've gone to Harrods hundreds of times."

"Never once. Oh, I was so busy finishing my studies and getting my job set up at the hospital, then working, I just haven't had the time. Besides, I know all Americans are expected to make immediate pilgrimages to Harrods, so maybe that's one reason why I've shied away so far. But I think it could be fun."

We took a taxi to Knightsbridge and entered the magical kingdom of Harrods. James walked through delighted and enchanted. We had fun. Together. *Fun* had never been a word with which I've felt particularly comfortable. It had always seemed to have two meanings. One appeared puerile: the thought of adults whirling about funfair amusement rides with sticky spun sugar stuck to their faces. Even as a child I had never enjoyed what adults assumed all children should enjoy as fun, although certainly other children around me often did like the *fun* activities provided for them by adults at birthday parties and village fêtes. I, instead, had always preferred solitude and books. Then there was the other kind of fun, what Françoise my other self had considered to be the only kind of fun, what the *chic élite* called fun, meaning revelling in the freakish, the unconventional. I had had more than my portion of such fun with Philippe and had learned all too painfully that the aftermath of this sort of fun was the queasiness of decadence.

With James *fun* came to mean something innocent and simply enjoyable, no shadowy premonitions of dangerous corruptions to follow. Side by side we walked through the different departments in the palatial splendours of Harrods. In the men's department, James amused me by trying on the garments of different kinds of English men. English clothes did not seem made for James. He looked preposterous in a bowler hat and I laughed. His frame was physically too big and too muscular to look at home in the restraint of a country tweed overcoat. But he did find something that suited him perfectly, a loose white woven Irish sweater with a round collar. He pulled the sweater over his head, messing up his walnut hair in the process, but not bothering to smooth it down with his hands, and looked in the mirror approvingly. "Yes," he grinned. "This ought to get me through next winter. Feels good. Roomy. Not too loose, not too tight . . ."

"And will you buy it?" I asked.

"You like the way it looks?" He looked at me with a smile in the mirror.

"Very much," I smiled back.

"Sure," he said simply. "I'll take it."

Life's decisions—even the little ones, like buying a sweater—were refreshingly uncomplicated for James.

In the ladies fur department I spent the better part of half an hour trying on minks and silver foxes and chinchillas I would never be able to afford. But James was enjoying himself, carefully considering how I looked in each coat or stole. "I think I like that one best," he said judiciously, like a buyer in a Paris fashion house, when I twirled in an elegant floor length mink. Its collar brushed wonderfully against my cheek.

I let out a laughing sigh. "Oh, maybe someday."

"Maybe," James laughed with me.

I did a turn and looked at myself in the three-sided mirror. The woman in the mirror looked like a woman whom I would have called beautiful. I looked again and I looked beautiful. For the very first time in my life I *felt* beautiful.

We had lunch in the Food Hall. It's impossible to remember what we talked about, we were so busy going from food counter to food counter trying a mouthful here and a mouthful there of delicacies from all over the world.

After lunch we continued our unhurried ramble through the many halls and departments. "It's funny," I said, without really meaning to bring up the subject, "I remember coming to Harrods with my mother. It was like a Royal visitation. All the salespeople in every department came up to her full of 'Hello, ma'am' and 'Nice to see you again, ma'am,' and 'Perhaps I could show you something from our new collection, ma'am.' They all seemed to love being able to serve her."

"I'm sure lots of people feel that way about your mother," James said.

"I suppose so."

"You know, Mary. It's all right to feel good things about your mother. There are too many people who never let themselves think anything good about their parents until after they're dead, and then it seems too late . . ."

"What are you saying?" Inexplicably, I suddenly felt myself cross with James, as if he was trying to manipulate my emotions. "Is this what you do with your psychology? Go around and share the benefit of your good advice with people whether they ask for it or not? Is that what made you a psychologist in the first place, so that you could tell people all sorts of things and they can never say anything back to you?"

"No, that's not why." James was calm. "You want to know why I went into psychology? I'll tell you. When I was in college I got hold of a book by an American philosopher named Henry David Thoreau. He's the man who said the famous saying, 'The mass of men lead lives of quiet desperation.' But when I actually read that line for myself—I'd heard it said enough times—I realized that most people read the line all wrong. They quote, 'All men lead lives of quiet desperation.' But that's not what Thoreau said. There's a big difference between saying *all men* and saying *the mass of men.* Do you see what I mean? I mean, *all men* means that there's no choice about it. Everybody has to live that way. But if you say *the mass of men,* then that means there are other people who *don't* live desperate lives. See?"

"I'm listening," I said.

"So I started studying psychology, because it seemed to me that we're all originally meant to live happily. God made us to live happily." I realized, as he spoke, that it had been a very long time since anyone had spoken to me, or I to anyone, of God. It was reassuring to hear James speak of God in a natural, unselfconscious way. God came naturally to James. "But," James continued, "most people don't. Why not? Because things happen to them in life, usually when they're very young, to twist life for them, to make everything unhappy and painful and complicated. But it really doesn't have to be that way. And I guess I saw psychology, and still do see it like this, as a way of sorting out all the crap that each of us has gone through so we can be happy again." He stopped. "Do you see what I'm trying to say?"

I said nothing. We walked past a department that sold antiques. In one display case I saw a collection of Russian silver. I thought of the former Russian aristocracy who, before the Revolution, owned such treasures as their ordinary housewares. I was reminded of the beautiful silver hairbrush and hand mirror which my mother gave me for my wedding. They had belonged to her mother, her Russian princess of a mother, now lost in the secrecy and the distance of a far-off land, a far-off time. I still cherished the hairbrush and mirror . . . I turned from the case and walked out of the antiques department.

James and I walked in silence through many more halls. Then we found ourselves in the pet department. We walked along the tanks of fishes and perches of parrots and cages of kittens and puppies and I smiled.

Such sweet creatures, so small and hopeful and innocent. I heard a sound, a familiar sound, the sound of
a fast wheezing breath, a snuffling through a short-
ened nose. I followed the sound to the next cage and
there saw the quivering excited pink tongue beneath
the stacatto sniffles of the nose. The Pekingese puppy
wagged its tiny tail at me. From the ball of fur that was
its body, two delicate paws climbed the bars of the
cage towards me and the eyes stared at me, full of
laughter. "Taiwan," I said. Suddenly I was back in the
sitting room in South Africa, my mother arriving home
from another shopping expedition, this time with a
present for me: a Pekingese puppy whom I had named
Taiwan.

James stood beside me. "I used to have a puppy that
could be this puppy's twin," I said. And I told him
about Taiwan, what a friend he had been to me in Africa—given to me, I felt, as a conciliatory offering from
my mother—what an ally in Paris. And then, while I
was away, my mother had him put down because he'd
messed the carpet. She'd got my father to tell me over
the telephone, leaving me to mourn alone miles away.
Couldn't she at least have waited for me to get home
before sending him to sleep? The ache of it all came
back to me fresh as I explained to James. "At times
she was cruel to me, you know," I said, lowering my
eyes and my voice. "It hurt. But I think we have forgiven each other."

James was silent for a moment, continuing to look
at the puppy who seemed interested only in enticing
our fingers through the bars so that he'd have someone to play with. "I believe you," he said at length.
"Hurts are nothing to build your life around. They'll
always be there. They'll always hurt. Still, I think
there's a way to leave the hurts where they are and
walk away from them and get on with your own life."

I looked at him. I did understand what he said and
for the first time I began to have a vision of living my

own life, not being dependent on my mother, or Patrick, or Philippe, or the next man to come into my life.

James looked back into my eyes. Then he laughed
suddenly. "Now you stay here a minute and play with
he puppy. I'll be right back." He walked away.

"Where are you going?"

"Play with the puppy!" he called over his shoulder.

I played with the puppy through the bars. The
puppy liked me, I could tell. Already he was doing his
standing-on-the-head dance for me. And I liked the
puppy.

In an instant James was back with a young girl who
wore a Harrods uniform. She started unlocking the
cage. "Oh, James!" I said. "You can't! I mean, really."

"Why not?"

"Look, James. Really. Thank you for the thought.
But I can't get another Pekingese. I mean, wouldn't
it be wrong to try to recreate what happened years
ago?"

"Who said anything about recreate?"

"It's a bit obvious, isn't it?"

"Mary," James sighed. "You like Pekingeses. Pekingeses like you. You're living like a prisoner in a
gloomy flat with your mother to look after and your
worried father at night. Don't get me wrong, you do
a champion job. But why not allow yourself another
little friend to keep yourself company during the
days?"

"James, it isn't as simple as that and you know it."

He laughed loudly. "You should have been the psychologist, you know. You analyze everything to death.
The trick is knowing when to stop. I got myself a
sweater today, and I'm getting you a puppy. Neither
of us leaves Harrods empty-handed. And now you've
got a new friend. Why not leave it at that?"

"Simple as that? Why not?"

"Simple as that," James said as the Harrods girl put
the puppy into my arms. "Why not?"

We stood outside the street door to the building containing my family's flat. "I enjoyed that, James. Thank you very much."

"Me, too, Mary." He smiled and looked at me out of the corner of his eye. "And did you manage to make it through the whole day without feeling guilty for not being home?"

"Mostly," I laughed. "Well, just a little maybe." I shook my head but smiled. "No, not really."

"You're getting there," he smiled. "Thanks for a great day. I'll see you soon, Mary." He turned and walked off up the street.

I climbed the stairs inside the building. I had to admit, I hadn't felt all that guilty. And I had had a good time. I caught myself beginning to feel guilty about not having felt guilty. I laughed at myself. I thought about James. I really had enjoyed his company for the day. I could tell I was beginning to feel for him a very deep affection—not needy like I'd felt towards Patrick, not passionately obsessed like I'd felt with Philippe—just a comfortable calm affection. I could learn to care about this man. And he seemed capable of caring about me . . . It felt good to have James as a friend, and I felt he would be a genuine friend.

My father was on his way out of the kitchen, a cup of tea in his hand, and walking back to my mother's bedroom when I turned the key and let myself into the flat. "Ah! A puppy!" he cried out at once, seeing what I held in my arms. "Lovely thing, Pumpkin. That should keep you company. What are you going to call him—her? Him?"

"Him," I said, "and I haven't decided."

"Looks just like your other one," my father said. "Taiwan, was it? Then there you are: Taiwan the Second. Taiwan II, eh?"

"All right," I laughed. "Taiwan II."

"Good," my father said with satisfaction. "Come and show your little friend to your mother. She'll be entertained."

"Do you think it's a good idea?" I asked. Old fears grabbed me, like cold wrinkled clawed fingers, by the back of the neck. The past could not be annihilated.

"Come. Come," my father said, proceeding down the hall. "She'll love it."

"Look, Mother," I said warily, "I've got a puppy. Daddy's named him Taiwan II." I held the dog and wondered if I'd said something wrong. This is a different dog, I reminded myself. A little friend to keep me company. *Why not?* as James had said. Why not? Boldly—resolutely pushing away the shadows of the past—I placed the puppy on the foot of my mother's bed. Immediately Taiwan II began his Chinese dancing, rubbing his small head against the side of my mother's blanketed unmovable foot. I waited for a response from my mother. Of course she could not smile or scowl. But it *felt*—as if she silently could convey her reactions and emotions by emitting invisible radio signals—that my mother did not mind the dog's presence on her bed. She lowered her eyes to where the puppy was and I could see her eyes follow Taiwan II's carefree gyrations. "And this one," I dared to say, but without rancour, without any hidden or sharp edges in my voice, "won't mess the carpet. Promise."

I sat in my armchair and watched Taiwan II roll about my mother's feet, my father chuckling with delight. As I watched I felt a queer and unfamiliar exhilaration not unlike the excitement of a newfound freedom.

Chapter 79

I'm not sure which day of the week it was, for the days of the week had come to fold their separate edges over each other, like a collapsed telescope, into a solid mess of unchanging routine and apprehension. Then the telephone rang. My father was at his office and my mother was resting in her bed. I half-jumped at the loudness of the telephone's bell. I could not recall the telephone in the flat to have rung before. Warily, as if expecting bad news, I answered. "Hello?"

It was my grandmother telephoning from Somerset. Immediately I felt reassured simply to hear my grandmother's familiar safe voice. "I've spoken to Peter several times from his office about your mother. How is she?"

"Not much to say, really," I said. "Not much change. The same every day, though I've been reading to her lately. Some E. F. Benson. And she does seem to enjoy that."

"And how are you, Mary?" I could hear genuine concern.

"Very well, thank you," I said, speaking with a reflexive, impersonal, polite rote learned over many years of Foreign Office stiff-upper-lip training. Then I remembered it was my grandmother I was talking to. "Actually, maybe not all that well." And, having admitted even partially to the anguish I was in, I found myself suddenly wanting to cry.

"Mary," my grandmother said quickly. Perhaps she heard a change in my tone and, in obedience to her own code of keeping a tight rein on emotions, was helping me to hold on to mine. "Mary, I'm coming up to London next week. I'll come and visit you." She paused. "And Lavinia. I shan't stay for very long. You know how busy life in the country is. We've another baking contest coming up, and I'll be hard at work preparing my entry. But it will be lovely to see my grand-daughter."

I felt comforted to hear myself called granddaughter. I was still my grandmother's granddaughter and she still loved me. "It will be lovely to see you, Grandma. I'll really look forward to that." Then, allowing my emotion to speak for itself: "I can't wait."

"Nor I," my grandmother replied with affection. "Tell me, Mary. What can I bring for you? Would you like a nice cake? Or I've just jarred some fresh strawberry preserves . . ."

I laughed lightly, reminded of innocent distant hours spent together baking and pickling and jarring. "That isn't necessary, Grandma. You don't have to bring anything."

"But I must. Very well, if you can't decide, I have to. I'll bring you some of the strawberry jam," she said with mock sternness. "I'll see you next week, Mary."

I sat in the sitting room thinking of my grandmother when I was startled again. This time by a knock at the door. Who knocks? I wondered. My father always let himself in with his key, and James never failed to ring the doorbell.

I knew before I reached the door, for through the wood of the door I heard a long phlegmy tobacco-filled cough. "Aunt Mary!" I said, opening the door. There stood my Aunt Mary, visibly panting from her climb up the many stairs. "I didn't think you'd come. How are you?"

"You know me. Mustn't grumble. Don't get to see this part of town much. And those bleedin' stairs are enough to make a person think twice 'bout coming again." She trudged into the flat.

We walked down the corridor together towards my mother's room. I hadn't seen Aunt Mary flustered before. She was breathless from the stairs, but more than that, I could tell, she was nervously agitated about seeing my mother. "Mother will be glad to see you," I said.

"I 'ope you're right," she said in a small voice.

I put my head around my mother's door, like an MC introducing the next act. "Mother? There's someone here to visit you."

" 'ello, Lavinia," Aunt Mary, red-faced, came in behind me, both hands clutching the top of her oversized handbag. "Recognize your old Aunt Mary? Surprised?" She sat herself down in the chair beside the bed. My mother's eyes followed each of her movements. Aunt Mary smiled. "Couldn't leave you stuck up in Chelsea without paying a visit, now could I?" She put her handbag next to the chair but kept her wool coat on. "So, 'ow's your Aunt Mary look? I'm an old lady, since the last time I saw you. A right OAP. But you 'aven't changed much. You still look lovely. Considering." Oh dear, I thought. Aunt Mary never was one for tact. Nevertheless, I always derived a distinct comfort from Aunt Mary's directness. I hoped my mother did, too. Aunt Mary turned to me. "Well, then. 'ow about getting us a cup of tea? Your mum and me'll have a good talk. We've lots of catching up to do."

"Back in a minute." I smiled and went to the kitchen to make a pot of tea.

When the kettle had boiled and I'd filled the teapot and let it steep—wondering all the while with impatient curiosity what Aunt Mary was saying to my mother—I poured out half a cupful into a separate cup and filled it to the top with cold milk. The milky tea would be cool enough for my mother not to burn her mouth.

In my mother's room I saw Aunt Mary had taken off her coat and was well on her usual way complaining that London was overrun by foreigners. "I'm not moaning, mind you, but it isn't the England I used to know." I put the tray on a little table, picked up my mother's cup and started to approach my mother with her tea and a teaspoon. "'ere, Mary," Aunt Mary stopped me. "I'll do that." She took the cup and saucer from my hands, dipped a small amount onto the spoon and blew on it, though it was already cool. She poured the tea through my mother's lips. My mother swallowed. "There we are then," said Aunt Mary. "There's a good girl," she said naturally. "We're used to this, your mum and me," she said over her shoulder to me as she continued to spoonfeed my mother. "Used to feed your mum this way when she was just a snotty-nosed little chicken."

I could never imagine my mother snotty-nosed, at any age.

"Just like the old days, in'it, Lavinia?" Aunt Mary wiped my mother's mouth with a napkin. "Remember?" And as Aunt Mary fed her, I thought of the old photographs of my mother as a child. Looking at her now, I could see her yielding like a child under the care of her nanny. I could still see the love with which Aunt Mary treated her.

When my mother had had about a third of the cup, she shut her lips. "Right," said Aunt Mary. "'ad enough?" She set the cup on the bedside table. I filled another cup, added the two sugars I knew she liked, and handed it to her. "There's a dear. Ta." Noisily Aunt Mary sipped her tea. "Ah, that's better."

She turned to my mother. "They was better times then," she said. "In the old days. Remember? Ever such a pretty thing, you were. And I'd take you for your walk every day, rain or shine. All over Shanghai we walked, 'til you knew the place so well you could've walked the city by y'self. And there was your mum, carrying on like the flippin' Queen of China! Such a woman, your mum. Not many in the world like 'er." She paused and took another loud sip of her tea. The picture I had seen of my mother's mother's face arose in my mind. Aunt Mary, I could see, was also envisioning the strange handsome woman, the grandmother

I'd never met. And my mother too. "No," Aunt Mary said again. "Not many like her.

"Then you and me was in South Africa," she'd stopped for a while before saying this, as if allowing appropriate moments to pass to cover their move from China to South Africa, a move that to me still remained concealed in mystery, "and that wasn't easy, those years. But we 'ad each other, and somehow we got by. We've been through a lot together, Lavinia." She smiled at my mother with obvious love in her eyes. "And I'll never forget the day you met Peter Freeland, and I knew he'd make you a good husband. I'd done all right by you, I told myself. And it's been all right for you ever since. 'asn't it?" The question hung unanswered in the air.

Aunt Mary put her teacup down on the table and, pushing her hands against her knees to raise herself from the chair, stood. She put on her thick coat with woollen tufts and the odd stray thread sticking out here and there. "I'd best be off," she said. "It's a long way back to Ealing." She picked up my mother's hand. "And you've done all right with this one here." Her eyes remained on my mother's empty face but she tilted her head in my direction. "Your Mary's a good girl with it all," she said. "And your mum'd be proud of you, and of 'er."

She leaned over my mother and stayed bent, her lips upon my mother's forehead, for many moments. When she straightened herself I saw slow teardrops sliding from mother's liquid eyes. Aunt Mary took a wrinkled hankie from her coat pocket and wiped my mother's cheeks. "I'll get back, if I can," Aunt Mary promised. "But you know 'ow it is. Me legs aren't what they once was, and these stairs you've got are a killer. Goodbye, Lavinia." She turned to me, but not before she'd wiped her own eyes with her handkerchief.

"I'll walk you downstairs and get you a taxi," I said. "Aunt Mary?" I held her arm down the last of the stairs. "Please tell me about my mother when she was young and about my grandmother. I really must know. Please tell me. Why did you and my mother have to leave China at all? You both sounded so happy there with my grandmother . . ."

"Mary." She sounded cross. Perhaps I had once again pushed too far. Perhaps she was too upset by my mother to speak any further. "I've said all I will say. If she'd wanted you to know, she'd have told you 'erself. And she never 'as, 'as she?"

"But now she can't, Aunt Mary, and . . ."

"Me mind's made up." That was all Aunt Mary would say while I, in a light cardigan, chilly in the gray autumn wind, stood beside her on the pavement and waved down a taxi.

"To Ealing," I told the driver, as Aunt Mary scrunched herself up to fit through the taxi's door, and I gave him enough to cover the fare and a bit extra. "Maybe someday you'll tell me?" I said through the slightly open window.

"Look after yourself, love," Aunt Mary said, and she waved as the taxi pulled away and raced ahead towards the evening traffic on the Kings Road.

Chapter 80

It's been a bad day today, a dreary autumn Saturday. I've had other bad days, but today was among the worst. In the aftermath of Aunt Mary's visit I've found myself more confused than ever. Since Aunt Mary shared her memories with my mother, my mother oddly has felt more of a stranger to me. She had a whole life before she met my father, before she gave birth to me, and neither my father nor I played any role in that early life which made my mother what she was, is. Why wouldn't anyone tell me about her past life, about her mother, about why she and Aunt Mary left her mother? The last brick in the wall between my mother and me, the many mysteries of her youth, stubbornly refused to be knocked down. And what did this stranger think of me?

I leaned out of the kitchen window to the little iron balcony to pick a tomato, my autumn harvest, from the plant I bought months ago at the nursery up the road. For some reason the tomato still felt warm, from some stolen moment of sunshine between the opaque clouds. Taiwan II amused himself with his acrobatic tricks round my feet while I cut the tomato into small pieces. Tomato skin, I remembered, can cause one to choke, so I cut the pieces even smaller.

My day had not been helped by my receipt this morning of a letter from a happily married Kim in Hong Kong. Philippe, she reported, had "gone native," as someone who saw him said. Well, that was no surprise. A Caribbean island was a good place for the flotsam of this life. I hoped he was happy.

I smelled the tomato and felt lonely because I had no one with whom to share the sensuous delight of the smell . . . What *did* my mother think of me?

I realized, slicing the peperoncini and wondering if their taste would be too hot for my mother, that trying to preguess her thoughts had too often been the center of my life.

I finished preparing my mother's supper and turned from the kitchen to carry it to her and feed her. What did I feel for my mother?

"Mary!" A voice roused me. "Mary!" It was my father's voice. He stood at the doorway to my mother's bedroom. "Mary, come quickly!" He was smiling excitedly.

I joined my father in the doorway. "She is trying to speak, Mary! She's trying to talk."

I looked at my mother's face. "Puh," I heard her lips say. She held her lips together, then, opening them, puffed out a breath of air. "Puh."

"You see?" my father said. "She's calling out my name. *Peter,* she's saying." He walked quickly to her, her eyes watching him move, took her hand, and sat beside her on the bed. "I'm here, Lavinia," he said happily, his heart in his words, joyful to be called once again by his wife. "Yes."

My mother's eyes gazed at me over my father's shoulder. Her lips rolled inwards in a line of effort. Slowly her throat made a noise to be squeezed between her closed lips. "Mmm," she said, then opened her lips. "Meh." She was saying *Mary.*

She is calling me. She does think, she does understand. She has heard all I've said and she understands. And she is getting better. This is the first sound to escape her mouth. She is healing.

I stood transfixed in the doorway watching my mother call the beginning of my name. I recognized in that moment, more than in any other moment of my life, that I loved my mother. I loved my mother. And if she died, I would miss her. So much, that I couldn't imagine how I would ever live without her.

❧ *Chapter 81* ❧

James visited yesterday, Monday, and was delighted by my description of my mother's efforts to speak. With all kindness and a gentle good humor, James asked her if she wanted to show him how she talked. But she couldn't. "Don't worry about it," James reassured her. "You can show me another time, if you're feeling up to it." Last night my father spent hours sitting beside her hoping she'd speak again but she made no sound. When she had fallen asleep and he rose to go to his own bed, he looked old and tired and haggard. Disappointed, I decided to remain hopeful anyway.

Today I was busy cleaning the flat. It was not particularly dirty, but my grandmother was due to arrive the next day for her visit. Merely the knowledge of her visit was enough to make me dust and redust every piece of furniture, change my mother's sheets again, and scour the tea-stains from the inside of the teapot, as if for a military inspection.

"Hello, Grandma." Why did I feel my voice shake? "I'm really glad you could come."

"Hello, Mary." She kissed me on the cheek as she entered the flat. In one hand was a basket with a linen cloth over the top. In the other was a bunch of autumn flowers. "These are for your mother." She handed me the flowers. "From my garden. And I've brought you the strawberry jam I promised and also some fresh bread I baked to go with it."

"Grandma," I laughed. "I told you that wasn't necessary."

"Never mind that," she said, putting her basket on a table in the kitchen while I put the flowers in a vase of water. "We'll have some with a cup of tea after I've said hello to your mother. How is she?"

I told her about my mother's few sounds and that we were hoping, my father and I, for more. My grandmother nodded approvingly and we walked to my mother's room. I was pleased, as we entered, that I had taken extra care brushing my mother's hair this morning, to look good for my grandmother. My mother, I thought, looked beautiful.

"Hello, Lavinia." I heard a practised civility in my grandmother's voice. It was friendly enough but lacking of any deep affection. "Mary tells me you're doing well . . ."

"Look what Grandma brought for you!" I interrupted a bit too eagerly, feeling a protective nervous-
ness of what my grandmother might say. I heard my
own words. Had I ever uttered the word *grandma* in
front of my mother before? I felt as if my endearing
naming of my grandmother was a betrayal of my
mother, revealing the hours I had spent with my
grandmother in a shared secret life apart from my life
with my mother. I put the flowers on the table beside
my mother's bed. "They're from her garden," I said,
hearing my own tone of apology.

My grandmother sat stiffly in the bedside chair. I
took up my usual post in the armchair against the wall
by the door, promising myself not to interrupt again.
I listened as my grandmother chattered to my mother.
Her conversation was not awkward; she had had far
too much training as an Army wife for her social conversation ever to be awkward. She talked of her garden
and this year's harvest and the winter crop she was
looking forward to. But she talked as if to a stranger
seated beside her at a formal dinner. I knew that my
mother, too, if she could have talked, would have
proved herself able to make small talk on any subject,
though she would have preferred to talk about the
winter collection of clothes from Paris's newest *coutu-
rier*.

"Lovely to see you," my grandmother said, rising.
I was stirred from my interminable habit of daydreaming. "I hope you feel better, Lavinia." My grandmother turned to me with a set smile on her face.
"Now, shall we have that cup of tea?"

My grandmother and I sat on opposite sides of the
dining table, the teapot and a plate of my grandmother's bread in front of us. I bit into my bread with strawberry jam on top and the taste carried me to Milton
Park in Somerset, to happy moments. For an instant
I felt I was betraying my mother simply by sitting at

the far end of the hall with my grandmother, as if in conspiracy against her. But I did not feel against my mother, and my grandmother, by her visit, seemed to have indicated that she did not either. "Grandma," I began. "I feel I owe you an apology. I *do* owe you an apology. I'm sorry I was not at Grandpa's funeral. I should have been there. But, you see . . ."

"Mary," my grandmother stopped me, "there's no need to explain." She took a delicate bite from her bread, chewed, swallowed, then spoke. "I know I may appear something of an old relic," she smiled, "but I am not a woman without understanding. You know, in many ways you remind me of your mother." I believed I heard almost a begrudging, unwitting, fondness in my grandmother's voice. "I do understand, and you needn't say any more."

I thanked her and repeated how sorry I was. "Grandma," I said, still trying to understand more fully, "surely you must know something of my mother's background. No one has ever told me. And now it's very important for me to know, while my mother is still . . . While I can still talk to her."

My grandmother stared at me, thinking, deciding. "You're a grown woman, Mary. I see no reason to keep secrets from you. All I can tell you is all I know," she said and I felt an excitement that at last I would learn the truth. "And this is much as I've ever known. Your mother's mother was a noblewoman, a princess, I believe, of a Russian family. Russia was promising unrest, even before the Revolution, and your grandmother had to flee. This was not at all uncommon, Mary. Many people from the Russian upper classes fled for fear of being killed and became émigrés in other countries and cities—New York, London, Berlin, Paris, Shanghai. That's where your grandmother went, Shanghai, taking the overland route across Russia and into China. As I say, this was nothing uncommon. And certainly she was a woman of position. A princess, no less." She cleared her throat. "But what your grandmother then *did* . . ." She stopped and shook her head. "What she *did* . . . Well, there simply is no excuse for it."

"What did she do that was so terrible?"

"She did what no woman should have to do, no woman should let herself do. Naturally, I've never met the woman, Mary. But I understand she was most disreputable. Earned herself a most unfortunate name: The *Snow Leopard.*" I could guess what my grandmother was avoiding saying, but I would not push her to cross her boundaries of propriety. "She was a wild thing, Mary." I remembered the woman I saw in the picture at Aunt Mary's house. I recalled only a face that revealed extraordinary beauty and a profound inner dignity. "And she had your mother. Lavinia was born in Shanghai, and Mary Higgins . . ."

"Aunt Mary," I added.

". . . was her nanny. Your mother was reared in the company of prominent but undesirable people." I thought of Philippe and his set. "And then, I honestly do not know why, your grandmother—who was quite wealthy by this time—came to believe that her own life and the life of your young mother were in peril. Goodness knows why, but it's hardly surprising, that sort of thing, among the wrong crowd. She seems to have had difficulty getting her money out of China, but in great haste arranged for your mother to be moved to safety. Somehow, Mary Higgins, or Aunt Mary as you call her—your mother named you after her, you know, but I'm getting ahead of myself—Aunt Mary managed to take her from China to South Africa where they lived virtually as refugees. Very poor, you know, with no word from the mother. You see, Mary, it is a question of breeding, of upbringing. Your mother grew among the wrong kind of wealthy and then among the poor. And that, if you ask me, is no way to raise a child."

"And then she met my father?"

"Not quite yet. We were in England much of the time, at Milton Park, of course. And then your grandfather was called for a tour in South Africa, near Kokstad. Peter, your father, was a young man when he met your mother, and she a young lady, hardly more than a girl. Young *lady*." My grandmother laughed slightly. "Nevertheless, your father insisted she was the most beautiful creature he'd ever seen. But, naturally, we reminded him he had his life to think of. And she, your mother, obviously was not suitable as a wife for a man with his future. We sent him . . . He went, he returned home to Oxford. And then entered the Foreign Office and rose, I might say, very quickly. But he's always been a determined man, your father.

"Unfortunately, during his absence, your mother had caused something of a scandal in South Africa among the British circle. Lavinia had found her way into the fringe of British society. One saw her at the odd party, though her name was never mentioned in the social column of the newspapers. And she fell in love, if that is the correct word, with a man—I remember it very clearly, a man not of very sound reputation, who already had a wife. Imagine the scandal! She was a married man's . . ." She stopped speaking and lowered her eyes.

"Mistress," I said without showing emotion. I felt a sympathy of spirit, for had I not been seen as a mistress in Philippe's château?

My grandmother wordlessly agreed with a sideways tilt of her head. "But it all went very badly wrong for her. You see, the man had no intention of marrying her or making their association in any way honorable. And ours was a very small world, Mary. You must try to understand this. The British were—are," she corrected herself, "a very small world indeed. We've all been to the same places—China, Singapore, India, Africa, Egypt. And a reputation gained in one country will follow you to the next. That was why, in Peter's interest, your grandfather and I had no choice but to object to any possible . . ." she searched for a word, "union. But, as I've said. Your father was a very determined man. He returned from England, his career already under way. And he came to marry Lavinia. He can be awfully singleminded, you know. He'd hear nothing of Lavinia's scandal, or her past, and promised her he'd never discuss it, with her or with anyone. We were frightfully afraid she'd be his undoing. After all, his career held so much promise. We could not very well give our blessing to such a marriage. Your grandfather and I were able to return to England. Your father wouldn't come with us, so we had no choice but to leave him to do what he felt he had to do."

"But she wasn't his undoing," I said, surprised at how defensive I was on my mother's behalf. "She wasn't his undoing at all. He was a Consul in South Africa when I was born, and he became the Consul General to France."

My grandmother looked at me with a resolute face. "And he'd have made an excellent Ambassador. Perhaps some day he will."

"Surely you're not suggesting that my mother is the reason why my father hasn't been made Amba . . ."

"I'm not suggesting anything, Mary." I saw an unyielding Britishness in my grandmother, an obstinate refusal to bend. No wonder my mother had steered clear of a woman who regarded her with uncompromising disapproval. How difficult and brave it must have been for mother to visit Milton Park for my wedding! As if reading my mind, my grandmother's face softened. "I know I must seem harsh to you, Mary. Perhaps even cruel. But it is not simply a question of class. More than just that. It was a matter of morals, of standards. We live the way we live and cannot apologize for it. That is how we were raised. It simply is not done for the daughter of a woman of ill repute to be welcomed into any good family. And the Freelands are a very good family."

"But I'm that woman's granddaughter. And my mother was a married man's mistress. Yet you've accepted me."

"You are my·son's daughter, Mary. Naturally, I've always loved you and always shall."

"And you've never forgiven my mother for her past."

"You must try to understand."

I did understand. My grandmother was right. I could not blame her for being what and who she was. And whether she sat here now for my sake or for my mother's, she had come. Maybe this was her form of forgiveness. Why should I expect other than what she could give? I could see she had nothing left to tell me. But I still had a question. "Can you tell me," I said, "who was my grandfather, my mother's father?" The question occurred to me only as I asked it. I had always been so concerned in trying to understand my mother and her mother that the issue of paternity had never crossed my mind.

"No, I can't," my grandmother shook her head, "because I don't know. Neither, I believe, does your mother."

"And what became of my grandmother?"

"Again, I don't know. Oh, I heard a rumour once. Among the old circle, you know, that she'd managed to get out of whatever danger she was in in Shanghai. But then of course so much has happened to China since then, the Japanese invasion, the Communists taking over. And people like her, *anybody* with money actually, were no longer welcomed." No wonder, I thought, my mother never liked Communists. In the revolutions of Russia and China, her mother had been personally endangered.

My grandmother and I had finished our tea. "Thank

ou for telling me," I said. "And thank you for com-
ng. I know it wasn't easy for you to come." I hesitated.
decided to risk saying what I felt. "I am glad you
made your peace today."

My grandmother stood silent, about to leave, and
hen smiled. "Yes," she nodded. "I suppose you're
ight. You are a grown woman indeed, Mary. I am
roud of you. Your father has done well." Her smile
idened. "As has your mother. God bless, Mary." She
issed my cheek and left.

t was getting dark and my father was a little late in
oming home. Perhaps some extra work had held him
t the office. I had made my mother some chicken
hich was easy for her to eat. Sitting on her bed I fed
er the mouthfuls until she wanted no more. I put the
late on the side table and was happy to be at my
mother's side. I was proud to be her daughter. I felt
more at peace with my mother than I had ever felt be-
ore. "Mother," I said, "I really want you to under-
tand that I love you. I know that I may not always have
cted as if I did, but I do." I held her hand in mine.
he looked at me with her amazing eyes bright. My
wn eyes, though I was trying to be brave, were weep-
ng.

This time I had no doubt. I felt a slight movement
f her fingers, trying to hold my own.

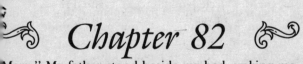

Chapter 82

Mary." My father stood beside my bed, waking me.
Mary, I've called the doctor. Your mother's had con-
ulsions. Come quickly."

I stood by my mother's bed. My father was behind
e with his hands on my shoulders. Her eyes were

closed and she breathed with great difficulty. I hel
her hand and I talked to her. "Mother, it's Mary. Ca
you hear me?" Briefly, very briefly, she opened he
eyes. She looked at me and again I felt the sligh
squeeze. Then my mother left her body.

Standing beside her bed, I felt her go. She absente
herself as if by will. Her body lay before us, empty an
dead.

I had not prepared myself for this moment, as I ha
had no experience of dying. All I knew was that in th
dreadful few hours that roared over me like a capsizin
wave, James arrived and I was clinging to him and cr
ing. My father sat numb in his chair in the sitting room
A doctor I did not know ordered us to stay out of th
bedroom. My father telephoned my grandmother wh
was back in Somerset. She said she would come an
help make the arrangements. I knew she would b
calm and efficient. My grandmother knew death. He
husband had died, and she lived in a village wher
there were many old people, a village where deat
called regularly.

I was neither calm nor efficient. The pain felt to
much to bear.

We stood for my mother's funeral at a churchyard i
Fulham Road. My grandmother stood beside my fa
ther, holding his hand to give him strength. Jame
stood beside me, similarly holding my hand. Au
Mary was not here. When I had telephoned her sh
had been distraught but had explained that she cou
not come to the funeral. "Your mum'd understand,
she had said. "Funerals are 'orrid things. I've said m
goodbyes already and Lavinia knows that. 'n it ju
wouldn't be right for me to be there. But you give m
a bell when it's all over and done, and I'll keep yo
company." Aunt Mary had been right, I realized, loo
ing at my grandmother. Perhaps she would have bee
out of place. The Lavinia of youth, of health, of Shan

hai and South Africa belonged to Aunt Mary, and I knew she would keep that Lavinia forever.

The men with the ropes around the casket started to lower my mother into the ground. James tightened his grip on my hand. I could not endure the thought of even my mother's body held captive in the ground that soon would freeze with winter, so with great will I thought other thoughts. Why was my mother to rest forever here? I suddenly wondered. Why London? And then I realized, where else should she be? She had no home. Shanghai was the city of her birth, but my mother's Shanghai no longer existed. South Africa? South Africa had never been a home to her. It had been a place that she yearned to leave. Paris? No, my mother had always been a foreigner to the French as, I was aware, she had been to many of the English.

Perhaps my mother should have been buried in Russia, her mother's country by noble birthright. But Russia would not have welcomed the return of the daughter of one of their lost princesses. It might as well be London in the Fulham Road. As good a place as any to house the body that had no home.

What was it Hattie had said? Something about exiles. Those of us in the world who were cut loose from our homes, destined to wander, trying to make homes wherever we went. My mother had been an exile, free in one way, lost and adrift in another. Captain Moses, had he been here (how I wished he were!), would have given the perfect eulogy for my mother: a long rich sermon, beginning inevitably with his recounting of his own life, on the merits of taking risks, of daring to be an outsider.

I blocked out the nasal droning of the priest, an anonymous man who had never met my mother, and silently I paid her my tribute. I remembered a picture I had seen of her in Aunt Mary's album. It was a picture of a small African shack. Outside the shack was Aunt Mary, a much younger Aunt Mary, and beside her was a little girl. The little girl was looking at the ground. She wore a woollen dress, long stockings, and thick poor-looking shoes. I could feel her embarrassment, even all those years ago, at being dressed so indigently.

This woman had come from nowhere and had taught herself everything she had taught me. She had taught herself etiquette and grace and charm. She was, as Madame Ferneux had said, an *arriviste* who taught herself *le style*.

A surge of pride filled me, as I finished my silent testimonial to my mother. Yes, I was the Consul General's daughter, but I was also my mother's daughter.

Her body was lowered and I looked upwards. She always soared, my mother.

My father and I sat alone, late that night, in the flat. We were at the kitchen table sipping the hot milk I had made to help us sleep. The flat, like our lives, felt bereft, empty and quiet. How strange that then the flat should have seemed quiet, for my mother when there had made no sound. But Silence had won its victory, leaving behind, after its conquest, only meagre quietude. My father, as if frightened to hear the sound of his own voice, spoke softly. "They've still some work for me here, Mary, so I'll be keeping the flat. You can stay with me as long as you like."

"Thank you. I will, for a while, until life . . . Until I'm ready to join the world again. It feels like we've been away from it for so long."

"I've felt the same way," my father said with a sad smile. "Even at the office. The world of the living feels very strange." He fell silent for a moment. "Do you know what you'll want to do? Eventually, I mean."

"I still have the inheritance," I said awkwardly, "from my other grandmother." My father did not flinch, so I continued. "I'm lucky to have it. I'll find a job later. And probably a flat of my own."

"Good," my father nodded distractedly. "Good." He seemed to be only half-listening to my answer. His thoughts, I knew, were with my mother. Then my father looked me in the eye. His eyes held a quizzical look. Evidently he managed for the moment to keep his grieving thoughts at bay. "That psychologist fellow, James, seems an awfully nice chap," he said kindly.

"He is," I agreed. "Quite unlike any man I've known before. I hope I will see him again," I revealed, perhaps more honestly than I intended.

"That would please me very much," my father said, and I was glad for his gladness.

We both sipped our hot milk. "Mary," my father said suddenly. He shook his head, "I'm no good at this sort of thing, but I feel I really ought to say something."

"How do you mean?"

He put his cup on the table and looked at the upper corner of the room, as if the words he was searching for might be hiding there. "There's a quotation from La Rochefoucauld," he said at last and I noticed his familiar correctness: diligently and with relish had he taught me, when I was a child in Africa, to say *quotation*, not *quote*. "Quite the wise man in his way, you know. 'We pardon to the extent that we love,' he said. Mary, I know that you and your mother—" He did not know how to say what he wanted to say. "For many years," he tried again, "it was rather hard, for *both* of you . . . Ah." He shook his head, displeased with himself and his own stumblings. He looked up at me. "Do you see what I'm getting at?"

I did. I had not forgotten my childhood feelings that my father had let me down by failing to protect me from my mother's sharper sides. I had not forgotten, and neither, evidently, had he. But I felt relieved, almost comforted to know that he noticed and cared. My mother was the stronger of the two, I now knew.

I took our empty cups to the sink and rinsed them quickly.

"You don't have to say any of it," I said, walking back to the table and standing behind my chair. "You know, I talked with Grandma, and I think I now understand mother pretty well. You gave her a new life. I know how much you always loved her. And I know that your first years together weren't easy, for either of you. You were both young and . . ." I sighed and stared into his eyes while they gazed into mine. "I loved her very much," I said and tears, suddenly plentiful and wilful, flooded from my eyes, making my body tremble with sobs.

"Mary . . ." My father rose from his seat and hugged me. "Your mother loved you, Mary. And I always will."

I returned his hug.

He held me for a very long time, until my cries had quietened and my body was still. My father's hands held the sides of my head as he smiled, full of sadness, at my face. He wiped my cheeks with his thumbs. "We'd better try to sleep."

His warm lips touched my forehead, a sweet and cherished remembered feeling from childhood. "Good night, Pumpkin," he said. "God bless."

"And God bless you." I turned and walked to my room. In my bed I felt calm sleep beginning to pull me away.

❧ *Chapter 83* ❧

The months after my mother's death dragged with leaden feet. For nearly half a year before she had died, my mother had been the center of my life, looking after her the whole of my life. Without her I had no routine, no reason. My father lived in a private hell of his own. He talked of her all the time. He seemed lost in our flat and spent most of his time in the office at Carlton Terrace. His work, I knew, gave him his routine and his reason to go on living.

I often visited him at lunchtime. We walked up the Strand together and lunched at various restaurants. He sat before me oblivious to the other diners, and I chatted in order to distract him. Later I wandered the streets alone as if walking could obviate my own pain.

One day I was in the British Museum. I was walking past the Elgin Marbles. Bloody (as Phoebe would say) British, wouldn't give them back to Greece. The marauding Victorians and Edwardians were no better than thieves. Then I remembered my mother's delight in her booty. Tears pricked. I remembered the look of childish pleasure she had on her face when she did a deal, especially if she had got the better of the barter.

I was high up in the museum. I walked slowly into the dead still calm of the mummies. There was a little woman curled up in a glass case. Her tight bones were sticking out of the wrappings. Her small head was haloed by a whisper of hair. She was thousands of years old. Poor woman, she lay naked and vulnerable . . .

I was alone in a room of death. Finally, though I'd tried walking all over London to hide, death and I had met. In this room. I covered my eyes with my hands and my body shuddered. I mourned for my mother . . . And suddenly, another spirit came to haunt me, I mourned for the baby I had had and lost, the baby that had lived in me but had never really lived, the mother I could have, should have, been. Would I ever be a mother again?

Many hours later I walked from the museum into the dusky bleakness of a London winter's evening. I felt ghost-like as I wandered.

Chapter 84

Patrick telephoned me. He had been transferred to the London home office of the British Oriental Bank. I agreed to meet him for supper. We arranged to dine at the Savoy. I felt safe there. I knew the staff and they knew me.

I tried to look attractive. I put on yet another of my little black dresses. When my mother died I bought six of them from Harrods. I couldn't bear colors. I had my hair, grown lanky, cut into a long bob. I was thin now. Thin enough to frighten myself in the mirror. My knees protruded. My ears stuck out at the sides of my head. I brushed my hair, holding the silver-backed mirror in one hand, with the matching silver-backed brush my mother gave me when I was marrying Patrick. I tried to smile in the mirror. Just before I left the flat, I clasped behind my neck the sunburst of diamonds that my mother had received on her wedding day, so many years ago.

Patrick was waiting for me alone without his new wife Sally. I walked towards him in the lobby. "Mary, you look lovely." He gave me a brief cordial hug, distant enough for our bodies not to touch, like teenagers shyly maintaining distance during a slow dance. "A drink?" he said. There was kindness in his eyes and I wondered if I ever should have left him. I needed kindness. No, Patrick was not for me. He was a kind tender man but I needed more than that.

"This way." The manager of the River Room restaurant drew us to our table. He was solicitous of me. He knew all about my mother's death. He had watched over my father and myself when we sat silently at our table.

Now Patrick and I were making polite conversation. I watched Patrick with my eyes behind my eyes. I felt

we had never known each other. Never been married.
I had never lain naked in his arms. He was talking earnestly about his wife Sally and about his two children.
The details were the same details any proud parent
talks of when they have children. I thought again of
the child I lost, but I had stopped hiding from the
pain, so now I could begin to think about it without
being obliterated by grief.

My thoughts were far from our well-laid table. I
looked out of the window at the Thames. I saw a boat
in Hong Kong and our much younger selves, still pink
from England, sitting on the deck with Ian and Isla.
We were laughing and talking . . .

I looked at Patrick chewing his beef now. There
were more lines on his face. He had put on weight.
"I am so sorry about your mother," he said. "Are you
coping?"

How like Patrick to have used the word cope. He
had been trained to cope by his public school education. Grace under pressure, as Hemingway had said.
Noblesse oblige, as my mother would have said. "Of
course," I said. "My father and I are doing well."

"Why don't you get a job? It might be good for you
to have something to do."

"I will," I said wearily. Everybody I knew, including
my grandmother, thought that a job would be the answer to my pain, to get through it. I must let it live
until it died of its own accord. I was at least beginning
to feel that I would survive the pain. I would outlive
it. "I see," I said, "your eldest is beginning school."

Patrick smiled broadly. "I know it's early days yet,
but I can see him making his way to Oxford." He
laughed the laugh of a parent contemplating his
child's long and successful future. "I couldn't hope for
more for him, after all it did for me."

I nodded. "Yes, indeed," and we ordered coffee.

I held the delicate cup in my hand and I smelt the
coffee. How many years ago did I drink coffee with

Mademoiselle in a Paris street café, I in my school uni
form? I took an after dinner mint from the plate. I un
wrapped it slowly. The paper was gold foil. How m
mother would have loved to be here. The Savoy cho
olates had been her favorite chocolates and when w
had stayed, as we always did during short trips to Lo
don, the manager had made sure she had a box
chocolates by her bed. Not for her the single chocola
on the pillow. The staff had loved her and had bee
mesmerized by her charm and beauty. When she use
to walk into the dining room she had a royal proce
sion of her own. A special light, all of her own, illum
nated her. I had always felt the River Room had lit u
when she walked in. A light had fallen upon the tab
while she took her place. I had no such light about m
self. "My mother sends you her regards," Patrick sai

I nodded again. "How kind of her," I said and ma
veled at how two human beings could spend time
social intercourse and say nothing to each othe
Nothing of feelings, nothing of passion, nothing
hurt and regret. We had hurt each other and we bot
had things to regret. I wondered, as I looked at hi
already sliding into middle age, if he was happy wit
his new wife, truly and deeply happy. But I knew n
to say anything. "I must rush, Patrick," I said, stan
ing. "Lovely to see you, and thank you for dinner."

"All right, old thing," he said. He stood and gav
me a peck on the cheek. "Cheerio, then," he sai
"And take care of yourself."

"I will," I said and I left hurriedly. Fred, the kin
doorman, waved for a taxi cab. The cab roared int
the courtyard. The Savoy Theater was just emptyin
Laughing happy people were pouring out. Most
Americans. They brushed past me in the doorwa
"Taxi, Madame?" Fred said, pushing the touris
aside.

"Thank you."

"Sorry to hear about your mother."

"Thank you," I said and I meant the thanks because I knew Fred was sincere. He understood my sorrow. He had known my mother for years and years. They used to tease each other every time she arrived. He, if he was on duty, always made it his business to see to her arrival. He, like Aunt Mary, shared a knowledge of the universe unguessed at by Patrick.

Fred pushed the door to the taxi shut and the taxi pulled away from the pavement. I sat back and my thoughts, too, left Patrick behind.

Now, I admitted to myself, I had begun to really care about James. He, quietly and patiently, had become a part of my life over the past half year. Slowly I was learning that I could trust him.

Part of me still waited, fearful that James might have a Mr Hyde deep inside. But I didn't believe he did. He took me out one weekend. We spent the morning at the Tate Gallery. James knew a great deal about art for a man from Texas. He had educated himself well. We both loved the Impressionist paintings. We both found it difficult to feel the same admiration for modernism. Our tastes seemed similar in so many spheres. We both distrusted experimental theater but would see an Agatha Christie play any day. We both read Graham Greene and Somerset Maugham.

In the afternoon we bought a bowl of geraniums for James's house. We bought them at Syon House. We looked at the great hall where King Henry VIII had lain dead and his blood leaked across the floor and the hunting dogs licked his blood, fulfilling a morbid prophecy about the King's end. Then James took me to see his own house, a rather frowsy Victorian building on Clapham Common. James said he loved geraniums. "Reminds me of Greece," he said. "One day I'd love to take you there." He cooked me a feast of Italian food in his kitchen and we drank Chianti. I offered to help but he wouldn't let me. "Men's work," he said with a smile. So I curled up in an old armchair and watched him work. He was a neat worker and he knew his tools well. He reminded me of my grandfather, also meticulous.

And always James was patient. He felt a fear in me and he had patience . . .

The taxi turned and raced off the Strand, cutting towards the river. We rushed down the embankment, the driver driving a little too fast and aggressively. People were everywhere. They walked and they talked and I looked forward with a small ray of hope to seeing James the next day. We were going to a party. And he had bought concert tickets for next week. James loved music as much as I did. He loved to eat and we both loved to cook. James, I found myself hoping, was in my future. The two of us together forever. Never to harm each other with bitter words. Love as peaceful and as calm as Hong Kong Harbor on a clear day. Aunt Mary would understand, I thought. "Cor!" I could hear her say. "Not another bloke!" I knew my father liked James, so he would be pleased.

I let my thoughts wander their river-course as I was driven through the night. What did I feel towards James? Not the urgent passionate physical longing I felt for Philippe. And not the myopic hope that he'd protect me from myself which I felt, in younger years, for Patrick. I simply wanted to be with James, to enjoy his company . . . My imagination ran free. What would our children look like? Like him or like me? I thought he'd be a very good father, loving and patient . . . I caught myself in my own thoughts and was relieved to discover that my desire to become a mother had not left me. I began to believe that some day I might have a child.

I sat and let the world slip by. We were now in Chelsea. Strangely garbed people were on the streets. The taxi turned and stopped. I paid the driver and tipped him extra in an effort to placate him. "Thanks," he looked at me. He was not really a daredevil, just a man yearning for excitement.

I smiled. "Thank you," I said and I walked up the stairs. Going home to a home that was no home, but now I had to make my own home for myself. And James? A small glow. A light lit. A sacristy candle waving in a small breeze of hope as I walked.

Chapter 85

My first party since my mother's death took place in Kensington, well-remembered Kensington. James invited me to go with him, explaining he'd been invited and needed a sympathetic spirit for moral support. The house was in Addison Gardens. "These people are socialists," he warned me, "so don't be amazed if you find them quite different." I was distracted when he invited me and therefore not really listening. "Your mother," James said, "never missed a party, did she?"

"I suppose not." She had been dead three months now. Twelve weeks. A short time and also forever.

We were walking together along the curved road that led to the house. "They must be very rich socialists," I remarked.

"They are," James laughed. "But they were all at university with me. And we used to be good friends. But you know how things change after university and you all have to enter the real world." We reached the gate in the metal railing. James opened the gate and held it for me. "Four of them live here together."

"Four bachelors together?" I asked.

James shrugged. "They all have live-in girl friends."

"Don't people marry any more?" There was an expectant silence and I felt a trembling question hang between us in the frozen night. We walked up the path and James knocked on the door.

I was suddenly aware how very little I'd had to do with practical politics of any sort, apart from listening to my father and his friends. I felt strange in this gathering. There must have been fifty people in the room. I recognized several faces from the television news. Tommy introduced himself to us and punched James in the shoulder. "Glad you could come, capitalist swine."

James laughed and squeezed my hand. "See?" he said. "They really love me."

"Got your Rolls yet, old boy?"

"Not long now," James said. "I'll give you a ride when I do." I knew the long days James worked at the hospital, and how tired he was after extra hours with his patients. I found myself feeling defensive on his behalf, but I said nothing.

Tommy was a big burly footballer. He spoke like Aunt Mary, but to me his voice sounded odd. Aunt Mary spoke naturally. Her voice could be heard all over London. But I could hear that Tommy had done something to his voice, as had most of the people in the room. Miss Standish, I thought, would have had a fit. We were all given elocution lessons in my day. Here, however, was Miss Standish's nightmare: a room full of successful people who could not "speak properly," as she said. I felt awkward to hear my voice sounding prissy and affected here. I looked different, and I was aware that my black pleated Coco Chanel dress stood out against the jeans and shirts of both the men and the women. I felt embarrassed for James, sure that I had let him down.

We walked over to the bar. On the bar were various bottles of drink. "Is there any wine?" I asked.

"Beer," Tommy said.

I shook my head. "I don't drink beer."

"Well, you should."

"Why should she, Tommy?" James's voice was sharp. "Why on earth should a woman drink beer? Beer's a man's drink. Don't worry, Mary. It's just old Tommy doing his boring working class act. You wouldn't think that he went to Eton, would you?"

"Good heavens!" I was amused. "Really?"

"You think he's always talked as if he came from the East End?" James laughed. "Why, his accent is the product of many hours of hard work and self-discipline."

Tommy grinned sheepishly. "Shut up, James," he said. "You'll ruin my act with the birds."

The women in the room could hardly be described as *birds.* Most of them were very masculine. Many wore men's boots and cigarettes hung from their lips. James poured me a "horse's neck," brandy and ginger ale. I remembered the drink from Macau and wished fervently that I was back there. Those people looked wholesome compared to this crowd. "Hey, James!" a raucous woman came over to where we were standing. "How are you, man?" She had frizzy red hair and wild blue eyes, and she wore a vibrant pink boiler suit. "Haven't seen you for ages. Where you been?" She had a bottle of beer in her hand and she was swaying. She threw her arms around James and lurched.

"Careful now." James propped her up.

"This your man?" she leered at me.

And I could tell I was blushing furiously. This was one of my more major blushes. I felt it rise from the soles of my feet, leave my unsuitable high heeled shoes, climb my nyloned legs, and then flood my neck and arms. I gazed miserably at James. We both stood looking at each other and I had nothing to say. "We are," I said stiffly, "just good friends. We're good friends."

"Oh. Ha!" The woman's face creased and split from ear to ear. "Hear that?" she screamed loudly. Everyone stopped talking. " 'We are just good friends,' " she imitated my accent. "Ha! Frigging ha!" She bowed from the waist. "Well, James, you were always too good for the likes of us."

James did not flinch. "Time," he said, "has not been kind to you, has it, Evelyn? Some of us grow up and others don't. Come on, Mary. Let's go and talk to some of my friends."

Some of James's friends were indeed nice. John Julius was a television reporter. They stood, those members of the media, in the middle of the floor discussing the intricate day to day goings on at the BBC. James seemed to know as much as they did about broadcasting. I stood mute. Again I had nothing to say. If I was asked, what could I say?

The television and radio crowd were deep in discussion. I looked across the room and saw French windows. Oh good, I thought, a garden. And gardens could be beautiful, even in their hibernal sleep. Quietly I slipped away through the French windows. The garden was quite large. In summer, I could see in the moonlight, there would be a lawn of sorts, but it looked bare and patchy. The people who lived in the house did not feel as if they had time to care for a garden. They were too busy waiting for the revolution that would sweep people like me with my private income away forever. I sat down on a plain wooden bench and breathed the night London air. Soot particles, fumes from cars, pollution. Night sounds: hoots and thumps. Cars wheeling and squealing. This was not my world. I didn't want to be with these people. They were all very new to me and I didn't like them any more than they liked me. No one except me in that room wore pearls. None of the women looked like women . . ." A penny for your thoughts? I looked up and it was James.

I shrugged. "Not worth a penny."

"They are to me."

I sighed, thinking *what-the-hell.* "I don't really fit with
ese sort of people, James. I'm sorry."

James sat down on the bench next to me. "Nor do
" he said. "But every so often I visit them. I attend
eir laborious get-togethers and see how they pro-
ess. For rampant socialists, they are a little sad. Ad-
son Gardens, the cradle of hot-bedded revolution."
e grinned. "They all amuse me. I like to tease them."
e bent down. "Here," he said. "Take this." His hand
ld a little nascent blue crocus. "First of the season.
und it over there in a warm spot next to the house."

I looked at the flower in his hand and I felt com-
rted: he *does* prefer me to those women in there. "I
ll you what," James said, as if mischievously. "Let's
ip all this nonsense and I'll take you to my favorite
staurant, the 'Gay Hussar.' The duck can't be
aten. Neither can the manager."

I smiled. "What about the revolution?"

"No revolution there. Victor wouldn't have it."

We left. We walked back to James's green Lagonda,
old car with huge pipes. As we roared towards the
nter of London I glanced at his face. In profile it was
gentle face with a very determined chin. I liked his
nds. They gripped the wheel with authority. I sat
ck and felt peace flowing through my veins. For the
st time I allowed myself to imagine, to dream beauti-
l dreams about James. The possibility of James and
or I and James . . . Either way, the thought warmed
e.

njoyed yourself?" James said, after a gorgeous din-
r, as he dropped me off at my door.

"I really had a wonderful time."

He put his arms around my shoulders and held me
ose. He bent down and kissed my cheek, a soft moth-
e kiss. I turned my mouth towards his. We kissed
ntly then I went upstairs, my heart singing.

Chapter 86

"What can I say?" Aunt Mary said. "You seem to kno[w] just about everything."

We sat at a table in Lyons Corner House. Everythi[ng] around me reminded me of my first time there, [my] first meeting with Aunt Mary a lifetime ago. She had[n't] changed, Aunt Mary, and I didn't expect she ev[er] would. One hand was on her teacup, waiting to si[p] and the other held a smoking cigarette in betwe[en] puffs. I had called her and asked her to meet me he[re]

I told her what I found out from my grandmoth[er] about my mother and her mother. I still had my que[s]tions. "For a start," I said, "who was the Snow Leo[p]ard? Exactly what did she do that made her so bad[ly] thought of?"

"But she wasn't," Aunt Mary said fiercely. "Only some, I mean."

"Some like my grandmother. But I must kno[w.] From what Grandma said, it sounds like she was . [. .] Aunt Mary, was my mother's mother a prostitute? W[as] that it?"

Aunt Mary squinted as she took her puff of cigare[tte] smoke and let a quarter inch of ash drop carelessly [on] the table. She did not bother to brush it away. "I[f I] say yes, you'll think she was, so I'll say no." Typi[cal] Aunt Mary. Answer a question with an enigma.

"What does that mean?" I sensed my own frustr[a]tion.

"It means you wouldn't understand. Times was d[if]ferent then. Not like the world you live in. You kn[ew] 'er as a princess, Mary. And that she was, so leave [it] at that.

"Can you at least tell me who my grandfather was[?]" I felt exasperated.

"You'd have to ask your grandmum that for y'se[lf.] If you could find 'er."

My heart jumped. "You mean she's still alive?"

Aunt Mary twitched her head to the side. "Can't say yes, can't say no. But she'd be older than Adam if she is. She was alive enough last time I saw her."

"When was that?"

"You never stop, do you? All right, Mary. I'll tell you this. When your mum and dad was married back in Africa, I knew I'd done me work. Your mum could look after 'erself, at least with your dad to look after 'er. But just before their wedding, I get a present from your grandmum to give to your mother. The same diamond necklace as you 'ave on." I clutched the necklace, my bejewelled link to the mysterious past. "Don't know 'ow she got it to us. Don't know 'ow she even knew about the wedding. But she 'ad friends. Connections. So I give it to your mum—a beautiful bride Lavinia was. And then, well where was I to go? Africa was no place for the likes of me. So I think, right, that's me done, might as well go back to London and live quietly. I'd 'ad enough of the rough life, you know.

"But your grandmother, along with the diamonds, had got 'er address to me somehow. An address in Hong Kong. So on me way back to England, I take the long way 'round and visit Hong Kong. And there she was, beautiful as ever. And she 'ad money by this time, so that's when she sets up your inheritance trust and makes me in charge of seeing you get it, only if you was born a girl."

"And if I'd been born a boy?"

"Then you'd never've got it, would you?"

"But why? Why only her granddaughter?"

"Men, she figures, can look after themselves. Women has to help each other out. But you was born a girl."

"And I was named after you."

Aunt Mary smiled. "Nice of Lavinia, that, wasn't it?" She drew deeply on her cigarette. "And after I was back in London," she continued, sipping her tea, "I wasn't sure you'd ever turn up. But you came back to go to school and I found you. Still keep me ears open, you know. And you 'ave to remember, Mary, every thing 'appened—your parents getting married, your dad's parents going back to England and going off in a sulk and all that—it all 'appened only a year or so before you was born. As soon as that. So it's no won der your mum spent her time hiding 'erself and you from your grandparents and me when you was over there in Paris, is it? I mean, it was all too fresh. But I found you, and you've come out all right. So it's all for the best really, i'n' it?"

"And how did you and my mother ever escape from Shanghai in the first place?"

"Ah," Aunt Mary said with unhidden delight in her foxlike eyes. "That's Captain Moses's doing that was. We made our way to Macau and Captain Moses got us out. To Hong Kong. But your grandmum, and it nearly killed 'er to see us go, couldn't come with us. She just couldn't."

"But Captain Moses said he knew my grand mother."

Aunt Mary smiled and said nothing.

I remembered the same smile in Captain Moses' eyes when he told me of my grandmother. "Aunt Mary, were Captain Moses and my grandmother lov ers?"

"He's a good man, Captain Moses, and your mum and me, we'd never've got out if it 'adn't a' been for him. But what you ask . . . You'd 'ave to ask 'er for yourself," she said again, still cherishing her enigmas.

"You do talk of her as if she's still alive."

"I'm an old woman, Mary," she tamped out her cig arette, "and I can't go round chasing up people on the other side of the world. I did try to get 'old of her once but that old address's no good anymore. Me letter was sent back."

"But she could still be alive."

"You'll 'ave to find out for yourself, if you ever get back to those parts."

I thought of myself walking the streets of Hong Kong, the alleys of Macau. Had I ever seen my grandmother? Maybe, if she was still alive, I had walked past her and hadn't even known. Maybe she had been a face in a window, a woman on the street . . . But it was enough. For now at least. I could see Aunt Mary gathering up her handbag and preparing to leave. But I knew enough. I felt the necklace around my neck, my legacy from my shadowy grandmother. And I had my mirror and brush from my mother, an inheritance to pass on to my eventual daughter. The circle had turned. I envisioned the ancient Chinese snake of time putting its tail in its mouth, the circle almost complete, waiting to unravel itself and reveal more of its secrets in a future unwrapping of its coils.

"Your dad tells me," Aunt Mary said, "and don't look so surprised! We talk on the telephone now, from time to time. I always did like your dad. 'e tells me there's a man in your life?" She grinned a knowing grin.

"I hope so," I grinned back. A momentary worry passed through my thoughts. We were supposed to go to the concert tomorrow, but James hadn't telephoned me since the party, since we kissed. Did he still . . .

"Trust you!" Aunt Mary screamed out for all of Lyons Corner House to hear, "Another bloke!" as I knew she would. "Well, good luck then, love. And you know where I am, next time you want a proper cup of tea." She turned and waddled her way, like a wise old duck, through the restaurant's door.

I paid the bill and walked out into the pre-dusk light that dimmed another London day. A warm gust blew against my cheek, a soft reminder that the melting of spring was inevitable. A chapter in my life had ended and I was beginning again. I waved down a taxi and headed towards Chelsea.

My hand opened the door. "Oh, there you are," m
father said. "I've been quite worried about you."

I smiled and I felt the unused muscles relax. "I re
ally am fine."

We kissed and he smiled. "James called while yo
were out."

"Did he?" I asked, relieved and happy. And w
smiled at each other, a complicit father and daughte
smile. I went to my room and I was humming.

*Tonight I lie in bed and for once I do not think of my mother
The future stretches ahead filled with possibilities. My future
a Mary-filled future, a James-filled future. I will sleep and th
same moon bathes both of us with her light. He sleeps unt
tomorrow when I shall see him and we will sit together at th
concert. I shall hold his warm firm hand. I dream and the moo
dreams with me, smiling at my thoughts. Taiwan II lies at th
foot of my bed, snuffling orientally to himself in his sleep. Th
night flees and I rest. My grandmother sleeps alone in her bi
bed in Somerset. Aunt Mary sleeps in her bed in Ealing. Cap
tain Moses and Jo Jo, no doubt, sleep on the China Sea in th
gently rocking Fat Shan. My father sleeps, snoring slightly
his hand stretched out to touch my absent, eternally slumberin
mother. We are safe now. I have come home.*

Erin Pizzey is the author of four novels, *The Snow Leopard of Shanghai*, *First Lady*, *In the Shadow of the Castle*, and *The Watershed*. Well known for her work with battered wives and their children, she is an accomplished journalist and has written a number of nonfiction books as well. She lives in Cayman Brac with her husband and children.